The Adventures of Elizabeth Stanton
Series            Volume 7

Abducted

Vic Broquard

# The Adventures of Elizabeth Stanton Series

## Volume 7: Abducted

Vic Broquard

Published by:
Broquard eBooks
http://Broquard-eBooks.com
author@Broquard-eBooks.com
103 Timberlane
East Peoria, IL 61611

Artwork by Crooked Willow Studios

For Morgan and L. Ron Hubbard

# Table of Contents

# Chapter 1 What Is Going On?

Today should be August 1, 657, assuming that now is tomorrow. Things have gone from the predictably mundane, workaday world to a total confusion.

My name is-was Elizabeth Stanton, originally anyway, and my dearest friends still call me Bethany. When that body died, my next lifetime I was called Bethany Madelyn Adid, until I married and became the wife of Jes Amir, who was the Great Messiah. I was then known as Bethany Madelyn Amir, and I discovered much later, I was called the Blessed Holy Mother. Next, I had a male body known as Ket Bethany. Yes, I have a fetish for the name Bethany and another for long hair, but those are just fleshly body things. Now I am Elizabeth Ann Rose Weston and am now twenty-two.

You see, I, like you, am a being — an immortal spirit. I've lived in many bodies and will have as many more as I desire, assuming the world, Tarra, our playground, is not destroyed. It began many years ago, I was part of a group of like-minded people, the druwids. In my group, I was revered as the Wid Bethany — the title, which I took nearly nine hundred years ago now, as I sit here and look back upon my past. I am Truth and Knowledge. Yes, you may call me a witch, a demon or a heretic, but, in doing so, you mark yourself as just another Blind One. I chose this road — this path I follow — knowingly and willingly. I do it for all mankind, even you.

Yesterday, Linda and I were working on reorganizing the Santi del Dio, the Knights of God, at the main headquarters in Velona, Sea Princes. It was my mom's estate until her body died last year. Her last order as the Supreme Commander of the Santi del Dio was that I, her daughter, take her place. Since I founded the Santi last lifetime, when I was called Ket Bethany, I had fully expected this to happen.

Reorganization — that's an understatement! Our organization has become huge in size and scope. How mom ran this group, I do not know! She was an amazing woman indeed. For the last year, I have been run ragged trying to cope with the myriad details that came her way.

I'm married to a fabulous fellow, Renzo Pazzio le'Goeur, and we have twins, Lena Jenna and Benjamin Andre, who are six years old and into everything, a daughter Danielle who is four, and a daughter Adrien, who is two.

Last night, if it was indeed last night, I remembered Renzo and me tucking in our children, giving them a good night kiss. In our bedroom, we passionately kissed and made love before I fell asleep. It was quite dark outside and in our bedroom.

Suddenly, the room was flooded with daylight, bright daylight, as if all of the walls in our house suddenly became transparent. I rose up a bit. I let out an involuntary squeal. This was not my bedroom, not my bed. I was not in bed with Renzo! Natale, struggling to sit up, was next to me, screeching in surprise; Linda awkwardly sat up cursing. We three were in a strange bed, naked, staring at an unfamiliar room and at each other.

Exclamations of shock and surprise came from two other beds nearby. I recognized some of the voices, other friends of mine. I struggled to get out of bed, only to find that I was not entirely naked. I had on some strange boots, whose heels were tiny metal spikes and quite tall, reminding me of those I had worn when I was visiting the country of Annelise, where the people insisted on wearing fancy clothing for every day. I got up, carefully watching my balance on these heels. I moved out of the way so that the others could get up.

Eight of us started in total shock and disbelief at each other. We all knew each other, we all were naked, and we all wore these impossibly high heels. We all panicked at the same time, looking at each other, the weird room, and our boots. What was going on?

The seven others here with me included Linda. Linda Sarah Amir d'Grange is our Headquarter's Judger and is the same age as me, twenty-two. We have been best friends since we could walk and remain inseparable. She is also blonde, though her hair is a shade darker than mine is, and she has deep blue eyes. After losing her first husband at the time she lost her arms, she fell in love with a man who came to our rescue, Chaucer d'Grange, a Protector. They have a daughter, Marion, age four, and a son, Samuel, age two. Her son Zachary Allen is six; her deceased husband Damien, my brother, was his father. She and I lost our arms at the same time to the mantis alien creatures.

Natale Angela Freeze is twenty-seven, our language translator with unparalleled language skills. She'd lost hers with the damnable metal encasements of the Holy Paladins some years back, and I had performed her therapy sessions. Natale married our ship's captain, Henry Freeze. She has beautiful, long, curly blonde tresses that extended down to her rear and she has enchantingly, pale blue eyes. They have a son, Charles Angel age six, a daughter, Gwenevere, age four, and a son, Barnabe, age two.

Enyo, now twenty-six, has thin lips and small breasts. Her eyes have a shade of green mixed in with the blue, enchanting some said, devilish, others thought. Her pale brown hair has grown a bit longer now, reaching her rear, of which she is rather proud. Enyo, the fantastic architect, mechanical device inventor, and engineer from the Isle of Right, once told me when I lost my arms, "Once you get used to it, you won't miss them. I haven't. I just keep on making new things. The world, Bethany and Linda, is full of arms, but there is a big lack of ideas, designs, and plans. That's where we fit in. I'm happy to help you any way I can." Enyo has become a full Planner, and at last, fell in love with a fellow Planner, Frank Westhall. Their children are Erika, age two, and Ben, age one. On the Isle of Right, Enyo was a member of the group of four women who were called the Rule Breakers.

Her nickname was the Foolhardy.

One of her compatriots is also here, Alexa, the Deep Thinker. Alexa, also now twenty-six, has bronzed skin with pale blue eyes. Her blonde hair now reaches to her upper thighs. Alexa is a very independent young woman, free spirited, and a driving force. She quickly became a Judger, a natural at it. She married Rene Reynaud, a Wid, and has a daughter, Airlea, age 2.

I also recognized two other women from the Isle of Right, both engineers. Aella, a twenty-seven year old blue eyed blonde, wears her hair shoulder length and is also a Planner. Similarly bronzed skinned, she is particularly pretty. She married Herbert Fry, an engineer of construction. Her specialties include the construction of roads and bridges, for which she has already become famous in these few years with ten fabulous bridges to her credit already. They have a daughter, Jannel, age three, and a son, Samuel, age one.

Natasa, twenty-five, is a Planner as well. Like her friends, she has bronzed skin, blue eyes, and wears her hair shoulder length. Natasa has an enormous number of freckles, earning her the name of Freckles, naturally. Her specialty is the building of great stone buildings and has drawn up the plans for four great cathedrals, which are in the early stages of construction. Her husband is Fred Spell, an architect of some renown in Velona. They have a daughter, Krysta, age two.

Kallisto Ali Williams is a Judger, is thirty-four years old, is from the country of Demokritos, and is the leader of the Kali band of Assassins. Her hair is coal black as are her eyes, penetrating cold black eyes. Her hair drapes in ringlets down to below her waist. Her long tresses cover the fact that she too has lost her arms. She married a fellow Judger, Frank Williams, and had returned to her mansion in Axos, Demokritos last year.

"I must be dreaming, having a bad nightmare. Someone please pinch me?" I muttered the only explanation I could fathom.

"I would but I don't have the use of my feet anymore," Linda said, fear in her face and a tremble in her voice. "I'll kick you instead." She stepped close and kicked me in the shins with the point of her boot.

"Ouch! This is real?" I exclaimed.

"I'm really scared," Natasa volunteered. "I have to pee badly before I pass out!"

"Hey, someone's copied my toilet invention!" Enyo pointed out. "Over here, Natasa." Her heels clicked on the hard surface of the floor as Enyo walked over to inspect the toilet. Natasa's clicks were rapid as she rushed to relieve herself. "Hey, they copied my Bottom Washer too," Enyo added.

All of us walked over to the toilet as well; suddenly we all had to go. Well, it was morning, evidently; at least our bodies told us so. We all talked at once. "Kallisto! I thought you were in Demokritos! Hello," I said. Her penetrating black eyes pierced mine, though I detected fear behind them for the first time ever. We exchanged our trademark bump welcome. Unable to hug properly, we bumped our bodies together and touched our cheeks together on one side and then the other side.

"I was. Where are we? What has happened? How can this be? I've a really bad feeling about this!" Kallisto replied.

As we each gave each other a welcoming bump, our fears only increased. Enyo, ever the practical one, said, "Bethany, Linda, how do you walk in these boots? They are so high! I feel like I am crippled! I cannot use my feet! Now I can hardly walk!" Alexa, Aella, Natasa, and Kallisto, all echoed her complaint.

"Take small, baby steps," Linda replied for me. Her voice was very shaky; fear took a hold of all nine of us.

"Well, can someone help me get them off me?" Enyo declared flatly. We all looked at each other's boots. They had no laces and came up to our knees. "Damn, it is all in one piece! It's as if they were molded onto our feet! How can this be?" Though we tried our best, these boots were impossible to remove, not without a knife to cut through the material somehow. Yet, there was not even a fraction of an inch spacing between our skin and the boot in which to insert the knife.

"Okay, the boots do not come off! Add that to the list of questions without answers!" I said exasperated. "Calm down everyone. Let's see what we do know. Me, I last remember being in my own bed, sleeping beside Renzo. Next thing I remember is this brilliant light coming on and waking up in here with all of you. I'm no help. Kallisto, you were thousands of miles away. What do you remember?"

"I — I — I was in bed with Frank in my own house. When I awoke to these bright lights, I'm here, wherever here is." She was definitely unnerved, and an assassin should never be unnerved.

Linda added, "I was in bed with Chaucer and next thing I know I heard you scream, Bethany, and awoke here."

"Me too," Enyo volunteered. "I was sleeping with Frank and awoke like this."

"Me too," echoed Natale, Natasa, Aell, and Alexa.

"Wait, this doesnt make any sense," the inquiring mind of Alexa kicked into gear. "How can we all be sleeping in our beds and wake up here naked and with these really awkward boots on? I was wearing a nightgown. Anyone seen any of the clothes we were wearing last night around here anywhere?"

Eight sets of heels clicked upon the floor as we all dashed about the room looking for our clothes. The room was large, perhaps forty feet across. The walls were stark white. The floor was brown. The bright lights came from ceiling panels some four feet across and two wide. Twenty of these provided the overly bright illumination. The rest of the ceiling, some ten feet above the floor, was also bright white.

A large table occupied the center of the room with eight chairs arranged around it. In one corner was the toilet and Bottom Washer. I also saw a bathtub with two knobs and a spigot, whose purpose was unknown to us at this time. Another of these, a miniature tub with smaller knobs and spigot was at chest height. Again, its purpose was unknown to us. There were no mirrors, however. "Damn, no mirrors," I found myself saying, in spite of our plight. Linda gave a laugh that bordered on terror.

Opposite the table was an open space or hole in the wall. There was nothing inside it, however. Just as we were all looking at the hole, a buzzing noise echoed in the room, coming from somewhere in the ceiling. Suddenly the floor of the hole began moving and a large bowl appeared, stopping when the bowl was perfectly centered in the hole. The aroma of food reached our noses at once. I noticed that the bowl had a large flange protruding out towards me and a thing sticking up in the air from inside it. I leaned over and picked it up with my teeth.

No sooner had I removed it, than the hole's floor moved and another identical bowl appeared. Heels clicking, I carefully walked it over to the table and awkwardly sat it down. Meanwhile, one by one the others retrieved a similar bowl and brought theirs over to the table. After Kallisto took the last bowl, the floor in the hole stopped moving.

However, another buzzing noise sounded and a batch of towels and wash rags appeared falling down from the ceiling near the bathtub. While we noticed that, we were more interested in breakfast. I stared into the bowl. A bluish semi-liquid mush filled the bowl. The protrusion item turned out to be a straw. Without the use of our feet to feed ourselves, the straw allowed us to suck up the mush. It was flavorful, nourishing we discovered later, but rather slimy, nothing to chew.

A few minutes of slurping later, we all finished. "Well, that wasn't too bad, I do feel full," I volunteered.

"It's about the same as what we all used to eat every day in the House of Right," Alexa replied, "right Enyo?" She nodded and took her last slurp.

"These straws make it a lot easier, though," Enyo replied.

"I wish we would have had them back then," Natasa added. Aella agreed with her.

"Now what?" Alexa asked. "We should figure out what has happened to us and where we are and how to get out of here, and in that order."

"I think I know how we might find out what happened to us," I offered.

"Good," Linda had calmed down considerably now. "Let's see, we have one Wid with us, three Judgers, three Planners, and one language translator. No Communicators, no Loremasters, no Healers, no Protectors, no arms, and no feet until we can get these damnable boots off. We are screwed! Everyone, be extra careful. If you are injured, we won't be able to do anything to help you. We are in a fine pickle this time!"

Enyo added, "Well, Linda, most of us are quite comfortable without arms, since we never had any to begin with. However, the loss of our feet is most troublesome, to put it mildly. We've depended upon them since birth. Perhaps a top priority is to find a way to get them off. After all, someone got them on us in the first place. What goes on must somehow come off," she added using her eternally optimistic engineering voice.

"We need to discover just how this can be done," Aella offered. "I'll get to work on it right away."

"Hold on a second!" Kallisto interrupted the continuous stream of conversation. "Bethany said something and I want to know how she can find out what happened to us all!" Her coal black eyes met mine and I smiled.

"Okay, I guess as your Wid, I had better take control," I chuckled. The others smiled at me, just giving me a nudge. "I can also handle the Communicator duties, but you are all right. I believe the therapy process might give us a clue about what happened last night. While I am working on this question, how about the Planners giving our room a good analysis? Judgers, work out our priorities and then lend the engineers a hand — okay a foot — okay a boot." We all chuckled. "I'll start with Kallisto because she ought to be several thousand miles south of where we all were located last night in Velona."

Kallisto took a seat next to me, while the others got up and began systematically going over our room, heels clicking on the stone floor. Yes, Enyo discovered that it was indeed solid stone, bedrock perhaps. "Okay, Kallisto, close your eyes and let's go back to last night. I want you to re-experience everything that happened. Tell me all about it as you go along."

"Well, Frank and I just had sex, and I was really contented, relaxed. I fell asleep quickly. I see blackness. It is nighttime. This is sure weird, Bethany. I see myself sleeping away on the bed. I am cuddling into Frank. Hey, hold on a second! I feel a tingle of energy all over my body, not enough to wake me up, though. The next instant I'm laying on a warm bed somewhere else. I hear a low-pitched humming sound, like metal, hollow or something. I hear a door slide open."

"Oh no! It is one of those mantis creatures! A big one! Its claws undress me. It slides these boots onto my feet and holds a device next to each one. My feet get hot, and the material seems to melt up tightly against my calves. Then I feel that tingle of energy once more, and I'm lying in the bed there next to Enyo. Ah, then the bright light and screeches wakes me up. That's all. Bethany! There is another mantis around! Why didn't it eat us? I mean eat our legs and such, as you saw elsewhere. What is going on? Where are we?"

"Kallisto, I do not know the answers to any of those. Why don't you help the others and I'll run the rest of us through last night." She agreed and clicked off to join the others, sending Linda back to me.

I ran Linda through last night with identical results. Sometime later, I finished all seven, and Linda ran me through my last evening. All of us experienced a tingling sensation over our whole body and then found the body had been somehow moved into a metal machine. My guess was that the machine was one of their flying machines. We had been brought here, similarly shod, and placed into the beds.

"There is only one explanation possible," Linda declared, after finishing me. "We have all been abducted by the mantis creature."

"I concur," Kallisto added.

"Ditto," Alexa put in, "and we are being held in some kind of prison somewhere. The purpose of these damnable boots is to render us even less able to do things, such as escape. It does not want us harmed, since it is clearly feeding us and providing for our basic living needs. For what purpose? That remains yet a mystery I intend to solve."

Linda fearfully said, "To eat our remaining limbs later or to serve as a host for their eggs or babies? If so, I want to kill this body somehow . I'm not going to play that game!"

"Let's not jump to such conclusions just yet," Kallisto cautioned and attempted to ease Linda's fears. "If it comes to needing to eliminate these bodies, I'm more than capable of doing so. However, that might not be their plans, eating us. After all, they could have eaten anyone of us eight last night. We were completely at their mercy and they didn't. Besides, if they were going to eat us, why put these boots onto our legs? Surely the boots are inedible. I'm sure they don't eat metal spikes."

"Let's look at who they have abducted," Kallisto continued.

"Powerhouses," Alexa interrupted her. "Bethany is the Supreme Commander of the Santi and the one who has killed the most of the mantis creatures. Linda is close behind her in that department, and she is re-organizing the Santi to make it even more powerful. To that end, I am also working on instigating all sorts of social reforms in Velona, helping others to prosper and thrive far better than they are now. Surely we three would be the first I would abduct if I wanted to attempt to regain control over the people of Tarra."

"Ah, following suit," Kallisto added, "Enyo already has invented any number of terrific inventions, so she needs to be captured. Likewise, Natasa and Aella, who are both top engineers helping to create a better Velona. Me, just look at the many social changes I have worked down in the one time, mantis controlled Demokritos with their marital Eight Degrees. I'd abduct me too."

"And don't forget Natale. She is the best translator on Tarra," Linda added. "Further, she is trying to decipher the mantis language and read their many books that we found. If she is successful, the whole world can read about what the mantis creatures have been doing. For sure, abduct her."

"But why not Renzo, Chaucer, or Rosina?" I asked. "They helped as well."

"Yes, but they are not going around changing things. You and I are — actually all of us are the prime movers of change in our areas," Linda explained.

"I see your point. Conclusion: they have abducted those beings most responsible for bringing about major, positive change on Tarra. With us out of the way, they have the upper hand once again," I replied, seeing her point clearly now.

"Ah, so they are making sure that we cannot escape this place," Kallisto added. "They want us out of circulation for a very long time. They must keep our bodies alive and us imprisoned within them. Hence, this elaborate prison cell here. Makes diabolical sense, something I would attempt, if the need arose."

"God, I am sure going to get mighty tired of sucking up that bluish slop they call food!" I exclaimed. "I could really use a cup of tea right about now!" Sipping tea always calms me down.

Worriedly, Linda asked, "Bethany, can you contact our husbands and see if they can come to rescue us? I'm worried about all our children. What are they going to do without us?"

"I have to relax first. Okay, no tea. Give me a minute, Linda. I am just as scared of this as the rest of you." I tried to calm my mind and finally did so. I expanded my awareness outward. About a hundred feet from where my body was sitting, I ran into an energy field of some sort, which zapped me. It caught me unaware; the backlash nearly knocked the body off its chair.

"God! Booby trapped! Got shocked," I explained to the very concerned Linda and Kallisto, who were sitting beside me. I tried again, but found no way to go around this barrier. Now I really got scared!

From my nervous shaking, both women knew something was very wrong. "I — I can't do it! There is some kind of electronic shield that is preventing me from making telepathic contact beyond about a hundred feet from where I sit! This is bad, very, very bad!"

"Maybe you can float up and out of this place and make contact when you are far from here," Linda suggested, trying desperately to think of something to help me with this. I sensed her fear rising by the minute. Me, I was nearly panicking. Never before had I encountered a telepathic block or shock!

I took a deep breath, tried to relax, and then floated up and through the roof. My plan was just to go on upwards a mile or two and then try. About a hundred feet up, I ran into a similar energy barrier of some kind. This time, the jolt backlash did send my body flying backwards; my head landed hard on the floor. At once, everyone came clicking over to help me. The heel noise was becoming annoying to me, and my head throbbed.

"Are you okay? Bethany, we cannot do anything for you. We are mostly helpless like this. Please wake up. Are you okay?" Linda was becoming nearly as frantic as I felt.

Moaning about my head, I awkwardly got up and the others even more awkwardly managed to set my chair upright. I sat down heavily in it. All seven were staring at me, terrified looks upon their faces. I had to tell them. "I can't get out of here. I tried going up. Around a hundred feet up, I was zapped and sent back down here. I'm really getting scared, gang. This is most certainly a nasty trap that we are in; my stomach is all in knots. I'm shaking like a leaf in the wind. God, for a cup of tea about now!"

Enyo apologetically said, "Will a cup of water be acceptable in its place? I've figured out how to draw water from the contraption over there, from the small one. The larger one is a bath. There is hot water at least."

"Yes, fabulous Enyo. Please," I replied, grateful for something to swallow, anything to relieve the horrible knot in my stomach.

"Where does it hurt, Bethany?" asked Kallisto. I told her the spot, and she used her head to rub it. Ah, that really helped me. We all watched as Enyo clicked with tiny steps over to the taller, smaller basin and demonstrated how to draw water. One pushed one's nose on a button. A mug came down. After picking it up with your teeth, you positioned it under the spigot, and then pressed the right lever. Out came cold water. She said the left one drew hot water. She carefully held the mug's horizontal handle in her teeth and clicked even more slowly back over to me. I had to use the straw from breakfast to drink it, however.

Slowly the knot lessened. "Gang, we are in really bad trouble here. I cannot break through the energy field to communicate to anyone outside of here nor can I even float up and out of here. Not only are our bodies trapped in here, but also we spiritual beings are likewise trapped! Even if we kill off our bodies, we cannot leave to go get new baby bodies! I am really scared this time!" I had to be honest with them; I loved them all too much not to be straight with them.

We eight women looked at each other; fear bordering on terror was in each of our eyes. "I got to go pee or vomit, can't tell which!" exclaimed Linda, who made a dash for the toilet, nearly falling down because of the high heels, which she forgot about in her haste. She managed not to vomit, however. We all felt very sick at this point.

"Why don't we all lie down a bit? I have to calm my nerves," I suggested. I was beginning to feel slightly faint and light headed on top of everything else.

Awkwardly, Linda, Natale, and Kallisto lay down beside me. Kallisto rolled her body up against mine, comforting me as best she could. "We'll think of something, Bethany," she whispered in my ear.

The others followed suit, lying awkwardly down on the second bed. My head began spinning. This time we were really trapped! I couldn't contact Renzo. I couldn't even get myself away from here. With our feet encased in these stupid heels, we were extremely immobilized, bordering on helplessness with daily life functions. I was scared, and the knot in my stomach only grew worse.

Kallisto, being the oldest here, began talking to us all. "Well, we got the first question answered. We know how we all got here. Enyo, what did you and Aella, Natasa, and Natale find out about our prison cell?"

Enyo's voice was wavering as she tried to control her panic as well. "The cell is not square, but is hexagonal in shape, nearly forty feet across. Strange shape, if you ask me. Perhaps it lies within a larger square room and the machinery and stuff to operate the devices is stored in the six corners. I say this, because a hexagonal structure is a solid building shape. The bees build their hives using hexagonal structures. Anyway, the floor is brown stone, probably bedrock. The walls are hollow sounding. We figured out how to operate the bathtub and the sink; I'm calling the smaller one a sink. We've got hot and cold running water, that's something anyway."

Aella added, "There are no windows, but I found something that might possibly be a door, though it requires much more study to determine if that is so and how it might operate. We could not find any way to reach the ceiling, however."

"These metal heels can scratch the brown stone floor," Natasa put in. "Here by our bed, I am constructing a calendar to keep track of the days. I made a long scratch mark for today. Each day, let's add another one. We must keep track of the days that we are in prison somehow."

"I found hairbrushes," Natale offered. "You press another button with your nose and a small door slides open. There are eight brushes in there on a ledge. Strange ones, though. Looks like we have to put them in our mouths, and try to brush out each other's hair with our heads. This is not going to be fun at all."

Just then, the overhead buzzer sounded. As at breakfast, a bowl of food suddenly appeared in the food dispenser, as we began to call it. One by one, we awkwardly got up and clicked our heels slowly over to the dispenser, picked up the bowl in our teeth, and even more slowly walked to the table. Again, a straw allowed us to suck up the same bluish slop, called food. Enyo discovered that if we placed the empty bowls into the dispenser, the dispenser activated, removing the bowl. Just where it went remained a complete mystery.

After disposing of the bowls, we all sat back down at the table and stared at each other; no one said anything. We were all growing quite frightened with our predicament. At last, Natale broke the silence. "Perhaps, the mantis will speak to us somehow and tell us what is going on. Maybe I can translate, if it does."

"You think it will speak to us?" asked Linda.

"Why would it?" replied Kallisto. "I wouldn't bother talking to my prisoners. Let them stew and rot."

"At least the temperature in here is uniform and constant. Naked as we are, we are entirely dependent on the temperature being just right. Some comfort in that," Enyo tried to cheer us up a bit.

I sighed. "Okay, gang. This must be the afternoon. Let's all go back over every inch of this prison cell and see if we can find out anything else that might be useful. That will give us something to do for a while anyway."

Each of us experimented with everything in the room. The beds were affixed to the floor with bolts and could not be moved. I even managed to get down and look underneath them, in hopes of finding something useful. I did find that there were blankets and spare sheets stored beneath the beds, but nothing more. Slowly the afternoon whiled away.

The buzzer sounded supper. Once more, the diet was blue slop. This was already getting old, though it was nourishing and filling and not un-tasty, just a weird color and texture. Yet, it had to be liquefied if we were going to suck it up through a straw. After supper, we decided to spend some time learning how to brush out each other's long hair. This turned out to be an exceedingly difficult a task, taking considerable time. Just as we were finally finishing up, the buzzer made a different sound and the lights flashed.

"I think it is a 'lights are about to be turned off' signal," I suggested, and we all headed for our beds. After we all awkwardly climbed in and used our teeth to pull up the sheet, the buzzer sounded again and the lights went out. Black, utter blackness filled the room. I could not see my hands in front of my face, even if I had them.

"God! What if I have to go to the bathroom during the night?" exclaimed a worried Linda. As if in answer to her fear, a small nightlight turned on and remained on throughout the night. I lay next to Kallisto, who lay next to Linda, who lay beside Natale. We all longed for our husband's arms; we longed for a loving snuggle. Instinctively, we four snuggled up close to each other, our bodies pressing against each other. At last, I drifted into a deep sleep.

Buzz! Blinding light announced the coming of a new day. Startled, we all rose and looked at each other, the fear returning to each of our faces as we faced another day in this prison. Nothing had changed, not even the bluish slop called food. After breakfast, we realized that we had nothing at all to actually do. "Look, we cannot just lie around here all day and sleep all night. Our muscles will simply atrophy. Besides, if we can ever find a way out of this room, we will need to be in peak physical condition. So let's continue with our usual stretching exercises; do as much of a work out as possible," I suggested.

"We should become very expert in walking in these heels," Kallisto added. "If we can get out, we need to be able to deal with walking long distances in them and with keeping our balance. We've enough room to do a lot of walking in here. Also, keep your eyes open for any way to escape."

We spent the morning doing all manner of exercises, including sit-ups, which kept our stomach muscles well-toned. If we ever could get the use of our feet back, we would still have those vital muscles at the ready. The long afternoon, we walked around and around and around the room. Finally, I decided to make a game out of it. "Let's play tag, since we don't have a ball for kick ball. We have to bump another to tag them. I'll be it first." I gave them a second to start moving away from me before I went after them. At first they were a bit reluctant to just play a game, considering how critical our situation was. Yet, before long, everyone was rushing about, well as fast as we could, given the circumstances, laughing and having fun.

When we finished, Natasa made the scratch mark on her calendar just as the supper buzzer sounded. After supper, we brushed out our hair once more and then it went dark again.

Slowly a week passed by, we continued our daily regimen but nothing changed within our prison cell. Depressing, unimaginably depressing. If the mantis creature was around, we detected no sign of it. Certainly, it did not attempt to communicate with us. Several times, we all yelled as loudly as we could, but nothing at all happened.

However, at the end of the week, while we were brushing out our hair, Kallisto said, "Bethany, I swear that your hair is growing longer by the day."

"Well, it does grow, but let me see." I stood up and measured how long it was. It did seem to be a bit longer than I remembered it being. This, however, did not displease me, as I have a fetish for long hair. In doing so, I also noticed my large breasts. I had spent my childhood hoping and praying that my small ones would fill out. Moms were quite large. They had become rather large after I had the twins. Now, however, they seemed even larger, they pushed up and outward more so than normal.

Kallisto saw me studying mine and examined hers more closely. "Could it be that our breasts are growing too?" she volunteered.

Natasa, who had the smallest pair, said, "Golly, mine are definitely getting larger! And I am not with child. Well, I won't mind this; Fred is going to love it if they get a bit bigger, assuming I ever see Fred again." Her voice nearly broke into grief. We all felt that horrible pang in our chests. Would we ever get out of here?

"Let's be practical about this," Enyo spoke up. "Let's find a way to measure them and then compare them say a week from now. Each of us went to a spot on the blank walls and pressed our chests up to the wall. Enyo then used her metal heel to make appropriate marks on the walls, also scratching in a letter to identify whose was whose. We barely got it done when the room went black once more. We all stood there waiting for the night light to activate. Thank god for the dim light!

Another week passed us by without the slightest change in our prison or its routine mechanical operation. Yes, we continued to exercise diligently, pushing our bodies harder and harder. If nothing else, we were going to be in excellent shape if we ever did get out of here! Our walking had now progressed to running, well more of a trotting in tiny steps. Along with strengthening our leg muscles, our sense of balance in these high heels was decidedly improving. Hence, we continued our daily workouts.

At the end of the week, duly announced by Natasa, we again measured our breasts. Yes, definitely all were growing larger! Mine had really firmed out and no longer sagged; rather they began to take on the shape of a rounded ball. So did the breasts of everyone else! Natasa was very pleased with hers, since hers used to be the smallest of any of us. I, whose breasts were decidedly the largest, began to worry about this growth spurt! Just how big were they going to get? I was more than happy to have them stop growing right now!

However, Enyo and Alexa both made the same comment at the same time, "I am really getting incredibly horny!" Both women looked at each other and started laughing. God, now that they mentioned it, so was I! Everyone began chatting about this at the same time.

I observed that all eight of us were experiencing the same phenomenon! I would have expected at any given point in time, one or two of us to feel this way, should we allow our minds to drift onto our husbands. Perfectly normal and understandable — but all eight of us at the same time? I asked if any had been thinking about their mates. No one had.

However, just my asking this of them produced an incredible effect. "My god, I've never felt this horny in my life!" exclaimed Linda. The next two minutes were filled with similar exclamations from everyone else, myself included! Somehow, I just had to relieve the pressure, the desire.

"It's okay to feel this way," Alexa broke in on our embarrassments. "We from the House of Right know what to do. It is perfectly natural. Our husbands are not here to help us. We four are experienced. When the lights go out tonight, let's trade sleeping partners. Enyo and I will take Natale and Linda's place; they can take our places."

"I've never felt this way before," I said very embarrassed about this sudden, powerful drive coursing through my body. "I don't understand what is happening to me, but I will do anything to relieve it! I am so embarrassed about this." Linda added a meek me too.

When the lights finally went out, Alexa and Enyo began working on me first. Kallisto watched and quickly caught on. Three did work better than two did. The relief that I felt sometime later, I cannot describe. I'd never felt anything like it before. One by one, all four of us got relief, and I overcame my embarrassment to help with my other three bedmates.

Sometime later, all eight of us were finally relaxed, the drive temporarily satisfied. Kallisto, snuggling up to me, concluded, "Bethany, there must be something in the bluish slop that is causing all this. First, our hair is growing far longer and far faster than normal, but none of us are worried about that. Second, our breasts are growing alarmingly, especially yours; they are now like small balls!"

Enyo said, "Bethany, I am estimating that at their present rate of growth, yours will be as big as the children's kick ball in about a month! That's huge by any standard!"

"E-gods! They are plenty big enough now!" I gushed, more than a little worried. "What's the third?" I asked.

Kallisto finished, "Third, the food must be making our sex drive abnormally strong and powerful. Mind you, I personally enjoyed this evening immensely, though I would prefer Frank to be in my bed. It has to be the food."

"So what do we do about it?" called out Linda from the other bed. "Stop eating?"

"No, we cannot stop eating, silly. I don't mind the first and third, I'm just worried about the second. Maybe when we get out of here and stop eating this slop, they will shrink back to their usual sizes," Kallisto tried to offer some hope.

"Gosh, I hope mine don't go back that small," Natasa teased. "I like them as they now are. Fred will too."

"Wait a minute, everyone! It just hit me!" I exclaimed, a revelation flooding my consciousness. "Look, this effect is driving us more solidly into our bodies! Look how we all could think of nothing but giving each other pleasure a bit ago? It's slowly driving us back into our heads!"

"We have got to get out of here and find better food," Enyo declared. "I'll be honest with you, Bethany. I often use this. After I get a round of intense pleasure, like tonight, I then get hungry, and then I begin to think. Some of my brightest ideas have struck me at such times. That's when I invented the toilet. The Bottom Washer I also thought of right after a pleasure time. When we have light in here tomorrow, will someone please pleasure me? I've just got to figure out a way for us to escape this prison." I thought that this was highly unusual, but I agreed with her. Just now, another wave of horniness was beginning to sweep over me yet again.

The next morning, after being pleasured twice more and helping to pleasure the others as well, we all arouse, somewhat bedraggled; our hair, a mess. We looked at each other and laughed as we got our blue slop breakfast. As soon as Enyo had finished, I pushed my body into hers, nudging her back towards the bed. I was ready to try anything to find a way out of here!

"Whoa, Bethany is really after me now," Enyo teased. However, Alexa and Kallisto joined me, as we laughed and continued to push Enyo toward the bed. A bit later, Enyo was very relaxed. She sighed, gave us three a loving kiss, and rose awkwardly as usual. For an hour, all we heard was the click of her heels as she slowly paced the room. Then, she paced around and around where the theoretical door was located.

"I have an idea. Look, if the mantis were in here, it would have to have a way to open the door to let itself out. It certainly isn't going to want to be trapped in here with us. So there has to be a way to open the door from in here. Now the mantis creature has only pointed appendages, and there is no usual keyhole as we have in some of our doors. The only thing visible at all is this tiny hole here. My idea is to stick something into the hole and see if it causes the door to open. Can you all come over here and balance me? I am going to stick this metal heel of mine in the hole. It is about the right size and it is the only thing we have that we could use anyway."

We seven clicked our way over to her as quickly as we could. We pushed our bodies up against hers, supporting her as she raised her leg high to reach the hole. It was a tricky move, and Kallisto bent over and used her back to help support and steady Enyo's leg. Yes, the tiny metal heel spike slid into the opening. "Golly, this is incredibly difficult. I have to somehow push it into the hole." I gave her body a push and that worked; her spike heel slid into the hole solidly.

We all nearly fainted in surprise as the door slid open sideways with a whooshing sound. Carefully, Enyo retracted her heel, and we all stepped outside out prison cell for the first time in about three weeks! "Someone look and see if there is a hole on the other side. We don't want to become trapped outside, if we cannot find food or water or a better place to sleep," Enyo hollered as we all began to step outside the doorway.

"There is an identical hole out here, Enyo," I replied. She was the last to step out of our cell.

"Ah, I was right, there is another space which lies outside our cell," she proclaimed.

"Gosh, it is much hotter out here!" I exclaimed. Already, I was beginning to sweat.

"It's so dark out here," Natasa observed, "brilliantly lighted inside, but dark out here and hot. Strange. I wonder if there is some light source that can be turned on out here?"

"I wonder if we should be very quiet out here? Perhaps a mantis is around and might hear us?" Linda added, somewhat fearful; after all, the prisoners were making a break for it.

"Well, let's look around where the light from our room shines out here," I suggested.

"Wait a minute, everyone," Aella broke in, "if the cell door closes, it will be pitch black out here. We will not be able to see the hole to re-open the cell door. If we are underground, there may not ever be any light out here. We could become trapped outside and starve to death."

"Good point, Aella," I replied. "Okay, Linda, Natale, and I will stay inside our door, just in case it closes automatically after a time. If it does, we will reopen it as fast as we can. Engineers, you be very careful out there and be quiet, just in case there is a mantis around. If one appears, get me at once, perhaps I may be able to handle it."

We three stepped back inside. Yes, I was dying of curiosity as well, but Aella was right. We could become trapped outside if the door closed and we found no light source out there. The five began exploring. The clicks of their heels echoed noisily, even though they whispered. One thing was for sure, with these boots, we could not move silently around here. Also, I could hear the hum of machinery in the background. Something was keeping our room at a uniform temperature while outside it was at least ninety degrees, maybe more. Yet, with the door opened, I noticed that the air circulation had stopped, our room began to heat up and was soon the same as the outer room, hot!

Sweating, I did not feel so horny. I could think a bit more clearly. Something I once heard during healing training years ago came to mind. I wish I had paid better attention to the Healer who was trying her best to teach me about herbs. Yes, that was it. Herbs. She was saying that certain herbs were aphrodisiacs. "Linda, what if the mantis creatures are injecting some kind of herbs into our food? That could account for our strange body behaviors?"

"I've heard of stimulants for sex drives, but I don't remember any specifics. Tonia would know, but I don't recall if any would cause our hair to grow abnormally fast or to swell our breasts so much. Yet, it could well be so," Linda answered thoughtfully.

"What could be so?" Enyo's voice interrupted us. She'd just returned from the first exploration of the small area beyond our door, where the room's light could reach.

"We think that the mantis creatures are injecting some kind of herbs into our slop which is causing our sexual drives to amplify, hair to grow abnormally fast, and our breasts to enlarge," I explained.

"Makes sense. Bottelo weed does that to us back in the House of Right, makes us more pliable when the men should come, or so I was always told. I've found the backside of the food dispenser machine. Man, it is hot out there. I'm dripping with sweat, and I've only been walking around. Jeesh, it is hot in here too! Ah, the machine, which kept our room at the constant temperature, is not working. I hope it begins to work when we close the door."

"Yes, or we are going to be awfully uncomfortable as well," I replied.

"Okay, I will go have another look at the food machine; back in a bit," Enyo cheerily said. She loved to examine new machinery! We listened to the rhythmic click of her heels as she walked out to re-examine the machine. The others returned to our room, finished with their initial search.

Aella said, "Look what Natasa has found!" We looked at Natasa, who held two long pieces of metal in her mouth. "She thinks that we can use these to open the door. When Enyo returns we should try it. If so, we ought to leave one hidden outside the door just in case we are trapped out there. Plus we have one for inside here."

"Well done, Natasa!" I validated her. She smiled and laid the two onto the table.

"We believe that we are inside another building," Natasa suggested. "Until we can get the outer area illuminated, we can't be sure. All signs indicate it may be so. What's Enyo doing?"

I explained our theory about the herbs or something akin to herbs being injected into our food. As I finished my explanation, Enyo returned. "I need Natale to see if she can decipher something. I found some writing. Why don't you come with us, Bethany? I'll show you what I found. I should probably get your okay before I tinker with the food dispenser machinery."

We three walked back outside our prison room, our heels making a racket in the large open space. Since no mantis had appeared yet, I relaxed a bit about the noise we were making. Enyo took us to what had to be the backside of the dispenser machine, the physical location was correct at least. There were three large metal barrels. Two were taller than I stood and six feet around. A tube ran from their tops into the back of the machine. The third cylindrical barrel was much smaller, about two feet tall and only a foot around. A tube likewise went from its top into the back of the machine.

"Look at this writing here, Natale," Enyo pointed with her toe. "It looks like lettering on the side of this smaller barrel. I would think that the injection of herbs or such chemicals into our food would not be of a very large quantity; hence, my theory is that it is coming from this smaller barrel. Can you read the writing?"

"Well, the lighting is not so good. I was making some progress on those books we got from the mantis creatures. I've worked out a possible alphabet and numerals thus far." She squatted down and looked closely at the letters. "Yes, definitely mantis in origin. Every cipher is in my alphabet. Unfortunately, I can't say more, Enyo."

"Well, I guess we can experiment. How can we undo this one?" I asked.

"Challenging, if only we had our feet available for use," Enyo replied. "We'll just have to use our minds on this one. I haven't found any tools yet, though I don't know how I would be able to manipulate them if I did find any. So we observe this cylinder thing more closely. Perhaps we could chew through the tube, but then if what it was injecting was important, we couldn't undo it. Hum, see this connection here at the top of the cylinder? It looks like it somehow moves. If we had a wrench, we might be able to loosen it. However, it may go up and down, kind of feels that way to me."

"Let me try," I volunteered. If something ill happens, I wanted it to be on my head, not our best engineer's. I sat down and awkwardly moved into a position where I could put the sides of my boots on the fixture right where it connected to the cylinder's top.

"See if you can push the metal sleeve down or up," Enyo suggested.

"Okay, you stand back in case something ill happens," I ordered and began to struggle with my feet. The boots did have a secure friction grip on the sides of the sleeve. I pushed up, but nothing happened. It was easier to push downward. Suddenly, it gave way. There was a giant spray of air and particles that hit me full in my face, but the tube disconnected from the cylinder.

I began coughing profusely from the fumes that entered my nose and mouth. I couldn't get up, but rolled onto my side and continued coughing. After several minutes, I regained control and struggled to my feet. "I feel woozy," I whispered hoarsely. Both Enyo and Natale pushed their bodies up against mine to steady me, and we walked very slowly back into the room.

"What's happened to Bethany?" Linda asked. I did not look at all well.

"She disconnected the tube that we think is injecting the stuff into our food. However, she got a back flash of the stuff in her face," Enyo explained.

"We should get her washed off fast," Linda ordered. I was not going to complain, struggling to keep my balance and not pass out on them. Somehow, they got me into the bath tub. The dust particles covered my face and hair, and it took all of them to get me cleaned up. I found it hard to get up and out of the tub, however. I sat on the floor, while they surrounded me, drying me off with a bunch of towels. "You should now go lay down," Linda ordered.

"Oh god! Something's happening to me, Linda!" My body's hormones began to rage! "Oh god! I can't stand it! Pleasure me! Please, I cannot even stand up!" My body was writhing on the floor, out of my control, begging for a release. A half hour later, I was finally relaxed, but still lying on the floor.

"No doubt about it, everyone," I managed to finally find my voice, "that cylinder contains the stuff that is making us so horny. Thank you all. I couldn't stand it any longer. I am okay now, I think, but I'll just lie here a while."

My seven friends looked very relieved at last. "Okay, Natasa and I are going to experiment with opening the doors then. If her metal rods work, we will have an easy way to get in and out of this room," Enyo explained. We watched them as they did their experiments. Yes, inserting the rod in the hole and pushing on it did shut the door. Another push and it opened again. They went outside and tried the other one, which worked perfectly in that hole as well. I relaxed considerably, for now we could go in or out of our cell here at will. That was a small victory. Coupled with the removal of whatever was being injected into our blue slop, I felt that we were making progress. So did everyone else.

The machine sounded our supper call. Linda got mine for me and I made a supreme effort to get up and to the table. The food tasted rather bland, we all noted. Yet, time would tell if I had actually gotten rid of the herb or chemical, which had been causing our problems. After supper, everyone else took a bath and the evening passed swiftly, especially working with so much long hair to dry and brush. Me, I was pretty wasted and spent the evening lying in bed, watching the others. On the positive side, once we shut the door after supper, the machinery, which kept our room at a comfortable, uniform temperature, turned back on, and soon the oppressive heat vanished.

I slept fitfully, tossing and turning all night. When the buzzer sounded morning and the bright lights once more illuminated the room, I had a very hard time rolling over to get up. Also, my hair seemed to be under my knees somehow, ouch. I got up and still felt a bit lightheaded. One by one, the others beside me got up as well, stretching the sleep from their legs.

"Oh my god, Bethany!" exclaimed Natale. "Your breasts! Look!"

Everyone looked at me and my chest. "Oh my god!" I exclaimed in shock and surprise. Overnight they had grown significantly! Mine were now triple the size of anyone else here! At least, they didn't sag, but protruded outward, nice and firm, but huge!

"Well Linda, your mom once said to me, 'Bethany, be careful what you wish for, you might get it.' I had tiny breasts then and wanted them to grow, but this has gone beyond even being ridiculous! They are even throwing me off balance. No wonder I was having a harder time rolling out of bed. Gosh, I hope that they now begin to shrink some, since that herb or chemical isn't in our slop anymore."

"Bethany! Your hair, look at your hair!" Natale exclaimed. "It's down below your knees!"

"Whoa! Now this is cool! Wow. Look at it, beautiful!" I exclaimed. Okay, so I have a fetish for long hair. This time it was now really long. My hair now touched the upper part of my ankles! Enyo and Alexa were my closest competitors, reaching their knees. Kallisto and Natale's hair now reached their upper thighs. Linda's now was below her waist. Aella and Natasa, who began with shoulder length hair, now sported tresses reaching their lower backs.

"Well, I love the hair, but the boobs have got to shrink!" I jested, and we all had a good laugh at my situation. I soon discovered that I had a new problem: I kept stepping on my hair when I got up from my chair. If I bent over, my hair swept the floor. We had nothing with which to tie it up out of the way a bit. Ah well, problems, we seemed surrounded with problems here in our prison cell.

"Well, I do think it is working, Bethany," Enyo volunteered. "I mean I don't feel so horny today at all. Thank goodness for small changes. Maybe we have licked the problem and maybe your breasts will now start to grow smaller." She sounded hopeful anyway.

After breakfast, with their help, I managed to get my hair parted and draped over my chest in front of me. At least this way, I could see where it was at and try to keep it out of things. Enyo then opened the door, and we all went outside to explore once more. It was early morning, according to our room. Yet the blast of heat we felt when we ventured out of the room was incredible, well over a hundred, almost unbearably hot!

"This is incredibly weird, Bethany," Natasa commented, tossing her head to either side to get her long hair onto her back. She was unused to having hers anywhere this long. "Yesterday, we were out here in the late afternoon and I would guess the temperature was maybe ninety or so. Now, it is morning and the temperature is a hundred twenty or more. How can this be? Mornings are the coolest times, not the hottest. Something isn't right here."

"Excellent observation, Natasa. Let's see if we can figure this one out today. Start searching everyone. Let's see if there is any kind of way to get some lights on in here," I replied.

Everything was exactly as we had left it yesterday. The light from our room still only illuminated a tiny portion of the outside room area. The clicking of our heels echoed in the huge space as we began wandering about once more. It didn't look too hopeful to me, however.

"Eureka! What an idiot am I!" exclaimed Enyo. We all stopped and stared at her. "We've been looking for a light thing where it would be located for someone our size. This is a mantis place and they are fifty feet not six. We should be looking for some devices way up there," she nodded her head upwards. We all began walking around, straining our necks upwards, looking for anything useful. Enyo spied a box with a tube running upwards from it. We all traced the route of the tube, which seemed to go to a location overhead and not to our room.

"Now, how do we press that button?" Enyo queried.

"Should I?" asked Natale.

"Sure, why not? Just be prepared to press it a second time if something awful happens," I ordered. She floated out of her body and gave the button a push. Presto, brilliant white light appeared in this whole section! "Thus, we have light!" I joyfully declared.

"Woo hoo, now we can really do some exploring!" the trio of engineers exclaimed together.

# Chapter 2 Missing?

August 1, 657, Renzo Pazzio le'Goeur was sleeping in. Our six year old twins, Lena and Ben, were hungry and crawled upon our bed. "Daddy, wake up," Ben said, shaking Renzo. Lena just tickled him when he groaned.

"Hey, what's this? Attacked by you two?" Renzo sat up and tickled the twins back.

"We're hungry, daddy," Lena explained.

"Go find mommy; it's my turn to sleep in today," he replied.

"We can't find mommy," Lena replied didactically.

"Oh, okay, I'll find her. Then, I can get back to sleep," Renzo replied. His head felt like he had a hangover, yet he had not drunk the night before. He staggered around our small house, calling out for me, the twins on his tail.

"See, daddy, mommy's not here," Ben explained. Now Danielle, our four year old, demanded some attention as well. Adrien also woke up, needing a diaper change. A bit harried, Renzo changed the dirty diaper, picked up Adrien, held on to the hands of Danielle, and walked out of our house and into the large mansion, where everyone was congregating for breakfast. The twins were right behind him.

"Hey, anyone seen Bethany this morning?" he called out as he began sitting the children down for their meal. Many voices called out no. Grumbling, he fixed our kids their breakfast and fed Adrien.

While they were eating, Chaucer d'Grange entered the huge dining room of the mansion, kids in tow. Zach, their six year old, came over to the twins, his constant playmates, while Chaucer got little Sam situated and Marion's chair adjusted. Zach whispered to Ben, "Mom's gone missing!"

"Oh, so's ours!" Ben replied, becoming more excited.

"Hey, anyone seen Linda this morning?" Chaucer called out. No one had seen her either, and he began to feed Sam his breakfast.

Renzo said, "Bethany's missing too, Chaucer. Our two wives are inseparable, always have been. I guess something must have come up. We'll probably find out about it at the morning's meeting. I sure could have used the sleep in today. My brain feels fried!"

"Funny, so does mine!" Chaucer replied, "as if I have a hangover or something. Funny, I don't remember having any wine last night."

Captain Henry Freeze wandered into the breakfast table, carrying Barnabe and Gwen, with Charlie walking at his side. "Hi gang. Anyone seen Natale this morning? I can't find her anywhere around. Here, Charlie, go get your breakfast, while I handle your brother and sister."

Charlie walked by his friends and said, "Hey, mom's gone missing!"

Ben and Lena chorused, "So's our mom."

"Mine too," added Zach.

Henry sat down close to Renzo and Chaucer. "This is not like her, going off without a word," he said, rather worried. "In fact, she's never done it. I'm beginning to have a bad feeling about it. Is everything else all right around here?"

"Nothing's going on as far as we know, but Bethany and Linda are also missing," Renzo added. "Probably something urgent came up and the three are off being busy," he tried to put an optimistic slant on it.

After the kids were fed, the men took them to the nursery, where the many nannies took over, while the older kids ran outside to play, chatting about the mysterious disappearance of their mothers.

"Why don't you come with us to the morning's meeting?" Renzo suggested to Henry. "Surely all three will be there. You can get an explanation and be on your way." Henry looked relieved and followed the two into the large meeting room.

Slowly the other members of the Explorers Circle, now the Headquarters Circle, whose task was to run the entire Santi del Dio organization, met each morning. Rosina, Renzo's twin sister, came in with her husband Cedric. Tonia and Emil wandered in chatting gaily, followed by Benet and Michelle, who parted with a loving kiss; she headed off to the Laird Foundation palace next door where her painting studio was located on the second floor.

"Hey, where's Bethany?" asked Emil.

"We don't know," Renzo replied. "Linda and Natale are missing as well. I thought that they'd be here. Bethany has never missed a meeting yet. I am starting to get a bit worried about her."

"Okay, brother, I'll contact her and find out," Rosina teased her twin. She was the Circle's Communicator, an excellent telepath in her own right. Rosina closed her eyes, expanded her awareness, and attempted to make contact with Bethany. Nothing. Blankness.

"Something is wrong! I can't contact her!" She sat down, relaxed, and tried once more. After a few minutes, she opened her eyes, a trace of panic in them. "I don't understand this! I cannot contact any of them, Bethany, Linda, or Natale! It's as if they don't even exist! What is going on? I'm getting scared."

"Okay, are we agreed that we have a problem?" Renzo asked. Everyone nodded. "Okay, then one of us must step into Bethany's shoes and lead us forward. I think it should be a Protector, since three women are missing."

Emil agreed, adding, "It should be Renzo, Chaucer, or me."

"Rule me out. I am too unfamiliar with things here," Chaucer spoke up very quickly.

Emil looked at Renzo. Renzo said, "Emil, you have been around here the longest of any of us, will you volunteer?"

"Okay, if no one has any objections?" Emil asked. None did. "First order of business, Rosina, go fetch whomever of Jenna's Circle that are still around the estate. Get them here as fast as possible. We need all the help we can get." Rosina left in a big hurry.

"What about others that might also be missing?" asked Tonia. "Shouldn't we start asking around?"

"Let's present that to Jenna's Circle. If we go around making inquiries, we might start a panic," Emil replied. "Keep our eyes and ears open for others, however. Let's sit tight for a couple more minutes. We ought to get some tea in here. I think we are going to need it."

A half hour later, the room was filled with Hank Weston, Loremaster and Bethany's father, Lilly Ann, Judger and Linda's mother, Beth Ann and Alan Donegal, Healer and Planner, Bennet's parents, Paulette, Communicator, and Adam, their Protector.

Everyone stared at Paulette as she began to search for each of the three missing women. Her face grew steadily whiter. After a half hour, she opened her eyes. "Nothing, absolutely nothing! I've never experienced anything like this, no contact, no nothing, as if they have disappeared utterly from Tarra! How can this be? Even if they had lost their bodies, I should still be able to contact them. I get nothing, total absence of contact!"

"Okay, let's go over all this once more," Lilly Ann, the Judger in her kicking into high gear. "Renzo, tell me everything you remember about last night."

"Not much, we put the kids to bed, we, ah," his face flushed, "made love, and then we fell asleep. I awoke this morning with a hangover and Bethany was gone." The other two told similar stories.

"Peculiar, all three of you say you have a hangover, yet none of you had anything to drink last night. Red flag goes up. We also should go examine the three women's rooms and see if they left us any clues. Meanwhile, Beth Ann, I want you to run a therapy session on these three. Find out what this hangover is all about. I hate inexplicable things. Let's get moving."

Everyone headed off to search the three rooms, while Beth Ann kept the three husbands here. "Okay, Renzo, you first. I want you to close your eyes and return to last night. Go through the night and tell me what you are seeing." She began to run him back through the night's events. On the third pass, the obscuring fog lifted from his mind.

"Oh, in the middle of the night, I felt this surge of energy over me, deadening me. It is covering Bethany too. One instant I have my arm over her body, the next instant she is gone, my arm drops down. What can this mean?"

She ran Henry and Henry through their nighttime sleep and discovered nearly the same story. One minute she was there, the next, she was gone. Both had felt a paralyzing blast of some kind of energy over their sleeping bodies, just before their wife disappeared.

Just then, the others returned en mass. Beth Ann reported what little she had uncovered. "The picture is becoming clearer," Lilly Ann replied. "We searched their rooms. The clothes they were wearing yesterday were piled on the floor; no clean clothes are missing. Conclusion, they left wearing next to nothing but a nightgown, not even shoes. Most interesting. Couple this with your report, Beth Ann, and I can draw only one conclusion."

"What?" asked a number of voices in unison.

"Who has the capability of using energy blasts? Who has the capabilities of carrying off a stunned woman? Who could possibly have the skill to block telepathic contacts totally? It has to be either the Grey Creatures or the mantis creatures behind this. I believe the three have been abducted during the night!"

"Damn, you might be right!" exclaimed Renzo. "That energy blast that I felt, it was exactly like the blasts I had before from the mantis creatures! Good god, Bethany's life is in grave danger, so is Linda and Natale! They cannot afford to lose any more appendages! Where are they at now?" he wailed.

"Why didn't they take me or Rosina?" asked Tonia.

"No idea, Tonia. However, we ought to see if anyone else is missing. This is very serious indeed, gang. Let's fan out. Cover every inch of the estate and the Laird Foundation. Find out who else might be missing. If we are very lucky, only these three have been abducted. Come on; let's get moving."

An hour later, everyone was back in the meeting room, a very disturbed, somber bunch. "Okay so now we know that Enyo, Alexa, Aella, and Natasa are also missing. That's seven of us. The picture is becoming clearer," Lilly Ann said.

"How? I am more concerned than ever!" Renzo exclaimed, a deep fear tightening in his stomach.

"They have picked out the seven most critical members of the Santi del Dio. Bethany is undoubtedly the most powerful of us all. Linda and Natale are a close second now. The House of Right women are the best inventors and engineers that Tarra has ever seen! Just look at the myriad inventions and works these have produced. I know Alexa has been working closely with Linda on the Santi reorganization plans. This is a very severe blow to the entire organization!"

She continued. "We should immediately contact all of the other Communicators, Tarra-wide! Let's find out if anyone else has gone missing within the last few days as well. I have a very bad feeling that we have lost others that we don't know about just yet. Tell the various Communicators to report to us immediately whenever anyone turns up missing in their zones. While Rosina and Paulette are doing that, I want the rest of you to fan out over the entire estate and spread the word. Any time anyone turns up missing, we are to be notified immediately. Next, let's get everyone to search this entire estate, from top to bottom, pantry to attic. We must be sure that their bodies are not here. Report in an hour, I'll see that lunch is brought in to us. Now action!"

Everyone jumped and dashed off to carry out her orders. Rosina and Paulette retrieved the lengthy list of all Communicators in the Santi organization. Slowly they began going down the list, contacting each, spreading the word.

At noon, everyone rejoined the two Communicators and the cooks brought in some lunch. "I do hope you find them soon," one cook told Lilly Ann, who bravely smiled back at the portly cook.

"Report," requested Lilly Ann.

Rosina, her face quite pale, said, "They got Kallisto too. Frank is going nuts down in Demokritos. He's calling out everyone to begin a search for her down there."

"No one else is missing," Paulette added. "That makes eight of them, and none have any arms. They are in big trouble; I just know it. I feel so sick at my stomach right now that I can hardly eat. We must find them before it is too late! I feel so helpless!"

"We all do, Paulette, we all do," Lilly Ann sighed.

Emil added, "Search of the estate turned up absolutely nothing, not a single sign of any of the seven. I am confident that they are not being held somewhere around here. God, they could be anywhere on Tarra!"

"Okay, we must think, use our brains, Renzo. We cannot make telepathic contact. That means that they must be alive and are being kept somewhere and behind some kind of telepathic screen that we cannot penetrate."

"Wait a second," Renzo interrupted. "If I know my wife, if she tried to contact us and failed, like Rosina and Paulette have, the first thing she would do is move up into the sky a couple miles, free from the mind shield, and try again! Bethany doesn't like barriers to her objectives."

Chaucer spoke up, "Then if that were so, why haven't we got her communication? Perhaps whatever is blocking her telepathic skills is also blocking her from moving a mile above where her body is being kept."

"Excellent point, Chaucer," Lilly Ann replied. "They must be being kept prisoners somewhere behind powerful shields."

"But if they abducted the eight most powerful of us, why go to all that trouble?" asked Tonia. "Why not just kill them outright?"

"Because they are very powerful spiritual beings and would immediately go pick up another body and jump back into the game of freeing all of us," Beth Ann answered her. "You see, body death for these eight would be acceptable, because each knows who and what they are and would just get a new body and be right back in action. This is certainly exactly the opposite of what the mantis creatures desire. From their view, these prisoners have escaped from their prison cells and are systematically going about releasing everyone else from their cells. As the prison guardians, the mantis must stop them from doing so. Killing them is not an option, they would be free to re-enter the game of life immediately. No, I rather think that the mantis creature's objective is to keep these eight somehow imprisoned in their current bodies for a very long time, totally isolated and out of circulation, so to speak."

"Oh god," Renzo exclaimed, "maybe they've eaten off their legs, leaving them to be a head and torso so they cannot move at all!"

"I don't think so, Renzo. I thought about that earlier," Lilly Ann calmed him down a bit. "You see, with those two in Wanakan, they left many other women around to care for their needs." She was referring to the two women who had lost their arms and legs to the mantis creatures. Wanakan was the port city on the new western continent that we had discovered a number of years ago. It lay thousands of miles to the west of our continent, the dog bone.

The narrow section connecting the two large lobes is an impassable desert. On either side, rise tall mountain ranges, which make overland travel into the Desert of Desolation impossible as well. Our civilization lies in the western lobe. Here, the Med Sea splits the lobe into two portions. The sparsely populated Southlands occupy the southern two-thirds of the lobe, while the upper third is divided into several pieces. The Med Sea, about seventy-five miles wide, spans nearly the entire western lobe, ending in a semi-arid land called Juda Arad. Some hundred miles north of the Med Sea is the eight thousand foot tall Appian Way mountain range, dividing this bottom northern third from the upper two equal sized long portions. Above Juda Arad lies the Northern Steppes, a hilly, grassland. Paralleling the Med Sea coast on the northern side and abutting the steppes are the Sea Princes, actually at one time called the Lands of the Seven Sea Princes.

The Zargarb sector abuts Juda Arad. Going on down the line are Solamina, Pieta, Bonilla, Vito, Barcella, and Velona. Fortress d'Grange, the eighth sector, lies in the mountainous lands just above Velona. On the other side of the Appian Way lies the Greenway and Langdoc regions. The Greenway has been broken into numerous small kingdoms, of which Mont Blanc, Langdoc, Calgary, and Southway are the strongest and controlled by us. The easternmost of these Greenway kingdoms abuts with the Northern Steppes. Further north beyond yet another mountain range lays Volksholm where the Axemen live, their home country, I should say, since many have now immigrated south.

Lying just offshore from Calgary, the largest city in the Greenway, is the island called West Reach, or Cymry by the locals.

On the southern shores of the Med Sea lies the Red Desert, largely uninhabited. Further south lays the Southlands, a huge land largely unexplored by us. Big game, diamond mines, gold mines, and heavy jungle regions abound down here. Much heavy, exotic timber comes from this area, which is used in the construction of our many ships.

Just off the western edge of the Southlands lies a series of hundreds of small islands, known collectively as the Spice Islands, from where we get our cocoa and teas, which I dearly love. Finally, on the eastern side of the Southlands, sitting just below the long stem of the dog bone shaped continent lies the huge island called Megalos. Its western side nearly touches the Southlands; a Narrow Firth separates the two, where the water level is only a few feet deep at low tide. A huge city lies there called Sud.

The Explorers Circle has opened up the rest of Tarra. The eastern lobe holds the country of Tashien, Empress Sho Lin rules there and is a good friend of ours. Far to the west across a vast ocean lies the peanut continent, peanut because of its shape. On the eastern equatorial coast lies the huge city of Wanakan. Far to the south lies the land of Konstantin, where the women rule and men are but mere slaves.

Lying far to the south of the dog bone continent lies the potato continent. Here barrier mountains separates the three countries. On the far eastern side is Annelise, home of the exquisitely dressed people. In the middle is Vladimir, a country of horsemen, similar to the Galts of our Northern Steppes. On the western side is Demokritos; these people share the same ancestors as those of Megalos. The two civilizations are remarkably similar, except Megalos had decayed, while Demokritos is thriving.

Lilly Ann continued her theorizing. "You see, if they remove these eight women's legs, then who will be looking after their basic needs? If they are not constantly moved, bedsores will develop quickly, infections will set in, and their bodies will die. This is exactly what the mantis creatures do not desire. My best guess, and this is only a guess, is that our women are being held prisoners. As such, their bodily needs are being well met so that they remain alive for a very long time, just imprisoned somehow, where escape is impossible."

"I so want to believe you!" Renzo was near tears. "What you say makes sense. We have to find them and rescue them somehow!"

"I have an idea," Rosina spoke up. "The mantis creatures might have taken them back to one of their secret bases. Renzo and I can go visit each one that we visited on our voyages. We can see if they are there."

"You mean take the caravel out?" Captain Henry asked.

Rosina countered, "No, that would take way too long, months. I mean we leave our bodies here with you all watching over them. Bethany has taught us to be where we desire. It might not take us too long to check on all of the ones that we know about right now."

"I like that idea," Lilly Ann replied. "We need to find them or to rule out locations where they might have been taken. Somehow, we must narrow our search area from all of Tarra! What should we do here?"

The twins explained and then took a half hour to quiet their nerves and block their anxiety from their minds. At last they were off, Mind Linked to each other and to Paulette, who linked them to the other members in the room.

*Let's be systematic about this. Let's go to Wanakan first. Then come back this way, stopping at each location,* Rosina suggested.

Instantly, the two floated over Wanakan and the remains of the Temple of the Black God. It was overgrown with jungle plants, totally deserted. No life was sensed anywhere near the ruins. Next, they appeared over the island of the giant statues. Quickly, they searched the caves where we had found much treasure. Still deserted.

They floated over the Island of Love, where the men of the New Order had slain all of the men of the Old Order, leaving only the Old Order women alive, the armless ones, who were slowly starving to death. The twins floated into the cavern at the top of the cliff. It was totally deserted, only a few spiders had now taken this as their new home. Next, they floated over the Isle of Right, where Enyo and Alexa had resided. Again, at the mountain cavern where the mantis base was located, they found absolutely nothing. The island itself was completely deserted.

They moved on to the Spice Island where we had battled a young mantis creature, who had eaten the lower arms of Alwanianon, the adopted daughter of Mireio and Roberto, the musicians. Again, in the secret cavern near the top of the tallest peak on the island, they found absolutely nothing.

From there, the twins moved over the island of Acropolis, whose people of Megalos ancestry had refused to allow us to land lived. High atop the tallest mountain was the cavern of the mantis creatures. It too was empty. Massive spider webs covered the entire inside of the cavern.

Next, they flew down to Demokritos and the Temple of Orthos, where we found a dead mantis body, which had been digging out the cavern. It too was empty — except the body of the dead mantis was still there along with thousands of donated appendages of the women of Demokritos who had agreed to one of the eight Holy Degrees, amputation of fingers, hands, and or arms.

From here, they moved north to the central area of the Southlands. Here at this isolated volcanic mountain, Bethany and Linda had lost their arms to the mantis creatures. Bethany's brother Damien, Linda's first husband, had died in the viper pit. When we left this fully operation station, the Protectors had caused a volcanic eruption and the entire mountain had grown enormously. The site was completely and utterly destroyed, along with the very evil Tikki tribe, who had caught us and fed Bethany and Linda to the mantis.

Sadly, the twins returned to their bodies. It was suppertime; food had already been brought into the meeting room. Neither twin spoke; words were unneeded. Everyone here had seen everything that they had seen via the Mind Link.

"Thanks for ruling all those likely locations out," Lilly Ann validated the twin's efforts. "I really didn't expect that you would find them. It would not make sense if these mantis creatures imprisoned our women at a spot that we already knew about, now does it?"

"No, I suppose not," Renzo tried to hold back his tears. "I was so hopeful though."

"I know, we all were, really we were," Beth Ann consoled him.

Hank added, "Don't worry so much. Remember, Lilly Ann's right. They are being kept alive for a long time; they are the eight most resourceful women on Tarra. If there is any way out of their prison, I am certain that they will find it. We have to be patient and ready to assist them."

The next day, they discovered that no additional people had gone missing. All experienced some relief over this news. Yet as they met discussing their options, no one had any real ideas of what to do next, save to continue trying to run the huge organization. Jenna's retired Circle volunteered to help, and from now on they all met together in the mornings.

Around noon, Paulette received a Mind Link from Julie, the first spiritual being that Jes Amir, the Guardian of the Anuir, had been working to free. When Jes and I were married and he was the Great Messiah of Juda Arad, sent from Jehosa to free his people, he meant spiritual freedom. Unfortunately, those in the Arad believed that he was sent to free them from their Megalos Centurion overlords. That uprising failed and now the few ragtag remnants of the ancient worshipers of Jehosa came out onto the uninhabited Red Desert and joined with Jes.

He was working his miracles of total spiritual freedom on a being by being basis. When I was a little girl, he had already achieved much with Julie, her husband, and the tribe's leader. Jes and I made a bargain. While he would continue to free beings one by one, I would do what I could to keep the overall human environment calm and tranquil, making wars and conflicts a thing of the past, giving him time to do his great work.

*Hi, Julie here. I bring you some important news from the Holy Guardian of the Anuir, Jes, I believe you call him. Last night, a mantis flying ship appeared over the Red Desert. It came in search of us, fully intent upon capturing us, and enslaving us within mortal bodies once more. It failed utterly. I will show you what happened.*

They watched in awe as the dark form of a huge flying ship hovered over the sands of the desert. The ship attempted to fire energy beams down upon the oasis encampment where they lived. The energy beams simply dissolved. Together, Julie, Karmanski, and Jes simply pulled the ship down to the ground. The mantis creature running the ship forced its engines to counteract their pull, quite unsuccessfully. The entire ship turned red hot and exploded. However, the fireball merely shot out in to the desert sands, completely harmless to the oasis, so forced by the powers of the trio.

*We destroyed the ship and the creature. Jes also picked up some mental thoughts from the creature during the brief encounter. Jes believes that the creature has imprisoned some of your people already. He also wanted me to tell you that the mantis creatures have returned, well at least this one ship has. Be on the lookout for more of them, he warns.*

*This is from me. If you find any more of these ships, let me know. My husband, Karmanski, and I had a lot of fun destroying those that have kept us on Tarra in prison these centuries. We would like another chance to teach them a lesson or two.*

*Please thank Jes and Karmanski for us. You have done what we are unable to do. However, you are right. It has abducted Bethany and seven others. We must find them and rescue them. If we see any more of their ships, we will let you know. They are beyond our powers to eliminate. Thank you, Julie.* She filled Paulette with hope and joy and then broke the connection.

At once, Paulette Mind Linked to the rest of the group and replayed Julie's message and images for everyone to see and hear. Many faces were white when she finished up.

"Damn, they really are back!" exclaimed Renzo. "We are in big, big trouble."

"Yes, but look at how powerful Julie and Karmanski have become! As Bethany used to say, we are buying time for Jes to do his miracles," Rosina countered her brother.

"Okay, okay, but look," Renzo argued, "they are down there and we are up here. We've lost eight of our people before they got the ship and mantis. We've got to find her and the rest of them!"

"Hold on a second, we don't even know if the mantis ship that Julie downed was even the same one that abducted our people," Lilly Ann cautioned everyone.

"How many of them do you suppose there are?" asked a white-faced Beth Ann. She was a Healer, not a fighter. She'd already seen thousands of these mantis creature's victims, more than enough to last a lifetime, though she'd nearly spent her lifetime entirely on helping their victims recover.

"We darn well better find out!" Chaucer declared, terrified over his imagined suffering wife, whom he could not immediately rescue.

Lilly Ann wiped a tear from her cheek, "I'm getting too old for this." She sniffled and recovered. "Okay then, Communicators, relay all this to all of the other Communicators. Give them an order to make inquiries discretely about anyone having seen any strange objects moving about in the sky, probably at night. Let's set about gaining more information. Are we facing a bunch of mantis creatures? If we are incredibly lucky, maybe only this one. Either way, we must find out somehow. Emil, you will begin constructing an observation map. Plot all known sightings, particularly the direction the ship came from and was heading. Perhaps from the patterns we can deduce their whole flight path and gain some clues to where our women might be being held."

"Yes, that does make sense, Lilly Ann. Come on, Chaucer, Renzo, let's go wake the night watch and interrogate them. Perhaps one of them saw something during the night," Emil requested. The three left to see if anything could be learned.

That night, Lena asked Renzo, "Where is mommy? I want mommy back." She held back her tears however. Ben looked quite sad too.

Renzo signed, keeping control of his grief. "Some very bad creatures stole mommy away during the night. We are all trying to get mommy back and all the other mommies too, Lena. I want mommy back just as bad as you two do. Come here; give me a hug. We will just have to hug each other harder for mommy. We must be brave and do everything we can to find her and bring her home." The twins hugged their father tightly, the three cried for a time. Starting that night, Renzo brought all four into his bed with him, "We will all sleep close until we get mommy back. I don't want anything to happen to you, my precious children, neither does mommy, wherever she is. I know she is thinking of us all every night when she goes to sleep."

A week later, Emil, Chaucer, and Renzo stared at their sightings map. Bits and pieces still kept arriving. A fisherman reported a strange thing in the night sky over Velona, moving southeast. Another report had a black shape going east, and so the reports trickled in. Emil dutifully noted each one on the map of Tarra, a copy quickly made for him by Michelle from Henry's mantis map of Tarra.

At the morning's meeting, as usual, everyone stared at the map, looking for any new additions and what it all might mean. It looked more like a bunch of tiny arrows pointing in many directions. "Well, thus far, we have had no new sightings," Lilly Ann began the meeting. "It's been a whole week now and no one has reported seeing anything unusual in the night skies after Julie destroyed the mantis flying ship."

"Does that mean there was only one of them?" asked Beth Ann.

"I am beginning to believe that," Emil sounded a hopeful note. "Yet, only one jailer, that seems unusual to my way of thinking. At our secure facility on Isla Roca, where we are keeping those who have caused great harm to others until they come to their senses, we have at least fifty guards on duty, to say nothing of the cooks, and other personnel. How strange to find only one ship, though who knows how many might have been on that ship."

"I'd like to take a look at what remains of that ship," Renzo declared. "Perhaps we might find some clues to their whereabouts in the wreckage."

"You are right, we ought to check it out," Lilly Ann agreed. "Since nothing else seems to be happening here, Renzo, why don't you and Emil take a party down to the Red Desert and see what you can find out?"

"Thanks, I am going nuts just sitting here all week doing nothing to rescue them!" he declared. Lilly Ann sensed the growing frustration in the three men, particularly the Protectors. "I had better take the kids with me.

They will feel really awful if I go off and leave them too."

"Take some nannies with you," Beth Ann suggested. He smiled in appreciation. Handling all four all by himself was becoming a chore. Renzo missed me in many ways.

"We can sail at high tide tonight, around midnight," Captain Henry volunteered. "I'll go see to the loading of food supplies for this quick trip. Someone get me the sailing directions, though."

Paulette made contact with Julie and relayed our request to examine the wreckage. *It's about a mile from our oasis. We will meet you where we met Jenna Rose when we accompanied her to Megalos, some years ago. Anchor in that bay and come ashore. We will meet you there. Contact us when you arrive, please. Is there any news of the women?* Julie sent to her.

*None, we've been plotting all of the sightings of possible ships. It's pretty strange. We have a map full of isolated observations, a big jumble, I'm afraid.*

"Kids, we are off to go search the evil ship that we think was used to abduct mommy. I want you all to get a sack filled with clothes for a few weeks. We are going down to the Red Desert," Renzo excitedly told our four children. Lena and Ben were naturally quite excited about taking a big trip in the boat once again and ran off to pack their sacks.

Late afternoon, many carriages pulled up in front of the mansion. Besides Chaucer, Renzo, and Henry with all their children, many of the others in the Explorers Circle went along. Specifically, Benet and Michelle went — she to make paintings of the wreckage — Cedric and Rosina, and Emil and Tonia went as well, bringing along their children as well. Only the musicians, Roberto and Mireio, stayed behind, since the trip had nothing to do with music and they felt that they would just be in the way.

As Hank, Paulette, Adam, Alan, Lilly Ann, and Beth Ann saw them off, waving goodbye, Hank said, "Here I thought that we were retired and here we are all back at the helm, running the whole Santi operation once more."

"Well, you do realize how much trouble the Santi del Dio will be in if we do not find and rescue these women?" Lilly Ann replied. "An organization such as ours can ill afford to lose its eight most powerful leaders at the same time. We are getting old, Hank. We need these younger ones to take our places. I have a very bad feeling about all this. Now that they are all gone, I can speak freely. Hank, we must face the possibility that we have lost these eight forever."

"Hell, Lilly Ann, I know that! I wouldn't dare say so around them, of course," Hank answered her. "What in the blazes are we going to do about it now?"

"I know, I know," Beth Ann sighed, then began mockingly teasing, "Beth Ann, will you prepare a full listing of all the Guardians in the Santi organization, along with their capabilities and ages? I know. We must take stock of our current position and come up with some viable replacements, just in case we have indeed lost all eight women."

Grinning broadly, Lilly Ann replied, "Beth Ann, will you prepare a full listing of all the Guardians in the Santi organization, please?" Everyone roared with laughter, releasing their unspoken tensions which had been steadily building up all week long. None dared say anything when the Explorers Circle was around.

"I feel so helpless," Alan mused. "Look at all Bethany has done for everyone here. Now she is in dire peril, so helpless herself and I can do nothing!"

"I know, dear, we all feel the same way," said his wife, Beth Ann. "I still see her as a six year old little girl, helping me with all that horrible surgery on the women we rescued who lost their arms to the Holy Paladins. She was always right there helping each one. Now she needs our help. By golly, Alan, I won't rest until I find her and get her safely back here, though I admit, I have not the faintest idea how that might be done."

"Well, we should use this time, while they are away, to engineer some replacement plans," Lilly Ann changed the topic. "Bethany certainly would not want our organization to crumble just because she is gone. We owe her that much at the very least, to keep this all going in her absence." Stoically, the small group entered the mansion and headed to the planning room.

The Sleepy Hollow, a sleek, fast caravel, slowly tacked out of the harbor in Velona. As soon as the ship was clear of the bay, the crew hoisted the large mainsails on the two huge masts. The white sails with the red fleur-del-is crossed emblazoned on them billowed in the midnight breeze. Henry trimmed the stern spanker sail, while boson Thad adjusted the two forward jibs.

She rode light in the water, carrying only provisions for several weeks, no trading cargo this trip. Their destination was far down the Med Sea, nearly opposite the great city of Zargarb, and very close to the Arad city of New Barq, which the Santi controlled. Normally, ten days sailing time would be required to traverse the length of the Med Sea. However, as light as they were, Henry knew he could cut days off that. His wife's life might depend on their speed.

Correspondingly, at dawn, he ordered every piece of sail to be raised. He set a new record, arriving at their destination, nearly the complete length of the Med, in just under five days. Although the Red Desert ran the entire length of the Med Sea, along its southern coast, the oasis where Julie and Karmanski lived was near the far end. There were no towns or even homesteads anywhere along this entire coastline of the desert. In fact, the desert was mostly uninhabited, except for the few tribes of which Julie's was one, and these people lived at the oases, which lay scattered around the vast desert.

The second night, when all of the children were finally asleep, the enthusiasm of the exciting boat trip at last calmed, Renzo and Chaucer strolled onto the main deck, leaning over the side railing. "I miss her so badly," Renzo said, "we always leaned like this. I'd put my arm around her waist and she'd lay her head on my shoulders. God, I love her."

"I know, me too. You know that there is a good chance that we will never find them, don't you? I know Lilly Ann suspects so, though she has been careful not to say any such thing around us. I can see how she looks, though, when she thinks I am not looking," Chaucer said melancholically.

"Don't say that, Chaucer, I will spend the rest of my entire life looking for her if I have to," Renzo declared. "Bethany is the best damn woman in the whole wide world!"

"No, now there you are wrong. I beg to differ; Linda Sarah is the best damn woman in the whole wide world!" Chaucer retorted.

Captain Henry, who had strolled over to join them, added, "Oh no, you are both entirely and completely wrong. Natale is the best damn woman in the whole wide world!"

The three men laughed. Henry added, "You know that I now own the Sleepy Hollow outright. I swear to you both that I am dedicating the rest of my life to finding them, alive or dead. I will never stop searching, even if I have to travel the entire length and breadth of Tarra in search of them."

"I cannot ever just lead the Santi and forget about Bethany," Renzo added. "I'm with you, Henry. The Santi be damned, Bethany is more important to me than the organization."

"Same with me," Chaucer put in, "Linda is my life. I will never rest until I find her. Lilly Ann can just find some other able Guardians to take our places, while we search. If we were the ones lost, Linda would leave no stone unturned looking for us. I won't ever let her down!"

"Then, you two are with me all the way?" Henry asked.

"All for one and one for all; we will never rest until we find them," declared Renzo. The three men shook hands, sealing their vow.

As the ship lowered anchor in the isolated little cove off the Red Desert, Rosina contacted Julie to let her know they had arrived. Renzo explained to our children, "Daddy is now going to be gone for a few days. We are all going to look at the destroyed ship that the enemy may have used to abduct mommy. She is certainly not here, but we are just looking for clues in the wreckage. Ben, I am putting you in charge, you are to look after Lena and the younger ones. Lena, you are second in command. I expect everything to be shipshape when I return. If we are lucky, we might have some clues about where mommy is at, okay? Will you be brave while I am away for a few days?"

"You can count on us," Lena said. Ben echoed her. She added, "Only do find out something. I want mommy back really badly, daddy."

He hugged her tightly, whispering in her ear, "So do I honey, so do I."

Emil, Renzo, Chaucer, Benet, Cedric, Tonia, Rosina, and Michelle, who had her sketchpads with her, used the longboat to row to shore. Once on land, they climbed up the tall sandy bluff to the desert proper, looking out onto a sea of red sand. Dunes rose and fell as far as the eye could see. Wind marks, like waves, dotted the surface of the mounds. Here they waited for the arrival of Julie and her people.

Late afternoon, riders appeared suddenly over a distant dune, and then promptly disappeared down the other side, only to reappear even closer. Such was travel across this vast desert. At last, Julie and Karmanski rode up the dune on which the group was standing. Karmanski called out, "Hail comrades from Velona." He led a long string of horses behind him.

"Greetings to both of you, though I do not know your names," Emil replied. I am Emil Amir, our temporary leader. On behalf of all free people of Tarra, we thank you for what you have done to the mantis enslavers." He thought this would make a good beginning anyway. After all, they must be the closest things to gods and goddesses there were on Tarra.

"I am called Karmanski and this is my wife, Julie. Forgive us, we seem to have both forgotten our sir name; it holds so little significance for us now."

"Very pleased to meet you both!" Emil exclaimed. He had heard the stories about how these two spiritual beings had gone with Jenna Rose Weston to Megalos, there to put an end to the mutilation of women by the Church of Jehosanity. The tales that Bethany had told of their incredible whirlwinds was daunting. Now he was face to face with these incredibly powerful beings.

"Oh, this is Renzo, Bethany's husband," Emil began to introduce the others to the pair. Once the introductions were done, they mounted up and began to make the return trip to their oasis.

Renzo noted that behind them a small whirlwind completely obliterated all traces of their passing. Julie noticed that he saw this and said, "We wish to keep our presence in the desert a secret so that the Guardian can continue to work his miracles."

"Very effective," Renzo replied.

"Darn effective," Benet added, as a Loremaster, this fascinated him, the complete obliteration of their hoof prints.

Julie spoke softly, "I see much of Bethany in you, Renzo. She chose a mate most wisely. There is a lot of love between you. I do hope that you can rescue her."

"She's the greatest woman on Tarra," Renzo bragged.

"Oh no, that is reserved for Linda," Chaucer interrupted.

"You are both wrong; that is reserved for Natale," Emil added, "I am upholding Captain Henry's view, guys." They all chuckled.

"Did you really pull that mantis flying ship down to the ground?" Renzo asked what he had been dying to ask of her, since he heard the words and saw the images Julie had shared with Paulette. "I know that I can do some incredible things, and Bethany is so much more able than I am, but pulling the ship down to the ground?"

"Yes, it took the combined efforts of three of us. You are looking at this body here, Renzo. I am not the body. In fact, I have so little use and need of it anymore that I sometimes forget I have it around. Yet, at times like these, it is useful, meeting you and bringing you to our oasis. Karmanski and I are nearly ready for the last step in our training, according to the Guardian. Yet we still need time of quiet to train, so we must all find Bethany so that she can continue to keep Tarra calm. There are many beings to free here."

"You can say that again," Renzo agreed. "I hope that one day Bethany and I will get a chance to become as able as you are."

"Oh it will come, if we all do our part. The Guardian has shown us that one person working alone cannot do it. We saw that again when the mantis ship came upon us. Only by working together can we achieve our goals. You are only half without Bethany at your side. Same with you, Chaucer, and even Henry. They must be found. I have been trying myself to locate her without any luck. I have talked with the Guardian about it too. Although he does not know where they are being held prisoner, he knows that they are alive. You may take some comfort in that; the Guardian always speaks the truth."

"Thank you for telling me. It means a lot to know they are alive," Renzo replied, barely able to keep his tears from flowing.

"Ah, here is our oasis," Julie announced.

"Hey, wait a minute," Benet exclaimed suddenly surprised. "I thought the oasis was twenty-five miles inland."

"Yes," Michelle added, quickly catching on to Benet's observations. "We should have only gone maybe five miles at the most."

Julie turned in the saddle to face the two very observant beings. Grinning, she said, "You don't mind if we shifted space slightly? Now we are here and there is still daylight for you to see the ship."

"How did you do that?" asked many voices at once.

"It is simple really, we decide we are here and here we are. Don't you do that all of the time yourselves?" she replied.

"Well, not exactly. Well, maybe," Benet struggled to find a way to answer her. "We ought to decide, but we, oh I see, we agree that if riding horses to your oasis which is twenty-five miles distant, that it should take us maybe half a day, and so it does take us a half a day. Is that what you mean?"

"Yes, by your agreements so are you ruled," she replied. Everyone looked completely baffled, so she added, "Make new agreements, simple. Come, let us put your things in our guest houses and then we will walk you to what remains of the ship."

They dismounted and looked at the village. Tall palm, date, and fig trees surrounded a large pool of spring fed water. Several fields of crops grew nearby. Hundreds of small adobe huts dotted the surrounding rolling land. People were going about their daily activities, hundreds of adults and nearly an equal number of children were at play, dashing about having fun. Many stopped to smile and wave at the newcomers.

After putting their sacks into the small bedrooms, they gathered beside Julie once more. "Karmanski has other duties to perform, if you will follow me, I will take you to the ship. It is not far." Slowly, the group walked out onto the sand dunes. Renzo watched Julie's footsteps carefully. He noticed that her feet barely made any indentation at all in the sand, completely opposite to his deep boot prints. "How does she walk so lightly?" He wondered.

Benet and Michelle also noticed this, but did not ask about it. A few minutes later, they crested a dune. Below them lay the remains of the alien flying ship. It looked badly burned. The ship was probably some five hundred feet long and rather cylindrical in shape. Two stubby wings lay mangled on either flank. Most of the burning had occurred near the rear, where several large openings lay. The other end had numerous hexagonal windows, joined together. However, all were cracked and shattered and thus blocked any coherent view inside. The ship was at least a hundred feet in diameter.

"Look for a way inside," Emil took charge as the group walked around the remains. Benet helped Michelle set up her sketch pad and attached her drawing utensils to her arms; then he left her to her work and joined the others searching for an entrance.

After about a half hour of searching, Renzo decided that this spot must be the entrance. "Look gang, see the outline. This must be a doorway, but where is the keyhole, the doorknob? How do we open it?"

Benet replied, "Well, you must put yourself into the point of view of the owner of the ship, in this case a mantis. They are about fifty feet long with all these insect-like appendages. They don't have hands like we do, Renzo."

"Oh I see what you mean. No hands, only pointy appendages. Well they probably touch something to cause it to open. I wonder what they touch?" Renzo asked.

Sometime later, Benet said, "How about that tiny spot way up there. We've been looking down here at our level, but the mantis creature's level would be likely that high up. Can I stand on someone's shoulders and see if I can reach it?"

"Try mine," Chaucer volunteered. Renzo helped Benet get up. Yes, he could reach it.

"Anyone got any tiny pointed thing I can stick into this hole?" he called down.

"Here, use one of my lock picks," Cedric volunteered. After a bit of effort, they managed to get the picks into Benet's outstretched hand without him having to climb back down.

"Hurry up, you are heavy!" Chaucer called out.

Suddenly, the door gave a lurch and opened a crack, nearly knocking the two men over. Once Benet had his feet firmly in the sand, they looked at the door. Yes, it was a door, and it had opened slightly. "Probably it is stuck or jammed by the crash," Renzo suggested. The men all gathered around and together pulled hard on the door which groaned and creaked and finally opened, crashing to the ground, revealing a walk ramp into the ship. "Now we are getting somewhere," he proclaimed.

Black soot covered much just inside the doorway. "Be careful inside; try not to touch too many strange things; some may cause us great harm," Emil ordered, remembering Bethany had warned us similarly when we entered the Grey Creature's cave down in Vladimir. One by one, the members walked up the ramp, activating their blue light spells as they entered the darkened hull of the ship. "Let's make our way forward, that seems to be where the pilot could see where he was going," Emil ordered.

All manner of strange things lined the sides of the ship, leaving the central portion wide open, to fit a fifty foot long creature. Hence, walking forward was not a problem.

"Hey, look at this!" screamed Renzo, forgetting he was in a very enclosed space. "Bethany was wearing this the night she was taken! It's her night gown."

"Hey, that one is Linda's," Chaucer added. They counted eight sets of clothes, which tallied with their estimates of how many women had been abducted. "Well, it is some small comfort to find out that only the eight were actually taken," he said. "Think what we would feel like if we found twelve not eight!"

"Gang, this proves beyond any doubt that our people were indeed aboard this very vessel," Emil concluded. "Let's see if we can find any other clues, particularly where they might be now located."

"What's that smell?" asked Benet, holding his nose as they moved further forward in the ship.

"Burnt mantis," Emil called back. He was in the lead. "I've reached its tail. Burned to a crisp by his own ship."

"Guys, I've found their earrings," called out Tonia from the rear. She had been going through the pile of nightgowns and undergarments. "Unless the mantis has made clothing for them, I would guess that all eight are completely naked; wherever they are at, that is not a good sign at all! I sure would not want to be held prisoner somewhere and having no clothes on at all!"

"Well, it's getting too dark to see well; let's return in the morning," Emil decided. Tonia rescued all of the earrings, however, along with our clothes.

The sun was low when they returned to the oasis. All of the villagers were now sitting on mats on the sand, facing the setting sun. "Come join us in our evening prayers, and then you will be served supper," Julie said. They found mats had already been laid out for them, and they mimicked the villagers, thought they did not understand the words being spoken; it was the Ancient Arad language.

The meal was delicious, a combination of grains, dates, figs, and lamb's milk, though it was a humble meal by our standards. Julie came over to us and sat down. "Did you learn anything today," she asked.

"Yes," Tonia replied. "We found the clothes all eight were wearing when they were abducted and their earrings, which they would never take off. So we know for a fact that they were very likely on that very ship at some time in the past and that the creature probably removed their earrings, because without hands, they would be very difficult to remove. Our conclusion is that the eight are being held somewhere and are naked. God, how awful."

Julie nodded, "I see. Yes, it does make sense, your conclusions."

"We want to go back in the morning when we have better light and search for more clues, like where they may have been taken," Emil said.

When they retired for the night, Rosina contacted first the caravel and then Paulette, relaying the news thus far. The guest quarters were small, but warm and comfortable. They all slept very peacefully.

The group spent five more days here at the crash site. Bit by bit, they examined every inch of the ship. Finding it entirely dormant, they began piling anything that might be either useful or informative into a pile outside the ship. Although covered in the black soot, Emil's plan was to bring the stuff back to the estate, clean them up, and look for further clues. Just in case location was somehow important, Tonia kept a ledger of where each artifact was originally located. Meanwhile, Michelle made sketch after sketch of the ship and its insides.

On the sixth morning, while standing around the large pile of blackened items, Emil asked, "Julie, I guess that we are done here. We wish to take this pile of stuff back, clean them up, and see if they can provide additional clues. By chance do you have a wagon we could borrow to transport this pile back to the ship?"

"So you are done with the ship? Can we bury it under the sands now?"

"Yes, we may want to return later, so don't destroy it," Emil replied.

"Okay. And this pile here is what you want to be moved to your ship?"

"Yes."

"Okay, I will see to it. Why don't you get your things together, and we will take you back to your ship now," Julie suggested.

The group began walking back to the oasis. However, Julie did not accompany them right away. Curious, Renzo paused and turned around to see what happened to her. He saw her standing over the pile. The next instant the pile was gone! Even more astounding, the next instant, Julie was now beside him, some fifty feet from where she had been, and walking slowly along with him!

"How did?" he tried to say.

"Oh, I just moved the pile to the beach for you all. You will find it exactly as you left it. Come, Karmanski has the horses ready for you," she replied. Renzo just stared at her for some time.

They mounted up, waved farewell to the villagers, and rode off onto the nearby dunes. This time, however, Michelle and Benet were watching astutely to observe their passage. At first, the land passed by under the horses as expected. Suddenly, both noticed that the next footfall was many miles from the last one. They had just observed the spatial shift that Julie and Karmanski had done. In fact, they shortly halted on the dune where they first met the two. Below stacked neatly was the pile of soot-covered artifacts they wanted to take back to Velona!

As they said their farewells and thank you's, Benet and Michelle whispered to Julie, "We both want to learn how to do that! We saw you do the spatial shift. One step here, the next twenty plus miles away! Fabulous. Is it hard to learn how to do that?"

Julie smiled, "Yes, it takes some learning, but one day you both will master it. It is a simple thing to do, really."

"Thanks for the encouragement! We both look forward to that day!" Michelle enthusiastically replied.

"Oh, one other thing I forgot to mention. After you find and rescue Bethany and the others, the Guardian wishes Bethany to send someone of her choosing down here to live with us for a time. The Guardian wishes to set one of your members free," Julie explained.

"Wow! That is terrific! Tell him thanks a lot!" Benet thanked her. Julie then turned to Karmanski, who had gathered up all the reigns. Together they rode up over the dune. Again, a whirlwind erased their passage. Benet and Michelle stood watching their departure very carefully.

"Watch closely. I bet anything they will not even appear on the next dune, but simply be back at their oasis," Benet said to his wife.

"No bet, I bet the same thing, dear," Michelle replied. Both waited and watched. They could easily estimate the time needed to go down and then up. That period came and went, but no riders appeared. After waiting twice the time both anticipated and still the riders had not appeared, both looked at each other and grinned. "Now that is an amazing skill to know how to do!" she said, as they rejoined the others who were loading the longboat with the soot covered items.

While they lent a hand, Benet said, "Did you hear Julie's last statement about having Bethany send someone down here to get freed?"

"Yes, someone is going to get a fabulous gift!" Emil said, and he meant it. "However, we have to find them first. Let's get this stuff onboard and cleaned off."

An hour later, the dirty items had been brought onboard, and Henry had set sail for home. Meanwhile, the group began cleaning off the black soot from the explosion of the craft's engines. As each item was finally clean, they examined it, attempting to ascertain what it was. Many of the items they could not do so.

However, they did find a small map of Tarra, a miniaturized version of the large-scale map Henry had in his cabin. Emil took this smaller one down to the cabin and began a careful comparison of the two, looking for any changes or alterations. An hour later, he gave it up and returned topside. "Nothing new on the map," he sadly reported to the anxious others. "It has the same markings as Henry's map and no new ones. Renzo and Rosina have already checked those sites and they are still empty."

"Makes sense really," Renzo commented. "After all, if I was the mantis and I discovered that all of my operation bases had been discovered by the enemy and if I had just taken some prisoners, I would find a new location, one which wasn't known to the enemy."

"Yes, but wouldn't you make some record of just where that location was at?" Rosina countered. "I mean, how would other mantis creatures ever find this new base?"

"Maybe it was killed before it had the chance to document its new base," suggested a gloomy Chaucer.

"Well, I'd sure make myself a note at least. How would I ever find it again if I didn't?" she countered. "We just have to keep on looking for a clue, that's all. There must be something here which will tell us something about where it has taken them."

"Did you find out where mommy is?" Lena asked her dad. While they were cleaning the stuff, she and Ben had come on deck to see Renzo. Their nanny was with them, of course.

"Oh hi, Lena, Ben. Not yet, but we did find mommy's nightgown, the one she was wearing when the bad bugs abducted her and also mommy's prized earrings. She was on that ship, that's for sure."

She looked saddened by the news. "But that means mommy is going around naked!"

"I know, that is not good at all, is it? She might get cold. We will just have to hurry up and find her, dear," Renzo said, barely able to keep his tears from coming once more.

"Well I don't think that it's a very nice bug at all, if it won't let mommy wear any clothes," Lena declared flatly. "Can we help?"

"Sure, why don't you two carry these cleaned off things down into the cargo dining table? Can you manage that?" Both children enthusiastically launched into the task, making numerous trips up and down the stairs. Of course, as soon as the other older children saw what Lena and Ben were doing, they insisted on helping too. This allowed the adults to concentrate on the massive cleaning project.

At suppertime, all of the items had been cleaned and the cleaners cleaned as well. It had been a very dirty job. After supper, they spent time with the children, whom they had not seen for nearly a week now.

The next day, while sailing at full speed towards Velona, the group began to examine each object systematically and very carefully. "Hey, this is another one of those books or journals, like Natale has," pronounced Rosina. "I know Natale was getting close to being able to read them. She told me she had their alphabet worked out, that's something. Maybe when we get back, we can find her writings and see if we can decipher it."

"I'll bet there is a clue in there somewhere," Tonia sounded a hopeful note.

# Chapter 3 Clues

September 1, 657, the Sleepy Hollow arrived back in Velona. The group had studied the items taken from the downed flying ship, but had found nothing that would suggest where the eight women were being held. A bunch of forlorn faces greeted Lilly Ann and the others as they arrived back at the Santi estate and mansion.

All of the items found were placed in the meeting room, in hopes that fresh minds might see something the group had missed. After three days of study, even Lilly Ann had to admit that there appeared nothing here that could cast any light on the situation.

"I'm going to take this book with me to Natale's room. Maybe I can use her alphabet and figure out something," Rosina stated.

"Go ahead, Rosina. Good luck, keep us posted," Lilly Ann replied. "What we need is a mystic visionary about now. We are exhausting all the leads."

"What about going over to West Reach and consulting with Cerys Laird? Maybe she can get a vision or something with that talisman of hers," suggested Renzo.

"Anything is worth a try at this point!" Chaucer glumly declared.

Beth Ann laughed, "Boy what a bunch of detectives we turn out to be! Seeking fortune tellers now."

Chaucer complained, "Look, we have all these strange things here and for all we know, we might be looking at its butt-scratcher!"

"Point taken," Lilly Ann chuckled; he was right, they well could be. "Let's all go take a walk around the estate and come back with a fresh mind and examine everything again."

After lunch, Michelle and Benet decided to study the map of sightings. No one had looked at this since they had gotten back from the Red Desert, mainly because nothing new had been added while they were gone. There were now over seventy sightings marked with date and times on the map of Tarra. It looked completely chaotic, except for the clustering around Velona. No pattern was apparent.

Rosina holed up in Natale's room with the journal book and Natale's experimental alphabet. Days passed by as she carefully wrote out the strange symbols using her alphabet, page by page. As she looked at the finished letters, to her it seemed nothing but a jumble of letters. Yet somehow these must spell out words, of that she was convinced. Dutifully, she kept at it until at last after a week, she had written out each page in the journal. She sighed as she looked at her many pages filled with an utter nonsense collection of letters, which must be words.

Six weeks had now passed since the abduction. Deep hopelessness had begun setting in on many of the extended group. Indeed Lilly Ann had given up all hope of finding the women, alive anyway. Still, she refused to admit her deep feelings to the others, refusing to rob them of whatever thread of hope remained in them.

Not all shared her deep sense of hopelessness, however. Benet and Michelle continued to study the map with all of the sightings. Michelle rubbed her short arms across her face and brushed back her hair, resting at last her head on the ends of her arms, staring at the map. She said, "You know love, maybe we have been looking at this all wrong."

"What do you mean honey?" he asked, intrigued. The two had not lost all hope yet, and they continued to tell each other that they must have been missing something. Her words sounded hopeful at least.

"We've been looking for a pattern out of all these sightings. Let's dump that approach. I need your hands. Let's go about this chronologically, hour by hour. How about using one of my chalks and coloring all of the observations between eleven and midnight in black. Then, midnight and one in blue, and so on, each hour range in a lighter color. How many colors are we going to need? Can you count the hour spread here?"

"I get twenty of them, have you got twenty different shades?" he replied.

"Hum, that is a lot, so we'll use successively lighter shades. That will work too. I can do the coloring but you know my speed is abysmal, compared to yours, love."

"Okay, you hand me the next chalk color to use and I'll mark them for us," Benet suggested. Slowly, the two began to color in the reported sightings. "Some of these are likely imaginary, you know."

"Oh sure, but we are looking for the overall pattern as it changes over time," she replied, handing him another color choice. A half hour later, the two stared at the colored map. "Now we can see the pattern! Look, it starts here over Wanakan. That is the earliest sighting. Then, it comes here over Velona, where it was seen the most."

"Indeed, several hours according to the three different colors," Benet added.

"Yes, but look at the yellow lines! That is what we are looking for! Benet, we have a clue! Get everyone in here now!" Michelle shrieked in excitement. A few minutes later, everyone rushed into the room, eager to see what the two Loremasters had found out.

"Look, everyone, we color coded the sightings. The darker shades occurred first, beginning over there in Wanakan. Next, for three hours the ship hovered over Velona. Now here come the critical ones. Look at the yellow ones which represent the next hour's worth of scattered sightings!" Michelle exclaimed very animatedly. She was certain this was critical information they had found.

"But they are all across the Sea Princes, random?" Lilly Ann questioned, seeing yellow tags scattered across the Sea Princes, from Velona over to Zargarb.

"Yes, notice anything different about them?" Michelle asked.

"I see it!" exclaimed Renzo. "They form more or less a straight line. I see it! They captured seven women here. Once it had them aboard the ship, the bug would then head to where it would imprison them. I certainly would do that — take my prisoners straight to their cells! It goes nearly straight eastward, right across the Sea Princes! It gives us the direction of travel! Well done, Michelle, Benet!" Renzo began jumping up and down; he was that excited about this first real break in the mystery.

Benet added, "We can draw yet another conclusion, if we make the assumption that this flying machine is capable of flying directly to its destination. If you had prisoners and desired to take them to their cells, then with the assumption that your machine would go where you desired, would you not fly directly there? That means, their prison must line precisely along this line somewhere further east from Zargarb!"

"That certainly narrows the search pattern!" Chaucer declared. "Very well done indeed, you two!"

"Ah there is more though," Michelle continued. Now look, hours later, this green line is coming back from somewhere to the east and is flying directly southwest to Demokritos. I know that we only have three of these green lines; most of the landmass is not under our control, so no way to get the observations. Then, the blue line seems to retrace the route, only several hours later. Then, we have only a few observations in white. See where it comes in from the east and ends up at Julie's oasis? They are located to the east."

"Unfortunately for us," Benet added, "the second and third lines have too few observations to rely upon for a direct intersection plot. Otherwise, we could triangulate it. Using these two, we tried, but they put the location either in the middle of Juda Arad or in the middle of Tashien. There are just not enough observations to plot the second two accurately enough to triangulate their position, I am sorry to report, mostly because the two lines are very oblique to the east line. Yet, we have a good primary line. Michelle and I will hang our hats on this east line. Their prison must lie along it somewhere."

"Woo hoo!" Chaucer gushed and began dancing around the room with Michelle. "You did it! Now we have a starting point at long last!"

Now the discussion centered on just how to go about the search. "We just cannot ride straight along this line, gang. Juda Arad is full of mesas and deep gullies, which make travel in a straight line utterly impossible, to say nothing about watering holes. It is a desert or nearly one," Emil volunteered.

"If they are not in Juda Arad, how the heck are we going to traverse a straight line across Tashien?" asked Renzo. "We don't have a clue what the land is like, and we barely speak the language, though I'm sure that Empress

Sho Lin would lend us any and all aid in our search for her Royal Consort. Yet, I'll wager that we still will be unable to just travel in a straight line."

"Besides, it is not really a straight line that we must search," Chaucer added. "The line of Michelle's is only an estimate. We would have to search at least twenty-five miles on either side of the line, even assuming that we could somehow know where the line is going across the landscape. There isn't going to be a nice yellow line drawn across the Arad for us to follow."

"We could spend years searching, going over this much landscape," Emil concluded. "You are right; we need more information to triangulate a more accurate place in which to start looking."

"The weak link is the very few observations from our fortress in New Barq at the southern edge of the Arad. If only we could get more observations from there," Benet suggested. "If we could, it might tell us that the location is in Juda Arad or Tashien."

"Why don't I contact them and ask them to redouble their efforts at finding more observations?" Paulette asked.

"It's been six weeks now since it happened. People will be very vague on the times of the sightings now. I doubt very much if such could be fully trusted. It's been too long ago now," Lilly Ann replied, dashing that idea. She was right; few would remember exact times of a strange sighting made over six weeks ago; even the exact day would be vague at best.

"Still, look at it this way. We kept going over what we have and finally worked out a powerful clue," Lilly Ann continued. "I suggest that we redouble our efforts. Let's all go over everything again. It may be that we have missed other clues as well as this incredible one."

Everyone began to restudy all the gathered items once more. Meanwhile, Michelle and Benet continued to study the map of sightings. "You know, if we had a few more observations, we might narrow it down a bit," she said. "Look, don't we have some people living in old Jerilum?"

"Yes, the women who evacuated Florintine Junction fled to Jerilum to gain their freedom," Benet replied. "What about the other Arads who live in secret towns somewhere out in here, the west central Arad? I know Lilly Ann is right about the observation timings. Yet, if they could give us a path that the ship traveled, that might help us pin this down more accurately."

The two went to Paulette with their request. She in turn contacted the Communicator in Jerilum and relayed their request. Now all they could do is wait, because it would take several weeks for overland travel from Jerilum to the secret towns of the old Arads and back again, assuming that anyone had actually seen anything that late at night.

Meanwhile, Chaucer made an observation. "Hey gang, I've figured out this device. It is its writing tool. See, it has no hands but if you hold it like this. See I am pretending to have two appendages. Hold it like this and press here on its side as you do it, see it marks or etches a line in the table top."

"Please stop gouging up our table, Chaucer," teased Beth Ann.

"Okay, so we now know that the bug can write with this," he said conclusively.

"Well, there are at least another ten of these markers in this pile. So we can conclude that the bug had ample writing utensils," Renzo replied. "What does that get us?"

"Like I suggested earlier," Rosina said, "if I were going to make a new secret prison that was not on the main maps, then I sure would leave some written record of its location somewhere. It must be in the journal somewhere. I will go back over it again. It must be in there somewhere."

"Wonder what this actually does?" Cedric asked, fiddling with a long cylindrical object. He found a button on it and pressed it. Nothing happened that he could see.

"Ieee! Stop that!" screamed Rosina.

"Eeeeee!" screamed Paulette.

"That is hurting my head!" yelled Renzo.

Cedric pushed the button again and still nothing happened, except everyone stopped screaming at the top of their lungs!

"What was that? That was excruciatingly painful!" Rosina was still screaming, holding her head with her hands.

"Damn, that really hurts!" exclaimed Paulette.

"I have a headache," muttered Renzo. "It feels as if I'm getting smashed into my head!"

"My mind is aching from that," Rosina finally spoke without yelling. "God, that really hurts!"

"Wow! It sure wiped me out," declared Paulette.

"I'm sorry. I just pressed this button on this gizmo here," Cedric said sheepishly.

"Wait a second," Lilly Ann interrupted. "Renzo, you were occupying the space which included the device, right?"

"Yes, I was moving over to see it because he was doing something with it. Why?" he asked.

"I wonder. I have an idea. Renzo, Paulette, Rosina, will you three go outside the mansion. Wave to us when you are there. We will turn this device on again. If you still are feeling it, scream as before. If you are not, we will wave at you three. If we wave, I want the Communicators to try to contact me in here, while Renzo you try to move into this room. Let us know what happens. I suspect you will again get blasted, so go easy with this, please."

The three quickly left the room and went outside the front of the mansion, Renzo waved for them. Shortly, Lilly Ann waved to them. "I don't feel anything," he said. The women agreed. "Okay, let's do our thing." Renzo moved toward the room. As soon as he was within about twenty feet of the room, he began to feel the same energy blasting him. He backed out to where his body stood.

"God! I can't make any contact. As soon as I try, I get this blast of energy over me!" his sister declared.

"Boy does that ever impact us telepaths!" declared Paulette, who began waving to Lilly Ann to turn it off. Neither of the three would reenter until Beth Ann came to fetch them!

When the three reentered the room, Lilly Ann explained. "This is a mantis weapon that is to be used against us, free beings. If you try to move into the space that this device is protecting, you get blasted with energy, forcing you away. If you try to make mental contact with someone inside the area this is protecting, you also get a mind blast of some kind. Gang, this is a diabolical weapon against us!"

"Damn, that explains why Bethany cannot contact me!" Renzo concluded. "Look their prison probably has one of these devices activated. I know she would try to contact me the instant she woke up. God, she probably was really blasted as I was when she tried. I'll bet she then would have done what I would have done, move way up in the sky, and try again. No wonder she hasn't been able to contact us. She is literally in two prisons, one is trapping her body, and the other is trapping her!"

"My god, this is a horrible weapon against us, the free beings of Tarra! How can we fight the mantis creatures if we cannot get close to them?" Lilly Ann declared, taking it further than just Bethany.

Alan, the older Planner, spoke up, "Well, as I see it, we have two problems to solve here, both are related. Somehow, we must experiment and find a way to defeat these energy blasts when we move too close or try to use telepathy. Second, once we have cracked those, we can then use that to contact Bethany and find out where she is at and set about rescuing the women."

"I'm game," Renzo said, "I'll do anything to help get Bethany rescued.

"Thanks, Renzo," Lilly Ann said. "Look, there are only three of you here who can work on moving into its space, Renzo, Michelle, and Benet. Only Paulette and Rosina can work on the telepathy thing. How about you five and Alan working together to see if you can find a way to defeat this device?"

"I'll volunteer too," Cedric replied. "Two Planners are better than one. Only this is more Enyo's specialty. I wish she were here."

"We all do, Cedric," Lilly Ann comforted him.

"I am getting close to figuring out that journal," Rosina said. "Can I see if I can finish that project first? If Paulette hasn't worked out a solution by then, I'll help her at once."

"True, yes, that is probably wise, Rosina. Say, how many of those things are in this pile of mantis stuff anyway?" Lilly Ann asked.

"Two," Cedric replied. "Let's go up to an unused room on the third floor where we won't disturb anyone with our screams." The five took the two devices and headed off to experiment. Rosina returned to Natale's room and poured even more diligently over the pages. The others continued to examine the mantis equipment looking for more clues.

Two days later, Rosina, carrying a copied page from the journal, came running into the meeting room, where everyone was discussing the morning's Santi business, which continued to demand part of their time. "I have something!" she yelled.

Laying the page on the table, she said very excitedly, "I've been a complete fool! I started at the beginning of the journal. What an idiot! Look, if you are writing a journal, where do you write the most recent things? Obviously at the next blank page! Look, this is the last page in the journal. It is a sketch, a rough one. See, there are these long lines on the left and right sides, as if someone moved a pen up and down rapidly and many times, as if they are drawing a barrier or a wall or something. Then, there are these two single horizontal wavy lines that connect, forming a large rectangle. Look what is in the very center! A circle! This must be a map of where they are being held prisoner, right there in that circle!"

"Fantastic!" declared Renzo. Then, his face fell, "But where is this place?"

"Oh, I haven't figured that one out yet. That's why I brought this to all of you. Does this sketch remind you of any place in Juda Arad or perhaps what little we know of Tashien?" she asked hopefully.

Everyone crowded around the table, staring at the map. "The real problem is that we do not have any scale here," Alan pointed out. "Is the distance across the rectangle a mile, ten miles, a hundred miles, a thousand miles?" Now, all understood his critical point. Without a scale, they had no idea what they were looking for, something small, something big, or something huge.

"Well, I am going to fetch all the maps I have," declared Captain Henry. "No one has more maps of Tarra than Natale and I do. Hang on a couple of minutes. Say, Cedric, come lend me a hand with them will you?" The two men dashed out of the room, running to his and Natale's quarters. Lining one wall was a wine rack affair, holding hundreds of maps, not wine.

"All of these?" asked Cedric in disbelief.

"Yes, who knows which map might be the right one," the seaman replied.

Their arms overflowing, the two men made their way back to the meeting room. Hours went by as they unfolded map after map, laying the journal sketch over a map and looking for anything resembling it. Nothing remotely matched. "Damn, I've got a map of nearly every known area of Tarra now, excepting the interiors of the new lands we just found, of course. Where could this spot be?"

Renzo, totally discouraged and feeling horribly let down, sat back in his chair and stared at the huge mantis map of the world, a copy that

Michelle had made from the master metal one that Henry had aboard the Sleepy Hollow. He folded his hands behind his head and stared at Tarra before him. Henry's words filtered through his mind, "known area of Tarra." His eyes shot over the Sea Princes, the Greenway, the Southlands, the peanut continent, the potato continent, Tashien, Megalos. All this was the known world. What wasn't known, he wondered.

His eyes moved up north. He'd never been to Volksholm, where the Axemen lived. Ah, but that was still the known world. Unknown, he reminded himself, but there weren't any unknown lands left. Perhaps, Henry was right, they were somewhere in the interior of the two continents they had not fully explored, only visited the coastal cities mostly. Ah, then there was all of Tashien; it was on the east line bearing of the sightings. His eyes followed the now memorized east-west line from the sightings map across Juda Arad to the impassable mountain range that formed the natural boundary of that land. He skipped over the Desert of Desolation to the parallel mountain range that formed another impassible barrier with Tashien. He recalled Empress Sho Lin telling them about her attempts to have some of her men climb these mountains. All had failed to find a passage through them.

The line went through the heart of the other side of the dog bone, Tashien. Golly, that was a very large, unexplored, by us, country. "Wait a second, Tashien cannot be considered 'unexplored.' There are millions of people living there." His eyes back tracked to the Desert of Desolation and fixed there. He muttered, "Well there certainly is an unknown area. No one can even get there!" Suddenly, Renzo cried out, "Damn! That's it! Not overland. It was flying! Where's that journal page!" He was so loud that he inadvertently had everyone's attention. He held the paper up to the Desert of Desolation.

"My god! It matches!" Henry nearly screamed in his excitement. "You've done it! You've found their prison!"

"Woo hoo!" Renzo screamed and fell out of his chair knocking Lilly Ann over. The two tumbled onto the floor. He sheepishly helped her up, but she was ecstatic as well.

"You did it, that must be the place," Lilly Ann exclaimed, ignoring completely having been knocked off her feet. "Look, it matches the sketch perfectly!"

For several minutes, everyone danced around the room, such was their relief! Jumping up and down, everyone yelled and cheered. Finally, they calmed down. Captain Henry interrupted the celebration, "Gang, we have a very serious problem here. The Desert of Desolation is uninhabited for a reason. Not only is it inaccessible, it is impassable. From what little I know of it, there is no water anywhere out there, and it is unlivably hot; temperatures have been reported to exceed one hundred thirty degrees! Some sea captains landed on the southern shores, walked a ways inland, and were nearly killed by heat strokes!"

Elation crumbled into despair in an instant. Renzo estimated from the sketch's position of the circle, they would have to travel some five hundred miles across a rough, barren desert in one hundred thirty degree heat with no water or food to be found there and back again. "Oh my god!" he muttered.

For some time, everyone sat in a stunned silence; the barrier between them and their loved ones seemed insurmountable! You've never seen such glum faces. Michelle brought them back to the problem at hand. "Well, the first thing that I would do is have Benet and me float over that land and see if we can find the location of their prison and scout out the land along the way."

Renzo responded at once. "Right, Michelle I could kiss you! Yes, let's all do it; let's go exploring. We ought to be able to know it exactly when we find them, because they are obviously being imprisoned with one of these energy devices. When we get too close to where the prison is located, we are going to get zapped again. That will tell us for sure that we have the right place. Besides, we will also be able to see the lay of the land. Maybe there are watering holes that no one knows about, there is always that possibility."

"I'm coming too," Rosina declared.

"Okay, let's do this properly," Lilly Ann took charge once more. "Renzo, you are the leader. Rosina, you are to keep the Mind Link with Paulette and your group up at all times. Michelle and Benet, you go with them. I want you to concentrate on the land and anything that we might make use of actually to travel over that desert. Paulette, you Mind Link the rest of us here to Rosina. We will take notes and observe. Between all our eyes, let's see just how desolate this desert actually is. Remember, stay alert for anything that can be of use in crossing the desert."

A few minutes later, the Mind Links in place, Renzo led the other three out over the mansion. He focused his mind on the familiar port of Constanza City, Megalos, where our archenemies lived, and the four arrived over the waters just off the docks there. Indeed, the Pope's yacht was docked there. Next, the group moved northward until they reached the coastline of the Desert of Desolation, only a hundred miles or so north of Megalos. Here, Renzo shot way up in the sky so that he could get a better view.

According to the map, the circle indicating the prison lay in the middle of the desert land. Hence, he needed to begin the search from the midpoint of the coastline between the two impassable mountain ranges. It took them a half hour to get into the right position at the coast. *Here we go,* he sent.

*We are going to skim over the surface,* Benet sent.

*I'll stay up high to make sure we are on course,* Renzo said.

*I'll be in the middle,* then, Rosina replied.

*God, it is boiling hot here,* Michelle sent. *Glad the heat doesn't affect me.* All four chuckled. Yet, they knew that if they had their bodies here, life would be nearly unbearable.

Renzo concluded that they had some five hundred miles to survey and about six hours of daylight left. Hence, he adjusted their speed so that they were covering what he thought might be a hundred miles in an hour.

The land was rocky in places; bedrock covered with smaller boulders would make foot traffic difficult. If a horse were used to cross this, great care would have to be taken. Low hills rose and fell. Occasionally, great patches of brown sand dunes covered the land. After a time, they realized that the rocky surfaces were about equal in size to the sandy areas. It was like a checkerboard layout of rough land to soft sandy dunes. The heat waves rising totally distorted the view of objects more than a few feet from them. It was a rather surrealistic view they all watched go by. Michelle would later paint a dozen magnificent canvasses depicting this trip.

No signs of life were spotted. No mice, not even a snake. Further, there was not a single blade of grass growing anywhere. This really was the Desert of Desolation! After an hour passed, a great windstorm blew across their path, nearly blinding them. However, the obscuration only blocked their view, unlike what it would have done to physical bodies caught in the dust storm. All realized that the terrain features were carved by the winds and not by rainfall. Perhaps it never rained in this land.

On they went, hour after hour, skimming along the broiling surface of the desert. Totally lifeless, a bleached land that offered no relief from the intolerable heat, no water to quench a thirst. Overland travel appeared to be next to impossible. As they four skimmed along, slowly the stark reality of the situation sunk into their minds, threatening to swamp their elation they anticipated when they would at last find this secret prison.

After five hours, Renzo estimated they must be in the vicinity; they all slowed down. He zoomed higher, to get a broader view of the landscape. However, he had no idea of what to look for, how this prison might appear. In this heat, how could it even be above ground? He wondered. Bethany and the others would have been long dead in this heat.

Then, slightly ahead of their position, he saw a strange, white ball shape rising from the brown rocky land. *I think it is dead ahead. I see a white ball. Let's make for it.* A few minutes later, the four floated close to a huge white ball, rising nearly seventy-five feet tall. However, its bottom was not rounded, as if the lower third of the ball was somehow underground. The surface of the white ball seemed to have the texture of cloth.

Experimentally, Renzo floated down to touch its surface. Wham! An energy blast sent him reeling backwards, landing on the broiling ground. Of course, without a body, no damage was done, mostly hurt pride. Rosina attempted to make contact with anyone inside the dome, and waves of excruciating pain swamped her, nearly forcing her unconscious.

*Ouch! We've found the place. I wish we could find some way to see if they are inside and if so, let them at least know that we have found them. We must find a way to give them some encouragement!* Renzo sent.

For a half hour, the four floated around the place, but no ideas came. Lilly Ann sent via Paulette, *See if you can find a door into the place.* That gave the four something to do at least. After going around the place a number of times, they gave that up too. It seemed to be a uniformly made ball. At last as the sun set, they had to give up and return home. That was blazingly fast. They made the decision to be back at the estate and immediately, they arrived back near their bodies. All four were very worn out by their excursion.

# Chapter 4 Problems in an Unattended Prison

As we looked about at the now well-lighted outer room just beyond our prison room, Linda reminded me, "Bethany, this must be October 1, 657, which means we have been here two months now. I hope Chaucer is not completely frantic by now."

"I know that Renzo and the others are very likely searching high and low for us, Linda. We must be somewhere secret or they would have found us by now. We just have to keep on trying to free ourselves as well."

"I know. I get depressed sometimes. By the way, I really want to thank you for having gotten that herb or chemical out of our food! I know that you have taken the worst of it, what with your hair being so long now. I can't imagine how awkward it must be for you with breasts so humongous. Yet, I do truly appreciate your having made that sacrifice. I have never felt so horny ever! I swear to you, Bethany, that I was ready to have sex with anything, even a dog, just to get some relief. That was utterly awful. Now it is mostly gone, and I feel about normal, all thanks to you. So if you need any extra help with your hair or because of your bust, let me know. It's the very least I can do to thank you."

"Thanks Linda. Yes, their weight is causing some back pains now and then. I just hope with that stuff out of our systems, they will shrink to normal, whatever that might be. Gosh, it is so hot out here. Enyo is right; something weird is going on; it seems backwards to me. I guess we ought to do some exploring, but help me keep an eye on the others, will you? In this heat, we can get a heat stroke pretty easy."

We two trailed along behind the others, who were excitedly exploring ahead. Still the clicking of our heels seemed louder than our voices. Well, if there were any mantis around, surely it would have heard us by now. I stopped worrying about that, worrying instead about the effects of this incredible heat!

"Will you look at all this equipment!" Enyo exclaimed to Natasa and Aella.

"What does it do?" asked Alexa. For her, function was more important than mere devices. To be useful, it had to do something that she could appreciate.

"Who knows," Natasa replied, "but is sure looks interesting! We could spend months studying all this stuff! Look, this part is blowing out very hot air, hotter than the air out here, while this side feels refreshingly cool. Maybe this device is what is keeping the temperature in our room constant. We could go close our door and see if it starts to work again." Sweat poured down the length of her body.

As we two walked slowly up to the group, I spied a small water puddle around each of the six women, who were standing around this huge piece of equipment. Yes, we were drenched, and we had only been lightly walking! I didn't like how this was materializing. Heat stroke would cause us major problems; the biggest would be how we could possibly transport one of us back to the room and cool them down in time.

Enyo said, "Gosh, I'm feeling a bit lightheaded, a bit woozy."

"Heat stroke! Come on; everyone, back into the room for now. Can you make it there, Enyo?"

"I hope so, it's so hot!"

"Come on, everyone. Let's put our bodies up against hers and help support her, give her some balance. I don't know how we would carry her if she collapses," Linda suggested. Well, I probably could move out of my body further and carry her, but the others had already begun to press together tightly. Slowly we moved back towards our room. Even I was feeling very lightheaded by the time we made the door. As we passed inside the doorway, Enyo began to sink to the floor. Our sweat covered bodies only allowed her to slip more slowly to the floor. "Shut the door fast," Linda called out. "We have to get her into the bathtub and get her cooled down fast!"

Natasa closed the door, but the others could not figure out how to lift Enyo up. As soon as the door shut, we heard the machinery turn on and a blast of much cooler air blew into the room. "I got her," I called out to their utter relief. Using my spiritual powers to lift things, I moved her over to the tub and gently laid her down. Natale already had the cold water running. We all grabbed wash rags in our mouths and began dabbing her face and chest with the cooler waters.

At last, she opened her eyes, "What happened? How did I get in the tub?"

"You fainted from the heat. I got you in here," I replied. "Close call, Enyo." Once she was cooled down, we dried her off. Then, we all took a quick bath as well, to wash off the sweat. We spent much of the day washing, drying off, and brushing out our long hair.

"I'm sorry everyone," Enyo apologized, while we were eating our supper. "That heat is something else. I don't understand this. How can it be so hot first thing in the morning? First thing in the evening — now that I can understand."

"Wait a minute," Natasa exclaimed. "What we are calling morning might not be the real morning! How do we know it is morning? The lights come on, that's all. What if morning were really the evening? Then, that would account for us being out there in the heat of the day."

"Well, that is easy enough to verify," I grasped what the engineers had already figured out. "When the lights go out tonight in here, let's check what is going on outside the room."

"Excellent plan," Enyo praised my quick grasp of her field of endeavor. "What shall we do in the mean time?"

"Gosh, if you want something to do, how about somehow massaging my monster breasts? They are aching now," I suggested. They giggled and agreed to assist me. As I stood up, again I stepped on my own long hair. "Ouch!" This takes a good deal of getting used to!" Everyone laughed.

After a lengthy massage, they did feel lots better. "Thanks gang. Much better. I wonder if they are now shrinking or still growing? Maybe I don't want to know!" Everyone roared. Suddenly the lights went out. We waited and shortly the nightlight turned on.

Quickly, Enyo walked over to the table, well, relatively quickly in these boots anyway, picked up the metal key in her mouth, and went to the door. When it opened, the heat was drastically lower, tolerable in fact. We had forgotten to turn off the lights when we were frantically rescuing Enyo; they were still on. Natale moved up and turned them off.

Imagine our shock and surprise to see that dim light was coming down from the white roof far overhead! "I bet it is now dawn!" Enyo declared.

"It's much cooler too," Natasa added. "Can we go exploring now, Bethany, before it gets too hot?"

"Okay, let's do it. Should we turn the lights back on?" I asked.

"Only if we need them. Come on. Let's take a quick walk and survey what is really out here, the whole place. Then, we can have something to think about while we sleep," Enyo suggested.

Heels clicking a percussive symphony, we eight walked around this outer area. I saw that it was indeed circular in shape but huge. While much machinery lay around and up against our room on all sides, one section of this outer area was very wide and empty. I immediately thought of parking one of their flying ships in here. It was big enough I felt from my memories of them. Conclusion, if they could get a flying ship in here, there had to be a door here somewhere.

We walked on past any number of fascinating machines and devices. Here was a worktable of some kind, a giant sized one. Its twenty-foot tall legs supported a large flat working area far above. I floated up to peek and saw a number of tools lying there. Then I spied something useful, well useful to us anyway. A spool of yellow ribbon hung from a metal spike, just what I needed to make a hair band! I floated it down to me and sat it on the floor. Now if only I could find something with which to cut it. I looked more closely at the tools, found what must be a knife, and floated it down to me. I smiled; it would work!

Now I had a choice, I could attempt to float these two objects around with me or just pick them up in my teeth. I chose teeth. I squatted down and awkwardly got them into my mouth securely. However, as I stood back up, I was once more standing on my hair. Argh. Well, this was going to soon be a thing of the past, I thought to myself, proudly carrying my find with me as I clicked hurriedly to catch up to the others.

"What do you have there, Bethany," Linda asked as I finally caught her. "Look everyone, Bethany has found us something to make hair ribbons with! Yes! Thank you!" Everyone grinned and looked pleased. An hour later, we found ourselves back where we started, the door to our prison room. I hastily went inside, dropped my find onto the table, and rejoined the others.

"Look how light outside it's getting," declared Enyo. "See, it is indeed morning. The mantis has us on an opposite cycle. I wonder if we can change that somehow? I wonder how big around this thing is?"

"I wonder where the doorway is?" I teased her back. She and the others laughed.

"Seriously, I think that big open space is where they park their flying ships. So this time around, let's see if we can find the exit?" I suggested.

"Okay, but we need to measure its size. I am going to do just that. I will take very small steps this time, you all ignore me," Natasa explained. "I will make them about one foot in length. Now there are too many obstructions to walk around the outer edge, so I will go about here. Aella, your task is to figure out the diameter of this circle enclosure and estimate how far out my circular path is at. Then, we can calculate everything we need to know."

"You got it, Natasa. Enyo, you find the door for Bethany," Aella replied enthusiastically. Engineers — always more interested in architecture than escaping!

Six of us clicked our way to what had to be the parking area. After an hour of searching, we all guessed that one button way up high was the switch. "Well, it might shut the whole place down; it might open the door; it might do any number of things," Enyo declared. "However, we won't know until we push it, now will we?"

"Foolhardy!" Alexa teased her lifelong friend. As one of the quartet of the Trouble Makers, Enyo's nickname was the Foolhardy. "Ah go ahead and push it. You realize there will be no living with her until it is pushed?" We all laughed. Once again, Natale floated up to the button, being careful not to get too high and run into the energy-blasting barrier. She pushed it and floated back down.

"Well, we didn't all explode," Alexa teased Enyo. We heard a large grating noise and some mechanical devices humming. Slowly, a huge section of the white wall began opening up! Fresh, but hot, air rushed inside. We bent low to get our first peek at the world outside our prison.

None of us was prepared for what we saw! Before us lay a vast expanse of rocky ground, bedrock covered with stones of all shapes and sizes. Far off in the distance we could see what must be a sand dune. No trees, no grass, no water, just an incredibly bleak and barren world. In addition, it was hot already. We walked outside the huge door.

Exasperated, Linda said, "Free but not free!"

"You can say that again!" declared Natale.

"Free but not free are we!" We chuckled at the hopelessness of our predicament. "Well, let's take a little stroll outside, shall we? Maybe Natale ought to stay here in case the door somehow automatically closes."

"Okay, I'll keep an eye on it. Just you all be careful out there. It doesn't look inviting. How are we ever going to walk out of here to home?"

We ambled outside, but found walking in these boots on this rough, stony terrain most difficult indeed! We kept losing our balance, barely keeping from falling over! While I was ready to curse these boots, I also realized that if we were actually barefoot now, our feet would be in very big trouble indeed!

From the angle of the sun, I estimated it was maybe ten in the morning, but where were we? The others turned to look in all directions and at the overall shape of our prison. It was a large white dome affair. The landscape was equally dismal in every direction as far as the eye could see. I tried to get my bearings, where was this place? I could not recall having seen any land like this ever!

"Keep an eye on things, I am going way up in the sky to see if I can spot where on Tarra we are at," I said to Linda. Off I shot like a rocket, loving every second of my newfound freedom that had been denied to me for two months now. Higher and higher, I ascended. The desolation only grew all the larger in all directions! I began to panic the higher I rose; nothing looked at all familiar to me! I kept going up.

Then relief swept over me. I recognized the bog bone! We were in the Desert of Desolation! In an instant I moved back to near my body. "Linda, Desert of Desolation, smack dab in the middle of it. No wonder it is so hot here."

"Well, now things make a whole lot more sense," Linda exclaimed. "Wow. Heat, desolate landscape. No one lives here, perfect place for a mantis prison. Say, you had better contact Renzo and the others; let them know that we are alive. Gosh, maybe a Mind Link for us all to chat with our mates, please?"

*Renzo! It's me! We have finally found a way outside the energy field.*

*Bethany! God, you are alive still! We've spent two months finding where you are! I missed you horribly! Are you and the others all right? We think you are in the Desert of Desolation.*

*We are smack in the middle of it and in a white dome thing.*

*We were there a bit ago. We know where it's at, but we cannot get through the energy fields nor can the Communicators get through. How are you able to?*

*We have managed to escape our prison cell and then found a way out of the whole complex. I'm outside right now, though it's getting hot, and we will have to go back inside soon. How are the kids doing? There are eight of us trapped here. We are all doing okay, unless the mantis comes back.*

*Kids miss you too. Julie and her group brought down the mantis flying ship; it burned up. The mantis who abducted you is burned to a crisp. No one has seen any others around. We are mounting a rescue somehow. How long can you all hold on?*

*Don't know on time. Fantastic to know we are not facing a return of the mantis creature. It's getting too hot for us to stay out here; we are totally naked, except for these infernal boots, like those in Annelise, really high metal spikes. They cannot come off, and it has rendered us pretty darn helpless. I'll make contact tomorrow morning when it is coolest. Have everyone there so the others can say hi to their husbands. I love you. Tell the kids mom will try to get home as soon as I can.*

This was the first time that I really, really appreciated my ability to communicate across space to another! Oh how I had missed Renzo and not even realized it! Yet, my body was rapidly overheating, and Linda was trying to nudge me back inside as fast as possible. I saw that she, too, was now sweating heavily. "I got through. They were here, checking this place out; they know where we are. I think they have done an incredible job of finding us. Renzo said he and Rosina and Benet and Michelle, all floated here the other day, but like me, they couldn't get through the energy field that surrounds this place. We will make the big Mind Link with your husbands tomorrow morning when it is cool again."

As soon as we were inside, Natale pushed the button to close the huge open door. Once we saw it was closing, we all headed as fast as we could safely manage back into our temperature controlled room and shut the door. The lights were off, suggesting that we ought to be fast asleep!

"Everyone, to the table. It's news time!" I said, rather excitedly. For the first time since we got here, things looked promising. "I found out where we are, smack in the middle of the Desert of Desolation!"

"Well, no wonder the temperatures are so unbearable," exclaimed Enyo.

"Now things make a whole lot more sense!" Alexa added.

I told them of my brief conversation with Renzo and that the others knew exactly where we were located. They all cheered me when I told them that tomorrow morning we would go back outside and make a big Mind Link with their husbands. The smiles looking back at me told all!

"How are they going to rescue us?" asked Enyo at last.

"No idea. I guess we will have to stay here a while longer, but we won't have to worry about the mantis returning."

"Well, then we can experiment with the equipment," Natasa replied. "It is day time now, but the room says we are sleeping. Worse, we need to be operational while it is cooler outside. Enyo and I have decided that the entire place must be running on some kind of timekeeper that knows what time of day it is. If we can find that device and figure out how to reset it, we can keep a better schedule."

"Let's not do anything until we hold the big conference tomorrow. We may be stuck here some time yet until they can get to us. We cannot possibly walk out of here. Actually, these boots are a blessing around here. The stone outside is broiling hot; our bare feet would be badly burned by now. Worse are the myriad of stones, which would injure our bare feet something badly. Yet, with these darn spikes, walking is precarious, but our feet are safe. So I guess there is something to be thankful about them," I replied.

"Now then, I found this ribbon spool and a knife. While you engineers give us your report, will some of you please try to tie up my hair in a ponytail, please? I keep stepping on it." They chuckled; actually, everyone wanted to put their hair up to reduce the heat on their necks, while we were out in the heat. I knew that without the use of our feet and toes, this was a challenging task that I had set for them. Yet, the benefits would be good for us all. It is amazing to see how resourceful women can be, using only their mouths. Yes, it took a considerable time to get everyone's hair tied back into a ponytail, but we did it. That was all that mattered to us.

"The outer dome is seventy-five feet tall," Enyo began to summarize their findings. "The outer dome covers our inner cell here. It is around sixty feet across here at the ground level. Our cell is off to one side, not in the center, probably because of the room needed for the flying machine. Most of the machinery adjacent to our cell is somehow connected to our cell. We know where the food dispenser equipment is located. Today, we believe we have found the water source. Machines seem to be bringing it up from somewhere underground, but how far underground, we don't yet know."

Natasa added, "The dome is very structurally sound and can probably withstand considerable wind. So we are safe as long as the cooling machine continues to function and as long as the food holds out."

Alexa pointed out, "I checked on the food cylinders. I discovered a new use for these spikes, actually. By kicking on the cylinders, I can hear how hollow they sound, since they are made of metal too. As you recall, there are two identical large cylinders connected to the food dispenser, ignoring that herb or chemical tank. One of the large ones is empty or nearly so. The other has only less than a quarter left in it. Gang, we are going to run out of food here within a few days. Perhaps Enyo can calculate how many days we have left."

"Damn, this is not good news," I replied, looking at Enyo for help.

"Okay, both tanks were full at the start — let's assume that anyway, though we have no way of knowing that detail. We've eaten one and three quarters of the food in sixty days. Taking the proportions into account, we have eight days of food left!" Enyo looked shocked at her own prediction.

"Well, top priority is finding more food!" I stated the obvious. "There's no way our guys can rescue us that quickly!"

"We have been too dependent upon all this alien technology of automation. Obviously, at some point, the mantis would have to return, if only to swap in a new set of food cylinders. Perhaps other pieces of the operation must be regularly serviced as well. What if the temperature control stops functioning?" Alexa pointed out. "We will not last one day in these temperatures, and only one of us can get into the tub at a time. Suppose the water machine runs dry? We'd die within days. I am afraid that with the mantis gone, our situation here has become dangerously perilous indeed!"

I looked at these brilliant seven women, and I couldn't help from commenting, "Gang, you know I have only now fully realized that I am in the presence of seven absolutely brilliant, intelligent, fantastic women. No matter how this all turns out, I just want you all to know that I am incredibly proud and honored to be your close friend. You are one incredible bunch of beings!" Tears of joy trickled down my cheeks as I ended my little accolade.

I continued, "Yes, Alexa, you took the very words I was about to say right out of my mouth before I could say them. Incredible. Yes, tomorrow, after we know more from our husbands, we must really begin to find out our true situation here. I have a feeling that this will become terribly vital to our survival. While I can lift and throw things, there is no way that I can get even one of us moved five hundred miles to the southern shores of this desert. We all know that we are not going to be able to walk out of here either, even if we had food and water somehow."

"In that case, we ought to make a test of how long the blue goo lasts before it spoils out in the open air," Linda volunteered. "If it will last days, we might be able to eat less and save some back." Thus began a lengthy discussion on just what things we could possible do and what avenues we ought to explore.

Finally, the lights turned on and the food dispenser doled out our breakfasts. After eating, we decided that lights or no lights, we needed to get our biological clocks reset to the real situation here. Hence, we all piled into bed. I got into ours last, throwing my head around to try to get my hair into a position where I wouldn't kneel on it trying to get into bed.

The next morning, well, night here in the room, we got up and got the food from the dispenser. Fortunately, it had not broken down by our not removing the lunch or supper bowls. It seemed to work fine, thus far. After eating, we all headed outside to make contact with our husbands and the others of our Circle. For over an hour, we exchanged news and private conversations. I insisted on Rosina sending us an image of what the energy-blasting device looked like in hopes that today we could find something similar here and somehow turn it off.

On the down side, Renzo was fully honest with us. Thus far, no one had any viable idea about how to actually reach and rescue us. Yet, we all knew that this would fully occupy their every thought until they did so.

Back inside with the door shut and the lights turned on for best seeing, I suggested we divide up into several groups, each tackling one of the many potential problems that we may soon be facing, food, water, heat, and the timer action which we might be able to change. I estimated that we would have four hours maximum before it became entirely too hot out here to continue explorations.

Since we were entirely dependent upon our three engineers, I went along with Enyo to assist her. Linda went with Natasa; Kallisto, with Aella. I had Alexa and Natale off in search of possible timer controls, which we might reset, figuring Natale's research into their language might give her some clues about such a device.

Enyo and I dealt with our food supply. We wandered about the outer area looking for additional similar looking cylinders. After some searching, we did find two more sets. "Darn, it looks like the entire batch of three must be replaced as a group. You only undid the input line in the group. Each of these groups is going to be continuing to inject that herb or chemical into our food."

"Gosh, look what happened to me when I cut it the last time! If I do it again, I will have hair below my feet and boobs that are giant balls!" I replied.

"Well, the alternative is for us all to suffer a little bit," Enyo countered. "No way can we ask you to do that again! God, I don't see how you are managing now. They are monsters. No, I simply won't let you do it, we all will just have to grin and bear it together," she said defiantly.

"Thanks, they are still aching today. I cannot imagine what life would be like if they got any bigger. Should we wait until the tank is completely empty or should we try to hook a new set up now? Perhaps, we would be able to somehow get what little food slop remains in the tank out of it by tipping it over or upside down, if we get desperate."

"It's going to be iffy, Bethany. I'd rather know sooner than later if we are unable to get a new batch hooked up and working. If we do it now, then if we have trouble and can make do with what remains in the one cylinder, it gives us a week's breathing room, but is it your call; you are the leader," Enyo deferred to me.

"Let's do it now. I will sleep better, if I know that we have another two months of blue slop to eat. How do we proceed? I will follow your orders."

"First, we must move this one over beside the other and then study all the connections." That was the easy part, at least for me. A minute later, the heavy assemblage was sitting close to the nearly empty group. Now we both began observing the obvious, following the three tubes to see where they went. At last, Enyo said, "It appears to me that only one connection must be undone and reconnected to this batch. This one here," she pointed with her heel, "it must be somehow unfastened and the similar dangling line here connected in its place. The question is how to undo it."

I sat down and tried to fiddle with the connection using my boots, which was a useless action. I accidentally stood on my pony tail getting up once more, ouch. "Okay, I am going to see what I can do with the connection. Any ideas how it should move?"

"Go easy on it. When you get the right action, it should come off easily. If you meet with resistance, it is probably the wrong motion. That's the best I can suggest," Enyo replied.

I pulled, tugged, and twisted, all to no avail. Disgusted, I gave it an inward push. A loud popping sound startled me, and the tube assemblage popped off! "Brilliant, Bethany, it goes inward. I would not have thought of that one."

"I didn't either," I admitted sheepishly, "I got pissed at it and pushed it. Lucky break. I'll move the old one out of the way and the new one into position." A couple minutes later, I had swapped the two units around. Actually, hooking the new one in was a snap, one strong push and it connected with a loud hissing sound as it pressurized.

"Well, if food comes out again, we have two more months of blue slop to eat," Enyo declared. "Let's go see how many more cylinders we can find. I think we saw another set, but there may be more stored around here." We set off in search of more. In the end, we found one more full set. If all went well, we could last four months in the food department, assuming you call the blue goo food.

Next, we tried to get what remained out of the cylinder. That frustrated us and in the end, we got none out. We decided to leave it be for now. Our four hours was up; the heat was beginning to get to both of us, so we headed back inside.

Meanwhile, Natale and Alexa wandered completely around the complex four times, their heels clicking endlessly. While Alexa looked around at our level and helped move Natale's body around, Natale move up and looked around at mantis height. "We are looking for something that has a lot of ciphers on it. If you see anything let me know and I'll check to see if they are numbers. I think a day-night timer ought to have numbers on it," Natale suggested.

"Well, if I were making a timing device, that's how I would do it," Alexa agreed. "Let's get going." Around and around the two walked. After their fourth trip, Alexa commented, "Well, if nothing else, I am getting much more used to walking in these heels. Actually, they are not that bad once you get used to them. They do make my legs look better defined. I just wish we had the option to take them off when I need my feet for something. Have you found anything? So far, I've only found five false alarms."

"Well, my attention keeps getting drawn to this thing up here. Why don't you back up a little so you can get a better angle to view it? What do you think? It's got numbers on it, part is white, and part is black."

"Is that a pointer thing there at the top? It looks like it is pointing from down here."

"Yes, yes, I think you are right. Let's see, what time is it really outside?" Natale asked.

"From the heat, I would guess around ten in the morning," Alexa replied. "What does the pointer show?"

"It is about a quarter of the way into the black."

"We should set it to be about a quarter of the way into the white. That would be my guess. Any ideas how to do that?" Alexa inquired.

"Well, why don't I try turning it? I am not very good at moving things, especially if they are heavy. I can only move very light things. Perhaps my light touch will not harm it. Should I try?"

"Heck, why not? If you were Enyo, the Foolhardy, you would have already turned it!" Both women laughed.

"It doesn't want to move if I move it to the left. I'll try to the right. Oh, it turns easily this way. Here goes, one quarter into the white. Anything happening?"

"I'll go see, be right back," Alexa replied and clicked back to our cell. "Hey," she yelled back loudly to Natale, "the lights are now off! Maybe you did it! Yes!"

Natale joined her and saw that the lights were indeed off. Both women gave each other our personal hug, three times, proud of their accomplishment. Then, they headed off to find me and relate what they had done.

"Great going ladies! Now we can sleep at the right times! Enyo and I have a new two month supply of blue goo hooked up. We don't know if it will actually work, though. I guess in two hours or so we will find out. I wonder how the others are faring?"

"Well, let's walk around this place some more," Alexa suggested. "I am really getting used to these boots now. It is so good to be able to walk around out here rather than in the tiny circles inside our cell!" We could not agree more and began strolling around the circumference, observing everything once more.

When noon approached, it was way too hot to be outside. We headed inside, our bodies dripping with sweat once more. The other two teams had little to report. Nothing substantial had been discovered about our water source nor had they found out much about the mechanism which kept us cool during the incredible heat of the day.

However, we were all surprised to hear the buzzer sound for lunch. As everyone headed to the dispenser, I had to warn them, "Gang, this new set of blue goo has the small cylinder that injects the herbs or chemicals into our food still attached."

Enyo hastily interrupted me, "There is no way that I will allow Bethany to disconnect it and suffer another massive growth spurt like before. I told her that we all would just have to grin and bear it together. Agreed?"

To my surprise, they all readily agreed, "I won't let you either,

Bethany," declared Linda and Natale in unison. We then retrieved our lunch of blue goo. Ah, it did taste much better with the herbs or whatever was in it, however.

After lunch, we took baths, dried our hair, and brushed them out. Since only one could use the tub at one time and since at least three of us actually had to bathe the person, it did take us all the afternoon to accomplish these tasks. It is just as well that it did, since it kept us otherwise occupied. I dreaded just sitting around doing absolutely nothing for the better part of the day!

What bothered me was the stuff in our food, which would begin to react on us within two more weeks, if it worked as before. As I lay on my back trying to fall asleep, I wondered how much our hair and breasts would continue to grow? My reasoning went thusly: if the overall plan was to keep us imprisoned here for the rest of our lifetimes and that lifetime was to be as long as possible, then having our breasts grow to monstrous proportions could only hinder that goal. Already mine were approaching the size of my own head, making simple chores much more difficult to manage. Normal life would become impossible if they doubled again in size. It just did not make any sense at all.

The nearly incredible growth of our hair also made no sense, though long hair posed a far smaller problem and was something one could deal with somehow. Ah, then there was the incredible sexual drive. I had nearly forgotten about that aspect. Now that was indeed a fitting part of the plan of entrapment, as I reasoned. Trapped like pigs in a cage, give the pigs an overwhelming sexual urge to be satisfied in any way possible and the pigs would be more content, well at least they would not have their attention on finding a way out of the cage. This was the only part that made sense to me.

Worse, such an overwhelming drive would tend to focus a spiritual being's attention solidly and nearly completely on the physical body, further entrapping them, perhaps even driving them into their heads maybe. Well, for now this is just my speculation only.

Okay, so if I accept that the fundamental purpose of the chemical enhancement was to generate this overwhelming desire for sensual pleasure, how did that tie in with monster breasts? Perhaps a mate might get aroused over them, but I certainly did not; they ached more now than during breast-feeding, when one of my children bit down too hard. This was anti-sexual, actually. Ah, the two phenomenon were opposites really. Maybe it was just a side effect.

This realization startled me. Damn, why didn't I think of this before! What an idiot I had been all along. Now I saw what I needed to do. Probably a Healer would have spotted this when it had begun happening. All that I needed to do was get into communication with my own body and find out what it was doing, how it was reacting, what it felt! After all, the body has its own life force, however thin compared to us beings that occupied them.

I relaxed and began to sense my own body. I felt first for my toes, then my ankles. Using tiny increments, I slowly began to sense and feel every part of my body. A long time later, I finally had a complete union with my whole body, boobs and all. I began to sense what it wanted, felt, needed, and how it was reacting to the chemical. I saw the side effect clearly. The breast growth was the body's method of ejecting the chemicals, which we were not allowing to be ejected in the optimum manner that the body desired! I thought to my body, *So how do you want to get rid of the stuff?*

I was surprised by the answer I received. We, the spiritual beings were in fact suppressing the optimum means that our physical bodies had to remove this poison from our systems! Only when the body sensations drove us nearly mad did we actually begin to use the means the body desired, pleasure stimulation. Well, if Renzo were here with me, probably my breasts would still be their normal size. We women had been trying to force our bodies to be civilized, and we had become our body's worst enemy with this chemical imbalance effect.

The next morning over breakfast, I explained what I had discovered to the others. "I know that it seems prurient, deviant, maybe even perverted or whatever, but I believe that it is our body's natural way to eliminate these chemicals we are eating. Since I am in the worst shape, I will be the guinea pig. After we report in to the others, I will return here, while the rest of you continue our explorations. I ask for one of you to volunteer to give me a work out. If I am right, we may have this side effect licked. I know that you probably will find this quite embarrassing. Please, let me try it and withhold judgment until we see if it works."

"I'll volunteer," Linda replied. "I'm pretty unhelpful on this engineering stuff.

"I will too," Kallisto added, "none of this is assassin's work." Everyone chuckled at her tease of herself.

A while later, without much news from headquarters, we three returned to our room. I laid down on our table so that Linda and Kallisto could have easier access to my body. "Okay, gang, have at it. Pleasure me utterly senseless. God, I hope I am right about this!"

I found that Kallisto was really quite the expert, though not as good as the women from the Isle of Loving, whose sole goal in life had been to give pleasure to men and women. What happened surprised even me. I will spare you the prurient details. By lunch time, both women could see a marked difference in my breast size! They were indeed shrinking. Finally, my body was ejecting the chemicals. We had licked this diabolical trap within a trap of the mantis creature! I also realized that these alien mantis creatures did seem to know an awful lot about the operations of our fleshly bodies, but then I shouldn't have been so surprised about this fact. They had been the ones who had engineered this entire trap for spiritual beings here on Tarra.

Natale and Alexa came into the room, heels clicking a happy tune. "We think we did it, Bethany," Alexa said cheerily. "We think we have turned off the energy devices. How about taking a minute and testing it, just to make sure?"

"Terrific!" I complimented them. I floated up, cautiously, unwilling to be zapped hard again. This time, I felt no resistance as I soared up above our dome prison. I returned to my body and made contact with Renzo to let him know we had the energy field down now. Once more, we had free communications at any time. Another small piece of the trap had been defeated!

When the heat of the day came, again we were comfortable within our cell. After eating our slop lunch, Enyo gave us a summary report of their findings. They had decided that if there was any way possible, they wanted to take as many of these devices as possible back home with them. Engineers! Already, they had been making mental lists of the priority of the items.

However, Natasa had made an interesting discovery. While exploring behind some equipment, the floor seemed hollow to her heel clicks. "We need your lifting help with this, Bethany. We believe that the metal slab on the floor can be moved, revealing what lies below. It appears this place has a basement! Who knows what incredibly cool things we can discover down there!" The engineers were excited over this discovery. "Oh, by the way, how did the pleasure session go?" she asked.

"Perfectly!" I explained, giving them the theory behind the results I had gotten.

From now on, right after lunch, we indulged in a round of heavy pleasure, took our baths, and brushed out our hair, filling up the long afternoon. Thank god the process worked; our breasts slowly began to return to their normal size or nearly so.

The next work period, early dawn til noon, we spent examining Natasa's discovery. I moved some equipment aside, and we definitely saw a metal slab covering the floor, not the bedrock of the rest of the place. The slab was about eight feet wide and ten long. The question was how to lift it up? Was it a trap door with hinges and would swing up?

The engineers concluded based upon the pattern of recessed bolts that it swung upwards toward the side of the dome. I found a small hole in the center of the opposite end. Ah, the mantis would insert its claw here and lift up. I did the same and the trap door creaked open. Enyo discovered a latch holder that would catch the slab at the hole and hold it open. It was out of our reach, so Natale lowered it, and I wiggled the slab slightly until the latch fell into the lifting hole.

Now we peered down into the darkness. A long sloping ramp of stone led downward. The mantis did not need steps, evidentially — made sense when I thought about it. "With these heels, we will not be able to walk down it — too steep," Enyo observed. "Guess we slide down on our butts."

"Hold on a second; we need to find the light switch," I cautioned. "A mantis must have a switch somewhere, I'm sure it isn't going to wander down into a totally black space and fumble around in the dark for a light down there. It must be in this vicinity. Start looking everyone."

Natale found the switch about twenty feet above our heads. Once pushed, lights went on down below. "I see a huge space," Enyo called out. "Can I go down now?"

"Let her rip, Enyo, the Foolhardy," Alexa teased her good friend. She tossed her head so that her long hair was in front of her, squatted down, and plopped her butt on to the ground. Using her feet, she edged to the ramp. "Whee, this is fun," she exclaimed as she slid down the thirty-foot long ramp. "Wow! Look at all this stuff! Come on down!" she called out.

I looked at Alexa, while one by one the engineers followed her lead. "Engineers!"

Alexa laughed, "She's always been like this, a fun loving, fearless explorer of the unknown. For that matter all four of us Rule Breakers have been. Come on. Let's have a slide!" She was just as excited as Enyo was. I brought up the rear, making sure everything else was okay. I tossed my ponytail out to the front, squatted down, and edged to the ramp. Then, down I went.

Okay, it was fun, but hard on the rear end skin. It would have been much more enjoyable if I had my pants on. Once down, for a moment I just sat there looking around. Enyo was right; stuff was everywhere, nicely stacked. Who knows what the stuff actually was, however.

"We will have to spend weeks in here figuring out what all this is!" declared Enyo. "I do hope the guys can bring a lot of transport vehicles!"

"Okay, let's take a quick survey. Everyone team up in pairs and let's see what we have found. Please be extra careful," I cautioned. "Kallisto, you are with me; let's try that way."

"This room is its nest," called out Linda, "no eggs. Good thing."

"Must be its pantry, lots of grass bales in here," yelled Aella.

"Bethany, this must be a study," Kallisto pointed out as we entered a side room which held a tall desk and a book rack filled with dozens of the books similar to the ones that Natale was studying, hoping to be able to learn their language and translate them. No sooner had Kallisto announced this than we heard the rapid clicks of heels behind us.

Natale rushed in to peek. "Oh my! There are more here than all the ones that I have! What a find! I have to look at these! Where is the light in here?" Natale was really catching on to where the mantis had placed its magical light switches. Within a minute, the room was well lighted, and Natale was at the bookshelf. We left her to the books and continued exploring.

As we two walked along, Kallisto said softly, "Bethany, something is troubling me. Has been since the first day we found ourselves brought here. I haven't said anything to the others about it yet. I didn't want to alarm them, but right now, we are by ourselves. Can I speak freely?" She looked worried.

"Sure, I'll keep my voice down."

"It's just this. How did the mantis creature, who we did not even know was here on Tarra, suddenly know just who to abduct? That is, how did it know to get us? There are millions of people on Tarra. How did it know about us eight, let alone where on Tarra we were? Especially me. I was in Demokritos while you all were in Velona."

"I see what you mean. I had not yet had time to think about such things, Kallisto. I have been more worried about keeping us alive and finding a way to be rescued. Yet, now that you point it out to me, I wonder the very same thing. I personally did not feel any alien mind probe in the days and weeks before we were abducted. I am sure that I would have. I sensed the Grey Creature down in Vladimir, when it tried to scan my memories. I feel confident that I would also detect a mantis making such an attempt."

"Thank you for being honest with me, Bethany. Really, I did not think that you would have been the one who gave me away," Kallisto replied. "Can you see where I am going with my thinking? Someone somewhere has given us away to the enemy. Even if we can be somehow rescued, and personally I sure do not see how that will happen, what is to prevent that very same person from giving us away to the next mantis who comes along to Tarra?"

"Kallisto, I will make you this solemn promise. As soon as I get us all rescued and back home, I will spare no expense to find out the answer to your question. Say, this tunnel is narrowing. What is that ahead of us?"

We stopped and peered into the dim area ahead. Indeed the tunnel sides had become rough and uneven. Only the floor remained smooth. A pipe lay at the very right side of the tunnel we were following; it ran on out ahead of us. "It looks like the tunnel is opening up into some kind of underground chamber," Kallisto surmised.

Just then, we heard an explosion or blast sounding noise coming from behind us, followed by a squeal of surprise from Enyo. Fearing the worst, everyone began jogging as fast as we could in these heels back toward the location of her noise. Another blast jolted the air down here. "Enyo, are you all right?" I yelled, trying to concentrate on running and not falling down. Perhaps I should not have let us divide and explore.

We two were the last to enter the workroom where Enyo was located. The others had gotten there before us and were staring at Enyo. She was sitting on the ground, her boots holding onto some mechanical device. A pair of giant, still smoking, holes were visible in the stone wall of the room. "Look what I found! I shall call it my Stone Cutter! Gang, it cuts through stone in the blink of an eye! Woo hoo! I get to keep this device!"

"Hey, are there more? Let's see it, Enyo. I want one too," Natasa replied.

"Hey, don't forget me! I want one as well!" declared Aella. Engineers!

"This is a most valuable find, Bethany," Enyo exuberantly exclaimed, as she struggled to her feet. She became quite as she picked up the device in her mouth.

"Ah, Enyo is now quiet at long last!" teased Alexa. We all roared with laughter as well as relief that she was not hurt.

"Hey, look, there is a whole bunch of them," Natasa exclaimed wildly excited. "We can all have several of them!"

We all continued laughing. Finally, Linda said, "We found a bunch of those eternal portable lights, all stacked in a box."

"Well, I found a large crate filled with all sizes of these boots. Also, there are several of the devices, which the creature used to seal the boots onto our legs and feet. Perhaps there is a way to reverse the process. In any event, I get the crate of boots. I think these heels look great, if only we can find a way to take them off when we want. They will bring a fashion fortune, I expect," Alexa explained her find.

"Okay, let's get ourselves each one of the eternal lights. I have something I want us to explore. Kallisto and I found something strange way back that way." A few minutes later, each of us holding a lantern in our teeth, shining its light ahead of us, we began walking on down into this strange cavern that Kallisto and I had discovered. The tunnel sloped gradually down to the uneven floor. The cavern wall was on the right of the sloping tunnel all the way down. However, eight feet to the left of the sloping floor, a steep drop off loomed, some thirty feet to the cavern's floor.

In the middle of the enormous cavern, a small pool of water shone in our lights. I noticed that the pipe, which had been going down the side of the tunnel, ended up immersed deep into the center of the pool. "Here is where our water is probably coming from," Enyo said through her clenched teeth.

"We won't have to worry about running out of water," I replied through my teeth, while shining my lantern about this space.

Natasa walked around a bit, shone her light up close to the rocky wall of the cavern. Promptly, she sat down and lowered her lantern to the floor. "There, now I can talk better. Gang, this is an amazing discovery. I bet anything that this was once an underground river! I mean before the desert became a desert. I've seen one of these on Megalos three hundred plus years ago, when we were building an aqueduct in the mountains there. We dammed up one section and used the rest for our water flow."

"Now I am beginning to see," Aella commented. "Back there, the smooth walls all looked fairly recently cut. Look at the sides down here. See the difference? I bet the mantis found this place and used these Stone Cutters to carve out its living areas."

"Any way to guess how recently it was cut?" asked Linda.

"Not with any certainty, I don't think. I'll look closely at Enyo's holes and compare them to the walls," Aella promised.

"Okay, so we have a nice supply of water," Natale said. "That is good. If only we had the food to last indefinitely."

"No, you don't follow me," Natasa interrupted her. "We've stumbled upon an ancient underground river bed. Don't you see?"

"Er, no," Natale replied. I didn't either for that matter.

"It goes somewhere. Look, in Velona, the creeks run into larger streams, which run into smaller rivers, which run into the big one at the border of Barcella. Where does it run to?" Natasa asked.

"Into the Med Sea, why?" asked Natale.

"Oh I get it!" I exclaimed, finally catching on to Natasa's idea. "At one time this underground river also likely ran downhill into the ocean. It is sloping in the right direction, south."

"Exactly, Bethany. At one time in the distant past, it very likely fed into the ocean, probably north of Megalos. Don't you all see what this means?" Natasa asked, painfully waiting for us to grasp her intent.

"A way out of the desert!" exclaimed Alexa. "Natasa, I could kiss you!"

"Yahoo!" we all chorused together, as the impact sunk into our minds.

"Of course, sections of the roof may have collapsed, but now we have these Stone Cutters. We can maybe cut us a hole through the obstacles," Natasa suggested.

"But how do we know that it ends up at the modern day ocean?" I asked, doubtful of her conclusion.

"We don't, it could lead into the middle of the desert. It could lead to somewhere under the ocean. It could have many side branches. However, it is the first real possibility that I can see for us to somehow get out of here," Natasa explained.

"I understand you now. Yes, that's what I was thinking, too, Natasa. Come on, we should be heading back. I am hungry and that means it is noon and far too hot for us," I ordered.

We headed back up the ramp and left our supply of lights at the beginning of this tunnel, in case we wanted to explore it further. The three engineers insisted on bringing a Stone Cutter back with them. Alexa insisted on carrying a pair of boots and one of the devices, which our memories showed the mantis had used to get them onto our feet so tightly. Natale, of course, brought back one of the mantis books with her. Me, I only brought thoughts, possibilities, and problems back with me.

I didn't say anything to the others, but we were all shivering by the time that we arrived at the ramp. It was quite chilly down there. Even if we decided to walk along that riverbed, naked, we would not last long at all. Yet, for the first time, we had a little hope.

It was easy to walk up the ramp. The blast of heat took us by surprise, reminding us of our precarious position here in this prison. I hastily shut the trap door. I brought up the rear, entering our cell. Linda pushed the rod into the hole, shutting it behind me. At once, the machinery kicked in and began to cool down our living quarters. Lunch was waiting for us.

As we ate, I pointed out, "If we are going to spend any significant time in the basement, we need to have some clothes on. I was shivering badly by the time we came up here. Has anyone seen any clothes down there?" No one had.

"At least we now have an even better safety net," Alexa commented. "If the air cooler thing for this room should break down, we can always move into the basement. If we leave the trap door open, that first room won't be too bad for us." Again, she was showing the others that we had once more gotten safer in our predicament.

After lunch and a mandatory pleasure session to help expunge our systems of the chemicals we had ingested, I decided to take a nap and ponder these new developments. Natale sat at the table, studying the book she had brought back. Alexa sat nearby, a pair of black boots on the table along with the device. "It's a shame they only come in black," she said. "Yet, black does go so well with nearly everything. Now let's see if I can figure out this device."

"Want some help?" Enyo could scarcely keep from insisting that she experiment as well. After all, it was a device that Alexa had brought back. The two soon became engrossed in their study. I contacted Renzo and relayed our latest discoveries. He was rather excited about it and gave me a nice validation, which I relayed to the others.

By suppertime, Alexa and Enyo had worked out how the boots were put on us. They demonstrated with the pair she'd brought back. "See, originally, they are very loose and just slip on. If only the creature had left it that way, these would be excellent boots. Anyway, when you use this device, it produces a great heat. Heat applied to the sides — see how Enyo is doing it now? Heat caused the material to shrink uniformly until it seals tightly against our calves and ankles."

"Yes, but how do we reverse it and get them off?" asked Linda.

Alexa's bright face fell slightly, "Ah, well, we haven't yet worked that out. At least we know how they were put on us. That is the first step anyway. Don't you think that these are just super boots? They are the sturdiest shoes I've ever worn. I'd expect such a tiny heel to break easily, but these are incredibly ruggedly made. I just wish they came in other colors, though."

"Just find a way to get them off us, please," teased Linda.

"You find anything, Natale?" I asked.

"I am sure that this volume is very old, very, very old. The style of writing is vastly different from the others. It is like a door into the distant past. Just wish I could read it, though. I have found some interesting aspects. I'll let you know when I get it figured out."

The ensuing days we continued to spend the mornings exploring the basement area. At last, I discovered something I found encouraging. In what was likely a storage room, I came across a bolt of the white material from which the dome was constructed. It was a soft fabric, lightweight, but strong. I wrapped a bit around me and found it was also warm, keeping the body heat inside.

Seeing my find, Alexa volunteered with a sigh, "I had hoped that I would never ever have to sit down and sew another dress. I hated those hours every day at the House of Right. However, if we are going to be down in the basement for long periods, we do need something to keep us warm. I will volunteer to sew us some dresses, if you can find scissors, needle, and thread. Oops, I forgot, Bethany, we need our toes to do the work! Rats. Well, maybe we can figure out something. We do need some clothes. So the first step is to find something with which to cut this material."

Several days searching later, I found a knife that would do the job. I already knew that we were not going to be able to manage sewing anything, not unless we got our feet back. Alexa also realized that. She and Enyo put their heads together and came up with a solution. Holding the knife in her mouth and with the rest of us holding the material flat, she cut out large rectangles of the cloth. Next, she cut a hole for our heads. Finally, she cut up numerous strips four inches or so wide. With all of us helping each other, we could slip our heads into the hole, draping the cloth over our bodies. Next, the strips were wrapped around our waists and crudely tied, holding it together. Instant dress. It worked and we retained all of our freedom of motion with our legs. If this was not enough to keep us warm, we could put a second one on over the first, and so on. Alexa and Enyo made each of us three sets.

Each day we found more and more interesting items to ponder in the basement. Natale, however, continued to be fascinated only with the mantis books. Finally, she had me come and look at a drawing that she had found in one of these very old volumes. "What do you make of this?"

I looked at a series of long, squiggly lines, with many side lines joining up, all heading into one main line which exited off of the bottom of the map. I was about to say "Squiggly lines," when I began to wonder myself. The overall area looked like where we were. "A map?" I suggested instead.

"That's what I keep concluding. It appears to be a relief map of that underground river system, probably made centuries ago. It would seem that we are here," she pointed with her spiked heel. "Could this be useful somehow?"

"Natale, you may have just rescued all of us!" If this proved correct or mostly accurate, then the old underground river did flow south to the ocean. "Let's get this info to the guys."

# Chapter 5 Exercises in Futility

Shortly after Renzo and the other three had returned from locating the dome, they were shocked and very happy when I made that first mental contact with them! It was the first week of October 657, and the entire staff at headquarters was put onto the problem at hand: how to rescue the eight women stranded in the Desert of Desolation.

"Look, if we leave immediately, it will take us nearly two months even to get to the shores of the desert! They may run out of food by then!" Renzo was getting even more frantic about doing something and doing it fast.

"Yes, but once you get there, how do you propose to cross the five hundred miles of scorching desert, Renzo?" asked Chaucer, equally ready to leave at once. However, he was more seasoned and practical. In one hundred thirty degree heat, they would not last a day.

"I don't know, take a lot of horses and wagons, loaded with food and water," he suggested.

"But wagons will only get mired down in the patches of sand dunes," Benet argued.

"All right, we go by pack horse, then. Take a hundred pack horses," Renzo countered.

Henry, who had been quiet during the heated discussion, finally made a suggestion, "Travel by night. Pitch a large canvass sail to keep the sun from directly frying you in the daytime. Perhaps that might work. I agree, we should get going at once. If the rest of you come up with a better idea, then let us know while we are sailing there. You would have nearly two months to work out something better. We could possibly pick up anything you might suggest in Megalos or even Tashien. As I see it, the longer we wait, the greater the chances they are going to run out of food. She estimates they have for sure two months of food right now. If they don't find more, they will be starving to death before we can get to them. If we delay longer now, we are risking their lives further down the road."

Hank agreed, "As senior Loremaster here, I say we should pack up a caravel with everything we think they might want and send them off immediately. Then, as he says, we have another two months to come up with some better plan. However, I would suggest that you take donkeys or mules instead of horses. They are hardier and may take less water. I would suggest you take two caravels, one loaded with mules and their feed and one with you and your gear. There is one other detail, by the time you get there, it will be winter, and the daytime temperatures may not be so intolerable."

Hank went on, "Let's send along a hundred mules to be on the safe side. We can calculate how much water and food to take with you while you are en route to the coast. And disagreements?"

"I still think overland is going to kill both the rescuers and the women," Lilly Ann replied. "One hundred thirty degrees is deadly. However, I will concur, if we delay and they only do have two months of food left, we have to go now. Let's bust all speed records, then, and get them sailing in a day or two at most."

Beth Ann added, "Renzo, please take everything you can possibly think of that might become needed. It will be hard to acquire other things along the way and doing so may delay matters if their situation worsens."

"Now hold on just a minute here," Alan, the older Planner interrupted. "You are letting your panic ruin your thoughts, all of you. Yes, it is two months by caravel, around the Southlands. Have you thought about overland? I think not! Eight to ten days to New Barq. Then, overland two hundred miles to the point where the mountains reach the ocean. From there, you could travel along the seacoast of the desert until you got to the middle, some two hundred fifty miles, give or take. Assuming you can make thirty-five miles each day, that comes to a grand total of twenty-one days, not sixty. Add another two weeks to get to them, and you have twenty-five days of their food supply to spare. See? There is still time to plan their rescue properly."

"I feel like an idiot!" Renzo said, his face red hot.

"Duh," was all that Chaucer said.

"Double duh," Hank, my father, added. "Renzo, we are just too close to Bethany; it's clouding our judgment. Alan is right. You should go overland. We can send the Sleepy Hollow around the long way and have it parked off the coast for your return. I suspect the women would rather sail home than ride mules such a long distance. This way you would have your choice of return methods."

"Could we pick up that many mules and the necessary supplies in New Barq?" asked Emil. "I am wholly unfamiliar with that area of the world."

"I'll check on it," Paulette volunteered.

Alan added, "We should contact some of the immigrants here that came from the Arad. Perhaps they can give us some good desert advice."

The next day, Al Tamir, a sixty year old man, who had immigrated many years ago from Juda Arad to Velona, came to the estate. Angel had gone to fetch him. According to Lilly Ann's inquiries, he knew the most about desert survival.

"I am honored to meet with the Santi High Council. How may I repay the kindness shown to me and my family when we came here so many years ago?"

After introducing everyone, Alan outlined the situation. "So we have eight women who are out there in the Desert of Desolation waiting a rescue operation. We had thought of taking mules and packing a lot of water on them. It is five hundred miles that they need to go, one way."

"I am so sorry that they are trapped there. Should I not ask how they got there in the first place?"

"Yes. That is another matter entirely. Let's just say that how they got there cannot be duplicated to get them back," Lilly Ann replied, hedging.

"Ah, it would not have anything to do with the recent requests of everyone: have you seen any strange things in the sky recently?" he replied, coyly.

"Well, yes. A flying thing took them prisoner and put them there. Now we have to rescue them," Lilly Ann still attempted to keep the information as detail-less as possible. After all, talk of aliens would only alarm the average person.

"Well, you should resign yourselves to their demise. It is not called the Desert of Desolation for no reason. The daytime temperatures cause the ground nearly to melt. If you walk on that ground with the shoes you have on right now, by the end of the day your feet will be nothing but burning blisters, as if you had stuck them into a fire pit."

"You cannot travel by day, only night. During the day, if you want any chance of not dying right away, you must find shade, which you must bring with you; there is none in the desert. Also, during the day, you must not put your feet onto the ground; sit on something. The ground will be one hundred sixty degrees if the air is one hundred thirty. Your mules will be in serious trouble rather quickly, I would think."

"Then there is the water problem. There is none there, not a drop. Even in the Arad, we can find water in many desert plants. Where you are going, there are no plants. There is no animal life, not even a snake can survive that desert. It is not called Desolation for no reason. In the Arad, you need a gallon of water a day if you are mobile in the desert. A mule needs more. Say you are to travel for thirty days and that there are ten of you going. Just for the people alone, you would need to bring along three hundred gallons of water. That amounts to two thousand five hundred pounds to carry, divided by ten people, you must carry two hundred and fifty pounds of water on your back."

"If you take mules for each, triple that. You see, it is a hopeless endeavor that you are asking. Yet, if you could find a way to carry the water, then wear white robes and turbans about your heads. It helps prevent water loss and keeps you cooler. Do not ever allow the baking sun to shine on your exposed skin. Take frequent rests to avoid overheating, especially with the mules. If you run low on water, do not eat food, for that only makes the water loss more severe. Wear thick, well insulated boots."

Renzo's face grew glummer and glummer the more the old man spoke. He realized that Al Tamar was not making this up. It seemed entirely reasonable; he'd just been avoiding directly looking at it. He wanted me back so badly that he would risk anything to do it. That had clouded his judgment.

Our group talked for several hours with Al Tamar, before thanking him. After he left, the entire headquarters group was as solemn as it had been the day they learned we had been abducted. Without saying anything further, the group broke up for the day.

Alan spent the rest of the day making water calculations. He estimated that one donkey could carry twenty gallons of water, or about one hundred sixty pounds. If he sent along one hundred donkeys, on the trip there, ninety could carry water. That meant eighteen hundred gallons, ignoring food and other essentials. He then estimated water consumption, based on it taking two weeks to get to the women. If they traveled in the heat of the day, the water would last a mere five days! Ah, but if they traveled at night, they could make it to the prison! Of course, then the water would have to be replaced from the prison. Did Bethany have enough water to supply the return trip?

At the next morning's meeting, Alan presented his findings. "Paulette, Renzo, the next time Bethany contacts us, ask her if they have enough water for the return trip, an estimated eighteen hundred gallons."

"Hey, here is another angle we could work," Cedric suggested. Suppose that when the caravel gets there, it takes a load of water out part way into the desert and leaves it there, sort of a make your own watering hole." Henry liked that idea, just in case of an emergency.

"I still like the idea of trying to take along several large water wagons," Benet volunteered. One water wagon can carry about two hundred fifty gallons of water. Take along four of them, and we would be in good shape. Renzo, Rosina, Michelle, and I can move out ahead and find routes around the large sand dune patches that we saw when we flew over the land in search of the dome. I know that it would take lots longer to get there, what with all the detours, but then we would not need so darn many mules, each one drinking a mountain of water."

"Let's do all three," Lilly Ann decided. "This is very likely a suicide run, so having three sources of water makes the odds much better. Renzo, half of you can travel by wagon and the other half leads the mules. Henry, the Santi on your ship can then make several runs inland setting up a water reserve. Maybe this way it is doable somehow. I'll be damned if I am going to leave them out there to die in the desert!"

The next day, Paulette got word back from New Barq. They could easily get the needed supplies there. With that decided, everyone decided it was time to get started. While the Planners and Loremasters continued to work on the problem, any new ideas could easily be relayed to the group, and they could respond until they left New Barq. The Explorers Circle dashed off to begin packing anything and everything that they thought might be needed.

Angel found Renzo in his room packing. "Sir, I know that we are sailing tomorrow to make the rescue attempt. I have come to beg you to allow me to accompany you overland. I have some experience in the Arad. I failed Bethany once, well I believe that I did, perhaps if I had acted sooner, she and Linda, well, you know what I mean." She was referring to her rescue of Bethany when they had their arms eaten by the mantis in the Tikki village. She had actually saved Bethany's life then, but still felt badly that she had not disobeyed Bethany's direct orders sooner. "I refuse to fail her this time! I will follow you, if you do not allow me to accompany you."

"Angel, you know darn well that you have no blame for your actions. Just the opposite, we all owe you our lives because of your actions back then. If you will give me a hug, I will let you come with us. I owe you so much, but I didn't dare ask you to come, because we may all die of heat stroke making the attempt. I cannot ask you to risk your life." She bolted into his arms and gave him a hug!

"Thanks, sir! I won't fail you all."

"I know you won't. Now go get packing; bring anything you might remotely need." She dashed out to carry out his orders.

The next day, everyone gathered at the docks to see them off. The food supplies and other cargo had already been loaded. Now it was time that each of the parents took the time to say farewell to the children.

Renzo said farewell to ours. "Daddy's going off to rescue mommy and the other mommies. It is a very dangerous mission, because the desert place where she is being held prisoner is exceedingly hot. It will take us a long time just to get to that desert. Then, they are located about five hundred miles into the desert. So I will be gone a long time. While I am gone, I expect both of you to do your studies really well, so you can surprise mommy with how much you have grown and learned while she has been away. Lena, I am putting you in charge of Danielle, and Ben, you are in charge of Adrien. Now come give me a farewell hug." The kids held him tightly for quite a while.

As he walked onto the gangplank, Lena said to Ben, "One day I am going to be a powerful explorer like mom and dad."

"Me too," Ben replied. Lena held Danielle's hand, while Ben carried little Adrien; together, the brave children walked back to the waiting carriage. The other children were also walking back there too, having said their farewells to their dads.

On October 9, the Sleepy Hollow set sail for the New Barq, the southernmost portion of Juda Arad. This very morning Bethany reported on their discovery of a basement and underground chamber filled with water. Everyone cheered, because we knew that we could refill our water supplies once we got there. Now we only needed to survive two weeks in the scorching heat!

The Loremasters and Planners began to investigate the possibility of using an underground tunnel as a safer way to get to us. They promised to keep Renzo informed.

With only a light load and knowing that time was critical, Henry put up all the sail the ship could handle. October 19, the caravel pulled into the Santi dock beside their fortress in New Barq.

Years ago when the Santi del Dio was formed during the time of the First Holy Crusade for Religious Freedom, the Centurions and Holy Paladins from Megalos owned New Barq. Here they stationed half of the army with which they planned to retake all of the Sea Princes once more. The mighty army marched out of New Bark and fought the Crusaders, while the Santi Strike force swept in behind them and captured New Barq, their only overland supply base this far north. At that time, the Santi began constructing a stone fortress from which to control and rule over this area.

Now it was a bustling port city once more, vast numbers of trading ships docked in New Bark, carrying cargo in and out of the city of some fifty thousand people. Most were of Megalos descent, though a few were of Arad origin. The Santi fortress was outside the city walls proper, as were most all of our fortresses outside of Velona that is. This way, if the city should fall, our fortress stood very independent.

Here at the southern extreme of the semi-arid desert land of Juda Arad, life and clothing were vastly different from that in Velona. Robes and sandals predominated, along with adobe houses. Only the wealthy could afford to build from stone. Water and salt were precious commodities, the salt coming from the distant salt mines, where anyone could go and help themselves, if they could not afford to buy it.

The group looked awfully out of place as they walked down the gangplank into the fortress. "Hi, Alfred Waincox, Fortress Commander and Judger. Let me welcome you to our fortress. We have already acquired most of what Paulette has asked for your trip. If there is anything that we can do to help you rescue our leaders, ask. I have one small suggestion, but let's take this inside the walls."

He led the way. Alfred was thirty years old, sporting a full beard, which allowed him to blend in with the Arad members of this society. His wife, Jill, was a year older, rather homely, but with vibrant eyes. Jill was rotund and jovial, a very caring person. She was waiting with a hot pot of tea and a tray of dates and figs. "This way. Pleased to meet you. Have a seat in our council room."

The ten sat down and observed how the pair had decorated the room. Arad tapestries hung on the walls. Jill noticed Michelle, Rosina, and Tania looking at them. "We're something of an Arad history buff here. You know, collect all things Arad. Here, you must see this! Our prized collection item. This is one of the cups and blankets that the legendary Elizabeth Stanton drank from and used when she and the Lightning Circle were here in New Barq, rescuing the mothers with their newborn babies when the Centurions went around the city killing all newborns, thinking one might be the Great Messiah! Isn't this just incredible? We found it in the sewers, where she dropped them during the rescue."

"Amazing discovery indeed," Tonia replied.

"Incredible," put in Rosina.

"Wow, the Elizabeth Stanton?" asked Michelle.

"Ah, come, let's sit down, Jill will talk about our many finds for hours," Alfred jested. She grinned and the group took their seats.

"Now as I was alluding outside, I have one suggestion that I would like to make, considering the perilous nature of this journey and the absolute criticalness of it. You need to take along with you, at least to the edge of the desert, someone who knows this area, a guide, so to speak."

"That would be useful," Emil replied. "None of us know the area at all; we've never been here, though Renzo and Rosina are from Zargarb."

"Yes, I knew their mother, one of the finest freedom fighters ever. Tremendous person!"

"Did you have a guide in mind?" Emil asked the obvious.

"Yes, myself. There is nothing going on around here, hasn't been anything for many years. I have traveled all of the way to the point where the Kathas Mountains reach the ocean, though no farther. I can get us safely and directly there. I thought perhaps that I could tag along with you along the coast and then stay at the point where you head inland, guarding your return point. Jill will run things here and stay in daily contact with me. Hence, if anything is needed, we can get it as fast as possible. Someone ought to be guarding your rear, just in case."

Emil was gracious, "Alfred, we would be honored to accept your assistance. Perhaps this is the most challenging mission the Santi has ever attempted, crossing this Desert of Desolation. So many have told us that it is impossible and that we are riding to our deaths. Yet, Bethany and seven others are out there and we have to succeed."

"So it is true then, the mantis creatures have returned to Tarra," Jill asked.

"One has and it has been destroyed," explained Rosina. "There are no signs that there was more than one. It took the eight prisoners and flew them to its new base out in the middle of the desert. Bethany has concluded, based on their imprisonment, that the mantis wanted these eight beings completely out of circulation forever. We must get them back."

"Is it also true that all eight have no arms?" Jill asked, curious about the true situation. She had not gotten the total picture from headquarters.

"Yes," Renzo answered her. "However, they are quite resourceful. They've managed to escape their prison cell, and even the outer base walls. They've been doing amazingly well, considering what they must be enduring. We just have to get there soon."

"Understood. We will have everything Paulette asked for by tomorrow. We can leave around midday," Alfred suggested.

Renzo suddenly gazed off into space, Rosina, likewise. *Hi. It's me again. You will never guess what Natale discovered today in one of the books of the mantis!* I had just made my daily contact with Renzo and Rosina. *She has found an aerial view map of the ancient underground river system that runs under this prison. It appears to go all the way to the seacoast. Honey, we have a huge number of alien items that we'd like to bring back with us if we can. Overland, this is not likely, considering the heat. Can the Loremasters and Planners consider following this ancient dried up underground river system? If so, and if it is large enough, maybe wagons could be brought here to carry tons of stuff back with us. What do you think?*

*We've just gotten into New Barq, dear. Alfred, the Commander here, is going to guide us to the desert. He says we can leave by tomorrow. I don't want to delay getting started; you may run out of food before we can get to you.*

*Okay, you guys get started, that will cheer the others up considerably. I'll let Paulette and the others have this information. I am going to impress an image of the map into both your minds. Is Michelle with you?*

*Yes.*

*I'll impress it into hers as well. Have her make a drawing of it, then everyone can see what we are talking about. Tomorrow I will begin exploring the river and see how feasible it might be to try that way. Love you both. Bye for now.*

"Oh!" Michelle said, startled by my sudden connection. "Okay I will," she said aloud, forgetting that she only needed to think her thoughts.

"Great news!" Renzo said. "That was Bethany reporting in. It seems Natale has made a remarkable discovery about the ancient underground dried up river that lies beneath their prison cell. It is a complete river system and exits along the southern coast. She wants us to consider bringing wagons up that river so we can bring back lots of alien stuff with us. I don't have the slightest idea about what she is talking, mind you. I'm just repeating what she told us. I think Lilly Ann will get back to us later on today with more advice."

"If you will excuse me," Michelle said, "Bethany wants me to sketch out the map image she sent me. It's of this river system. Benet, can you come help me get set up? Jill, is there somewhere where we can stay?"

"Sure dear child, follow me." The three left at once. The others began discussing this new turn of events. None quite knew what Bethany was suggesting, an underground river that wasn't a river anymore?

In one of the tower's guest rooms, Benet unfolded Michelle's art box, containing mostly sketching supplies this trip. Travel light; make rough sketches; that was her plan. Certainly, there would be little spare time actually to complete a painting. Besides, she doubted her oils would survive in the predicted heat; her supplies would dry out in a day. Easel set up, he helped her slip on her arm extensions and put a blank page on the board for her. Usually, she would do this herself, but it took a lot of time. Bethany was most urgent in requesting this sketch, so she had him speed things along.

Jill, who had only been around the many men who had lost limbs during the First Crusade, watched quietly. Hundreds of those men had been housed here in New Barq after the war. Most had lived rather pathetic lives she had noted. However, Jill knew that Jenna Rose had rescued hundreds upon hundreds of women who had lost limbs to either these mantis creatures or the Holy Paladins and their brutality toward women. She'd heard many tales of how this Laird Foundation and Jenna had somehow trained these women into productive artists once more. To Jill, this had always seemed a contradiction in terms, based on what she had seen here. Jill had been born and raised in the Zargarb-Arad region and had never been to Velona.

Jill watch fascinated as this young woman, whose arms were missing below her elbows, began to sketch the image Bethany desired. Michelle couldn't help noticing her staring over her shoulder, and said, "Lost mine in a warehouse accident. A heavy crate fell on them and crushed both arms. Hurt bad; lost them both. Jenna gave me therapy, and the wonderful women at the Laird Foundation helped me work out alternate means to continue to do my paintings. I know. I am really, really slow, compared to what I used to be. Still, I have time and patience. What amazes me is how those without any arms left manage to paint."

"Now you take Dione, one of those from the House of Right. There, they removed the arms of all baby girls immediately after they were born. Dione grew up believing that women were born without arms, can you believe that? Well, you should see the fantastic paintings that Dione creates! I swear you can see pure love and beauty literally flowing out at you from her paintings! I will never be one tenth as good as she is. I just try to capture the essence of the sea. That's what I'm interested in painting, the sea. Always have, since I was a little girl." Michelle chatted on, while making her sketch. This way, she didn't feel Jill's eyes burning into her back.

"Dear child, you are absolutely amazing. I had no idea. You do incredibly well," Jill complimented her.

"Oh, look in that bag there. I have one of my finished sea paintings in there. I got it done while we were sailing here. It's dry now, so you don't have to be careful of it. Now when I got back from the last trip, for some reason, my paintings are really selling unbelievably well. I left two dozen on display in the Art Gallery and when I returned, only one was left, and that one was spoken for! They've even gone so far as to taking advanced orders for me now. Well, they are just going to have to wait. I am too slow to make that many that quickly."

"You, you did this?" asked Jill, as she stared at the image of a caravel in full sail, leaning into the wind, spray flowing up its bow. "This is fantastic, so realistic, so powerful! You've captured power in this painting!"

"Yes, I like that one. I was going to put that one up in our bedroom. I even got to take watches at the helm on the Sleepy Hollow. It reminds me of my true love, sailing the sea."

"We don't have such fabulous art works out here in the dregs of civilization. How I would love to have such magnificent art works adorning our drab and sometimes dreary fortress! Perhaps when you return, I could hire you to purchase several paintings from the Art Gallery for me? I would reimburse you well for your trouble. At least one ought to be one of your paintings."

"Oh sure, we can discuss it when we get back. There are so many to choose from. We ought to really figure out just what you would like here."

"Oh that would be so fabulous! Wait until Alfred hears of this!" she said jovially. After a pause, she continued onto a different line of questioning, one that she really had wanted to ask before, but hadn't quite figured out how. "I suppose that you will be bringing the rescued women back through New Barq to your caravel."

"Probably, but I don't know for sure. Why?"

"Our leader, Supreme Commander Bethany, well, I've never met her, nor any of the other famous women with her. I mean she, they don't have any arms and I was wondering how I should greet them. With you, why we just shake as normal. I once met Jenna Rose and shook her arms. What an honor that was, but I mean, well, our Supreme Commander hasn't any. How should I properly greet her?"

"Oh, just give her a big hug! She loves hugs. Actually, they all enjoy them. They have their own special type of hug that they do among themselves. Bethany calls it the bump hug. Honestly, you will get along just fine with them. Remember, just allow them to do things for themselves. They will ask when they need something." Michelle knew that Jill was unused to being around people who were not "normal," but then so were the vast majority of people for that matter. The Laird Foundation was their true lifeline, their safety net.

"There, I believe that does it. Bethany only sent a black and white type image. Not much more I can do than reproduce what she sent. I've no idea what I am looking at. Do you?"

Jill and Michelle stared at the lines on the page. "Well, this does look like the coastline of the desert, I believe," Jill said hopefully.

"Say, as long as you are here, lend me a hand putting this stuff away, please. I can do it, only it takes so long. Bethany wanted me to get this to the others right away." A few minutes later, Jill carried the sketch and escorted Michelle to the meeting room once more.

The others were in the middle of a heated discussion. "Ah, here comes the map," Renzo said as the two women joined them. Jill laid the map out on the table and everyone gathered around it.

"I still say this is foolhardy," Emil continued his arguments. "Look, for all we know, this dried up underground river could still have deep sink holes in it; parts of its ceiling may have collapsed, totally blocking passage. Parts might be too low for us to traverse. Who knows how impassable this could be."

"Ah, look at the map," Benet argued. "You can see my point. Look at how it twists, turns, and winds around. Even if we can go the whole way without trouble, it is going to add at least another couple hundred miles to the journey. We would have to take much more food and grain for the mules. Remember, they don't have an unlimited food supply there, we have to bring along enough for the return trip, except thankfully for the water."

"You are forgetting that Bethany has got her hands on a whole bunch of this alien technology. We must try to find a way to retrieve it. Who knows how valuable this stuff might be to us," Cedric countered.

"Well, she did say that they were going to explore the river channel some today," Renzo countered. "We should wait for her next report before making any firm conclusions. After all, if she reports that it is impassable, then it becomes a moot point."

"At least this route would spare us the heat and provide all the water we could use," Rosina sounded a hopeful note.

"But it is totally dark underground!" Tonia put in her viewpoint. "How are we ever going to be able to travel in pitch blackness? Have you thought of that?"

"Well, we could all carry lanterns," Renzo answered. "How much oil would say a dozen lanterns need if they burned continuously for over a month?"

"Gosh, that will take some figuring," Cedric replied. "I should get onto that one. We may be facing having to bring along a mountain of oil instead of water."

"We do have four of those eternal lights of the mantis creatures with us," Renzo offered. "I thought to bring a few, just in case. Looks like that may have been fortuitous on my part."

"You know, the more I think about journeying along an underground river system, the more I am beginning to think of the possibilities. There may be new and unknown fish in those waters. We might find gold and silver veins exposed. All manner of interesting things might lie in there," Benet thought to change the mood of the group with other ideas.

"Well, I say let's have lunch. After that, why don't we women go shopping? We didn't know the sizes of the women so we haven't yet purchased clothing for them," Jill broke up the meeting.

Shopping appealed to Rosina, Michelle, and Tonia. Angel, though she wouldn't outright admit it, love to as well, and she accompanied them. While she too needed appropriate clothing, she suggested that she would provide Santi protection for the women. Wandering the hard packed dirt streets of New Barq, filled with strange shops, the women were in heaven, pausing frequently to examine the many wares offered for sale in the bazaars.

At last, they entered the clothing shop, run by an Arad couple. Jill explained what they needed and quickly the women were trying on various styles of robes. "We need complete freedom of movement from the waist downward," Tonia explained, ruling out several fancier styles. After some examinations, they opted for the plainest style.

"Now on these eight, would it be a problem for you to remove the arm sleeves and sew the holes shut somehow?" Rosina asked. "The women these are for have no arms and the sleeves will only get in their way."

"Oh my goodness! Those poor women. No, it will only take a few hours for all eight. They won't look so good, but then, as you say, without arms, the sleeves will only get in their way. Those poor women."

"Can you make my sleeves much shorter?" asked Michelle. "I can manage better with very short sleeves."

"Yes, you poor thing. Let me measure your arms." She was kindly, but had never seen a woman with both arms missing. Yes, she had seen numerous men, the survivors of the Crusades, here in New Barq. They were a pitiful lot, leading such miserable lives. Fortunately, so many of them had already died. She said a quiet prayer to Jehosa for their souls, as she recalled the men she had seen around the city.

Don't let women go on shopping trips! With several hours to kill before the robes would be ready, they headed back into the bazaar and its many shops. When the group finally returned to the fortress, they needed a push cart to carry all of the items they had purchased, including Michelle's find, a copper water urn, which she declared would look fabulous on her mantle back home. She ignored a suggestion that it would come in handy on the trip as a water dispenser, which it actually was.

Tonia had bought a fabulous tea making apparatus, which she planned to give to Bethany as a welcome home present. Each woman had also purchased several different styles of local footwear, including open desert sandals and working boots. They added dozens of scarves of various colors, which they thought might be useful for the eight women and their long hair. So it went. Many packages had to be unloaded and sorted out. Some would remain on the caravel, while some had to be packed for the trip.

Word had come from Headquarters: hold off leaving for a couple days, until they had time to evaluate Bethany's idea of the underground river. Renzo commented, "This whole affair is full of totally contradicting plans! I just want my wife back safe and sound!" The others echoed his sentiments.

# Chapter 6 A Hike Along a Dead River

Early next morning, Bethany ordered a full-scale examination of the river cavern. While they ate their breakfast, she explained, "We need to do some significant hiking today. Object: find out if we think this river chamber is passable and a safe route for our rescue party. We all know that if we have them come overland, they may well die of heat stroke on the way. I do not want to lose Renzo or any of the others, nor do I wish to spend any more time here than needed. I want to go home to my children as soon as possible. If the river cavern is passable, it may be the best way out of here. Besides, Enyo, we ought to be able to take a whole lot more of these things with us than if we have to return overland in the heat."

We spent an hour getting ourselves ready. We had to put on the crude white dresses and see that they were securely tied around out waists. Further, we all put another tie into our long hair, so that once more, we had ponytails, which would help keep it out of our way. Next, we each got one of the eternal lights and held it between our teeth. Satisfied we were ready, Linda opened our cell door, closing it after we exited. I undid the metal slab, revealing the basement. Natale turned on the main light, and together, we slid down the ramp.

The eerie silence of the underground area was broken only by the sharp clicks of our heels, as we walked directly to the long tunnel that led to the cavern and river bed below the basement. Here, we stopped, sat down, and fiddled with the lights, turning them on. "I know this will be awkward for us, but we must see if this river passage is usable. Can a wagon come through it? Can a horse? Can people? These answers we must find out today. Our men are in New Barq and ready to head overland to get to us. We must let them know today if this river system is a viable possibility."

"You have our full cooperation!" Linda replied. "I want Chaucer on his way, like yesterday!"

"Thanks," I grinned. "I know this is going to be very tough on us, as we are. Please watch your step. I will go first. I want Natale to come last. If she sees one of us starting to fall, she may be able to hold you still until we can get you upright again. Questions?"

"How far are we planning to go?" asked Aella.

"Several miles at least, unless there are so many barriers that this whole idea of mine proves pointless." We bent over, securing our lanterns in our teeth. I looked back at my group, who nodded they were ready. Off we went into the pitch blackness and utter silence of the underground, mostly dried up, riverbed. Only the sounds of our heels broke the stillness.

Here where we began, the width of the chamber was over a hundred feet. A thin water channel flowed down its middle. The floor, though uneven, was worn smooth and was quite dry. I found walking easy here, though arms would have been most welcome.

Alexa called out through her teeth, "Say, these boots are working out well. They grip well and provide great ankle support. I wouldn't have thought they would. Just wish I could keep better balance, and then we could go faster."

The height of the undulating roof above varied between ten and perhaps fifteen feet, plenty high for wagons or riders, I thought. So far so good, we could travel along here just fine. Our progress was pitifully slow, however. I longed to have Renzo's strong arm around my waist to steady me, then I could go much faster. However, I found that Alexa's observation was quite right. Had we been wearing our normal shoes, our ankles would be quite sore by now, if not outright sprained. The floor was too uneven, though smooth. Perhaps our heavy hiking boots would fare better here. I made a note to tell Renzo to bring those kinds of boots along.

About a mile further down, we came upon a gravely patch. Loose gravel covered the whole floor, making footsteps quite slippery. "Hey, these boots handle the gravel well," Alexa commented. "While they do slip like any boot would, my feet are not being punctured by the gravel like my normal boots. The soles of these boots must be softening the jars somehow. I must remember to look inside and see if I can see how that might be." Again, I noted she was right. Except for constant slipping, the sudden, unexpected pressure of a stone against my foot was not there as it should have been. Again, Renzo would have to bring heavy boots or his feet would take a bruising over these patches.

The ceiling now dropped considerably, just over our heads. That meant one could not always ride along down here. We continued slowly along. Now the sides began to narrow as well until we had only a small path to walk on without stepping into the water. Here, the slope was a bit steep and we moved ever so slowly, keeping our balance here was tricky. If only I had Renzo to support me, this would not be a problem either. Ah well, he wasn't here and I was determined to see this through. If they could come this way, I would not worry about all of them dying of heat stroke.

"Hey, hold up a second," Aella called out. We stopped. When I carefully turned around, I saw her shining her light on the side wall. Something was sparking or reflecting her light. "I think this is a gold vein, a rather large on at that. Now this is very interesting, Bethany," she muttered through her teeth. "We could easily mine gold here! Okay, keep your eyes open for more veins!"

I grinned in spite of myself. These engineers were something else! Here we were utterly trapped prisoners barely able to function, in a crisis, and she was thinking about the possibility of mining gold here! "I see where it is at on the other side!" Natasa called out, just as we began to continue.

Further on, a new problem arose. Our little ledge finally ended. Water covered the whole floor. Near my feet, it did not seem deep. Just as I was about to step into the water, I saw something that almost made me drop my light! "Oh no, look here! A body!"

Sure enough, the nearly decomposed remains of a woman lay in the shallow waters! We stared. "She is wearing the same boots as we are," commented Alexa.

"Anyone recognize here?" I asked, I didn't recognize her at all.

Kallisto turned white, nearly dropping her light! "It's Kalio, the leader of the Kali Assassins, who led us before she disappeared, and I was able to become our leader. We thought that she had had some kind of accident. She was, like me, of the Eight Degree. Accidents can be more deadly for us. The general opinion was that she accidentally fell into the river. We had no idea that she, too, was abducted like us. God, she was imprisoned here until she died. They just dumped her body into the river, not even a proper burial for her."

"Can you imagine living in our cell all by yourself?" Enyo exclaimed. "She couldn't even get any relief from the horny drug effect. My god that must have been awful for her."

"It proves Natale's assertion that this base has been around for a while," Linda commented.

"Look, in the deep part, there are more bodies, well, bones and boots anyway," Natasa observed. Indeed, I spotted at least three sets of boots with many bones and three skulls staring up at us from the clear water depths. These were old, very old.

"They probably floated down to this deep pool and sunk. When we are rescued, I'll have the men give these women a proper burial and the final respect they deserve. Kallisto, I'm sorry about your leader, Kalio," I sympathized with her.

"She worked hard to help undo the Eight Degrees, but was unsuccessful," Kallisto replied.

"Well, let's see if we can get by this area. I'm going to go through the shallow waters here. If I make it okay, then you come too," I got us going again. I sure didn't want to end up like Kalio. I stepped into the waters and felt the chill on my feet and ankles. Although I expected these boots to be very slippery, in fact, they were not. I was able to keep my footing reasonably well, with only a little wobbling to keep my balance. A little ways further on, the bare floor reappeared once more. One by one, we made it past this obstacle.

Enyo estimated that we had gone some five miles, when we reached a real barrier. Part of the rocky ceiling had fallen down. A mound of jagged boulders blocked our path. Without assistance, we could realistically go no further. Well, we might have, but we'd take hours to cross this barrier in these boots and without arms to grab onto the boulders. I decided not to push any farther forward. Since I knew the men were anxiously awaiting my report, while we took a break, sitting on the rocks, I made contact with Renzo and explained what we had found.

*I don't think wagons can get through here, but pack animals might be able to get through. The only problem we've run into is this ceiling collapse here. We'd have to climb over it. Without your help, we'd be hours at it, instead of a few minutes. I would plan on coming across partial ceiling collapses, dear.*

*Okay, we will see if we can find the entrance. Either way, I'm leaving today if possible; tomorrow at the latest. I want you back! Love you. Be careful. I'm coming.*

I relayed Renzo's suggestion that they would be starting out today or tomorrow. That cheered the others up considerably. Sitting on the boulders, Kallisto said with a sigh, "You know, for years I knew that I would never ever miss any man. Now I find that I miss Frank something awful. I miss him so badly that I could scream. Funny the strange twists life has for us."

"I miss my Frank too," Enyo added. "I had pretty much given up all hope of having a man in my life. Then, Frank came along. Here I am stuck out here, and the one man for me is so far away I could cry. Yet I know he has to take care of our two children; god I miss them too. I am getting so homesick, just sitting here doing so darn little." I began to suspect that Enyo's heavy attention on the mechanical things in our cell was her way of dealing with her loss.

"Well, we have found a safer route for our rescue team. I was horribly worried that they would not survive the long trip across the desert. We've proven that they can get to us underground, though it will probably take them longer to get to us this way. No telling how many of these boulder fields lie between us and the sea," I commented.

We headed back, taking our time, lost in our own personal thoughts of our loved ones. As we walked, Enyo said, "If only we could find a way to bring some food along with us, we could begin to make our way down this river and perhaps meet up with them a whole lot sooner, but then we would just have to retrace our steps back here to retrieve all of the neat stuff."

"Well, I would not mind it, retracing our steps, if everyone else was with us. God, to be eating real food again, to have someone helping me keep my balance down here, why, I wouldn't complain one little bit," Alexa answered her.

"If Chaucer could hold me and help me, I wouldn't mind going back either," Linda added her feelings too.

I had not thought of this option. "What about the rest of you? I mean if we could find a way to bring food along with us, then we could slowly walk toward them and meet up sooner. Yet, we would just have to return the way we came. We must take as much of the alien stuff back with us as we can."

"Well, we could use the Stone Cutters to remove some of that boulder field so we and they could pass through it more easily," Natasa volunteered.

"I'm all for trying it, if you think we can safely do so. We will have to find a way to bring blankets, lights, Stone Cutters, as well as our food supply. Honestly, I am going out of my mind back there in the cell! Any action is better than just sitting around there. I know that we are comfortable there and all that, but if we can even make it a quarter of the way down the river, we meet help a week sooner at least."

"Hold on a second, Paulette is contacting me," I called out.

*Hi Bethany. I have some news. Frank, Kallisto's husband has just arrived from Demokritos. He and the other husbands are now on their way to join up with the rescue party. They don't want to hold up the first rescue team; they think that they can catch up with them before Renzo reaches you.*

*They are really going to appreciate that! All of us miss our husbands something awful. Did Rosina let you all know what we found today, that the river is passable?*

*Yes, that convinced Lilly Ann to allow the other four to try to catch up with Renzo. Underground has to be a whole lot safer.*

*Okay, one more thing, we are going to explore the possibility of somehow walking part of the way down to meet them. Of course, then we will just have to walk back here, but we need to be with them badly.*

*I'll let the others know. Is it safe enough for you to do this?*

*So far, we believe so. Yet, we have many other problems to solve first. More later, and tell the four that their wives are just dying for them to hold them and kiss them and hug them. They have been horribly missed.* I sensed Paulette grinning broadly.

"Well, Enyo, Alexa, Natasa, Kallisto, I have some news for you. It seems that your husbands are on their way to join up with the rescue party. If we can somehow manage to head down the channel to meet them sooner, you have something to look forward to sooner!"

Their exclamations of happiness, relief, and joy echoed in the tunnel! Four women had just gotten the best news they desired. "We've got to get ourselves way down stream!" Enyo said exuberantly.

It was near suppertime when we finally clicked our way into the cell room. Again, the oppressive heat swamped us as we climbed up out of the basement. Fortunately, we only had a short walk to our cell and comfortable temperatures once more. Quickly, we ate from the food dispenser. Next, we cleaned up and barely were ready for the automatic lights out. To get the alien chemicals that we'd ingested today out of our systems, we had to pleasure ourselves while in bed this night.

The next day, we began to make our plans. "If we can make some kind of large carrying platform, I can move it along with us," I offered. "Let's take stock of our food supply, which is the single most important detail."

"We've about a month left in here," Enyo estimated. "There is one more set over there, it is full. Three months' supply is what we have. How much should we take?"

"Let's opt for the two month's fresh one. Experiment with it, you engineers. See if there is any way that we can fill our bowls from it without it being hooked up to the machinery here. If you can surmount that challenge, then I see nothing to keep us from leaving here at once."

"Woo hoo!" Enyo exclaimed. The three engineers began a careful, close observation of the device. I decided to watch them for a spell. "The cylinders are vertical with the hose coming out of the top. Hence, we can rule out gravity flow," Enyo declared.

"That means that either the machine somehow sucks the food up and out or that the cylinder itself has pressure inside it to force food out," concluded Natasa.

"Or perhaps the machine forces air inside which forces the food up and out," Aella added. "How do we decide which it is?"

"Let's experiment with this old one, which has maybe a week's worth of food left in it," suggested Enyo. A while later, the three stared at the fastener, which I had unhooked from the machine dispenser.

"Looks like there is something in there that moves," Aella observed. "We need something like the spikes we use on the doors to cause them to open." Finding nothing convenient except their heels, Aella volunteered hers. The three sat down, Aella carefully positioned her heel into the fixture's open end. Now the other two used their feet to push it hard onto her heel.

Psst. A bit of pressure from inside the cylinders shot blue slop out onto her heel, making a small mess. "Ah ha, there is air inside which pushes the food out," Enyo concluded. "Now we only need to find an easy way to control this. Let's look around for something that we can use."

A while later, rummaging through the basement workshop, Aella held up a device in her teeth. "How's this?" she asked. It looked like one end would fasten into the fixture. The other end had a lever and a hole in its center. "I think if you press the lever food may come out the hole." The three headed up the ramp to put her theory to the test.

They had an awful time getting the device onto the fixture, however. Here hands would have been most welcome indeed. Since it was so hard, they chose to try to put it onto the real fixture of the full food supply rack. If it worked, they would be done. If they had put it onto the old one and it worked, they would have to somehow get it off and then back on to the real one. As hard as this proved, they opted to switch gears and put it onto the real set. In the end, it took Natale and me to accomplish their task. Natale held the fixture rigidly still, while I pushed the device into the hole. I discovered that it took a good deal of force to insert it into place, just as it had required when I pulled it off when I switched the tanks.

A quick test proved it worked; blue slop squirted out onto the floor. "Woo hoo!" Enyo exclaimed. "Problem solved, now we can get on our way at long last! Frank, here I come!"

This apparatus was on a small platform, which I decided would serve to carry everything we needed. However, we would need to find something to build sides on the platform so things would not easily fall off. This the engineers solved quickly, though I needed to do the work. They found some pieces of metal, which would insert vertically into the long sides and would hold things in place. Alexa made three long tying strips of the white cloth, which we carefully wrapped all around the contraption. Once we tied these securely, the metal pieces could not fall off. Next, because it was now getting too hot to work out here inside the dome, I moved the whole thing on down the ramp into the basement.

An hour later, we had it loaded down with the eternal lights and a few Stone Cutters. Now we made numerous trips to and from our cell and the basement. We took all the blankets we could find, ate our lunch, and brought along the bowls and straws. We piled all our makeshift cloth dresses on the platform as well. By suppertime, we were ready to go. However, we decided to eat supper and take along those bowls too, as well as more towels and drinking cups. Satisfied that we had everything loaded, we were ready when the lights went out for the night.

I slept very soundly that night. Perhaps it was a result of the pleasure release of the chemicals; perhaps it was the idea that we were leaving our prison, making our own way out of here. Whichever it was mattered not. After eating breakfast, donning our crude dresses, and tying up our hair as best we could, we carried the last of our stuff down to the platform. Linda did the final honors; she shut the cell door for the last time. Once we were all in the basement, I managed to maneuver the metal trap door down, shutting us in the basement.

My idea was to leave very little clues as to our whereabouts should another mantis appear on the scene. Alexa volunteered to take the lead, while I brought up the rear, hauling along our platform. Never in a million years would I have ever suspected that I would be putting this hard won skill mom taught me to this kind of use! Once I had the platform down to the river bed, Natale turned off the main basement light. Now we could really see just how dark this was going to be! Only now did I consider what might happen to us if the eternal lights went out!

Our pattern of movement was simple. Together we would walk a hundred feet and stop, while I then lifted and brought the platform up to our position. Simple, but slow. None of us cared how slowly our progress actually was. No, we were doing it ourselves, walking out of the most diabolically designed prison which we ever could conceive of!

At one of our breaks while I was moving the platform, Alexa commented, "You know, as hard as these heels have been on us, without them we would be still trapped back there. Yes, we would manage daily chores better, but we could not possibly walk in the desert barefoot, nor could we be walking barefoot down here. In fact, I bet that mantis warden never thought that his diabolical boots would be our salvation." We all gave a chuckle at this thought, having turned the tables on our prison warden. We eight felt we'd achieved a small victory over the mantis creatures.

Around lunchtime, we made it to the barrier of fallen ceiling stones. While seven of us held our lights on the boulders, Enyo sat down, turned the device on with her boots, picked it carefully up with her mouth, and directed its energy flows to the pile in front of us. Bits of disintegrating rock dust flew into the air, slowly falling to the ground. A half hour later, we looked at the results. Enyo had burned a nice footpath through the obstruction. Pretty darn amazing we all thought.

Now we took a time out for lunch, our first experience with making our own meals. It took the combined efforts of all of us to manage this. Three were needed to operate the lever end, so that the blue slop ended up in the bowls. The rest of us were kept busy maneuvering the bowls. With great satisfaction, we eight slurped up out first meal on the road, as we called it. Oh no! Once more, I was saddled with dishwashing detail!

Natale was in charge of directions; to that end, she brought along her book with the map in it. Only near suppertime did we finally need guidance. We'd arrived at a fork in the system. I thought it obvious which direction we should go. Off to our right a smaller opening joined this main passage, coming in from an oblique angle, surely a side river joining up with the main one. While several of us held our lights so she could see and turn the pages to the map, Natale verified the observation.

However, it also gave us a point of reference by which we could tell the others our new location! After eating our dinner, we were all too excited to sleep, and pressed on for a while longer, choosing a wide spot in the tunnel to make camp for the night. I say night, but it was always night down here. We only needed to turn off the eternal lights. We managed with some effort to get blankets spread out. My plan was to have us lie down on them and then sort of roll up in them, two to a blanket, to stay warm. It was quite chilly down here, especially when we were just lying around.

Our final worry was the lights. Did we dare turn all of them off? If we did, while it would be completely dark, fine for sleeping, in the morning, how would we see to either find them or turn them on in pitch blackness? Yet, none of us knew whether they would eventually die out of their own selves? Enyo suggested that they could not truly be eternal rather that they lasted for a considerable time before dying.

Without light, we would be doomed! How could we see where we were going, what lay ahead? We'd be completely blind. Worse, with these boots, we constantly had to watch our every step to maintain our balance. If that wasn't enough, we could not see to fix our meals or even find water to drink, which was always nearby. "We need to experiment so that we can know," I decided for us. "We will leave Linda's light always on and see just how long it will last. I pray that it doesn't go fail while we sleep. Just in case, ladies, always before you close your eyes, know where your light is at so that you can find it if it becomes totally black." That was a disturbing thought for us to sleep upon.

Kallisto and I rolled up to snuggle together. We had forgotten to pleasure ourselves to rid our bodies of the chemicals we'd ingested today, so this all of us had to do before we actually slept. "How will we know when it's time to get up?" Linda asked as we finally were about to sleep.

Darn good question, I thought. "Okay, when you feel really hungry and have to go to the bathroom, it's probably time."

I relaxed and found Renzo. I brought him up to date with our action. He sounded very pleased that we were making our move instead of waiting helplessly for them to reach us. I had a brilliant thought. I asked him to have Rosina make contact with me when it was morning again. Now we had our clock!

# Chapter 7 Finding an Entrance Long Dead

"They are planning to walk down the river bed to meet us part way," declared Renzo, as the group met in Alfred's meeting room. "We ought to get underway today if possible."

"Everything is ready," Alfred answered. "We can leave after breakfast, which is coming now. Sleep well?" They had. "I'm something of a local cuisine buff. I hope you don't mind eating Arad style."

A few belches later, Renzo was full and ready to get going. He was itching for action, tired of all the waiting. The group walked down to the huge Santi courtyard. Already the Santi had been packing up our mules for them. After tying their bags onto their saddles, the group mounted their mules.

Alfred took the lead, since he was the official guide. Emil and Tonia came next. Cedric and Rosina followed them, with Benet and Michelle right behind them. Chaucer, Renzo, and Henry rode after them, with Angel bringing up the rear, her long bow at the ready. Each of them also led a string of a dozen more mules, loaded with food, water, lantern oil, new clothing for the eight they were rescuing, and a few needed camping supplies.

They rode down the paved Centurion made roadway that angled nearly due southeast. "Sure are smaller than the horses I'm used to," Renzo called out to the others.

"True, but dependable and surefooted," Alfred called back. "Wise decision, I believe, to use mules and not horses."

The day was sunny and warm, even though it was early October. This was still the Arad and winters here were simply a relief from the heat of the summer. It never snowed or even froze this far south. The countryside was stark and bleak, sandy to gravely soil lay on either side of the road. Desert plants grew in what appeared to be random locations.

At first, they passed a number of shepherds tending flocks of sheep. Renzo wondered where the grass was located that kept the sheep alive. The newness of the land soon wore off, and the group became very bored. This was going to be a long, monotonous trip; of that, he was convinced.

Since speed was needed, the group pushed on until near sunset. To save on oil, they made camp quickly, tended the many animals, and ate their rations as rapidly as possible. Just as Renzo was about to drift into sleep, I made contact with him, telling him of our day of hiking down the river to meet up with them.

At dawn, the camp came alive. Renzo relayed to everyone what I had said to him last night. Haste became the byword for the group. Everyone pitched in and worked together to get underway as quickly as possible.

Indeed, by the time they reached the edge of the mountain barrier, where it met the ocean, this bunch of travelers had the chores down to an extremely efficient action!

As they got underway this first morning, Alfred said, "We are making good progress, forty miles yesterday. Let's push it a bit more today. We ought to reach the edge of the desert in a week, if we push it."

The next day, Rosina began by making her morning wake up telepathic notification to me, which was highly appreciated by us women. That afternoon, Alfred veered the group off the paved road. "We are paralleling the road today to avoid any contact with the Centurion northern outpost, where the road crosses the river, about five miles south of here. Tomorrow, we will veer to the southeast again until we hit the river. From there, we always want to stay on this side. I once was down here where the mountains touch the ocean. If we are on the other side, we will not be able to cross the river; it's too deep and wide where it hits the ocean."

Each night, Michelle put a new mark on her map, showing approximately where we were at in the river system. Okay, it was often just a wild guess on my part. Only when we passed a side river passage that was on the map was I sure of our location.

True to his word, Alfred led them straight to the point where the Kathas mountains reached down to the ocean, exactly one week after they set out. Here the jagged boulders and rock outcrops of the mountains made passage along the coast treacherous, but passable with care. Sometimes a small black sandy beach a few feet wide offered easy going. Just as often, they had to dismount and carefully pick a path through the rocks and boulders. More than once, they were covered in foam spray from the waves crashing upon the rocky fingers of Kathas. It was a duel between the ocean and the mountain to see who would win.

Two harrowing, tense days later and the black sandy beach grew wide; the Desert of Desolation lay before them on their left. For several minutes, the party stopped and stared at their first glimpse of the terrain. Bleak, stark, relatively flat land stretched out before them. Areas of boulders gave way to areas covered with smaller pebbles gave way to great mounds of sand dunes. It varied from one to the other at undefinable intervals.

However, the heat told all. As they looked inland, the heat waves rising from the ground caused their vision to waver as though they were looking at an image that reflected like a flag waving in the wind. Any correct estimate of distances was completely impossible. However, this close to the moderating ocean, it was only hot, tolerable, only in the nineties. At night, the rising air from the desert sucked in cooler, distant ocean breezes, giving them relief from the heat.

Alfred suggested a short experiment the third day along the coast, around noon when they stopped for lunch. "I would like to see for myself what this desert is like. I don't want to risk taking a mule up there, so I propose to walk out there a little ways. Anyone care to join me?" They all were wearing their white robes with turbans around their heads.

"I'm game," Renzo replied. The Loremasters also just had to go as well. However, Alfred insisted many remain behind, just in case of trouble and to watch over the mules. Alfred, Renzo, Benet, Michelle, and Chaucer walked upon to the rocky desert floor. Here small pebbles dotted the hard brownish black surface, undulating and rolling along, as if a massive hand of god has swept all soil from its surface. "Ouch! Damn these stones. It is awful to walk on these," Renzo called out at once.

Wham, they ran into the massive heat being reflected up at them from the ground below their feet. They found it difficult to breathe properly. All were sweating within a couple minutes. All around them, their vision was swirling masses of waving lines; heat wave distortions made everything look surreal.

"Oh my god, my boots are melting! My feet are burning up!" Renzo called out. "Let's get back fast!"

"Which way is back?" called out a much disoriented Chaucer. "I think it's this way." He began heading deeper into the desert.

"No it is this way," Alfred yelled, moving off in another direction, which led obliquely deeper into the desert.

"This is madness," Benet whispered to Michelle.

"Think of the sea. Can you smell it?" Michelle suggested. Both could.

"Hey, everyone, this way; we can smell the sea. Please you are going way out into the desert! Hey, this way." Now both began yelling and jumping up and down to attract the other's attention. Of course, with the heat distortions, to Renzo, they looked perfectly usual.

Only after screaming and yelling their heads off did the two finally get the other three headed back towards them. All five collapsed from the heat when they finally reached the ocean's edge. Tonia was right there with water skins. "You had a very narrow escape," she pointed out to the five as their body temperatures finally cooled down and their thinking ability returned.

"Man, I now believe every word I've ever heard about this desert!" Renzo exclaimed. "If we had to cross that for five hundred miles, we would never make it!"

"I don't think that we would last one day out there," Chaucer added.

"I'm sorry my curiosity nearly got us all killed," Alfred apologized.

"Accepted, but realize that I had to find out for myself," Renzo added. "Can you look at my feet, Tonia?"

"Jeesh, you've got burns on them, Renzo. Let me fix you up. You will have to stay off them for several days. Gang, we now have our new dishwasher here," she teased him. Renzo merely grumbled. The others fared better; their feet, though hot, had not been burned.

That night when I made contact to report on our progress, Renzo told me what had happened. I nearly cried.

*Oh Renzo! If we had not found this underground river, you would have all died trying to rescue us, and then we would have died out here later on when we ran out of food. Please, don't take any more chances like that. I love you too much. I need you, please.*

*I won't, but we had to see for ourselves. How is it that your feet were not burned when you were outside the dome?*

*It's these mantis-supplied boots. As Alexa says, they are the most fantastic boots she's ever heard about. They do not conduct the heat, they are sturdy, they don't slip easily, and we don't feel the sharp punctures of gravel beneath our feet. If only they did not have these enormous spiked heels, they would be the greatest. You will see what we mean when you get to us. Walking in them is something else for us. Yet, we are managing, though you won't believe how slowly we have to go.*

Renzo replied, *But you are going and that is all that matters to me, honey. Keep up the good work. Somehow, we will find the entrance and get moving toward you soon, I hope. Hang in there. I can't wait to put my arms around you. Remember how I like to do it? Imagine my arms are around your waist now. I love you.*

A week of coastal edge travel brought them to roughly the location from which they had intended to strike due north to the dome prison. They had been traveling for two weeks now, we only a day less. They had covered an amazing five hundred fifty miles. We had made a whopping sixty-five! Yet, we had made this on our own steam and that mattered the world to us. We had been delayed an entire day, cutting our way through a large ceiling collapse, one which opened up to the outside world, allowing light and heat to reach the river bed far below the surface above us.

We had another problem. On the twelfth night, Linda's eternal light died. Everyone began to panic, until we realize that, stupid us, we could just as easily cast our blue light spells. At once, seven appeared. Only Natale could not cast one. We all realized that we were also suffering another side effect from the chemicals we were ingesting: loss of thinking power. We had become so internalized into our bodies that we forgot such simple things as casting our blue lights. We all had a good laugh over this one. God, I couldn't wait to stop eating this awful blue slop!

Now I had a new worry, would they be able to find the entrance to this river system? Did it come out under the ocean? Did it come out long before it reached the ocean? From Renzo's experience with the actual desert, I prayed that was not so.

"Well, now comes the hard part," Renzo said. "Find the entrance. Any ideas?"

"Why don't the four of us sweep down the coast, using a methodical search pattern?" Benet suggested. "Michelle and I do that all the time when we are at sea searching for islands and storms.

"Okay, let's agree on a search pattern then," Renzo replied. The pattern had Michelle sailing along the actual coastline. Benet would parallel her a hundred feet from her. Renzo would go along a hundred feet from him, Rosina, a hundred from her brother.

"The map is too low a scale for accurate measurements," Michelle added. "Let's error on the side of caution and go at least another hundred miles east before we double back further inland, if we don't spot it." They agreed. While Tonia kept watch over the four bodies lying down under the canvas tarp, shielding their bodies from the direct sunlight, the four took off down the coast searching for the entrance. The others looked after the mules and chatted among themselves.

*Sailing along the ocean is much more fun, Benet.* Michelle sent to her husband. The two could communicate telepathically when they both were out of their bodies like this.

*Absolutely, my beautiful babe!* Tonia noticed a slight flush on Michelle's body and wondered what that was all about. These two often held very private, very intimate chats when they could not be overheard by another soul. This was their very romantic sharing, which bonded them so tightly together, a sharing beyond words.

Up and down the coastline, the four traveled until their bodies intervened with hunger pangs. After eating, they took off once more, traveling even further inland. Four very disappointed people sat around the supper grounds, poking at their food. "Nothing, nada, zero, complete bust!" declared Renzo.

Michelle sighed. "Why don't we take another look at the map, guys? We must be missing something significant." In the evening twilight, the four stared at the map, hoping something would pop off her drawing at them. Nothing did.

The next morning, Cedric pointed out the obvious, "Water runs downhill."

"What do you think? That I am an idiot?" Renzo grumbled. He'd slept poorly, terrified that he would not be able to find the entrance, that I would end up dying far underground, while he wandered around on the surface unable to find me.

"No, I mean we need to use our heads here. Let's estimate the elevation where the dome is at, where they started. Then, since water must flow downhill, we estimate the fall. That is doable because we know that they are following the main channel, which leads to the ocean. That means the fall is not very great, particularly where it finally met the ancient ocean. We know Bethany's depth estimate where they began, adding in the total distance to the sea and the fall along the way, we can get an estimate of how high the entrance might be."

"I'm afraid that I cannot work all that out," Renzo muttered, realizing that this was way beyond his knowledge.

"I know; this is stuff we Planners must work with every day. Give me a few minutes." He began writing out figures in the sand of the beach. "I'm assuming that they began about thirty feet below the surface. We have a great break here because you have already been to the dome and have said the land is very flat, overall. So now I'll guess that we have five hundred miles of fall from there, the tricky part is estimating the fall per mile. Say, didn't you say that they encountered a total ceiling collapse the other day?"

"Yes, it cost them a day to get past it. Why?" Renzo replied.

"Rosina, contact Bethany now. Ask her to estimate how far from the surface they were located at the ceiling collapse spot, please."

Presently, Rosina spoke, "She says maybe fifty feet."

"Okay, then plugging in that drop, guessing that with all the winding of the river, they only made fifty miles not sixty-five, that means the exit is two hundred feet below the surface here."

"You mean it is out there under water?" Renzo's face fell.

"Not necessarily, Renzo. While the land appears very flat to us, it must be rising a little in those five hundred miles. I don't understand how you and your sister can do this moving about out of your body stuff, but can you go in a straight line, without looking at the ground as a guide? I mean can you start out here and like close your eyes and zoom off inland a hundred miles?"

"I suppose so, why?"

"We need to figure the rise in the land here. Can you find the dome fast, where they were at?"

"Sure, we can be there in an instant."

"Okay, I want you to go there and then be a foot or so above the ground. Then without paying any attention to the ground, come back here at the same elevation. Once here, we need to see how high above us you are, that gives us the total land drop."

"Okay, come on Rosina, let's do this," Renzo cheered up. He was at least doing something.

Five minutes later, the two swooped back down behind their heads. "We think we were about a hundred eighty or so feet up when we got back here."

"Ah, then that means the entrance is perhaps ten to twenty feet below the edge of the land. Given that the beach here is say ten feet below that, the entrance should lie ten below the sands."

"Ah ha. Wait for low tide!" Captain Henry interrupted. "That's the answer. At low tide, the entrance may well be open for travel! I don't have my figures for tides around here; they are back on the caravel. Well, actually, the data is scant for this part of the world. We mostly judge it from the sea itself. I've had little to do but watch the sea. Low tide will be in a few hours. Why don't you make another attempt around then?"

"Can you go along just under the water?" Cedric asked. "If so, you might find it just below the surface, though I don't know how that will help us."

"Now that is an interesting question!" Michelle answered. "Can we do that Benet?"

"I don't know. I don't see why not. Let's try it, dear. Renzo, you and Rosina go along the coastline, while we see if we can parallel you while underwater. It might not work, we'll see."

"Well, we won't drown," Michelle teased her husband, who chuckled at her jest.

Off the foursome went, spiritual beings flying along the coast once more. *Oh, this is unbelievable neat!* Michelle sent to Benet. Skimming along just under the water's surface, she saw all manner of underwater life. Both were incredibly impressed, vowing to do this more often! Fish and plants moving by them almost totally distracted them from what they were supposed to be doing, finding the river's exit.

Twenty-five miles on down the coast, Renzo finally found a large, dark opening. *Hey, I've found something, he sent to his sister,* who was maintaining their Mind Link. She swooped over to his position, and both stared into a large, dark opening. *Should we enter and check it out?*

*Let's,* she replied.

The ocean waves lapped over the rocky floor. Both could see that the sides and ceiling were wet. When not near low tide, the entrance here was underwater. Soon, it became too dark to see, and they cast their blue lights to peer on ahead. After a mile, the ceiling was dry, after two miles or so, only a stream of water flowed down the dry, stony floor of the river. Having decided this was it, Rosina let the others know, both twins returned to their bodies.

Benet and Michelle were chatting about their discovery that they could skim along underwater, and the two paid little attention to Renzo's description of the river entrance. However, in an hour, camp was broken and the group began moving on down the coast toward this entrance. By the time that they arrived near the river's underground exit here at the ocean, the seawater was already halfway to the ceiling. They would have to wait for the next low tide to enter.

"Delays, always delays," Renzo cursed, "I just want to get to my wife!"

"Calm down; we are almost into the river system," Chaucer replied. "I can't wait to get my arms around Linda either. We must be patient. They are certainly safer now than ever before, as long as their food supply holds out."

"True guys," Cedric cautioned them, "expect more delays when we are inside the river. Bethany says that in places the ceiling has collapsed. I don't know what the device that Enyo has that burns rock, but we don't have it. Expect delays, as we have to dig our way through to them. Chaucer is right, patience. I, too, am most worried about their food supply. Renzo, next time she chats with you, get a new estimate on how long their food will last."

*Renzo, it's me. We've run into a new problem. We're maybe another seven miles along now. Ahead of us is a deep pool. We aren't sure that it can be easily walked through. It looks deep. The water is very cold, and we are very limited on anything to dry off with or to be rewarmed up by if we chill. We've been staring at it all day now.*

He replied, *Why don't you just lift everyone across it? Or is it way too large?*

*Duh! Why didn't I think of that! Oh, it's this damnable food slop that we're forced to eat. They have a chemical in it that tends to drive us into our bodies, turns on these incredible sexual sensations, and dulls our thinking. Can you believe that we all forgot about our blue lights, and just panicked in the total darkness when Linda's went out the other day? God, I will be glad to get real food in me. I hope these effects aren't permanent.*

*Hang in there, my love; we found the entrance today. It is underwater, except at low tide. We'll be entering at the next low tide, less than a half day away. We are soon going to be on our way. Say, what's the latest estimate on the remaining number of days of your food? This has us most worried.*

*Gosh, with our screwy thinking now, I wouldn't count on our accuracy. Enyo thinks that maybe five weeks are left. We seem to be eating more than normal, probably because we are moving and not just lying around.*

*Okay. We will be coming as fast as we can. Cedric says we may run into more collapsed ceilings, which will hold us up. Gosh, I hope not! I want to grab you and hold you so tightly!*

*I hope you do more than that! This food slop makes us so horny; you are going to get a workout, until the blue slop and chemicals in it are out of our systems!*

*You are on. We'll see who runs out of energy first. Looser becomes the winner's slave for a week this time.*

*God, I missed our play! Okay, deal. I'd better see if I can get us over this barrier. Bye for now.*

I told the others, "Gang, they have found the entrance!" We all cheered. "It's underwater, except at low tide. Renzo believes they will be entering the river tunnel heading our way in twelve hours! Best news in a long time. Now, for our current predicament: the chemicals are clouding my mental facilities again. I will just carry our bodies over the pool, simple. Hang on to your lights and shine them ahead of us so I can see where to put you down."

The seven squatted down and picked up their lights, holding them secure in their teeth. One by one, I picked each woman's body up, and then I moved them forward over this large pool. Once I could see the smooth surface of the riverbed once more, I sat them down and returned for my body and the platform carrying our food and supplies. A few minutes later, this barrier was passed.

"We didn't make too much progress today," Enyo suggested. "Perhaps we should continue for a while yet before we stop to eat and sleep." The others seconded the idea, and once more we began to pick our way carefully along the undulating riverbed. "I sure will welcome a steading hand. I have to go so slowly so as not to lose my balance," Enyo stated what we all felt.

"I bet when the guys reach us and we have to go back for all the alien stuff, we will be able to go much faster with them helping us," Natasa added. "Oops, I nearly lost it there. Oh for Fred's arms!" She'd nearly fallen.

We made roughly another two miles before stopping for the night. We ate hungrily. While I did up the dishes, okay the bowls and straws, in the river water, I told them Renzo's fears. "We need to be patient; there are likely to be more cave-ins along the way. We can get through them fairly easily, but our rescue party will have to dig their way through or find some way around them."

Enyo commented, "I wish there was some way we could get one of our Stone Cutters to them, but I don't know how we could do that." She echoed all our wishes, anything to speed up their getting to us!

Oh no, I began thinking of them, and the chemicals I had ingested chose this time to activate. "Kallisto, get our blankets out fast; it's coming in a wave over me again! I don't know how long I can last without relief. This is crazy!"

"A little of this goes a very long way with me," Linda declared.

"Oh, you need to lighten up a little; we're enjoying it," Enyo teased, though from the way she was walking, I knew she could barely hold it at bay as well. You never saw eight women trying to get to bed so darn fast as we did this night! Kallisto and I didn't even bother to roll up in our blanket. An hour later, the chemical was out of my system sufficiently for me to relax at last. "Thanks, Kallisto."

"Thanks Bethany. This sure is getting old! While I truly enjoy sex, enforced sex, I do not! I'd love to get my hands on the mantis who dreamed up this torture. I'd teach it a thing or two!"

Enyo giggled, "But Kallisto, you don't have any hands." We all roared with laughter.

"Well, I'd like to get my hands on the mantis who invented these marvelous boots," Alexa added.

"Ask it how we get them off, will you?" Aella teased her.

"I'd like to get a trading arrangement going, perhaps boots for gold or something; they seem to always desire gold. I could make a fortune with boots of this quality, if only they could be removed when we needed our toes or feet," Alexa continued. "Say, you know those people down in Annelise that you were telling us all about, Bethany, the ones who are insane on being formally dressed for a royal ball at all times?"

"Yes, they wear these tight corsets with huge billowing skirts with enormous hoops," I replied.

"I saw the boots that they gave you, oh and the outlandish clothes too," Alexa continued pondering something. "Their boots are somewhat similar to these, just with a much thicker heel and far less well made. Do you suppose that their people were at one time influenced by these mantis creatures?"

"Now that is an interesting line of conjecture," I replied. "We didn't find a single trace of the usual mantis activity: appendage removal."

"They didn't really tell us much of anything about their history," Linda added. She was lying alongside of Natale.

"You didn't know about these boots before then," Alexa replied.

"Well, the mantis sure infected Demokritos," Kallisto added. "We wear flaring dresses as well, but use a number of petticoats to poof them out, not those incredible metal hoops that the Annelise women wear. Also, we often have boots or shoes with higher, rather blocky heels on them. Similar, but not the same."

"Ah, the corsets fit in here somehow," Linda offered. "They are so tight, so constricting, that they literally force so much of your attention inward on your body. At least I found that terribly true. It was so hard to stay behind my head, when my attention was enforced into my waist."

"Golly, you are right, me too. I felt and acted the same way. It drives one into the cell, to use the mantis term for our bodies. I wonder just how much of our cultures have their genesis with these mantis creatures?" I answered.

'This was their prison colony long before the Grey Creatures came," Natale pointed out. "They've likely had centuries to experiment on us."

"I don't think that it is fair to put all this blame onto the mantis creatures," Alexa commented, surprisingly. "Look, we women do many things to attract our mates. We try to look pretty, wear attractive clothing, arrange our hair — so many, many things we do just to draw their attention. I remember when I first came to your mom's estate and Natale gave me my first silky, form fitting dress without armholes, it was so sleek and emphasized our true body shape. I felt so sexy in that dress the first time I wore it! The men at the dance couldn't keep their hands off me. I felt like a million, and for the first time in my life, I was actually attracting men. There were none back in the House of Right, you see."

She went on, "Now that I have Rene, I find that I do really enjoy dressing up sexily and flirting with him. We have such fun together. There isn't anything I wouldn't do for him, and I know he feels the same way about me. Then there is the social must fit in idea. We all want to fit into our society. If everyone else was wearing tight fitting corsets and poufy dresses, I would feel very out of place wearing my working leathers. It's our need to blend in with our friends, families, and groups at work here as well. So you cannot go blaming the mantis for all our faults and frailties."

Enyo took this opportunity to inject her thoughts as well. "Another thing, if I were to be in the mantis creature's position of having to create and keep spiritual beings trapped in these bodies, I would certainly conduct any number of experiments to see what worked the best. You would have to keep those experiments separated from each other or you would get cross-contamination of results. Some of us are the results of one kind of experiment — we here from the House of Right, as are so many others that you rescued, Bethany. Perhaps, they also experimented with tight fitting clothing and poufy dresses, which make everyday actions a chore. To keep cross-contamination at a minimum, I wouldn't dare make anyone there lose appendages."

"Kallisto's country is another example of such an experiment, in my opinion. Imagine establishing a whole culture based on Holy Degrees in a marriage — a different social experiment yet again," Enyo said.

"Hey, what about Tashien?" Linda broke in with her thoughts. "You know there they place an insane value on women having the tiniest feet, so tiny that they can scarcely walk! Add to that their use of corsets as well, and their extremely long fingernails and face paint to look attractive, doesn't this also sound like a mantis experiment in progress? It sure does to me. Empress Sho Lin can only walk if someone supports her. She needs others to help her with nearly every personal thing."

"Doesn't their incredible reliance on maintaining honor play a key role here as well?" asked Natale. "I mean where would Sho Lin be if everyone else was not so keen on maintaining honor with everyone, even their dead ancestors? Without that support, she'd be completely useless, except perhaps as a sexual toy."

"I think that we can see mantis influence all over Tarra, except in the northern areas which were under the control of the Grey Creatures," I concluded.

"Say, what effects did the Grey Creatures have?" asked Enyo. "They didn't cut off appendages as far as I know."

"No, they fomented endless wars so that many were killed and the spiritual beings would be sucked into their mind scrambling devices and sent back to get a new body. I think that they were just being perfectly direct in making beings so confused that they just stayed tightly inside their heads, like good prisoners," Linda suggested.

"Hey you all — see what I mean about deep thinking after pleasuring oneself?" Enyo giggled, making her point. We all stopped for a second and realized what she had said to us back in our cell. We all burst out laughing along with her.

"We'd better get some sleep before we solve all the world's problems. Save some for tomorrow," I teased, and the laughter continued.

The next morning, our routine began once more. Breakfast, clean up, put our things onto the platform, and then move out. Well, we, slowly and very carefully, moved out. Just as we got started, I received the news I'd been waiting for all night. Renzo and our rescue party had entered the other end of this ancient river system! With a round of the House of Right's woo hoo's, we pressed on forward, knowing that each step brought us closer to our mates.

"Let the mules find their way," Benet ordered as the group began wading into the swirling waters of the gaping hole where the ancient river had once emptied into the ocean. This was a tricky move, riding through the water with no idea of the footing beneath the mule's feet. Yet, they did a great job of it; only one stumbled. "We've got about two hours before the water level begins to rise. We must get to where Renzo has said the ground is dry. I don't want to be caught along here when the tide rises!"

Sometime later, lanterns lighting the way, Renzo and Cedric in the lead, called out, "Water is rising. I hope we can make it!" Cedric moved his lantern to shine onto the ceiling; it was dry! He relaxed a bit, knowing that there would still be air in here if they didn't make it all the way in time.

"I see dry land ahead," Renzo yelled back to the others, strung out a very long way behind him. They were going in single file, a one hundred mule train. Only he and Cedric did not lead a long string of pack mules. Leading the way, they needed freedom of movement, in case of trouble. Now he realized there would be a new problem while in the riverbed.

Outside, they just tethered the mules into a small group. Here inside, they would have to be strung out in a very long line indeed. He resolved to make sure tomorrow that the mules with their food and camping supplies were up front where they would be more accessible. "We are making pretty good time, don't you think, Cedrick?"

"Renzo, we've only been riding two hours! Calm down. There are hundreds of miles and obstacles ahead of us!"

"Hum, how are we going to know when it is night time?" Renzo asked, and then laughed. Bethany had asked him the same thing. Rosina had been giving them the wakeup call.

"We'll have Paulette contact Rosina each morning, and then she can wake up Bethany."

"I heard. I'll get a hold of her tonight," Rosina called out from way behind her brother. "We should alternate; tomorrow you get to lead the mules!" She didn't like having to pull along thirty or so mules behind her.

As the monotonous hours passed them by, the novelty of their adventure soon wore off. When they finally made their first camp that night, or whenever it was, they were all quite tired. Now came the endless chores. The hundred mules had to be fed; at least watering them was not a problem. The river's trickle ran down the middle of the floor. Next, a camp of sorts had to be made and dinner fixed. Charcoal was used for cooking; they could not have brought remotely enough firewood for that purpose. Still, they used as little of it per meal as possible, which meant that cooking times were longer than normal.

"At least, we're snug in these robes," Tonia said to Rosina, as they sipped their after diner tea. "How far did the guys say that we came today?"

"I heard them debating it, but perhaps thirty or there abouts. I think that tomorrow we will be able to cover more distance, we had to wait on the tide today."

A week passed by slowly. The rescue party then ran into their first real barrier, a ceiling rock fall that blocked their way. While the men worked on making a path through the boulders, Rosina contacted Bethany.

*Hi, we are temporarily stopped at a rock fall. The men are out there moving rocks around. We estimate that we have come over two hundred miles so far. How goes it with you?*

*Not so good. We are down to two eternal lights now. We are surviving only on our blue light spells. Spooky indeed. I think that we are at least a hundred twenty miles down this riverbed, but it winds so much that I don't know how close we are. Have you figured out where you might be on the map?*

*Hang on, Michelle has it. I'll see. Here, I'm sending you my image of the map. The black dot is where Michelle thinks that we are. Where are you at on the map?*

*I'll send you our image, where we think we might be. Gosh, we have been walking for two weeks now and only gotten this far, but you have been at it only a week and are at least three times as far as we! Great going!*

Exhausted by their efforts to move enough boulders so that the mules could pass, the men collapsed. The women fixed them a hearty meal and took care of the endless chores that day. The next morning, they had to lead the mules over the obstacle course of the boulder field. Only then, could they mount up and continue making progress.

Two days later, they, too, came to a water pool. There was no way around it, only through it. This became tricky as the mules continued to lose their footing. It took an entire hour to pass this barrier. Then, it was smooth sailing once more, as Henry put it.

That night, they heard a distant, "Hello!" It was the other husbands, who had finally caught up to the main party. Frank, Herbert, Fred, Rene, and Hank had seen their lights ahead of them.

Renzo halted the group and rode back to greet them. "Hail and well met indeed! How do you like Bethany's path?" he said jovially. He knew that they were getting close to us.

"Sure beats the desert!" exclaimed Frank. "Alfred told us about his little excursion into the desert. You could have died of heat stroke!"

"Tell me about it. My boots melted and I got burns on my feet! Say, how many mules did you bring along?"

"Fifty," called out Hank. "We came prepared with extras of

everything, just in case you run out of something. Sure glad you allowed us to come. Kallisto is probably dying to be in my arms."

"Yes, I am glad you are all here for your wives. They've had quite a time of it. Incredibly brave, resourceful women! We are a bunch of incredibly lucky men!" Renzo added.

"You can say that one again!" Frank, Enyo's husband, replied. "Enyo is the most incredible woman I have ever met!"

"Oh no, Natasa is the most incredible woman," Herbert insisted.

"You are both wrong, it's Kallisto," Hank teased.

"Nah, you are all wrong, it's Bethany," Renzo couldn't help adding to the fun.

"Oh no, you have it all wrong," Chaucer had come up behind him. "Linda is the goddess here." The men chuckled. "Come on, daylight's a'wasting," he teased. Of course, there was no daylight here at all, just pitch blackness, broken only by the feeble light from their always burning oil lanterns.

That night while they ate, Cedric pointed out that they were going through oil at a slightly faster rate than anticipated. Frank had brought along a resupply, thinking this might happen. Renzo shook the Planner's hand, "Thank you! We don't want to meet up with the women only to find ourselves totally in the dark, now would we? How could we tell which woman was which?" The men roared. Tonia simply smiled.

The two-week mark came for the rescue party. They had covered some four hundred fifty-five miles of winding riverbed. However, now they faced a serious problem. Ahead, the ceiling had collapsed; daylight shone down onto the massive pile of rocks. While a person could manage to climb them to get to the other side eventually, the mules could not get past this barrier.

*Where are you?* Rosina sent to Bethany. *We've encountered a bad place. The ceiling has fallen in, and we can see daylight overhead. While that is a very welcome change, the mules cannot get over the giant rock pile.*

*Hold on. I'll find out. Okay, here comes the image. Natale has made a mark where we think we might be. How about sending us your position?*

*Here comes Michelle's map.*

The two women compared their image in their minds with the maps before them. The two dots were nearly upon top of each other!

*Yahoo! You must be only a little ways ahead of us! Don't do anything about the cave in; wait for us. We will be along as soon as we can. Just be ready for us to come blasting our way through the rock pile. Have everyone far back please; we don't know the range of our Stone Cutter. Yahoo!*

"They are stopped just ahead of us by a cave in that they can't get through. We are going to meet up with them very soon now. I told them to stay well back while we cut our way through the stone. Can you believe it? We are nearly there!" Eight women began jumping up and down, our heels clicking on the bedrock. Elated, that would be an understatement of the greatest magnitude.

"Hey, slow down, careful does it. We don't want to take a fall this close to being rescued," I called out, as Enyo began to walk too fast for the rest of us.

# Chapter 8 Rescued at Long Last!

It was now November 1. After two hours of patient, careful walking, we could see daylight ahead of us. Through my teeth, which held one of the remaining non-eternal lights so that I could see to bring up our platform, I called out, "Let's turn off the lights. Enyo get out your Stone Cutter. Let me warn them before you cut us to freedom at long last!" I could almost feel Renzo's arms around me. The chemicals in my system were raging once more, but tonight I might find real relief!

A few minutes later, we eight walked up to the enormous cave in. I brought the platform up for the last time, sitting it far out of the way against the side of the wall. "We are here. Please stand way, way back. Enyo's going to cut us a path. We don't know how far out the device cuts, so stay way, way back!"

Renzo yelled back to me, "We are all way back. God, it is so great to hear your voice! Tell her to hurry up! Or I am going to scramble over these rocks and get you myself!"

Enyo sat awkwardly down, as she had many times before. Using her heels, she activated the button, being extremely careful of its initial direction. Then, she picked it up in her teeth, pointing it forward. She slowly moved to the rock pile, and the cutter did its job. Rock dust flew high in the air as she cut us a pathway some four feet wide. As the path progressed, she stepped forward to extend its length. A half hour later, she broke through to the other side, dust flying in all directions. She sat down carefully, the energy blast arcing out in front of her slicing only the air. Carefully, she pressed the off button.

The clicks of our heels echoed through the passageway, as we seven came up right behind her, just in time to see Frank running toward her. She awkwardly got to her feet just as he reached her. He picked her up, held her tightly, and swirled her around and around and around in a small circle, her long hair flying outward!

One by one, as the rest of us appeared at the end of this new passageway, our husbands greeted us similarly. Being the last one through only made Renzo even more excited. When we finally saw each other, he raced to me, picked me up, and swirled me around like mad as well. Our lips found each other's, and we had our first loving embrace in months!

Yes, I was crying like a baby. My emotions were totally out of my control, and I didn't want to control them. I only wanted his arms around me, holding me tightly, my lips on his! I ignored everything else in the universe for a long time. Later, Tonia said that we were like this for a half hour. Thankfully, the others stayed quiet and allowed us this time together.

Finally, Renzo said, "Okay, my love, let's get you cleaned up and into some decent clothes. Then, would you care for a cup of tea, my dear?" I banged him hard, my style of hug, and he grinned.

"Oh, hi everyone. Sorry, we were a little carried away there. God, you don't know how fantastic it is for us to see you all once more!"

"We are just as glad to finally get you all back with us," Tonia said. "Renzo is right; I need to check you over to see if anything needs healing. You are very dirty, comes from sleeping in here in the dark. Let's get you cleaned up, shall we?"

"Hey, I want a look at you, my love," Renzo said.

"Look all you want to, but keep your arms around me, bud! I don't want you away from me for days and days!" I replied. "Seriously, everyone, we have two major physical problems for you. First, as you know, the blue slop, which we have been forced to eat for four months plus now, is filled with some kind of chemical that causes us to be incredibly horny. This is embarrassing to talk about so openly, but you must understand." I took a deep breath. "At first, we all suppressed these incredible sexual urges we were having. That resulted in our hair growing excessively fast. Of course, I didn't mind that so much at first, but then our breast enlarged to enormous proportions. I kid you not, Renzo, mine were nearly the size of my head! Then, I discovered that the body's method to remove these chemicals from its system was through sexual pleasure. Once we got accustomed to doing it for each other, the intense pressure lifted, and our breasts shrunk. As you can see, mine are still much larger than before. I'm rather hoping that once we are off this chemical, they will continue to shrink back to their normal big size."

"Hey, you look fabulous, Bethany," Renzo commented, lending me some moral support.

"The second problem that we have had to deal with since we were abducted is these strange boots that we woke up wearing. They cannot be removed by us."

Alexa said, "Actually, having these boots has been a godsend; without them, we could not have escaped at all, though we could have helped ourselves so much more easily. We know that the mantis used heat to shrink them down tightly to our calves. In fact, when we take baths or go into deeper water, not a drop has ever gotten inside the boots! That's how tightly they are sealed onto our feet, making us extremely helpless without our feet and toes."

"Well, I must say, Alexa, that you are the most helpful, able, and powerful 'extremely helpless women' that I have ever heard of!" Chaucer declared flatly.

"You wouldn't say that if you had to walk around in these heels," she retaliated. "Yet, these heels are just fantastic in all other ways." She began a litany of their virtues; the only drawbacks were they wouldn't come off and of course the high spiked heels themselves.

"Well, I think you look sexy in them," Rene whispered into her ear.

She smiled and whispered back, "I thought they might excite you." He blushed.

"Anyhow, while you are cleaning us up and checking us out, you might see what you can do with these boots. Alexa has one experimental pair back there on our platform. Just do not eat the blue slop, unless you want to grow enormous boobs," I teased them.

Quickly, the others set to work on us eight. I just relaxed for the first time in five months. I had gotten us all out safely, now I was more than willing to sit back and let everyone else fuss over me. First, while the water was heating up, we were undressed. One by one, Tonia inspected each of us. Other than a few bruises on our knees, we were in excellent health. However, Tonia whispered to me, "I can tell that there is a lot of a foreign substance in your body. I'll monitor its level each day. Keep our fingers crossed. Well, you can keep your toes crossed. No, I guess like this you can keep your legs crossed." We chuckled. It was so good to hear her voice once more, to be playfully teased.

Next, our doting husbands gave us a hot bath. However, our exceedingly long hair was beyond them. Angel, Tania, and Rosina had to do our hair themselves. However, they then made the husbands dry it and brush it out for us. I felt clean, as if somehow the many months of imprisonment had been washed off me.

Next, our men dressed us in our new desert robes that they had brought along for us. After Renzo had me all fixed up and my hair straightened, he commented, "Do you realize that your hair goes down to your ankles? Incredible indeed, immensely beautiful."

"I know; it now gets in the way, and I keep stepping on it. Perhaps I have too much of a good thing going here." We both laughed. He then began wrapping it up in the turban. Soon, I looked like he did, white turbaned head without hair. His arm around me giving me support so that I could walk without constantly staring at the ground, he led me to the eating area. "Allow me to present you with the first cup of tea," he said mocking a great ceremony.

As he poured my favorite cup full, he and the others suddenly realized just how helpless we really were without the use of our feet. The magnitude of just what we eight had managed to do finally sank home to our rescuers. "You are the most un-helpless helpless women that I have ever seen!" Renzo declared as he held the cup so I could sip. Ah, tea! Ecstasy! Heaven!

"Here, I've cleaned up your straws; this will help you a little," Cedric said, inserting my trusty blue slop straw into the teacup. Now Renzo could sit back and just hold me, which suited me just fine.

Cedric sat beside us. "I inspected the boots back on the platform. You are right; they are very alien and have strange physical properties. What troubles me the most is that my knife will not cut through their sides! Can I see your feet? Maybe I can get some ideas by actually seeing how they are on your feet."

He pulled up my robes and stared at them, moved them around, even tried to wedge something between my skin and the boot top, to no avail; there was just no space there at all. The boots were sealing up my lower legs and feet.

Alexa, who saw Cedric studying my boots, suggested, "Cedric, what goes on must somehow come off. We just have to discover the proper means. I take it you cannot cut them off?"

"No, my knife cannot cut this strange material. While it feels like leather, it most definitely is not leather. Yet, they are flexible up here above your ankles. I don't understand this problem at all."

"We didn't either, alien technology at work," Alexa said. "Please keep trying, though. If you don't succeed, you will have to care for our every need."

"Yes, madam un-helpless helpless," he teased her. She grinned. From now on, our men referred to us eight as the un-helpless helpless women.

"Right now, I just want someone to feed me some real food!" Linda declared. However, we already smelled the odors of supper on the way. Yes, without the use of our feet, we now depended upon our husbands to feed us. There was no other choice, except to eat the blue slop, which we never wanted to touch again as long as we lived!

"While Renzo alternated between sticking a bit of fish into my mouth and then his, he commented, "The mantis must have been pretty darn intelligent to have created a prison cell in such a way that you would somehow be able actually to live and not die. I'm surer than ever that it wanted you eight out of circulation permanently, for many, many years, but I've got you now, and I am never going to let go of you again!" I rested my head on his shoulder, something I had been dreaming about doing for so many months now.

After dinner, Tonia said, "Bethany, we are letting you out of chores around here until you get the use of your feet back."

"Thanks, Tonia. I don't think you have too much choice in the matter. In our cell, everything was set up so that we could deal with things using our mouths or heads. Out here, very little can be done that way. Sorry, but until the boots come off, we are dependent on you guys."

By now, it was getting dark up in the desert. Finally, Renzo laid out our bed, a pile of soft blankets and sheets. He helped me undo my turban and then the robe. At the speed of light, he removed his clothes. I let him gently lift me up and lay me down on the blankets. I had to have him arrange my hair, though. He pulled the blankets over us, we kissed, and the chemicals inside my body exploded into action. I heard the other seven similarly exploding as well. An hour later, Renzo was exhausted, "Don't stop now, do it again. I need it, please honey," I begged him for more.

The next morning, Renzo woke me up with a kiss and a whisper, "Okay, love, you won that one. I'll be your slave for a week. I cannot believe it. You are insatiable, but I love it!"

"I know, partly it is the chemicals still being expunged from my body. Partly I am trying to make up for missing it for so many months. I love you. Come and snuggle with me yet a while." Our lips met once more.

Over breakfast, I put on my leader's hat once more. "Okay gang. Status time. We have uncovered an awful lot of alien stuff back there that we would like to confiscate. However, I've no idea of your situation. Do you have enough supplies to go back to the prison or not?"

"We've misjudged our consumption of oil, but Hank came to our rescue," Emil reported. "I believe that we have more than enough to fetch all that these mules can carry out of the dome. Are you women up to going back there? I am rather worried that you might dread it."

"Alone and like we are now, I would never make the attempt," I replied honestly. "However, with you all with us, we are eager to go. I'm sorry that we are going to be such a burden on all of you, however. Yet, I cannot see how we can be of much use, though I say this for all of us, we will do all that we can possibly do to help around here. I only have one request to make of you. If we have to walk at all, please let our husbands have their arms around us to steady us. These heels and the riverbed do not mix at all well."

"Is it possible to ride much of the way?" Emil asked.

"Yes, there are a few places where we will have trouble riding, but I think that we may be able to ride much of the way," I replied.

"Then, let's get going." We helped with the packing as we could, lifting, and carrying things in our mouths. I know it wasn't much, but we had to do something, however small. The men lifted us up onto our mules, and they led them behind theirs. Unfortunately, that meant the others had to bring along enormous strings of mules with them.

As we rode along, just what we women had accomplished slowly became apparent to everyone, including ourselves. It had taken us over two weeks to go a little over a hundred miles down this ancient riverbed. Three days later by mule, we were back where we started, in the underground basement of the dome structure!

Natale moved out of her body and did the honors of turning on the basement light, which she had done so many times before. We left the mules here near the water and walked up the sloping tunnel into the basement proper. Our party was amazed to see all the stuff that we had discovered here. Next, I floated to the metal trap door and opened it, securing the locking bar. Up we walked free beings into what had been a formidable prison. Heels clicking away, we gave everyone a tour of the outer dome area, which here in the middle of the daytime, was incredibly hot.

Enyo then retrieved our metal spike and opened the cell door. After everyone piled inside, she shut the door. Once shut, everyone heard the cooling mechanism turn on once more. In a few minutes, it was nice and comfortable again. We showed and demonstrated all the features of our cell. "That you even got out of here is utterly amazing! You are the most resourceful, un-helpless helpless women in the world!" Renzo exclaimed. He meant it too.

The rest of the day was spent estimating what we could realistically carry back with us. Alexa insisted on bringing back all of the boots and the devices which were used to seal our legs in them. Natale insisted on bringing back all of the books and anything which had lots of writing on it. Enyo, Aella, and Natasa tried to bring back everything else in the place, including the cooling machine!

"But Enyo, my beloved," Frank protested. "The machine is too big to fit on a mule!"

"Well, can we somehow take it apart then?" Everyone roared with laughter. Engineers!

"Enyo, if you don't take less stuff, I am going to have to throw you on that bed and have my way with you to teach you not to be so greedy," Frank teased her.

"Oh, please let's do it now!" she exclaimed seriously.

"Oh god, not after last night!" Our men really looked haggard. Frank had been had by Enyo. Once more, we all had a good laugh.

We spent the night below with the mules. At dawn, Cedric and several others went back to retrieve the dead women that we had found. Enyo, Stone Cutter in mouth, led the rest of us outside the dome. Her plan was to cut a crypt in the bedrock to bury these women properly.

It was dawn and the coolest part of the day. The ground was uneven and covered with small pebbles. Frank put his arm around Enyo's waist, Renzo, his arm around mine. Together, we walked out onto the desert proper, looking for a suitable burial site.

"It sure is a whole lot easier walking out here when you are supporting me," I said.

"Honey, I don't think I can take much more of this walking. The stones are hurting the bottoms of my feet!"

"Hey, same here," Frank replied.

"Gosh, we don't feel them hardly at all, just hard to keep our balance is all, right Enyo?" she nodded, the device still firmly between her teeth. Both men once more looked at our boots in amazement. Enyo then picked a spot closer to the dome. Reluctantly, she let Frank do the honors of cutting a burial hole in the bedrock.

While we waited for the others, we stared off into the distance. "Sure is desolate out here," Frank mused. "No water, no trees, no grass, no nothing, just bedrock and stones with a little sand here and there. I wonder how it got this way?"

Just then, Kallisto and Hank came out, along with Cedric and Rosina, carrying two sacks for us. "Ouch! Holy cow!" Hank exclaimed. "Honey, be careful of these stones, they hurt our feet."

"You can say that again," echoed both Cedric and Rosina, who were now very carefully picking their way over to where we stood. Kallisto just walked normally.

"We don't feel them much, just hard to keep our balance is all," she said to Hank. Like Renzo, he stared at her boots once more.

We ceremonially placed the two sacks of remains into the hole. I said a few words of respect. While the others headed back inside, I began sweeping up the loose gravel from all around, filling in the hole. "Thank you for making the path back to the dome gravel free just for me," Renzo said lovingly. I smiled, as his arm slid around my waist, supporting me as we walked rapidly back inside the dome.

We spent the rest of the morning sacking and tying as much stuff as the mules could carry onto their saddle packs. While we were able to retrieve most all of the smaller items, Enyo had to leave the room cooler machine behind. Frank promised that one day they could return to retrieve it.

By suppertime, we were fifteen miles on down the riverbed, finally heading for home. Emil's estimate was that we would need fifteen days to reach the ocean. From there, we could load the gear onto the caravel to be taken home. It would be faster for us to return overland with Alfred, taking the Sleepy Hollow back to Velona. With luck, we would arrive home in early January.

In fact, it took us only thirteen days to reach the ocean. Retracing their path turned out to be far easier, for we had a very clear trail to follow. We did very little but ride the mules all day long and far into the evening hours, each day. By the time that we finally reached the outside world, the chemicals in our systems had pretty much been expelled. Our somewhat cloudy thinking cleared up. Even Enyo was now laughing about her insistence on trying to bring the huge cooling machine back with us in parts! We did little talking, though. While riding, one had to pay attention to the path ahead. At night, we just wanted to make as much love to our mates as possible.

Seeing the light of day once more rejuvenated us all. My spirits rose as I breathed in the salty air, felt the warm sunlight on my face instead of the burning of the desert heat. Now I really did feel free. I was back in the world once more.

Alfred was introduced to us, and he chatted about his long wait here for us. Thankfully, the extra caravel had arrived to keep him company. The Santi crew gave us all a hearty welcoming cheer and then set to work using their longboats to haul our finds out to the caravel. Most of the gear we sent back with them, keeping only a few items with us, among them was the test boots that Alexa had brought with her and its fastening device. Now that we were in the daylight, Cedric began to put his full attention on our remaining problem.

Two days later, we began the overland journey back to New Barq and the Sleepy Hollow. Alfred spent time with me, getting acquainted with his Supreme Commander. He began telling me how much he admired one of our ancient founders, Elizabeth Stanton. He told me all about how she and her Lightning Circle had been in Al Barq the night of the Baby Murders. He animatedly described how she had helped so many new mothers flee the city with their babies, by cleverly using the city sewers. Alfred described his most treasured historical items that he and his wife had found down in the sewers during the lengthy construction of the fortress of New Barq.

Actually, New Barq was built somewhat south of the ruins of Al Barq. I had explicitly chosen the ruins as the location for our fortress there, knowing that the sewers would provide a secret escape route, should those in the fortress ever need it. He was so excited about all this, that I didn't have the heart to tell him that he was talking to the spiritual being who had been Elizabeth Stanton!

Talking with him brought back many memories of those early years to mind. Besides, it helped pass the long days on mule back. As we neared his fortress, I remembered a small thing. "Alfred, Bethany Stanton left behind another item. She had a dagger, which continually got in her way while she was helping the women through the tunnels. She dropped it in a secret spot, intending to retrieve it on the last trip. Unfortunately, circumstances of that night prevented her from making that last trip; she had too many women outside who needed care." I then described the precise location to Alfred, who could not believe his incredible luck.

"I promise you that I will go in seek of this incredible historical treasure as soon as I see you all safely on your way back to your many children! How can I ever thank you?"

"You already have, by helping get all these mules and supplies, and for patiently waiting for our return, guarding our exit point. Thank you." I smiled.

On December 25, I saw the tops of the masts of the Sleepy Hollow in the distance, beside the tall tower of the fortress. I would know those masts anywhere! Never was I gladder to see that caravel than this day!

Alfred introduced us to his wife Jill, and she begged us to stay one night longer. She wanted us to have the chance to clean up and to wash the trail dirt and mule smell from our clothes. Besides, she wanted the chance to meet us as well. We agreed, but not until we hugged all our friends on the Sleepy Hollow, who were very pleased to see us all back in one piece. It was a happy reunion.

After a long, hot, lilac fragrance bath, a good hair washing, and lengthy brushing session, our husbands brought us our usual leather dresses. These we were used to wearing; with our feet and toes, we managed life quite nicely in these. However, as we were, our husbands became our hands, lovingly so, that's for sure. I rather enjoyed being so doted over by Renzo, though I knew that it would not last. I had to become more responsible for my own care and soon. This evening, I had Renzo part my hair and drape it over my shoulders down my front side. This way I could manage it better.

His arm around my waist, we headed down to join the others in the big meeting room, where Jill was to serve our welcome home feast. As I walked in, Alexa said, "Gosh Bethany, you do look good in your leathers. The boots go fabulously well with the outfit! See, guys, they really do look great on us, if only we could take them off when we need to use our feet." I had to admit that they did look good on us, particularly so now that we all were wearing our leathers.

Jill served us an official Arad meal. Oh, I enjoyed that! It had been half a century, maybe more, since I last had such a unique meal. Lamb laced with Arad spices, dates, figs, and local vegetables, oh what a delicacy! While the others were not enamored of the cuisine, I certainly was and validated Jill on how good and historically accurate her well planned meal actually was. I learned later from one of her Santi helpers, that she had planned this meal in my honor ever since she'd received word that the rescuers had reached us!

The next day, while the others were busy loading our things onto the caravel, I took the two aside. "Alfred, Jill, as your Santi Supreme Commander, I want to take this opportunity to tell you just how great a job I think that you two are doing here in New Barq. Very well done. I know it can be rather lonely out here so far from the rest of us, but you are holding the frontier at bay here, a very valuable service to us all. Thank you both for a very good job." Both were very pleased for the direct validation, and they gave me a nice hug.

With my hair nicely in front of me, I walked up the gangplank onto the caravel unassisted, as did we all, eight very proud women. Henry issued the orders to raise anchor, and slowly he and our crew backed out of the small harbor here in New Barq. Once clear and turned toward Velona, Captain Henry called out, "Okay Commander, sailing orders?"

It was just like old times! "I guess we ought to sail for Velona, Captain Sir." I said it just as formally as he had to me. Everyone began laughing and I added, "If for no other reason than to get these darn boots off!"

We had not gone a mile before we eight women experienced a great difficulty in keeping our balance in these heels on the swaying, moving decks! Rats, yet another barrier to handle. First thing that I ordered was a conference in the galley, where we could sit down and have some tea. I felt that I could never drink enough tea for all the time I had missed it!

Sipping mine with my straw, I began, "Gang, there is more to all this than we have said. I didn't want to discuss this in the presence of others. This is for our ears only." I gave them a quick, firsthand account of all that we had learned and concluded. Finally, I brought up what was bothering both Kallisto and me the most.

"Kallisto has raised perhaps the most critical issue. Just how did a mantis creature, who was not likely here on Tarra before, certainly we have seen no trace of it anywhere for all these years, over a quarter of a century, how did it suddenly know that we eight were the most critical spiritual beings to be taken out of circulation? How did it know where we were located? Particularly, where Kallisto was at?"

"Further, it headed after the Guardian and Julie's bunch, but only after we were abducted first. Clearly, those in the Red Desert pose a far more serious threat to our jailors than we did. I am amazed that they are now so able that they could bring down that flying ship! Pretty incredible deed. If I were the jailor, those would have been my first targets, not us."

"What are you suggesting?" asked Emil.

"We have a traitor somewhere on Tarra," Kallisto replied, interrupting me, and getting precisely to her point.

"Either a willing spy for the enemy or an unwilling one," I amended her pronouncement. "I suspect that while I was knocked out by the mantis creature's energy device, it may have learned about those in the Red Desert from me. That makes me an unwilling one, Kallisto. Yet, Tarra holds millions of people. If I were the jailor and had the means to probe minds, still it would take centuries to probe so many to learn about us. Hence, I am inclined to believe, as Kallisto does, that somewhere on Tarra is an alien spy or at least an informer."

"He or she ought to be sought out and eliminated," Kallisto replied.

"Or captured and kept at Isla Roca until they come to their senses," Tonia added.

"That's the first order of business. Now then, the second order must be for us to find some way to defeat the energy devices, which make it impossible for telepathy to occur or for free beings to move through their protective fields. I nearly panicked when I could do neither back there that first day! I swear I will not sleep nights until I can crack this problem, this barrier."

"I agree, Bethany. I felt so awful when I could not reach you after we discovered you were all missing. This has never happened to a telepath!" Rosina concurred.

"The third order of business must be some kind of early warning mechanism whereby we can be alerted to the arrival of more of these mantis creatures on Tarra. Although I don't know that we could have prevented our abductions had we known that a mantis was about, still we would have been on our guard."

"If I had known a mantis was on Tarra," Renzo replied, "the minute I missed you, I would have bet on mantis treachery."

"Yes, but then what Renzo?" Emil pointed out. "We had no idea this dome place existed. You would have only panicked even more."

Renzo sighed knowing that Emil was right. He would have gone insane with panic over my safety. "Well, you have me there. What say we just relax a while and enjoy our wives for the next week or so? There's not much we can do at the moment while we are at sea."

I agreed. "Just be thinking about these three; we will deal with them as soon as we get back. Now then, please refill my teacup, will you dear?"

The brief meeting was over. I had them thinking about what needed to be done. Now, I leaned my head on Renzo's shoulder and sipped my tea. I could and did just relax and enjoy such a simple thing as this. Oh, how I had missed it.

That afternoon, Cedric came over to Alexa, who was standing by the railing with Rene. His arm rested on her shoulder, she had her head on his shoulder. "Sorry to interrupt, Alexa, but I have made an important discovery for you. We have all been utter fools with these boots! I had this grandiose plan on how to remove them back at the estate, probably would have worked too. However, there is a stupidly simple way."

"Out with it man," she teased, though a trifle unwilling to have them removed just yet. Rene enjoyed seeing her well-defined legs.

"The device which shrinks them down to a sealed fit also undoes them completely, without harming the boots. We were always pushing the switch forward, but it also goes backwards, which undoes the shrinkage process perfectly. Would you like me to undo yours now?"

She sighed, but realized that she could still wear them. "Yes, please. I guess that mantis chemical really did block my reasoning powers. I ought to have worked that one out for myself." Five minutes later, the tops of the boots looked like all of the others she'd brought back with her, loose fitting. Rene was about to help her pull them off, when she insisted, "No, let me see if I can get them off by myself. If I can, then I will feel comfortable wearing them when I desire. If I cannot, then you and I will have to agree because I would need your assistance with them." She found that she could easily slip them off now that they were loosened.

"Thank you, thank you, thank you, Cedric!" Alexa exclaimed. "My feet, I have my feet and toes back at last."

"Does this mean that I don't get to dote over you any longer, my love," Rene teased her.

"Oh don't be silly, I love you doting on me! You can dote right now, give me a kiss!" They embraced.

"Ah this feels so good, to have my feet feeling the air once more." She then stood up and ran into a new problem. "Ouch!" I can't seem to put my feet flat on the floor anymore! I have to keep standing on tiptoes! What's happened to my legs?"

"Don't do anything. I'll get Tonia right away!" Cedric dashed off to find Tonia, who was relaxing in Emil's arms in their cabin. "Excuse me, but we need you, Tonia. I've got the boots off of Alexa, but she has a problem with her legs."

A few minutes later, after Tonia pervaded Alexa's legs, she reported her diagnosis. "Well, you wore them so long that your leg muscles have adapted to them. The muscle has shortened on one part of your leg, which is why it won't let your feet go flat. I've no idea how we can fix this. If you force them flat, you could easily damage your legs. Perhaps in time, if you keep stretching them gently, they will stretch back out."

An hour later, we eight women were now tiptoeing about the ship, finally free of the boots. Well sort of, I discovered that it was too painful to do much walking this way. It was far simpler to don the boots when I needed to do any significant walking. Ah well, at least, we now had the use of our feet back. We had a choice. I guess if this was the only permanent result of our narrow escape from the mantis creatures this time, I could live with it. After all, this was a minor inconvenience, not in the same league with losing your arms.

On January 5, 658, the Sleepy Hollow pulled into Velona. Per our request, only our children were there to greet us. They had been without us nearly a half a year, and I wanted our return to be very special for their sakes. Of course, Lilly Ann and the others were there to meet us as well, looking after the many children, who were very excited about seeing their mothers once more.

As Renzo and I walked down the gangplank to the docks, our four came running up to me. Lena carried Danielle so they could get to me faster, while Ben carried little Adrien. As they came rushing up to me, I squatted down to their level so they could hug and hold me. What a joyous reunion! All around me, the other mothers were similarly greeted by their children.

"Oh I like your hair, mommy! It has grown so long," Lena commented.

"You two, my how much you have grown in just six months! Amazing. God, how I have missed you four! Just hold me tightly will you all?" It was a mom-kid bundle for quite some time. Yes, I kissed them repeatedly, until Ben became somewhat embarrassed by my motherly affection.

Then, we walked to the carriages and headed to the estate. "You look good, Bethany," Lilly Ann said as we rode along. "Hair long enough?" she teased me. She knew my fetish for long hair very well. "Those boots are something else. I don't know how you can walk in them, but Rosina has kept us informed. I am sure glad that Cedric was able to work out how to get them off."

"You can say that again. You look good too, Lilly Ann. I'm sorry that your retirement days were so short lived."

"Ah, well, you are back safe and sound. Now we can retire once more," she jested with me.

# Chapter 9 West Reach Uprising

Early October of 657, Bishop Hercule Thopolis of the Church of Jehosanity of West Reach, paced his study in the rectory here in Bregia, Layamon, West Reach. He'd just received the best news ever. The Church's archenemy, the Santi del Dio, was indeed leaderless. All their top commanders had vanished without a trace, rumor had it. "Women leaders, we all knew that spelled their doom," he said to his assistant. "Our illustrious Popes have been predicting the downfall of the Santi for years now, ever since women took over its leadership. Now is the time for action, to spread the Holy Word of God to the heathens along the western side of this isle."

"Should I send for the General?" his aide asked.

"Not yet, let's not be hasty. I should confirm this leader, whom I understand not even has arms, a complete cripple, has indeed deserted her post. Bring me my traveling vestments. I shall pay a call on the Santi fortress at once." He had a scheme in mind to verify the rumors.

A short while later, the portly man, dressed in his sky blue traveling robes with the plain white cross adorning its front and back, walked out of the rectory and headed across Bregia to the Santi stone fortress on the northwestern edge of the city. At the heavy gates, he knocked and announced himself to the gate keeper. "Bishop Thopolis to see Commander Romerez." He heard a flurry of activity behind the gate, just before it open.

A woman soldier, a complete joke as far as the Bishop was concerned, escorted him into the stone tower. At least they build good stone works, he mused as he walked along. She led him into the formal meeting room on the second floor. Plainly furnished, it was a comfortable room, with a large table and numerous chairs. Hector Romerez, the Commander and Judger, was just entering as the Bishop stepped into the room. Lucinda Romerez, his wife, was just in front of him, she was their Communicator. Sue Ellen Leeds, their Healer, was not present.

"Good day, Bishop Thopolos. Please have a seat," Hector, twenty-four years old with blonde hair and blue eyes, said as he adjusted the chair for his wife. "To what do we owe the pleasure of your company? Care for refreshments?"

"Good day Commander. I've just eaten, thank you for offering. I've come to make a request. As you know, it is nearly harvest time in Layamon, and this year, you may have heard that we will be holding a Holy Blessing Ceremony in two weeks to bless the harvest and raise goodwill among men and women of Layamon. In keeping with the spirit of this ceremony and festival, I would like to extend my hand of friendship to your Supreme Commander of the Santi del Dio, Bethany le'Goeur, I believe is her name. It is time that we make peace and learn to work together for the betterment of the people of Layamon. Would you be so kind as to extend our offer to your Commander for me? She would sit at my table at the ceremony as befitting someone of her highest rank. I believe this is a great opportunity for both of us to get to know each other and work out how together we can best serve the people of this land."

"This is wonderful news indeed. Thank you Bishop for extending the offer. I agree, we have been antagonists for far too long. Working together, we can do much for the people of this fine country." Hector was stalling for time. Lucinda had already linked to his mind. *How do I answer him?* he asked his wife.

*It's no secret that Bethany has been abducted. Tell him the truth that she is away on assignment. Ask for a rain check.*

"Perhaps you have not heard the news yet, but Supreme Commander Bethany le'Goeur is temporarily unavailable, away in a distant land on assignment. I beg of you, could we perhaps conduct another joint ceremony, say in the spring, when we expect she may be back?" He'd picked a random date in the future. No one knew if the women could even be rescued, but by then, if Bethany was lost to the Santi, he felt sure that a new Supreme Commander would be appointed.

"I understand fully. Yes, we leaders have so many responsibilities with which to deal. Yes, springtime would be most acceptable, a time for the blessing of a new crop. I look forward to that meeting then. Thank you so much. I must be returning to the Church. I have a High Mass to deliver shortly." He rose and the two men shook hands. The Santi warrior led him back to the gate. As the Bishop walked back to the rectory, he wiped his hand onto his robe, trying to get the heathen touch of his enemy's hand off his.

As he entered, he stopped before the basin of Holy Water. There, he washed his hand, purifying them from the heathen touch. Satisfied he was now clean, he turned around and walked to the military compound. Shortly, he entered the office of General Thaddeus Kellas, the twenty-five year old replacement Holy Paladin General.

"Good day, Bishop," the boyish smile of Thaddeus greeted the older Church official. "What brings you to my office? Tea? Wine, perhaps?"

"Pass. May I sit?"

"But of course. How may I assist our most holy man?"

Hercule thought the younger man was pouring it on rather thickly. "I have just confirmed that the Santi del Dio is, as we thought, completely leaderless. This insane action of putting a total cripple, an armless, helpless woman, as their leader and then surrounding her with more of the same, has indeed led to their downfall. As we speak, they are leaderless over in Velona. Now is the time for you to launch your campaign to bring the Word and Truth of Lord Jehosa to the heathens of Tewdwr, who cannot even speak proper words. You have my blessings for a totally successful campaign."

"This is the best of news. My forces are already in place. We will strike swiftly and accurately. This heathen land will be under our control before the harvest is done. Expect our granaries to be overflowing this fall!"

The Bishop smiled, yes, that would be wonderful. Full granaries would mean he could send some back to the homeland and earn accolades from his Pope. "Keep me posted periodically. May Jehosa guide thy fighting arm." The two men shook hands and the Bishop walked back to his rectory, confident of a very bright future indeed.

"Aides, front and center! The time has come at last!" General Thaddeus called out, scarcely able to contain his enthusiasm. Now finally he could prove his mettle on the battlefield, as his predecessor, Hellas Konas, had. Indeed, Hellas had single handedly wiped out the entire kingdom of Brea, led by the woman who would be king, Lachlan Laird. True, he has died shortly afterwards, but his fame was widespread among the troops. Now Thaddeus would demonstrate once more the true power of the mighty Holy Paladins, an unstoppable force.

His aides filed in and joined him at the large situation map on his office wall. "Our recruitment plans have paid off handsomely. By visiting all of the towns and villages, no matter how small, demonstrating our skill and prowess, we have enticed many young men into the ranks of Holy Paladins. Here we have our ten legions of short bow men," he pointed out a location on the western coast of West Reach, just at the border with Tewdwr, near a ghost town called Cuch Glen. "Here at these four key positions we have arrayed our forty legions of cavalry."

"We know that most of the larger towns lie within twenty miles of the seacoast. I aim to take the entire country, this entire half of West Reach by November at the very latest. Cavalry Group One will sweep wide through the heartland to this northern area, where we know little of the towns. There, they will sweep down to the sea. Group Two arcs and sweeps just south of them. Group Three sweeps up and to the left down to the sea. Group Four and the Archer Group will be with me. We will angle into the heartland and be in position to come to the assistance of any of the three strike groups. Questions?"

"Sir, it was most brilliant of you to have arranged this fall's mock battles at these locations. Conveniently, they are now in position to strike. Well done, Sir."

"That was no accident. I have been planning this for a year now. We've been waiting for the perfect time to strike," General Thaddeus replied.

"Sir, what is so special about right now? We are nearing the fall harvest, is that it?" asked an aide.

Thaddeus laughed, "That's why you are only an aide." The man's face reddened. "No, the time is right because our archenemy, the Santi del Dio, is currently leaderless; their joke of a Supreme Commander, this armless, helpless woman, has deserted her post and no one can apparently find her. Their leadership ranks are in complete disarray. They will be unable to counter any move that we make. In addition, the last of the fighters have now gotten their chain mail. We are now as invincible as the best of the Santi used to be so many years ago when they defeated our illustrious Emperor Justinian in Barcella."

"Then it is true, these rumors that their leaders are hopeless cripples, women without arms?" another aide asked. "It shows you just how stupid these Santi really are. A woman leader is like a shaft of wheat in the wind; she goes whichever way the wind blows. Yet, armless, that is the absolute height of folly! What's she going to do to us on the battlefield, spit on us?" Several laughed.

Another aide joked, "Now, Herman, she's going to kick you in the crotch!" Their laughter continued unabated, as more jokes were bantered about the room.

"Okay, we take my last private legion and leave tonight, under the cover of darkness," the General ordered. "I do not want to be seen by the Santi in their tower, though I shouldn't be worried about them any longer. Yet, prudence I will follow. Now get to work on the final preparations. Pack your bags. See you at the stables around midnight."

Lucinda asked Hector, "Do you think the Bishop was serious? I mean about working with us?"

"Not a chance in their Hell! Look, we know that he is just a puppet of the Pope in distant Megalos. The Pope pulls all of the strings. If the Pope actually wanted to mend his fences, he would contact the Supreme Commander directly, just as Jenna Rose Wilkins did with the Pope so many years ago. No, this Bishop knew that Bethany has disappeared. He had an entirely different purpose in coming here than what he said."

"Well, perhaps he wanted us to come out and say that Bethany and the others are missing," she replied, curling her tresses in her fingers.

"That would be the obvious; we were forced to outright say so. Yet, why would he want to know for sure that Bethany is gone?"

"Well, their General has called for field training exercises near the border with Tewdwr this fall. We've had many reports of their gatherings along the border for the past few weeks," she said thoughtfully.

"If they are planning an attack, it must be against Tewdwr. His forces are totally out of position to go after the Highlands and Fergus. Yet, why Tewdwr? They do not have any armies, simple fishermen for the most part, though some tend sheep and grain crops further inland. Why Tewdwr? They have little of any real value there, hardly any gold at all. Even gemstones are a rarity there."

"I will alert our garrison here to keep a sharp lookout for any movement of the General and his staff. That will be a dead giveaway that something is up, though it may be he will only be conducting the supposed field exercises," Hector added.

"I'll let Paulette know at headquarters; she can let Lilly Ann know. Perhaps they will be able to tell us what they want us to do, dear."

"Good idea." He left to meet with all of the Santi officers in the fortress.

"Oh good grief!" exclaimed Lilly Ann. "Haven't we got enough to worry about trying to rescue Bethany? Damn those Unholy Paladins anyway."

"Yes, but what are we going to do about it?" Paulette asked. "Lucinda wants some orders."

"Tell her we will get back to her as soon as we can. I guess we should bother Bethany about this. It is her call, though she has more than enough problems of her own."

That evening, Paulette had her nightly contact with me, as I reported in our status to her. *Lucinda says that in all likelihood, the Holy Paladins of Layamon are about to attack all of Tewdwr. Lilly Ann wants to know what you wish her to do about it? We don't know that they will be attacking for sure yet, possibly within a week or so.*

I felt more helpless than normal, yet I kept this information from the other seven women. We had our own horrid situation to handle. I needed their full attention on our survival. *Okay, let's play it smart. Mobilize the entire Strike Force One. Send them to Tewdwr. See if Elona will loan us some carracks. If so, the only port that could possible handle such deep draft ships is Dwyr way up in the northern part of Tewdwr. Tell everyone to keep their movement a secret, that this is a mobilization training exercise, at least until we know that Tewdwr is under attack.*

*Who will command them? Plot their strategy? I'm not qualified to do so, Bethany.*

*Let's leave the entire campaign up the General Lem. It will be his big test. Can our Strike Force operate successfully without constant headquarters oversight? Besides, we aren't in any position to guide them. I've my own problems to face here. Tell Lucinda to try everything they can to find out if the General there is planning to attack Tewdwr. Let Lem have everything he may ask for, okay?*

*Thanks for relieving me of this additional burden, Bethany. I'll see to it. Bye.*

General Lem walked into the meeting room at our estate. He knew something was up; he'd seldom been called directly here, never when his Supreme Commander was missing. Perhaps it had something to do with her rescue.

"General Lem," Lilly Ann began, wiping her hands through her greying hair, "it seems that General Thaddeus Kellas is about to attack

Tewdwr. Hector suspects that he has one thousand short bowmen and four thousand cavalrymen. He says that all are chain mail clad. They are stationed along the Layamon-Tewdwr border. We don't know yet if they are going to invade, but Bethany has issued you your orders, Lem. You are to mobilize the entire Strike Force One. Elona is loaning us a number of the new carracks, so they can transport you over there. Bethany wants you to keep this whole movement as secret as possible, call it a field training exercise or some such."

"Wow! I had no idea they were going to begin fighting once more. Who's going to be issuing the orders in Bethany's absence?"

"You are. Bethany has given you carte-blanche to do whatever you need to stop them. Just keep us here at headquarters informed, and we'll send you what supplies you ask for. Congratulations General, you are now the one in power." He smiled.

"Supreme Commander Bethany must have a tremendous faith in my leadership to leave the entire operation to me! How is she doing? Holding up? How's the rescue operation going?"

"She and the others are alive and doing as well as may be expected, under the circumstances. The rescue is well underway. We don't know how much time you may have. Oh yes, Bethany said that you will need to disembark in Dwyr. She says that is the only deep-water port that the carracks can use. Keep us posted, General." He saluted and raced back to begin his plans.

Two nights later, Hector paced his nearly empty meeting room. Lucinda watched him pace around for an hour, though she said nothing. She knew that he was working out something important. They'd received word from Paulette that Bethany had ordered out the entire strike force. Still something was worrying her husband.

"Nearly all the soldiers are gone, dear. I've decided to sneak into the general's office and see if I can find any clues about what his ultimate plans might be. Lem is going to need all the information I can find. Time is so very short."

"Well, take a bunch of our forces with you, dear."

"No, that will only draw attention to me. I will go alone. I do not want anyone there to know about it. If I find anything useful and they know we found out, they would only change their plans. It must be a secret. I'll use extreme caution, my dear. Please don't worry."

"Don't worry you say? Ha! I'll be biting my nails until you are back! However, I do see your point. Just do be careful. I love you." They kissed and he headed to his room to change.

Around midnight, a man wearing dark clothing snuck through the deserted streets of Bregia. A careful watch allowed him to bypass the routine patrols of the night watch soldiers, who always followed the same path through the town. The shadowy form slipped over the low fence, which surrounded the army barracks, here in the southeast section of the port city. From earlier spy sessions, he knew the building in which the general held his strategy meetings with his aides. A lone sentry stood guard at the main door.

He chanted a brief spell, and the guard dozed off, asleep while on duty. Carefully, the shadowy form picked the lock on the door and slipped inside. Another chant later, and a faint blue light illuminated the entrance room. Now the form had to search in earnest, since he didn't know where the main meeting room was located. A quarter of an hour later, Hector found the meeting room. On the wall was a large map of West Reach. He moved his light close to the map and stared at it. "Thank you General Thaddeus for showing me your entire campaign strategy!" he said to himself. The great arcs showed their precise intended troop movements. Quickly, he memorized the map and made his exit, going as silently as possible, pausing only to relock the door.

"Mind Link me to Paulette and then have her get me linked to General Lem! I have their entire battle plans in my mind now. The fool of a general left them in plain sight on his wall!"

"We've got a serious problem. The attack will begin in a couple of days, and we will need a couple of weeks to mobilize and get to Dwyr," Lem reported to Lilly Ann, the next day.

"Could Fergus d'Aine and his army help in some way?" she tossed out. He was the only one she could think of on such short notice. Field battles were out of her area of expertise.

"Yes, can you put me in touch with him? If so, let me work via our Field Communicator directly with him, please."

"You got it. I'll have Paulette make the contacts. Will noon be an acceptable hook up time?"

At noon, General Lem and King Fergus d'Aine were Mind Linked, via their Communicators. After explaining all that was about to happen, Lem asked, *Is there any way you can stall them a couple weeks until we get fully fielded up around Dwyr?*

*What if my thousand cavalrymen sweep down from the Highlands, laddie, and come arcing up into the heartland of Tewdwr, right where they are passing? I can harry them and perhaps pull them off their intended targets long enough for the Strike Force to get prepared.*

*Just don't put your army at risk, please. This would be immensely helpful. What good is the Strike Force, if we arrive long after the invasion is done? Have our Communicators stay in touch. Again, thank you, King Fergus.*

Unfortunately, I only have second hand accounts of this whole situation. Thus, I will merely summarize that of which I am fairly confident. For two weeks, King Fergus raided far out onto the central green plains of Tewdwr, harrying the Holy Paladins. This continued action forced at least two of the enemy cavalry groups to pull back from their intended towns and give chase to the forces of King Fergus, who continually eluded any actual stand upon the battlefield.

After two weeks of chasing armies, General Thaddeus realized that if he were going to force King Fergus to do battle, he would have to abandon his plans of conquest, putting all four groups into play to corner King Fergus. This, he was reluctant to do.

Two weeks was just what General Lem needed to get our Strike Force One mobilized, loaded, transported, and unloaded around the northwest town of Dwyr. I didn't actually see what our forces looked like until long after the battle. In order to support the heavier weight of the plate mail, heavier horses were acquired and trained. Many of these horses were also given chain mail protection, though only those who would actually be at the head of a charging line. We had not yet made enough horse armor to outfit all our force. Five thousand in our force formed into their units on the plains of Dwyr. One thousand longbow men and women rode in the rear. One thousand chain mail light but fast cavalry split to either flank of Lem's main force. Three thousand of our plate mail men formed into a long frontal attack line.

Lem's force then swept down the central plains of Tewdwr, engaging the forces of General Thaddeus wherever they were found. A week after Lem began pressing our forces to the south, Thaddeus realized that King Fergus had only been stalling him from his objectives, while the Santi heavy forces appeared as if from nowhere! Undaunted, Thaddeus retreated, pulling all of his forces into a solid battle line, determined to rid West Reach of our forces. He placed his archers behind his main lines, just as we did.

On November 7, somewhere in the central rolling grasslands of Tewdwr, the two forces met. The short bows of the Holy Paladins were nearly ineffective, save for wounding a number of horses; their arrows bounced off the plate mail. Our longbows were more effective, but only when the enemy lines were close to ours. Archers shot over the heads of the front line combatants, striking those coming up to engage us. Here, they were effective.

The superiority of the plate mail over chain mail became apparent when the battle was over. Only one thousand of the Holy Paladin forces limped back to Bregia that fall. General Thaddeus was not among them, dying at the hands of General Lem himself. We had five hundred fifty-nine wounded men, but only six lost their lives. The tin men proved their worth that day. They could wander the battlefield at will with little danger of being harmed. However, a good deal of effort was required to slay the enemy in chain mail. Hence, the battle raged all that day.

On December 5, the combined mayors of the six largest cities in Tewdwr formally requested a permanent Santi presence in Tewdwr. General Lem, acting on the authority granted him by me, via Lilly Ann, received permission to construct a series of Santi fortresses along the southern border with Layamon. The concept was to ensure that these Holy Paladins could never again invade Tewdwr, who still had no army of its own.

By the time of my return, the wounded men had been brought back to Mont Blanc to recover, while General Lem positioned his forces long the southern border and had identified seven key sites where the series of interlocking fortresses should be built. Planners had been dispatched there and already the long, laborious construction projects had begun. The ghost town of Cuch Glen became the Santi port fortress. Strange how things have developed around that small fishing village where my Ket Bethany body had been born.

While the results were excellent, the campaign, run entirely without coordination and leadership from the top of our organization, left things in a mess. Supplies went awry, critical items ended up at the wrong locations. Other locales, in meeting the needed requests, were then overly short themselves as the winter arrived. In short, when we returned home, we had a supply debacle on our hands. I appreciated what my mother, Jenna, had been doing all these years even more than before!

# Chapter 10 Organizational Changes

January 10, 658, the complete headquarters group met for the first time since our abduction. Renzo had explained to me that the Guardian of the Anuir wanted me to send someone from our group down to the Red Desert for some time. He had promised to help set that spiritual being free. We would then have one very able person at headquarters. The question was who should I send?

All were more than worthy; all were most deserving. I could not send one of the seven off without sending along her husband and children, for that would be very unfair to him and the kids. We had only been back a few days, and I wanted to send Enyo as my first choice, but we quickly realized that she would not want to go off and leave all these alien objects. Already, she was attempting to learn how many operated. She would see this more as punishment, not the greatest gift imaginable.

"But I need to work on the organization," Linda replied, when I asked her if she would go to the Red Desert for a time.

"I'll have Alexa, Kallisto, and Hank fill your boots. This is the greatest gift that I can possibly bestow. When you come back, you will be unimaginably more able to help us all. Please, will you do it? I will send Chaucer and your children along as well. I don't know if they will get any training or not, but I refuse to have you all parted. Please say yes," I begged her.

"We've never been parted," she began, and then suddenly stopped short. "Duh, that is a dumb thing to say. Yes, of course, I will go, as long as my family comes with me. Thank you, Bethany. I will do my best." We hugged, resting our heads on each other's shoulders for a time. Two days later, they were packed and on their way, and Captain Henry and Natale took them to Julie's village in the Sleepy Hollow.

As we met at the meeting, I announced that Kallisto, Hank, and Alexa were now officially taking over Linda's position as Judger. "You are charged with working out a re-organization of the Santi. We are too big for one person to run everything. I do not know how mom ever did it."

"Rosina, I want you to work with Paulette. She is attempting to find a way to use telepathy when the mantis devices are trying to prevent it. Paulette has been studying it while we were being rescued and has some ideas about how it may be done."

"Sure thing," she replied. "Not being able to communicate made me so utterly blind to all of you that I couldn't stand it."

"Renzo, you and I are going to see how we can move through the blocking action of these same devices. Unable to get out of the dome was awful. I do not want any of us to become trapped like that again."

"Benet and Michelle, you are to see if you can work out just how the mantis creature found us eight and where the creature came from in the first place. Emil and Tonia will join you, once they return from Mont Blanc, where they have gone to lend a hand with all the healing of our strike force fighters."

"But what about this incredible backlog mess? Who is going to deal with that?" asked Cedric?

I grinned, "You my fine young lad. You deal with it, please." He feigned dying, as if I had stabbed him in the heart. We all laughed.

"Okay, gang, we will meet each morning as usual to compare notes and ideas. Let's get busy. Who knows when the next mantis will appear?"

We dispersed, Renzo and I headed to our little bungalow, where we would begin our experiments. My heels clicked away, though my steps were small. Renzo had to keep himself from out pacing me. Yes, my ankles and calves ached something awful when I tried walking barefoot. Right now, I didn't want to deal with that. The fear of another mantis abduction was too real.

"What's the first thing we try?" he asked once we were in our small home.

"You are going to cut my hair, please, butt length. I keep stepping on it, sitting on it."

"But I love it long like this," he lovingly and sincerely complained.

"If I had hands with which to properly deal with it, I would leave it long like this. I know; it is nearly sacrilege for me to cut my hair. Yet, it is just too long for me to manage without arms. Please, Renzo?"

"Okay, you have enough problems with having to still wear those boots. I'll do it. Only if you ever want it to grow longer, I promise to take proper care of it for you." I felt rather sick as I watched nearly two feet of my blonde hair fall onto the floor. Yet, I knew it had to be done. I just could not manage it as I was.

An hour later, we sat down on our bed. "Okay, you turn it on, but be ready to turn it off if we get suddenly zapped or something." I laid down so that I wouldn't fall down if the energy blast somehow hit me.

He clicked it on; the device made a low-pitched humming sound. Neither of us felt anything. Slowly he and I rose up into the air above our bodies. Soon we found the energy barrier, a sphere, some fifty feet centered on the device in his hands. I made my body say, "Okay, now let's experiment. We need to find a way to get through this energy wall."

We worked on it until lunch, getting nowhere at all. After having lunch with our children, we were back at it most of the afternoon. An hour before supper, we gave up for the day. I needed to get completely away from the problem. We went into our private Modified Torque Ball arena, back of our bedroom.

This had always been our favorite game to play with each other. A pair of white lines marked the in play area on the wall facing us. The objective was to kick the ball with some part of your body onto the wall between the two lines. The other player had to do the same before the ball bounced on the floor for the second time. Usually, it is played using one's hands, however, after the mantis creature had eaten my arms, we lowered the line and added the top line so that I could more readily use my feet in place of my hands.

Now, however, we faced an even greater challenge for me. In these heels, how could I possibly play? We tried, but it was dismal. I had no speed to move around the court. Only when I took the boots off could I manage a somewhat better game. However, it was very tiring, continually moving around on my toes. When we finished at suppertime, Renzo slid my boots back on my feet. "Gosh, they feel like heaven now. I can see that getting readjusted to not wearing them is going to be a major problem. Let's see how kick ball goes with the kids after supper; perhaps that will be more doable for me right now."

"Okay, dear, you are on. Of course, I will have Lena and Ben go after you," he teased me.

As everyone finished supper, I made an announcement to all, "From now on, after supper, I will be playing kick ball out front with all the children who want to play, as well as all the grownups who want some fun as well. Mom always did this for the children, and I am going to follow her example. So kids, let's play ball!"

"But you are so slow, mom!" Lena sympathized for me. "You walk so slowly in those boots."

"Oh, I suspect that won't make a huge difference, but we shall see. Dad says you are all going to gang up on me tonight?"

She giggled, "You bet. You can't run at all, so we are going to get you good!" she declared, forgetting about my boot problem. Outside, some fifty children gathered along with Renzo. I was surprised to see that Enyo, Aella, Natasa, Alexa, and Kallisto came out to join us as well.

"If you can manage, then so can I," declared Alexa. "Besides if I am going to market these boots, I need to prove that you can still do just about anything you want while wearing them. Well, excepting perhaps running. How do we play? I sort of forgot the rules."

Hundreds of us were laughing our heads off as dark fell. From those who could barely walk to us grownups, everyone had fun. We women discovered that with our pointed toes, we could deliver a very powerful kick; all the force of our swing was concentrated in a tiny point, sending the ball fast and hard. In fact, I knocked Renzo flat on his back twice, much to the yelling and cheering of the kids. Lena's last comment as we panted for breath walking back to our bungalow was simply, "Wicked mom, you are wicked out there! You got dad good! I'm going to have to get me a pair of those boots when my feet get bigger!"

After a long and frustrating week of experimentation, Rosina, Paulette, Renzo, and I had made a significant discovery. The devices were outputting an energy field of a particular pattern of oscillation or frequency. Rosina made the break through comment, "Perhaps we just need to somehow alter the frequency that we are somehow using for our communications."

Another week later, and both Communicators were teaching me how to slide between the frequencies of the telepathy blocker! Now we could get through no matter what. I had those two teach all our other many Communicators just how this was done. I wanted this knowledge and skill spread far and wide! Never again would one of our Communicators ever be stopped by these devices of our enemy!

Using the same principle, Renzo and I were also able to break through the energy barrier as well! We then set about drilling all the others here who could move about outside of their bodies. I did not want any of them to be trapped either. By the first week in February, we had defeated this weapon of our enemy, and I could finally relax.

On the betrayer of us women front, Michelle made a key observation. The first reported sightings had been in Wanakan. Dutifully, she and Benet had sent messages to our Communicators there for more information. During these two weeks, there was little for them to do until they heard back, so they helped Cedric with the daily operational details, which by now were in shambles.

On March 1, the two received back a rather large amount of information, which they shifted through for several days, before making a formal report at our morning's meeting. Benet said, "I will let Michelle brief you, since it was largely her observations, which have led us to the answer."

Michelle, a painter, was not used to addressing us as equals, and she was somewhat ill at ease and embarrassed at first. As she got into the details, though, it left her. "You see, the first sightings were in Wanakan. We asked for more specific details. Ten people there agree that when they first saw the strange object flying overhead at night, it came in this direction." She pointed on the map. "Our conclusion or speculation rather, is that it came from that location there." Michelle pointed to the spots on the western side of the peanut continent to which we had not yet gotten to explore. Those locations were not made using the same symbols as all of the other mantis secret bases had been. At the time, we thought these might not be important. Now, however, we looked at these two sites in a new light. One was mantis; one was Grey Creature.

"What is really bothering us," Michelle continued, pushing back her hair, which had flopped onto her face while she was pointing on the map, "is the fact that both of the two Wanakan women who lost both their arms and legs died that same night! We thought that very strange indeed. So we had the Communicator there in Wanakan see if she could locate one of the two spiritual beings. She found one who had already acquired a new baby body. She checked and sure enough, that night the mantis creature made some kind of mind contact with her. It forced out of her, who had been there and learned about you, Bethany. I believe that the mantis found out about us from those poor women. It then killed her body, for which the woman was grateful."

Benet added a little more, which we all found exceedingly scary. "We learned that both women had been cremated and their ashes scattered at the base of the Sun God Temple. I was wondering how this mantis creature could so quickly find these women. I had the Santi there go examine the ashes or what was left. They found a tiny bluish object, two of them actually. Bethany, I am wondering if the mantis creature has left one of these bluish things inside your body after it ate your arms. If so, it might be how the creature can so readily find you."

I felt sick, so did several others in the room. "We should draw up a list of all those who have lost appendages from the mantis creatures," I ordered. Rosina began making the extensive list. When in doubt, add the person to the list, became her motto.

A week later, Emil and Tonia returned from Mont Blanc. After briefing them fully, I took Tonia with me and went into our bungalow and laid down on my bed. "Okay, Tonia, I want you to go over my entire body. We suspect there is a tiny blue thing somewhere inside my body. I need to you to first find out if it is there and secondly find a way to remove it, please!"

She looked very pale, but she relaxed, and I soon felt her moving into my body. How long she observed, I don't know, but it seemed ages! I was terrified that she would find such a thing; yet I would be relieved if she did, for that would explain many things. In fact, she spent two hours studying my body diligently. Finally, I felt her moving out of my body and back behind her head.

She sighed, "You are right, Bethany, there is something foreign inside you. It's very small and lodged inside your belly. I will have to cut you open to get to it. However, I found out something else, Bethany. I don't know how to tell you this. It's awful."

I sighed. What could be worse I wondered. "Just tell me outright, please."

"All those chemicals that you ingested while you were imprisoned, they have made you infertile. Bethany, you won't be able to have any more children! How awful!"

That hit me hard. I love kids. "Well, I have four, so I guess that will have to be all. I wondered why I was not having my monthly cycles. I thought I might be with child again, but I was not getting any bigger. I wonder if the others are also infertile now. Well, one problem at a time. When can you operate? I want that thing out of me as soon as possible."

"I'll do it in the morning, Bethany. Tonight, don't eat much for supper. I think I will use the anesthesia that we got from Wanakan, maybe I won't need to knock you completely out. We'll see. Should I examine the others now?"

"Yes, Rosina has the lengthy list. Start with the other seven, well, six. Linda is down in the Red Desert by now. We'll have to do her when she gets back."

Of our group, only Kallisto had a thing inside her body. Those from the House of Right had their arms removed by the men who carried on after the mantis had left. However, the older members from that house would likely have one of these things inside them. They were on the extensive list to check out. On the positive side, the other six were still able to bear children. I must have become infertile because of that wild overexposure to the chemicals when I disconnected the cylinder.

With a bit of anxiety, I walked into the infirmary the next morning. Tonia was already there, making her last minute preparations. "Hi, I am going to try to use the stuff we got from Teyacapan. If it doesn't work well enough, I'll use other means. I am hoping to find this thing easily."

"What do you want me to do?"

"Take off your dress and lie down, belly up please. Here, I'll help you; it will be quicker."

She felt around on my right side for a bit. "I'm going to have another look and see if I can pin point it more precisely before I start," she sounded encouraging. She made a small mark on my belly. Next, using one of the pots of anesthesia we had brought back from Wanakan, she pinpricked the area, which quickly felt quite numb. In fact, I didn't feel the knife cutting into my skin.

"Oh, I feel that, bit more please!" I called out; obviously, it was only numbing what it was in contact with, so she added more as she went along.

"Ah, I see it, Bethany. Just a little longer. Got it. Now to sew you back up." I felt her tiny needle pricks as she stitched up the small wound. "Here, take a look, I made the tiniest of incisions. At most, you will only have a tiny scar there." She was right; it was only an inch long. Carefully, she put healing salves on it and then a small bandage.

"Here is the alien device," she said. "It sure is tiny." I stared at the thing, barely an eighth of an inch square and a sliver in thickness. "Amazing that something this tiny can be used to find your body out of the millions here on Tarra."

She helped me dress and adjusted my hair for me. "On your way out, send in Kallisto, please." Kallisto looked at me as I came out; she was more than a little afraid.

"It barely hurt at all, very tiny cut, only an inch. Tonia is an expert at this," I gave her encouragement. I chose to wait outside for her. A half hour later, Kallisto came out to join me.

"I can't believe it was that small! How do we destroy them?" she asked.

Just then, Alexa arrived to see how we were doing. "Gosh, you are both done so quickly? Did she get the things out of you? Can I see them?" We three headed back inside.

"They are lying there," Tonia pointed to the two blue objects. "How are we going to destroy them?"

"Well, fire won't do the job, the Communicators over in Wanakan proved that, the two devices inside of the two women who were cremated were undamaged by the fire," I pointed out.

"Can I try to see if I can destroy them?" asked an eager Alexa. Kallisto and I grinned at each other, and I told her she could try, figuring I would have to get Renzo to figure out something.

We watched as she used her nose to move one of them off the table, allowing it to fall to the stone floor. Carefully, she positioned the spike from her right boot heel squarely over the blue object. "Da ta!" she said as she stepped down hard on her heel and twisted her ankle from side to side. We heard a distinct crunching sound. When she moved her boot, the blue device was smashed into many tiny bits.

"Ironically, their own boots destroyed their tracking devices," Alexa said, doing the same to the second one. "These heels have their uses!" We three grinned.

Tonia said, "Okay, I believe I have my work cut out for me." Again, we all chuckled. We thanked her and headed to the morning meeting. During the next three weeks, Tonia removed several hundred of these devices, all dutifully crushed by Alexa, who was enjoying the new use for her heels. I also contacted Julie and told her about the likelihood that one was inside of Linda. The next day she reported that there was and that it had been eliminated; I didn't ask how they did it, however.

Next, I had to know what was at these other two, as yet unexplored, sites on the far side of the peanut continent. We debated this issue for several days. All agreed on one point: some or all of the Explorers Circle should make the trip in the Sleepy Hollow. In the end, I had to make the final decision. Considering the mess that the headquarters operation was currently facing, I decided to send Captain Henry and Natale, of course, with Emil and Tonia, Benet and Michelle, and Rosina and Cedric to do the exploration once there.

Renzo and I would stay behind and try to run the organization. He and I felt really awful as we watched our caravel slowly tack out of Velona on March 21, 658. Our dear friends were off on another voyage of exploration, and we had to stay behind. Yet, we both knew that if they ran into any trouble at all, we could instantly be where they were located and lend a hand. He and I could move around Tarra at will and use our spells there.

"You are going to have to play a lot of ball with me to make up for keeping us both behind here," Renzo stated, but soon his attempt to make me feel guilty failed and we ended up in a loving embrace.

Back at the estate, I faced a new minor difficulty. Always before, we bunked four of the armless women either together or in close by so that we could aid each other in daily life chores. With Linda and Natale both gone, I only had Mireio. Since the cottages of the others were now not in use, I asked Alexa and Kallisto to move their families temporarily into two of the vacated cottages so that we four could manage our daily chores, like brushing our hair, making our beds, picking up after our many children — all the usual little things those with arms take for granted.

Finally on March 15, Alexa proudly announced their grand re-organizational plans for the Santi del Dio. Hank carried in their piles of papers, while the two women walked in standing tall — our heels now help with this detail. "We've done it. Wait until you see what we have here," Alexa said excitedly. "As Enyo is so fond of saying, the world has many hands but so few ideas. Well, we've solved that one." Even Kallisto was grinning ear to ear.

"Aye, we've done it," she added.

"Yes, broken my back carrying all these papers," Hank teased his wife. Yet, he had a hand in all this as well. I had placed my faith in three Judgers for this re-organization. If they could not find a way to run this vast organization of Santi, then we were doomed; we'd become far too large for one person to manage, yet alone cope.

Hank said, "Alexa, will you begin the explanation? After all, it was you who had the major breakthrough that allowed all of this to develop." Hank always gave each person full credit for what they had done.

Alexa began, "Well, our current organization has all of these titles, like Supreme Commander, Commander, General, and so forth. Yet, in reality, the organization doesn't work that way. What is an organization? I asked myself and found the answer to be a collection of people working together for some common purpose or goal. It is people and people communicate to people to get things accomplished. The key is communication. Yet communication must go between two people, not two titles. So what we are looking at here is people and the tasks that they perform, not titles."

"Next, we examined just what those major tasks that are being done were. We found a complete disarray of those and had to back off from what we have now and ask ourselves to start to build the organization up from scratch. This was my breakthrough; before I had it, we spent weeks wallowing in the mess we have currently, getting nowhere."

"Putting our heads together, we came up with seven large scale activities that an organization must have in operation. We are calling these Groups for want of a better name at this time. The first Group is responsible for creating and populating the remainder of the organization, the hiring, the training, the handling of grievances, the handling of communications, and the making inspections to see if things are running properly. We call it the Establishment Group."

"Next, with an organization there, we must acquire new shipping contracts, for example, from our existing clientele. This we are calling our Marketing Group. Their tasks include advertising to our clientele about what services we can provide, seeking out what they currently need from us, and signing contracts for services. Next, this leads to a Treasury Group, who handle the incoming funds, pays our expenses, and keeps track of all the things that we own and acquires the materials that we need."

"The largest group is, of course, the Production Group. Here is where we must really break the things the Santi do down into key subgroups. We have the Attack Subgroup, the Fortress Defense Subgroup, the Shipping Subgroup, the Warehouse Subgroup, the Constructions Subgroup, the Healing Subgroup, the Archives and Museum Subgroup, the Education and Retraining Subgroup, the Weapons and Armor Construction Subgroup, and the Research and Development Subgroup. I never knew that we had so many different things going on until we worked this all out."

"Then, since things can go wrong, we need a Corrections Group to monitor what is produced and to correct things that have gone astray. Our Explorers Circle in finding new lands has led us to add a new group, the Outreach Group, whose task is to open up new markets for our services. Finally, to provide the overall coordination, advance planning, and the routine maintenance of our facilities, we propose the Headquarters Group, which is where we all fit into the scheme. What do you all think of this?" Alexa ended, with a huge smile on her face. She waved her head to throw her errant locks back over her shoulders.

"If I had arms, I'd hug you all!" I exclaimed. We did our usual bump hug instead. "Alexa, Kallisto, Hank, this is just fabulous. What a giant step forward! No wonder we have been completely swamped here, we're trying to run everything ourselves!"

"Oh, it gets even better," Kallisto added, "we've broken all of these down into their logical working subgroups as well. You see, the executives, we folks here at headquarters, would only need to chat with the six main Group leaders to know what was happening. The Group leaders would then issue the necessary orders and so on to the subgroups below them, and so on down the line."

She went on, "We expect a large volume of communications or dispatches to go up and down with a group, you see, as they work on accomplishing their goals and tasks. However, say an armorer needs more iron ore, he sends his request up the lines to his Subgroup Leader, who okays it and sends it on up to the Production Group Leader, who okays it and sends it on over to the Treasury Group Leader, who okays it and sends it down to the Materials Acquisition Subgroup, who then knows that it is okay to go acquire the iron ore, because it has been okayed by all the relevant leaders."

Kallisto ended by saying, "Now those of you at the top of the organization are no longer going to be swamped with all the details. They will be handled by those in the appropriate Groups. Isn't this is the greatest organizational setup?" Yes, we all totally agreed with her.

Hank added, "Once we finalize this, we need to setup the operational posts and assign personnel to man them. Each member of the organization should be given a copy of this chart, and we should drill them all on how this organization will now operate. Vastly smoother, I will lay odds on that! The more we three have worked on this new scheme, the better we like it and the more problems of organization it solves. Personally, I want to thank Alexa and Kallisto, because they were the ones who invented the overall plan. It's incredible. Had this been in operation when you were abducted, you would have returned to a still well-running organization!"

Alexa continued her description, "You see, in the Establishment Group, one subgroup, the Procurement Subgroup, is in charge of hiring new personnel. The Communications Subgroup handles the delivery of all communications within the Santi and to the outer world, while the Inspections Subgroup handles making inspections to see how all the groups are working, and it handles the whole Isla Roca system for reforming those who harm more than they help. It all works out very nicely."

"Well, then, let's set about getting people appointed to these new positions and get it up and running!" I declared with a passion.

"Alexa, how would you like to be the first Establishment Group Leader?" She was thrilled. Kallisto volunteered to take on the Inspections Subgroup Leader, since she was good a spotting things that were right and wrong. Hank wanted to be in charge of the Procurement Subgroup, so that we got the right people for the right job. Enyo accepted the position of Research and Development Subgroup Leader; this was her passion. Later, Natale took on the position of Archives and Museum Subgroup Leader, while Captain Henry took on the Shipping Subgroup Leader position.

Slowly, but surely, our new organizational methods began to be implemented across our far-flung enterprises. Once one of our members fully understood the new operational methods, they soon swore by it. Problems were being solved right and left just by having the proper system established. By the end of the year, the Santi del Dio organization was running like a nicely trimmed caravel. Production problems were quickly isolated and remedied in a timely manner, something that had always been a mess to fix.

Even more importantly for me, as the Headquarters Group Leader, I now did not have to worry about thousands of minor details. These were worked out by the Subgroup and Group Leaders. I only had to work on large-scale plans and goals, though at any time I could go and inspect any portion of our organization. Now I could just be the leader! No longer were we in Headquarters totally overworked. Fabulous.

Even more interesting, as the years went by, Alexa began having other companies asking her about our methods and how they could be applied to their business. The first of these was the closely associated Laird Foundation for the Arts, which was also growing beyond easy means for one person to control everything. Alexa spent the early months of 659 helping them rework their own organization.

In December of 658, the Explorers Circle made their final report on the two unexplored site on the peanut continent. They had stopped for resupply at the southernmost city of Konstantin, Kostya. From there, they sailed up the western coast, discovering some smaller civilizations, which they ignored this trip. Once they arrived off the coast from the two sites, it took them another three months to hike up into the mountains to reach the two sites, which were about five thousand feet above sea level. Both sites were within a few miles of each other, strange since the mantis and Grey Creatures were enemies.

At both sites, Emil and the others found nothing at all. Well, nothing resembling any kind of city, base camp, or facilities. Rather they found strange markings on the landscape, which Rosina viewed from high above. She sent back mental images of any number of strange pictures sketched into the dry ground of this high plain. When they inspected these etched lines, they found that the soil had been removed, revealing a lighter soil beneath. Thus, the strange images would only be visible from high in the sky, which added credence to these aliens using their flying crafts.

These sites were both remote and uninhabited. The nearest small settlement lay down near the coast, a fishing village, some hundred miles away. Yes, the locals did tell Natale about seeing strange lights and flying objects high upon the mountain plains, but they did not appear very often. The last reported sightings coincided shortly before our abductions.

The only thing that I could conclude was that these spots must somehow be the arrival points on Tarra for the aliens. However, they certainly did not spend any time there.

Captain Henry received permission to make contact with some of these smaller coastal villages on the return trip. Hence, I updated their approximate return date as being sometime in the summer of 659. Yes, I really missed all my friends and looked forward to their return.

One final note, by the end of the year, by working with my legs and feet some each day, I was finally able to wear normal shoes once again. All seven of us finally were not dependent upon these alien boots. However, Alexa still loved hers and had sold a few pairs to her close friends.

Now she had some others studying them, in an attempt to make similar boots to mass market. While she knew that they would not be anywhere the same quality nor have quite the remarkable properties as ours, she wanted to develop boots as comparable as possible. Then, she would begin her mass sales. I was quite surprised to hear so many other women commenting how they loved our boots and how they looked on us. They wanted a pair to wear to dances and other formal gatherings. Yes, they certainly did attract attention.

# Chapter 11 A Strange Visitor

On October 20, 658, our day Gatekeeper, Helen, came to find me. "Commander, an unusual man is at the main gate asking to see you. He called you Bethany Rose Weston. Besides his rough appearance, he doesn't know that you have been married for years now. I thought all this rather unusual and have him waiting at the gate, under watch of course. Your orders?"

"Have you ever seen him her before?"

"No. He looks as bad as he smells."

"Hum, perhaps I should come with you to the gate. We don't need an unsavory man wandering around the estate grounds." Renzo was off doing something, so I decided just to go myself. Helen and I walked down the half mile of cobblestone driveway that led from the manor house to our main gate. I was still wearing my boots and had to walk slowly. I did have Helen throw a cloak over my shoulders to ward off the late fall chill.

"Your boots do look beautiful," Helen commented. "Are they hard to walk in or wear? I've been meaning to ask Alexa about them. She's been getting a lot of requests from many women wanting to get a similar pair." We chatted about boots all the way to the gate, where I saw three other guards facing someone, but I could not see the man directly.

The guards stepped aside to allow me to face the visitor. I'd never seen him before. He wore filthy, ragged clothes, many times patched. He smelled of fish and stale beer. His hair was long and unkempt, ragged and bits of straw suggested he slept in barns or lofts recently. He had not shaved in ages, and his beard was just as rough as his hair, but with less straw bits and with the residue of food quite noticeably present. I was glad that I had not had him come on up to the manor.

"I am the Santi Commander Bethany Rose Wilkins Pazzio le'Goeur," I said formally. "You wish to see me?"

"Ah, yes. I did not know that you were married. Excuse me." He held out his arm, as if to shake my hand.

"Er, sorry, but I don't have any arms. Lost them some time ago. A bow will do instead." Strange that he did not know about this.

"I am so terribly sorry! I did not know. You are such a beautiful young woman. Those boots are very attractive. I would tell you my name, but only in private. Can we speak in private? I have a very urgent message for your ears only."

Helen said, "Commander, I don't think that is wise." She nodded at him, as if to say, look at this unsavory character. I saw no weapons other than a cheap dagger fastened to his boot.

"If you will leave your dagger here with Helen, we can walk a ways inside the grounds where we will not be over heard, sir." I replied, taking Helen's advice. He unfastened the dagger and handed it sheath and all to Helen.

I nodded my head to indicate he should follow me. As we walked, he had to adjust his steps to keep pace with my very small steps. He said nothing until we were out of earshot range. Then, he said, "This will do. Thank you for hearing me. This information is for your ears alone and those who protect you. I am in disguise. When you hear my name, you will know why I have insisted upon meeting this way. I am Hecate Lox, formerly the Holy Paladin General of Solamina." He paused, allowing me a moment to grasp the significance of just who he was.

Years ago when Emperor Justinian had conquered many of the Sea Princes, in this case, Solamina, he had placed one of Pope Yazi's Holy Paladin Generals in charge of the occupied sectors. Later, he had directly ordered General Hecate to kill the nobles of Solamina, who ran the country. After that, things deteriorated there, until he recanted and of his own volition returned the control of the sector over to the Santi, ordering his own troops to go home, while he just disappeared into thin air. He told the Santi there in our Fortress, that he was a soldier, not a governor, nor a butcher. He could no longer support what his own church was doing to the women of Solamina who did not agree to become slaves as the church demanded.

"The Santi Headquarters never got the opportunity to thank you for what you did in Solamina. Please accept my thanks at this late date." I thought this should set him at ease and let him know that I knew who he was. "I see the need for your disguise, Hecate, or should I call you by another name?"

"Enrico, that would be better. Thank you Commander Bethany. I have come here at great personal peril to warn you. If anyone discovered my identity, I would be a dead man within days, if that long. The Church of Jehosanity has long arms in their Mano del Dio. These past many years, I have been enjoying myself, shall we say somewhere in the Southlands. Recently, however, I have discovered a highly secret organization known only as the KASL, Kill All Santi Leaders. I have other disguises; one is Phillepe. As Phillepe, I was quietly and rather secretly recruited by the KASL to become one of their members. Curious, I passed their tests for admittance into their group."

"These are very evil men, who have an irrational hatred of all Santi, especially those of you in leadership positions. From what I have learned, they are an invisible underground, living and operating undercover and in disguise. If what I am told is true, they have operatives or members in most major towns and cities of the Southlands and the Sea Princes, very probably West Reach and the Greenway, though I am not so sure about these two. Just now, they are content to foment hatred and distrust of Santi. Yet, always they plan mass assassinations to take place on some unspecified date. To my horror and disgust, I found that they are practicing their killing skills on local derelicts and drunks who would not be missed. They do everything possible to not call any attention to themselves."

I tried to think of how best to reply, but said, "How can one identify one of these KASL members?"

"As part of their initiation ceremony, you must prove your determination, your resolution, and your power. You must pick up a heated bowl with your arms. This is the result." He slid up his sleeves revealing a pair of intertwined snakes of scared flesh where the bowl had burned his arms. "I did this so that you would believe me." He quickly pulled his sleeves back down. "Know this. I will not ever kill again except in self-defense. Yet, these men may yet one day strike. When they do, it will not be one that is struck down. Hence, I have risked all to deliver this warning that you might be somehow prepared against these evil men."

"Thank you, Enrico for what you have done on our behalf. Is there any way that the Santi could repay you for your assistance?"

"If one of your caravels should find an old sailor adrift beyond the harbor tomorrow, it would be a great service if the caravel could rescue him and set him on the coast of the Red Desert, near your Fortress there. I must go now; they may have already penetrated this disguise."

"Thank you, Enrico. I give you my word that the old sailor will be so rescued." He bowed, turned, and walked back toward the heart of Velona. I walked back to the manor as quickly as my boots would allow. An hour later, I had sent the orders to the Lucky Swallow to assist the "old sailor," which I guessed was Enrico.

"Well, what do we do about this threat?" I asked everyone at our next meeting. "Bad enough having the Mano del Dio assassins after us and the mantis creatures and the Grey Creatures. Now we got to contend with more malcontents!"

"Do you trust what his man said?" asked Kallisto, who knew the least about Sea Prince history.

"He went to an awfully painful way to prove it to me if he is lying. Those were some severe burns, terribly painful. Besides, he didn't look like he was lying, though I am not an expert in this area," I replied.

"Well, with assassins, there is little you can do once they have their minds set on a victim," Kallisto continued. "Based on my experience in the Kali, of that you can be sure. They will stop at nothing until they kill their mark. About all you can do is to always travel with a group and avoid meeting anyone alone. Assassins often use disguises. I'd advise that we use extra caution when outside the estate here."

"I think that perhaps it is time for a little underground work ourselves. What say we see if we can learn anything about this KASL, Kallisto?" Hank volunteered with a twinkle in his eye; he was ready for some exciting work in the larger cities. She grinned and nodded.

"Look, you two be careful," I cautioned, "we are going to be shorthanded around here until the others get back in the middle of next year."

A few days later, I found myself looking over the map that Michelle had made with all of the colored flags indicating sightings with their dates and times, which she had used to help work out where we had been held by the mantis creature. For the life of me, I cannot tell you why I chose this day to study her map, but perhaps it was a bit of paranoia from learning of yet another bunch after our heads.

As I mentally traced the various routes that she had colored in, I marveled at her powers of deduction. She'd done a marvelous job finding the patterns among the chaos. I did notice that there were a few that didn't seem to be used, that didn't match the well-defined routes that the mantis ship had taken. In fact, they appeared somewhat after our mantis had left Wanakan. The first of these was nearly a week later. I found several more over Fortress d'Grange and Mont Blanc of all places! They stopped however, in the Appian Way, the mountain range, which separated the Sea Princes from the Greenway. All told, there were just six of these, not much to work out any kind of long-range pattern, especially since they did not fit with all the myriad of other colored bits of paper marking the mantis creature's flights.

Then, I had a horribly bad feeling; these hovered over where the Grey Creatures used to have their base in the Appian Way! Could one or more of those aliens also have returned? Why should it only be the mantis who returned? I suddenly felt rather sick and went to find Renzo.

"By golly, you may well be right, dear," he said in a very serious tone as he looked over what I had just discovered. "Now we can add a fourth antagonist into the mix! We had better let everyone know about this."

I called a special session and told them of my suspicions, backed by Michelle's map. "I've no experience with these Grey Creatures," Kallisto said, rather worriedly. "What kind of behavior should we anticipate from them? They don't go in for mutilations of bodies, I hope."

"No, my own experiences over several lifetimes," I answered not only for her sake but for the others as well, "is that they often are able to disguise themselves as a normal person and go around getting normal people to engage in fighting, wars, I mean. Several times, we've seen them capture a prominent figure and then 'take on their identity' and create havoc. Can you imagine the chaos one of them could cause if they disguised themselves as me and started issuing orders to the Santi that you all would believe came from me?"

"Gosh, how are we to know you are you? Or maybe one has already infiltrated our group here? Maybe Renzo isn't Renzo even!" Kallisto replied, becoming very alarmed. "That is possible, isn't it?"

"Absolutely possible, Kallisto. It could assume the identity of anyone of us, very convincingly from what I have seen in the past. However, you could tell by making a mental contact with them. Also, you can tell by the feelings you sense when you look them in the eyes. I felt an utter coldness when looking into Goran's eyes. He was the Grey Creature that we encountered down in Vladimir. An inhuman coldness, that's the best I can say."

"Well, can you make sure that none of us here is a Grey Creature right now?" Kallisto was in a near panic. Even Renzo looked worried.

I quickly touched everyone in the room. "You are all you," I said with a grin. Kallisto still was not completely convinced.

"But how do we know that you are you? I mean you could be a Grey Creature and are just saying that we are we, but no, I did feel your touch. It felt like it always does, but then how would a Grey Creature feel? I'm getting confused. Do you know what I mean?"

"Yes, that is their stock and trade, create confusion all around. All I can say is that when you feel one of these, you will really feel ill at ease, Kallisto. You will know it. I won't feel right to you."

I looked around at the many faces; none looked particularly satisfied. "How about at least once a week, we have Paulette touch each of us in a leadership role here at the estate? You've all sensed her at least once, so you will know it if it is her, just like you know it if it is me."

"What the devil do I do if I find a Grey Creature?" asked Paulette. "It's going to blast me or something nasty, I just know it!"

"Here's what you do. We make a list of our people to check. You do straight down the list and put a checkmark beside each name as you contact them. Then, if something bad happens to you, all we have to do is look at the list and the first unchecked name is the guilty one."

"Hey, I like that, it gives us some way to know who is not who they are," Renzo replied.

"Yes, but what happens to me?" declared Paulette.

"Okay, then I can do it," I volunteered. She looked immensely relieved, so did the others. "Someone will have to be with me to make the checkmarks, however." Renzo volunteered his services.

He then said, "Should we send out scouts to explore the Appian Way and see if we can spot anything amiss up there?"

"Probably a very prudent thing. Let's let some from Mont Blanc handle this, since they are closer to it. Make sure that they travel in at least a foursome. At the first sign of trouble, one must ride at top speed back to get help and warn us," I ordered.

"Okay, Kallisto and I are heading into Calgary tonight. We are going undercover for a time to see if we can learn anything about this KASL organization," Hank informed us. "We've discovered that when you wear these long cloaks over you to stay warm, they completely hide the presence or, in this case, the non-presence of her arms from passersby. However, the boots are going to be a giveaway. We haven't decided whether she will wear long pants or a long dress. Suggestions, Bethany?"

"Pants, definitely, less confining and easier to deal with, until you need to go to the bathroom," I replied without hesitation. "Sometime put on a big dress with many petticoats and then lie on the ground and try to get up without using your arms. Pants, Hank." Kallisto grinned. She knew what I meant, but had not yet convinced Hank.

"Oh yes, Hank, we have not yet seen how these boots with their high heels will function on snow or ice. Be extra careful of her; my own hunch is that they will be really treacherous under those conditions," I suggested, wondering how I was going to get by when it snowed heavily here. However, my legs were actually recovering, and I hoped that soon I would be able to wear my normal boots without heels, just dressing up fancy in these at dances and such.

"Should I contact you each night?" I asked Hank.

"No, we will be most likely active at night and sleeping much of the day. How about checking in on us around noon, say every couple of days? It may take us weeks to find out anything, especially if this is a very secret organization," Hank replied. I agreed and the meeting adjourned.

On November 1, it snowed a half-inch transforming the world around us into a soft white paradise. Renzo hooked up the sleigh and came inside our bungalow. "Okay, kids, mom, it is time for a little relaxation and fun. Anyone care for a sleigh ride?"

The four children yelled and jumped around quite excited about the prospect of a sleigh ride. He helped me into my heeled boots and draped a heavy cloak over my shoulders, making sure it was securely fastened. "Hair in or out, dear?" I decided to leave it out. Lena and Ben had already gotten their warm clothes on and quickly got the littler ones ready. Danielle was very excited, but little Adrien looked more like a snowball, a brown one at that. Renzo carried Adrien, and we all went outside and around to the front where he had the sleigh waiting for us.

I took the opportunity to test the boots in the snow. Yes, walking was now twice as delicate, for they did indeed tend to slip in the snow. Ah well, Alexa would have a new problem to face with her boots. We climbed in and Renzo tucked us all in under a warm pair of blankets and off we went. For two hours, we drove around the countryside a few miles beyond the estate here on the northwestern edge of the ever-growing Velona. With red faces and eyes filled with delight, we ended back at the estate, warming up with cups of hot chocolate. I gave Renzo a very loving embrace as well. We had quite a family indeed.

# Chapter 12 Response

G'Kar growled, he'd arrived on the penal colony with supplies two weeks ago. He hated this supply run stint. Three times now, he'd been turned down for the Warden position at the colony. Twice, he'd even put in for a jailor's job there and had likewise been rejected. "We need good pilots; you are not replaceable." That had always been the justification that kept him from his goal of becoming the Warden of Penal Colony Number 914, located in a remote, deserted section of the galaxy.

He longed to control people, to force them to his will for a change. Yes, maybe even punish them. G'Kar often dreamed of just how he would punish recalcitrant prisoners. Instead, he found himself once more making the half-year supply run to this remote penal colony, alone with nothing to control but the flying machine, which hardly counted. It always did what he commanded it to do; it was a machine, nothing more.

Imagine G'Kar's utter shock and surprise to find absolutely no trace of their main prison colony base high in the mountains. Nothing was left, not even a trace of where it had been a quarter century ago when he had made his last run to this forsaken planet. "The Kronids must have done this!" He spat on the ground. G'Kar hated these insect creatures more than anything else. His race of highly intelligent and evolved giant humanoid bodies had been at war with these insects for two centuries now.

He got back into his ship and headed for the known locations of the Kronids, in a band across the hot southern portion of the penal planet. He loaded every weapon in his ship's arsenal, preparing to blast these vile insects to oblivion. He failed to send a report to headquarters, however. G'Kar wanted to prove his mettle; he would single handedly wipe out these meddling insects once and for all. Perhaps then, he would make the report. Then he realized that with everyone else dead, he could become the warden by default. "No need to report anytime soon," he chuckled to himself as his ship approached the city the locals called Wanakan.

Wise, he flew about only during the dead of night in the prison. Less chance of anyone seeing his flying ship and asking the wrong questions. Soon he stared in disbelief at the hole in the ground where the Kronids' temple had once stood. "Maybe our side blew this base up. Good for us." Quickly, he punched in the coordinates for the next base, and the next. Base after base was deserted or destroyed. He floated over the remains of the base at Mount Hudu. The volcano had erupted, wiping away all trace of the base here. In fact, Hudu was now twice as tall as it had once been.

He steered his ship back to the old warden's base in the Appian Way. He activated the ship's chameleon screen so that it appeared like a large boulder on the mountainside. "Gone, all gone. No Kronids, none of us. Good grief! That means the prisoners can escape their cells! I must assume emergency Warden Status." He went below to his cargo room and pulled out his official warden's uniform, which he had often worn about the ship, while pretending to be the warden here. Now G'Kar was the warden. He looked at his profile in the reflector, satisfied that he looked completely official.

Then he remembered their secret Experimental Station One in the far north. "First order of business: check out that station. Second order: mingle with the prisoners and find out what has been going on this last quarter of a century. Wish I didn't have to wait for nightfall, grr."

Shortly after midnight, G'Kar sat his flying ship down outside the gates of Experimental Station One. All around him, heavy layers of snow and ice covered the land, which he knew was some twenty feet below his feet. He walked up to the alarmed perimeter. Ah, the base looked untouched, a hopeful sign. For a second, he panicked. What if the actual warden had fled to this base? Swallowing hard, he decided that he would just pretend that he was ordered to assume the position because of the wide spread destruction of the facilities here on the prison colony. He pushed the activation buzzer, wondering if anyone would actually answer it. From experience, he knew that it would be several minutes for the guard inside to get this far up to the surface to enter the security codes that would allow him access. Still he paced back and forth impatiently.

Just as he nearly lost his patience and began considering breaking his way inside, the red light changed to green accompanied with a slight buzzing sound. He quickly entered his access code, and the gate opened for him. He walked inside, opened the main door, and descended the many steps to the outer control room, where whoever had allowed him access would be waiting for him.

"Ah, H'Kan, it's you. G'Kar here. I'm now the new warden. How many of us are there?"

H'Kan was very old, having spent nearly two hundred years here on the penal colony. His later years had been spent entirely inside the Experimental Station, looking after the many experiments the previous warden had ordered. "Just me, G'Kar. Good to see a familiar face. I haven't heard from the warden in a quarter century or more. We could use more supplies. You did bring them with you?"

"Well, yes, but they are all long dead! You don't know what happened here?"

"Not exactly. Over a quarter century ago now, I believe somewhere around there anyway, we got an all hands to battle stations call from the warden. The Kronids were planning to attack our base. I'm too old to fight any longer and was ordered to man this station until relieved. Are you here to relieve me so that I can go home?"

"Heck no! We have an entire prison on the loose! No jailors for a quarter century, man! Think about that for a second, will you! There's no telling what these prisoners have been up to all these years. Okay, give me a hand unloading your supplies. Then, I have to go find out how rebellious the prisoners have become."

An hour later, H'Kan watched sadly as G'Kar, the first of his people he'd seen in ages, fly off to the south. "He's angry, not good company anyway. Guess I will go below to watch over the experiments once more." He activated the security fence and went back inside.

G'Kar buzzed quickly over the Sea Princes, because these were their main charges over which they had dominion, along with some lesser folks even further north. "What has happened here?" he commented as his scope revealed drastic reductions in prison cells in the cities below him. His night scope allowed him to see the shapes of the warm prison cells miles below him in the cities. "Has there been a devastating war here? Perhaps a viral plague?"

"Good god! They've all moved to Velona? That backwards area? My god, there must be nearly a million warm prison cells down there!" He didn't wait for the machine to finish making an accurate cell count, however. He put his ship down in the hills north of Velona and activated its chameleon screen once more. Next, he fastened two blasters, one on each side of his legs. He thought it looked more impressive to be able to fire a blaster in each of his hands.

Finally, he made sure that his Disguise Belt was fully charged. It was. He punched in the code to activate it and watched his giant eight-foot tall frame appear to shrink to six feet. His appearance quickly took on that of a normal prison cell, rather what it looked like a quarter century ago anyway. He would update its illusion as soon as he spotted a prison cell here in Velona. He walked determinedly out of his ship, entered the security locking code, and began a swift walk into the huge city. He saw that the city had indeed grown tenfold or more since he last saw this backwater town. "Something has happened here, probably the prisoners' doing. I must get them back under my control and domination. Boy, I do hope I get to punish some of the prison cells!"

Sitting in the various inns and pubs around Velona, G'Kar heard everything about our recent history. He spied on the Santi del Dio headquarters for a time and his mouth spat out curse after curse. Things were far worse than he had ever imagined! The prisoners were not only on the loose, but they were in large measure escaping their cells. Worse, they were creating all sorts of things from art to great engineering projects. This had to stop, but he soon found out that there were many thousand in the Santi organization, far too many for him to eliminate alone, especially since so many were out of their cells already. "I've a full scale prison riot on my hands here! My god!"

He returned to his ship to ponder his first move. "Prime Directive Number One: no prisoner should ever see the true image of the warden or the jailers. I must follow that one. If I go in there with my ship's guns blazing and eliminate them all, then every prison cell will suddenly realize that we jailors are actually here. That would cause tremendously bad repercussions. Prime Directive Number One was only violated one time, and after it had, the prison became uncontrollable, and the entire planet had to be disintegrated, the prisoners scooped up and transported to another facility, after their minds had been wiped, of course. No, I dare not break that one. The warden who broke it found himself in the prison after that calamity. I must utilize some of the prisoners; get them to do my work for me, without suspecting anything."

For the next six months, G'Kar was very busy setting up his network of assistants among the prisoners. Actually, he sought out those that were locked entirely in their cells and who had been, in fact, criminal beings, which was why they had been sent here to the penal colony in the first place. Now very widespread over the northern sections of Tarra, he was satisfied that they would respond when he gave the orders for action. The Santi del Dio leadership had to be destroyed utterly. Once that was accomplished, then he could go after the other individuals, such as the engineers who dared improve the prison life!

However, G'Kar knew that before he could use his forces and act against the Santi here, one being in particular had to be somehow eliminated. This one alone could completely foil his attempt to retake control of the prison. For a week now, he had cleverly been inside the estate, scouting out the details he needed before he could make his first move.

# Chapter 13 Abducted, Willingly

January 3, 659 was dark and ominous. Snow began falling heavily. By late afternoon, two inches covered the grounds of the estate, far more than normal. Renzo appeared at the stables, surprising the stable hands. "Saddle up our sleigh. I am taking the family out to see the snow," he said, adding as an afterthought, "please."

"Okay, sir. I thought you were in the planning meeting. It will just take us a few minutes. I'm sure the kids will really enjoy the outing. They certainly did the last time," the Santi woman made idle chat, while she quickly harnessed the horses to the sleigh.

"Thanks," Renzo forced himself to say. "Will you be so kind to go fetch the kids? It is a surprise for them. I've not told them that we are going yet. Tell them to come here to the gate. I know, better yet, I will be waiting for them just outside the gate, add to their surprise. No need to bother Bethany; she will be coming along shortly after the kids are here."

She grinned, "Aye, sir, will the children ever be surprised! I'll get them right away. Snow clothes as usual?"

"Yes, please," Renzo forced himself to say to this repugnant Santi woman cell.

Renzo drove the sleigh rather awkwardly out and through the gate, halting it just outside of the gatekeeper's view. He waited, "Patience," he told himself. Everything depended upon this working properly, everything.

About twenty minutes later, the four children came dashing through the gate. Lena, now nine, was holding Danielle's hand; she was five. Ben, also nine, was steadying Adrien with his hand; our youngest was now four and able to walk. "Look daddy's got the sleigh! Yeh!" exclaimed Danielle very excited about another sleigh ride in the new snow.

"Hi, dad," Ben said.

"Climb up and get under the warm blankets. Mother will be along soon now," Renzo ordered somewhat briskly, Lena thought. Somehow, dad's voice didn't sound quite right. Maybe then, he had a cold coming on, she thought, as she helped her sister climb aboard. When the four were aboard, she wondered why dad had not adjusted the blankets for them, instead she and Ben did.

"How soon is mom coming?" Lena asked.

"Oh very soon now; we are surprising her," he replied and then pressed a button on a device he had concealed beneath the blanket over his legs for just this purpose. The device activated. Suddenly, Lena could not move! She could feel, hear, see, but could not move a muscle in her body! She tried to yell out, but nothing happened. Fear seeped into her mind, as it had already done so with her other siblings. They were trapped.

"Ah, stasis works every time on prison cells," Renzo muttered to himself. Now that he had the children secured, he could go to step two of his plan.

Inside our meeting room, I was saying, "Well, we had better set about making more markers on the map, like Michelle did. Already, we have had a dozen strange nighttime sightings in and around Velona. Perhaps another mantis is shadowing us."

"I'll double the guards," Renzo said, "but I don't know if that will be at all effective."

A cold, inhuman mind contacted mine. *I have your children. Look.* I saw their four terrified faces frozen and immobile. *If you do precisely what I say, I will not harm them. If you do not, I will kill them, one by one, until you do what I tell you to do. Is this clear?*

My face went white with fear, without thinking, I touched Renzo's mind, and he saw what I saw and heard. *Yes. If you harm my children, I will hunt you down and kill you in the most painful way I can invent!*

*Ha! Now I want you to put on a coat and walk out through the main gate, where I am waiting with your children in the sleigh. You will come alone and tell no one where you are going. If Renzo attempts to continue listening in, I will kill the one you call Adrien. If Renzo attempts to follow you in any way, I will not only kill both boys, but him as well. In fact, I will kill anyone else who attempts to follow us. Is this perfectly clear, Bethany, Renzo?*

Renzo nodded, and I dropped my connection with him. Renzo yelled, "They are attempting to abduct Bethany right now. They say they have our children. Someone, run and check if the kids are actually gone. Fast!"

Half ran out of the room to go find our children; the others were hastily briefed on the little bit that Renzo had overheard. "Should we sound the estate-wide alarm and go after them?" Alexa asked, terrified for everyone's safety. She had suddenly felt herself so helpless without arms, something that had not bothered her for many, many years. I believe it was the suddenness of the attack that took her completely off guard and by surprise.

"No! It said that it would kill our boys if we don't do as it asks. It will kill anyone who tries to follow or intervene," Renzo fairly shouted, causing Alexa to breakdown into tears, unable to think any more. Renzo stalled, slowly fetching my cloak. Fortunately, I was now finally able to wear my normal boots, which he also helped me into, tying up the laces for me.

Mireio dashed into the room, nearly falling over Renzo. "They are gone! The stable hand came to tell them that Renzo wanted them bundled up to go for a surprise sleigh ride, but that cannot be; he's been here all this time. You are you, aren't you?" She looked at Renzo as if he were an alien.

"He's the real Renzo," I said, barely audible, my fear for our children growing by the moment. "I'll do what it says until I can get back to you.

Right now, don't do anything that might make him kill our children, promise me that!"

"I won't, dear. I will find you, wherever they take you and the children. You make sure the kids stay safe, and I'll come after you somehow," Renzo replied, and gave me a hug and passionate last kiss. My knees shaking, I began the long walk out and down the snow covered cobblestones to the gate, a half mile distant. I spotted Renzo floating up and out of the building, intent on following me. I hoped that the creatures would not see him up there. If so, we had a chance to rescue our children.

I finally made the gate, and the gatekeeper said, "Enjoy your surprise sleigh ride. The kids and Renzo are waiting you that way. See you in a little while."

The gatekeeper had no idea that anything was wrong! My face was white as a sheet. I muttered something and kept walking in the direction he pointed, though the sleigh tracks were highly visible. Then, I saw the sleigh and the face of Renzo staring at me.

"This way, into the sleigh, Bethany," I detected the cold inhuman tone in his voice. While he might be able to look like Renzo, his voice gave him away. Of course, I needed help getting into the sleigh. As it was lifting me up, it said, "I told you to come alone. Who's that floating up there?"

"Please don't hurt my children!" I begged him. He pointed his blaster at Renzo, and I watched as my husband took the blast; he went spiraling down into the estate. I knew his body was probably out cold from the blast, but not dead. If his body had died, he would not have gone back into it nearly that fast. I looked at my kids. "What have you done to them?" I fairly screamed at him.

"Stasis, unharmed for the moment. Now sit down and cover up. Do as I say and they will come to no harm. Disobey me and I will shoot them one by one until you do. Got that?"

"Yes, just don't hurt them!" Zap! I felt my body suddenly freeze up. I could see, hear, smell, but I had no control over any voluntary muscles. Only the involuntary muscles continued to work unaffected by the stasis blast. I felt the jerk as the sleigh began to move, taking heart that the sleigh would leave a trail that anyone could follow for quite some time, perhaps even days.

We rode for less than a mile, halting behind a hill. Only the hill wasn't there before! Strong arms carried my motionless body into the hill; it was its flying ship. My heart sank. I felt my children's bodies being laid up against mine, so it was taking us all prisoner. The voice said, "Enjoy the ride." I felt a humming vibration; the ship was flying, taking us away with it. If only the children were not with us, this creature would be dead by now, I swore. I controlled my intense anger. I had to keep my children somehow safe, somehow.

After a while, I felt a bump and the low vibrational humming ceased.

We must have landed, but I could not move my body to see where, assuming I could see anything from where I was at in its ship. Strong arms carried me outside. I saw snow everywhere. I made the hasty conclusion that we must not be far from Velona. It carried me down many steps, underground, placing me at last on a bed, facing a wall. I couldn't see anything like this. I moved out of my head to look around and soon saw him returning, carrying the four children under its arms like sacks of potatoes! I knew at once that this must be a Grey Creature and not a mantis!

"Ah, I see you are out of your cell already, Bethany. That will never do! I am going to release you and you will come with me. If you leave your cell, your body you call it, I will start harming the children, beginning with the littlest. Do you understand me?" I couldn't move to indicate either way.

"Renzo" pressed a button on his waist device, and I could once more move my body. "The mantises have had their way with you. Okay, I will assist you up," his powerful arm lifted me onto my feet. "Walk to the door and stop." I did as told.

"You will come with me and do as I say. As a token of good faith, I will now release your children. Remember that if at any time you disobey me, one push of the button and their cells are dead. Understand?"

"Yes," I muttered faintly, not even recognizing my own voice. I watched as the kids suddenly could move again.

Lena called out, "Mom! What's happening?"

The creature turned off its belt illusion-creating device. We could now see this eight foot tall, Grey Creature, with three toes on each foot. "You have been captured. If you four behave yourselves, you will not be harmed. If you disobey me, I will hurt your mother. If your mother disobeys me, I will kill one of you children. You can decide among yourselves who I kill first. Do you understand me?" The four nodded, petrified. He then pushed me through the door. It slid shut, and he bolted it securely from the outside. They could not escape that room; my heart sank a bit further.

He led me to another room, filled with machinery and devices. He said, "Bethany, you are posing the greatest challenge to me. I am Warden G'Kar of this penal colony. You continue to escape your prison cell, this flimsy body here. Evidently, the mantis work on you was not enough to keep you in your cell. I know that at any moment, you can zip up there somewhere, be back at your base, even open up a communication line to anyone. I'm sorry but that is not going to be allowed around here anymore. This special place is known as the Experimental Station One. I am going to fix you up now. If you disobey me, try to leave, try to communicate to anyone other than me, believe me, I will kill one of those other little cells that you are so attached too. Do I make myself perfectly clear?"

"Yes, but why are you doing this to me and my children?" I asked.

"We will talk much more and at length, once I have you in your cell." We both knew that his command over me just now was very tenuous indeed.

If I could find any way to get a hold of his belt devices, I could then safely attack him. The instant I knew my kids were safe his life would be forfeited. He knew that as well as I did. He said nothing, but stared into my eyes with his cold, inhuman orbs.

Zap! Once more. I felt the paralyzation stasis taking over my body. Involuntarily, I began floating further out of my body. "Now, now, what did I say about leaving?" His hand was on a button. "Ready for me to kill whichever one they decided gets to die first?" I dashed in close to my head, frantically, yet unable to say anything or even move my body. "There, that's being a good prisoner."

I heard the door open and a second Grey Creature entered. Though I could not see him with my body's eyes, I did see him myself. He looked much older and was carrying a large box, some six feet on a side. I watched helplessly, as they fully undressed me . What were they going to do to me? I began to panic. One lifted me up, while another began doing something to my bottom. No, it was sliding something foreign, cold, icy cold, into my womb! Are these just a bunch of perverts, I wondered? I heard a click. Now I saw the older man reluctantly, I thought, hand what looked like a corset to G'Kar, a strange one, though. Well, I had worn these before in Tashien, Annelise, and even in Demokritos, awfully uncomfortable, and crippling for one without arms who needed flexibility to be able to care for herself. Perhaps that was his intention, to make me more helpless?

Ugh. I felt it being tightened mercilessly, until I could scarcely breathe. Yet, I could not move a muscle to counter it. I just tried not to panic, though I wondered what the body might do if I did panic? Next, I saw him with some metal golden rings. These were similar in nature to the ones we captured women had worn when the mantis had taken our arms. They fit tightly between your chin and shoulders, making any movement of the neck, such as turning your head to see to the side, or even looking down, impossible without turning the whole body or bending at the waist, which I knew would be tough with the corset this tightly around me. God, I remembered just how helpless I had been when I worn this before. Now I was panicking, and yet the body did not respond in any way. I felt some strange heat on the back of my neck going up and down repeatedly. Perhaps it was somehow sealing it onto my neck?

Next, the older one lifted me up, and I saw the G'Kar putting boots similar to those of the mantis creatures onto my feet. Damn, I had just finally gotten my legs back to normal, and he was fitting me with these tall-heeled boots again! I felt the surge of heat on my legs and soon felt that familiar tightness, as the boots shrunk down and sealed my legs inside the boots. Well, we had the devices, which would undo this process, so I didn't worry too much about this. I could see that he was just trying to make it impossible for me to escape here.

The older Grey Creature said, "No, G'Kar, please; this is more than enough." G'Kar glared at the older one and took another device out.

"This will hurt a bit." I felt an excruciating pain in my lower back and then in my neck. I passed out or blacked out. The world disappeared from me.

Sometime later, I came violently awake; a horrible smell was being moved around my nose. I jerked awake and alert, but it was entirely black. My neck and lower back ached. "What's happening?" I called out into the darkness."

"It's all right mom, you are back with us in our cell. You are sitting on our bed. What awful things have they done to you?" It was the voice of Lena.

"I cannot see you. They must have the lights off."

"No, the lights are very bright. He gave me this tube to stick under your nose. He said it would wake you up. It worked. Mom, we're all very scared. What have they done to you?" she asked, her voice bordering on terror. I had to keep her calm, while I was panicking.

"They put my waist in a corset. I can barely breathe in it and cannot bend much. They put my neck in a metal restraint as well, like the mantis creatures did, remember, I told you about that. I cannot move my head." I tried just to be sure. I couldn't, but it didn't make any difference that I couldn't, since I was now blinded. "And I cannot see anything. It's all black."

"We know mom, your eyes arc now all grey. They did put a dress on you and you have boots like the ones you used to have to wear. We will help you mom, don't worry. We'll find a way out of here." She tried to sound brave, but she was only nine years old.

Just then, the door opened and someone came in. I recognized the voice of G'Kar once more. "If you will come over here to the table and sit down, we can have that talk now."

"But I cannot see," I protested.

"We'll help you mom," Lena said.

"Try to stand up now mom," Ben's voice said. I felt their arms awkwardly around my waist, and I tried to stand up, nearly losing my balance and falling over. Except for the kids, I would have. Something about these heels was different; they were much taller. I could barely take a step in them. I kept taking tiny, feeling steps toward the direction my kids were pushing me gently and bumped into a chair. We had a devil of a time trying to get me into the chair safely. I ached badly and was horribly disoriented. I'd never been blinded before.

Once seated, I relaxed a little. "Now we can talk. You are completely under my control now. Inside your private area, I have placed a device, which senses when you are straying too far from your cell. It will activate and send you into some discomfort until you return to the cell. Go ahead, try it."

Hesitatingly, I tried to move somewhat out of my head. I only got a few inches out when something triggered inside me, sending a horrible, painful shock into my insides! I nearly fainted in the chair! I sat there gasping for air, which I could not get easily.

"See, you will stay in your cell now. If you try to communicate with your telepathy, it will activate similarly until you cease communicating that way." There was smugness in his voice, as if he really was enjoying seeing my body in so much pain and discomfort, me so helpless and humiliated.

"I must say, I have not had this much fun in, well I can't ever recall having so much pleasure. Giving these cells, these bodies, such punishment is quite a thrill! For once, I believe our archenemies, the Kronids, or the mantis as you call them, were on to something with all their punishments and tortures of these bodies, these cells. What fun they must have been having all these years. Well, I, G'Kar, am now the Warden of this prison colony, and I make the rules. The mantises are gone, and I am in charge of the penal colony now. So I make the rules; you obey them."

"Your kids, whom you so foolishly value so highly, will now look after your needs, since I don't believe you will be able to do much of anything anymore," he laughed cynically and sadistically. "You are in Experimental Station One. This has been our base where we have always conducted experiments on the cells, the bodies, to find the best ways of keeping you all incarcerated in your cells."

"During my last trip here, over a quarter century ago, the Warden had made several secret raids on the mantis secret colonies way down south, bringing back some of their specimens for us to study, just in case their methods worked better at keeping you prisoners firmly in your cells. Back then, I admit I thought such was mere foolishness. Our mind scramblers work so much better. Yet, now that so many of you prisoners have escaped your cells, more drastic measures must be taken. You have the honor to be the first of many. In a while, you will have lots more company here, Bethany."

"I will be leaving you in the hands of our capable jailor and watcher, H'Kan. He has been watching over all the many experiments all these years. We don't want you starving to death or dying, no, not for a very long time, not until we are certain that the next baby cell you get you will stay inside it permanently like a good prisoner should behave."

"Remember, there is no escape for you. If you try to move out of the cell or try to contact anyone with your telepathy, you will meet with excruciating pain until you stop or pass out. It will not kill you, so don't get that idea either."

"Why are you doing this to me?"

"Because you are the only one capable of killing me. You are the one who is letting the prisoners out of their cells with your therapy sessions. You must be stopped from doing this forever. Now that I have you completely under my control and being punished by me for all those that you have thus far freed, I am now able to go after all the others in this damnable Santi organization of yours. Since you aren't going anywhere and since you can't do anything anymore, I can tell you this."

"In a week, my forces will be attacking all the Santi positions, going after all your leaders, dead or alive. While I wish to capture as many of them alive so that I can bring them here and torture them as I'm doing with you — I'm finding that I really do enjoy torturing you, Bethany — I wanted to remove all your teeth and your tongue as well, maybe even puncture your lips and spread them out, but H'Kan here convinced me that your cell longevity would be drastically reduced if I did that. Ah well, I do hope you try to escape a few times; the pain should be really something to feel there inside your flimsy cell, by the way. Where was I? Oh, while I want to capture as many of your other leaders as possible, my forces are not as capable as I am, so many will likely just die and have to go get a new prison cell. No matter, that alone will give me another dozen plus years to get everything back under my control here on this penal colony you call Tarra."

"So you see, Supreme Commander Bethany, this is the end of your Santi and all this talk of freedom. This is a penal colony, after all. Also, all those new inventions, such as that aqueduct, those have to go. I have to keep the cells fully occupied on just staying alive, not taking time off for those silly dances of yours. No more of what you pathetic people call art works. Ha, just a bunch of oils on a canvas. Plow the fields, grind the grain, I'll get heavy work out of you all yet. Well, H'Kan will see that you get a work out here too, won't you H'Kan?" I heard the other man grunt something. Work out of me? Ha, I cannot even move on my own any more.

"Well, now I hope I've answered all your questions. I must be off to make all the final arrangements to assault the Santi next week. I'll be back in a couple weeks with lots more of your friends to join you in torment. I think I can keep you tormented like this for at least a hundred more years, because we feed you right. Look on the bright side; you won't be getting any of those commonplace illnesses your cells out there in Velona are so prone to acquiring. H'Kan will see that you reach at least one hundred years of age before we send you off to get a new baby body. Just make sure you stay in it this time or I will be back, and we can go through this again. Actually, this is so much fun, please do do all this freeing stuff next time; it has been thoroughly enjoyable torturing you thus far. I look forward to doing it some more when I get done with all the other Santi leaders in a week or so."

I heard him get up from his chair, and I figured that was all I would get from him. However, he paused at the door and added, "I added a special program to your device. You will discover it tonight when you go to sleep. I hope you enjoy it," he said with a horrible sneer in his voice, bordering again on a sadistic, insane laugh.

I heard the door shut. Then, I heard the other voice speak, H'Kan. "You must be in a good deal of pain and confusion at this time. I will allow you some private time today to recover. I will bring in food and water shortly. Your children will be able to look after your needs. However, I would recommend that they help you learn to get around with their help. You can't just sit there all the time. Around here, everyone helps out in some way, but I will talk of that later, once you have recovered some, healed, and are able to walk with their aid." His tone suggested kindness, a gentleness that I had never thought existed among the Grey Creatures. I heard him leave and the door shut.

"There is a lock on the other side of the door. Kids, we can't get out of this room unless they let us out. Are you all unharmed?"

"Yes, mom," Ben said. "Please don't cry; we are going to look after you somehow. Lena and I will figure out some way to get us free from here. How are you supposed to move around like you are anyhow?"

"I honestly don't know, Ben."

"Mommy, I'm scared," Danielle whispered.

"I know honey, come here, and hug mommy. I'm very, very scared too. For now, let's all do as they ask; we must stay alive and well. Eventually, we'll find a way to escape." I felt her little arms around me, but I couldn't lower my head to reach her, to comfort her.

Lena said, "Mom, dad and everyone else are in grave danger. We have to find a way to warn them somehow."

"I know. I will try later tonight. I guess I had better start learning how to get around. Damn, I can't see anything, and these clothes, shoes, and neck thing are making it nearly impossible for me to," I didn't finish my sentence, but sighed instead. Right now, I realized very suddenly that I had to show my children by example. I had to demonstrate that no matter what happens to you, you adapt and move ahead, either that or succumb and die, and I wasn't about to do that just yet!

"Come on, I know my back is aching terribly badly and my neck is too, but I've got to try." I tried to stand up and nearly fell over. All of the body motion I used to make to keep my balance was gone. I depended upon my eyes to judge and my head and body bending to compensate. All three were gone now. I felt the arms of my two oldest children around my waist steading me. I have never felt as scared in my life as I did just now, trying to take tiny steps in these impossible shoes, unable to see anything. My only connection to the universe around me was the balls of my feet and toes inside the damnable boots.

"You are doing it, mom!" Lena tried to encourage me. I thought I felt her crying quietly to herself, but I couldn't see. I felt terribly frightened, scared, and sick, in horrible pain, with a terrible pressure around my waist. Yes, I was forcibly smashed into my head. Baby steps, that's what it felt like to me. I had no sense of direction at all; I just let Lena and Ben guide me around at a snail's pace. More than once I nearly fell.

The door opened and the jailor entered. I could smell hot food. "I've brought you some lunch. It is good that you are up and learning to get around. I'll pick these up when I bring you dinner. Keep up the good work, Bethany. That is what you call yourself is it not?"

"Yes, thank you. I cannot do this on my own. I cannot see. I cannot keep my balance. I might be able to if it wasn't for these horrible boots. Let's get me to the table, kids." I felt the eyes of the jailor watching me. At least I didn't hear him leaving, not until I nearly fell into the chair sitting down.

"Come on, Danielle, Adrien; we get to feed mommy," Lena said stifling back tears. I hear her sniff quietly to herself. I couldn't turn my head to eat either. I found I had to pivot my whole body toward Lena so she could feed me. I wanted to cry, but tried to eat and keep up a positive face.

I found that I could barely eat, my waist was so constricted that I filled up rapidly. Well, that left more for the kids. "Are you all getting enough to eat? I cannot see, so please tell me the truth. I have to know this, Lena."

"Yes, mom, we are all full. It wasn't very bad, really. Ben's found the chamber pot. Let us know when you need to go. I'm going to help Danielle and Adrien now, before we walk you some more. You just sit there, mom, for a couple minutes. We won't be far away."

"God, don't leave me kids! I won't be able to do anything by myself like this," I suddenly realized how utterly dependent I actually was on my own children!

"Don't worry, mom. I'm right here with you," Ben said, resting his arm on my shoulder. I found that touch incredibly reassuring. While I sat there, hearing the sounds of Lena helping the younger ones go to the bathroom, I suddenly remembered our blind Santi soothsayer, Jolina. We had taught her to get around, and I began to remember bits of what her training had involved. Counting steps, yes, she would count her steps and that provided space between objects in the universe.

I explained this to Ben, who I hoped understood me. I couldn't see his face, though and had to rely on his voice and what he said. "Mom's going to count out the steps between things in the room," he explained to Lena.

"Hey, that's a great idea mom!" she called over to me. I instinctively pivoted in my chair to face her. Silly, I couldn't see if I was even close to facing her.

A little while later, with the littler two children sitting on the bed, I began learning our room by counting steps. Yes, these were my steps, probably six inches at the most per step. I didn't dare take any larger ones in these boots; I couldn't see to balance myself. All afternoon, we paced the room. Forty steps one way, thirty the other. Ten steps from bed to table. Fifteen from table to door. Now I realized another thing. "Kids, it will be very, very important for mommy that you leave nothing in the way where I could stumble over it. I can't see it. It is important not to move anything around. I know where things are by counting steps. If you move something, I won't get the right number of steps and will stumble and fall. So if you move something, remember to put it back exactly where it was. Everyone understand? Four chorused, "We do, mom."

Later with my feet and ankles now aching, supper came. The jailer said, "After you all eat, I think that you have done enough for one day. Please, touch this panel here, kids when you want the lights out. A small nightlight will come on in its place. Bethany, you haven't seen the bed arrangement, so I will tell you. The smaller one is for the children, the larger for you, unless you wish one of the larger children to sleep with you. I know that you may find sleeping terribly difficult for some days, but the pains you are feeling will eventually pass. Kids, you probably should let her sleep alone until the pains are gone."

"Thank you, sir."

"H'Kan, ma'am. Just old H'Kan. I bid you good night now. I will bring you breakfast in the morning." I heard his footsteps leave and the door shut.

"Here mom, have a bite," Lena said, from somewhere off to my right. Awkwardly, I used my feet to pivot my body and hence my head toward roughly where I heard her voice. I felt the spoon in my mouth. Slowly, I began to eat. Again, I filled up rapidly, and I listened to my kids eating away for some time. Thus, I concluded that they must have been getting enough to eat.

Once they were done, Lena helped me back to the bed, which would be mine. "God, I cannot see to even get into bed!"

"Wait a second, mom. Are you going to sleep in your clothes?" Lena asked.

"Yes, I don't think it matters much to me. I can barely move around anyway."

"Okay, let us get the sheets pulled back. There, now turn around. Take one back step. There you feel the bed edge against your legs?" I did. "Now slowly see if you can sit down, mom." God, this was terribly difficult, scary. I had no idea what was behind me, how far down it was, were my body was in relation to the bed, and no arms to feel for it. I just fell sitting down and landed on the bed, thankfully.

"How am I ever going to lie down like this?" I panicked once more.

"I got your back mom and Lena has your feet; we will lower you down," Ben explained. I mostly fell back onto my back, on top of my hair, which the very least of my worries now.

"Okay, we will pull the sheet up. If you get cold, holler," Lena said sympathetically.

"Now it's your turn, Danielle, Adrien. Into bed with you. Lena will snuggle with you, and I'll be on the outside snuggling with you, Adrien," Ben took command. "After you are all in bed, I'll turn off the light and make my way to the bed." Shortly, I heard Ben walking across the room and then heard him come back. All was still utter blackness to me. I began crying silently to myself.

How long I lay there crying, I don't know. At last, I heard all four sleeping and took some comfort in that. Now I knew what I had to do, pain or no pain. I had to warn Renzo and the others. Far too many lives were at stake, besides, G'Kar said that it wouldn't kill me. I relaxed as best I could. At least, the pain in my legs eased up, but my back and neck were killing me.

*Renzo. It's me.* A massive bolt of pain shot through my womb and innards, I nearly fainted. *Can't talk. Can't get out of head.* I writhed on the bed, forcing my mouth to say nothing to wake the kids. *Pain device. I'm blinded, and trapped, dependent on the kids.* Renzo felt my pain. As it subsided, I sent, *Grey Creature. Plans attacking all Santi leaders. One week. Save everyone.* I passed out from the pain jolts.

I woke a little later. My back ached; my neck ached. I began to cry once more. I couldn't move at all. Suddenly, the device activated again, only differently this time. Waves of stimulated pleasure flooded from my womb! Damn, the Grey Creature was now torturing me with sexual sensation! That was his little surprise, I concluded. In a way, it did help me relax from the pain that my body was in, and I believe that I somehow did get to sleep.

The next morning, H'Kan came in and turned on the lights. "Good morning everyone. How are you feeling this morning, Bethany? Hi kids."

"My back and neck hurt like the devil," I replied honestly.

"That is to be expected. I wish G'Kar had not done that to you. I tried to stop him, but he wouldn't listen to me. Ah, well, no one in command listens to me anyway. Say, the others here in our little family heard of your arrival and would love to meet you all over breakfast. We all eat our meals together. If you feel up to it, we would love to have your family join us. There are seven children around the same ages as yours. They could all play together after breakfast."

"Others? Are the children harmed or imprisoned like me?" I began to worry once more.

"Oh no, they are like yours. We do not harm children. That is not our way, unlike our enemies the mantis creatures, the Kronids. What say you, Bethany, come join us and meet the others?"

"Can we, mom?" asked Ben.

"Okay, but H'Kan, can you help me to my feet? I doubt with this pain I can manage. Lena, I need the chamber pot first. Probably all of you should use it first, before we go to eat," I asked and suggested.

The strong arms of H'Kan gently lifted me out of bed, carefully putting me on my feet. A short while later and after I heard four uses of the chamber pot, we were ready to go. Ben and Lena both held on to me, their other hands held Danielle and Adrien. Again, I was taking most hesitatingly small steps, terrified of each footstep. "How far is it?" I asked pitifully.

Soon I heard noises, talking, cheerful voices steadily growing louder. We turned and entered a room. The voices stopped. I figured everyone was staring at us. H'Kan said to me, "Do you wish to introduce yourself and your family?"

I heard male voices whispering, "What's she look like?" I heard other voices, some probably children replying, "She can't see either. She has no arms, but beautiful long blonde hair, the longest of anyone here perhaps. She's wearing the gold neck stretcher, probably a corset; she has a small waist. Four children." On the whispering went.

Lena said, "Mom, I see eight adults and seven children. All of the women have the same neck thing as you. Three don't have any arms either and one is like Jovanna, at the elbows. Three men, they seem to be blinded too. Kids are like us, normal."

H'Kan said, "We speak many languages here, Bethany. Wanakan, Isle of Right, Southlands, and Sea Prince. Why don't you introduce yourself and family now? Everyone is eager to hear you."

"I can't see you, but here goes." I tried to face the group. Lena rather pointed me in the right direction. "I am Bethany Rose Wilkins Pazzio le'Goeur, Supreme Commander of the Santi del Dio. These are our children, Lena, Ben, Danielle, and Adrien. We've just been abducted by the Grey Creatures, the aliens. The goal of the Santi is to help free all the peoples of Tarra, particularly from these beastly aliens, the mantis creatures and these Grey Creatures. I lost my arms fighting against the mantis creatures, but I killed them all, with help from my friends. I've also killed a couple of these Grey Creatures, like our captor here." I repeated this in the other three languages H'Kan had mentioned.

I heard many voices saying, "She speaks our language!" I detected shock and surprise that I spoke in their own tongues.

H'Kan said, "Bethany, they want to meet you. Why don't you all come up and meet her before we eat? Let's start with the oldest, Sophia, from the Isle of Right. Come on up here and bring your family with you, Sophia." I head numerous heel clicks on the stone floor as the sounds approached me.

"I am Sophia. I'm fifty and the eldest. I was born without arms, as was my daughter. I too wear the neck collar and waist constrictor that you do, but at least I can see." I felt her body against mine and her head touching mine. Our necks clanked together. "This is my daughter, Delia."

I felt another woman press against me and our necks again clanked together. "I am thirty cycles old now. I have no arms like you, born that way. Our necks are the same, but I can see and wear no waist constrictor. I have married Pedro whom they brought here before you came, and we have two children, which is why they are not making me wear that device so we can have children. Here is my brother, Lexos. He is blind. I hope you don't mind him touching you. It is his way of seeing you."

"Hi, I'm Lexos. I was born here and have seen twenty-eight cycles. I cannot see, but I have arms to help everyone. I will help you as I can, Bethany. I have married Citalmina, and we have three children, but I am supposed to wait to introduce them; H'Kan wants us to go in family order.

May I feel you so I can see you?"

"Sure, I wish I could feel you," I replied. His hands were gentle, and he felt my face, lips, hair, and body. When he finished, another group came towards me; I could tell from the noise of their boots.

"I am Chimalma a Blessed Holy Maiden from Wanakan. I'm forty-five now. I'm like you except I can see. When they abducted me, I was with child. I had twins here. Citalmina and Aduviri, both are twenty-eight. It has been so long since I heard someone speak my language. Thank you for that present."

"I am Citalmina. I wear a neck thing like you, but that's all. I am so fortunate this way. I have married Lexos here, and we have two children. Mom loves to be hugged, so if you do too, I would love to hug you." I was delighted to receive her hug. "I look after most of us women's hair here. I would be please to do yours as well." I gave her a big thank you for this small detail.

I felt the groping hands of another, "I'm her twin brother, Adiviri. Like you, I cannot see, but I can feel. Lexos, Pedro, and I try to do all the hard, heavy work around here for everyone else. I will help you too, as I can. You have such long, fine hair. Your husband must be proud of you. I have married the young woman from the Southlands, Yida."

"I am Yida," another voice said timidly. "I can sort of hug you. I have some of my arms left." I felt a simple hug from her. She had lost hers at the elbows. "My skin is different than all the rest, black, but that doesn't make a difference to Adiviri. We have two children."

Another male voice spoke, "I'm Pedro Amirez, thirty, from Bonilla. They took me when I was a young boy. Like the other men, I have been blinded, but we still work hard to provide and take care of our women and our families. Delia and I are blessed with three fine children. Not being able to see takes readjustment. We three know. Try counting how many steps things are apart. That's what we do. Of course, the children are a really big help to us all."

Pedro added, "Can you tell us any news from our world out there? We have heard nothing for a quarter century or more. We tell stories to our children at night, perhaps you can tell us much news."

"Right now, that's about all I can do — tell you about the current situation in our world. I cannot tell if the rest of you are interested in this or not. I feel so helpless at the moment," I replied honestly. Many voices encouraged me, and I smiled.

Next came breakfast. While we were eating, H'Kan explained, "After we eat, we all do what chores we can. The children wash the dishes the best. Here we have to grow all of our own food. We have a big garden. The men pull the plows and the carts around, while the women give directions and often lead them. Well, you will just have to see for yourself, oops, I mean feel and hear, that is. However, I will not let you do any real work until your back and neck have healed, and you have no more pain there. Oh yes, there is one other detail I must ask you about, Bethany."

Out of habit, I pivoted to face from where his voice was coming. "The floor here is quite cold. Probably your children are already experiencing cold feet. The only boots we have that can withstand the cold are boots similar to those you are wearing. They are insulated. All the other children are wearing them. In fact, everyone here does, except me, since my three toed feet are used to the cold. However, all the children's boots are loose fitting; children's feet do grow, and we have to exchange them for larger ones quite often. With your permission, I would like your kids to help themselves to a warm pair."

"He's right mom; my feet are freezing," Lena whispered.

"All right, as long as they can take them off when they desire, like before going to bed."

"Lena, would you like to lead your mom so she can come with us to listen to you getting just the right pair of boots to keep your feet warm?"

I lost count of the steps on the smooth stone floor. However, by the time we reached wherever this was, all four were complaining of cold feet. "Gosh, mom, our heels are not as tall as yours are," Lena said.

"This is weird for a boy to be wearing these boots," Ben said. "Oh, they are totally warm! I guess these will have to do." I heard H'Kan asking about where their toes were at inside the boots, so I could tell that he was making sure they had the right fit. Strange consideration from a Grey Creature, I thought, though I said nothing.

Now came the long walk back, many heels clicking on the stone. "I see what you mean mom," Lena said. "You have to take very small steps, compared to what we are used to taking, but we are managing, mom. Don't worry."

When we got back, several of the other children came up to mine and asked if they wanted to go play and see the world. I was terrified of being completely alone, but Citalmina came to me. Putting her arms around me, she said, "I have much experience leading the blind men around. I will be here for you. Let's get you used to walking from your room to the dining hall, shall we." Thus began a long day of counting my steps, learning to measure space by my footsteps. "The guys have pretty much got it all memorized, but they have hands for balance and in case they bump into something. It will be much harder for you, I suspect." That was an understatement.

In the evening, I listened to the men and women telling stories to all the children. Of course, soon everyone wanted to know all about the outside world, especially their homelands. For the next ten days, I spared no details. I told them about all the women we Santi had rescued and had retrained and aided, about the Laird Foundation and all of the armless women there in the arts. I told them about our adventures exploring the world of Tarra, including the feat of being the first people to sail all around the world. I told of the events in Wanakan and elsewhere. I particularly described how the mantis and Grey Creatures were manipulating our lives. At any moment, I expected H'Kan to interrupt me or smack me in the face, because I was telling these people the absolute truth of the situation here on Tarra.

Yes, they asked hundreds of questions. Even the children wanted more details, and Lena and Ben backed me up in places. Finally, I told them about our fabulous therapy sessions and what the results were, about the fabulous gains that many of my friends had made, erasing the encounters with the Grey Creatures as well as the mantis.

"So we are all spiritual beings?" asked Sophia.

"Yes, every one of us. They have a device in me that is preventing me from moving out of my head at the moment, though the pain, the tightness of my waist, and neck are more than enough to drive me into my head anyway."

"Can you do this therapy on us here?" asked Chimalma. "I would be free, if I could."

"We are constrained mostly by these boots, corsets, and neck things. If you were not wearing them, once the therapy was done, I could show you how to do nearly everything with your teeth and feet. After all, I did win that horse race."

Yida said, "Bethany, you offer us the first real ray of hope here. We all would do anything to have this therapy of yours. Can you do it while we are here?"

"I can't see. I don't know if I can do it without being able to see you and what is happening with you," I lamented. "I promise you if I can ever figure out a way to see you, I will give all of you my therapy sessions." They stomped their boots on the floor, which I gathered was their way of cheering me, after all, only a few had hands to clap.

By the tenth day, what I found interesting and slightly hopeful was that I was able to walk by myself alone and unaided from my bedroom to the dining room table. That was a major victory for me.

# Chapter 14 Countermeasures

January 6, 659, every major leader of the Santi stationed in and around Velona had come for Renzo's critical meeting. The dining room was packed. "I've called you all together today for the most critical meeting we have ever had. Bethany and our children have been abducted by the Grey Creatures, who have returned." Gasps and exclamations of shock and surprise drowned him out for some time.

"It is not for Bethany's plight that I have called you here. Just after she was taken, she was able, under tremendous pain, to get a warning to me. At least one Grey Creature, along with a large number of human henchmen, is planning to attack us. Their goal is to kill as many of we leaders as they possibly can. It seems that we are undoing all of the suppression of people that they are doing." More talk again drowned him out.

"I am proposing that we take advantage of this advance knowledge that cost Bethany dearly to give us and throw a surprise party on our enemies. The attack will probably come at night, not in broad daylight, sometime in the next few days. Enyo, how many of the Stone Cutters do we have?"

"Ten, Renzo," she replied.

"Here's my plan. Hear it out and then let's improve it. I want to kill every last one of these vile men and aliens!" For six hours, various personnel offered suggestions and modifications. At last, they all agreed. "Let's get cracking!" Renzo cheered them on.

During the nighttime and in secret, all of the armless women at the estate and in the Laird Foundation were taken to the eight Santi Fortresses along the border with Barcella. Here inside strong walls, they would be safe. The Grey Creatures would undoubtedly be with those attacking our main headquarters. On the return trip, the carriages brought along all their Guardians except the Communicators of the fortress garrisons. Every available Santi fighter in d'Grange and Mont Blanc were brought in at night, staying in hiding in the vacated rooms. Fully four thousand heavily armed Santi, many wearing plate mail, were now inside the estate, not the usual thousand.

Renzo had fifty-three Guardians with him and had dispensed the ten Stone Cutters to some of these. All stayed inside the manor house, out of sight. During the daytime, many of the artists came to work on their works at the Laird Foundation, as usual, though some wondered where all the armless artists were. Attending a special seminar for them was the pat answer Renzo ordered given. The cooks and other working crews went about their daily chores, as if nothing was amiss. They waited impatiently.

Around midnight of the 12th of October, a loud smashing noise woke everyone up. Actually, they were sleeping days and awake nights. However, all were startled by the sound of our outer wall being smashed down. The break in occurred along the northern wall halfway between the manor house and the stables and women's dorms. The garrison for the usual one thousand Santi was further to the east along the north wall. Many eyes watched them from the second and third floor windows of the manor house, as well as the rooftops of our many buildings.

One tall man came through the break first. He waved his arms and hundreds of men came pouring through the breech in the wall. Half moved east toward the known barracks, while the tall man led the others west toward the manor house. As ordered, the gate man, seeing the break, sounded our feeble alarm, as if we had been taken completely by surprise. "Steady, steady," Renzo whispered to the Guardians beside him. He was on the second floor, gazing out the opened window above the dining room.

More and more men swarmed through the breech. Finally, the men reached the manor house, just as the last stragglers came through the hole in the wall. "Now Tal, sound the attack!" Renzo ordered. Bard Tal played a very loud trumpet-attacking tune.

Action suddenly came everywhere. Several walls of fire appeared at the breech, blocking any escape or retreat through their entrance point. A hail of fire sheets dropped down on the men running up to the manor house. Renzo spied the tall man pointing a something in his hand toward one of the Guardians, who had just unleashed burning fire on the men around the tall man. He saw a flash of energy and heard the Guardian being thrown back against the wall, with luck only knocked out.

"That's the one, let him have it," Renzo ordered. He pushed the full on, maximum range button of the Stone Cutter he held. The blue arc of energy flashed out and nine more followed his. The tall man jumped and dodged the sweeping, slicing, cutting arcs, while pieces of the ground went flying in all directions. Repeatedly, the tall man eluded the ten sweeping beams. Bard Tal called out to Renzo, "I'll cut a hole in the ground just in front of him. When he stumbles, cut him." Tal carefully aimed his cutter a bit lower, throwing up a large cloud of dust and debris, temporarily confusing the tall man.

He lost his footing and stumbled. Renzo anticipate his fall and had his cutter sweeping in an arc to the spot. A hideous scream of intense pain drowned out the wild noise of the battlefield. The top half of the tall man became instantly separated from the lower half! "Good job, Tal!" Renzo yelled. "Sound the charge!" He raced down the steps, three at a time! Bard Tal played another loud trumpet chorus, and all the Santi in the manor house began wildly rushing down and out onto the battlefield.

Meanwhile, as the first of the men reached the Santi barracks where they anticipated finding just awakening fighters, wearing their nightclothes. They got the shock of their lives. Plate mail clad fighters stormed out to meet them. This was not how the slaughter was to have happened. Momentarily stunned, they halted and tried to defend themselves. Those in the rear decided to retreat. Unfortunately for them, from the women's dorms hundreds more armored Santi stormed out, surrounding the entire bunch of would be assassins.

One gruff man, who had taken a wound to his leg and was lying on the ground, cried out, "Mercy, mercy," to the female Santi warrior who came running up to him. She stared at him as he begged again. Without batting an eye, she thrust her sword into his throat and then cut his head off, before moving on to the next assassin. Renzo's orders were being strictly followed, especially by these women Santi fighters. Ten more brought up the rear, going from body to body, stabbing each in their hearts, just to make doubly sure the man was dead and not playing possum. Santi thoroughness was once more at work.

An hour later, the last man, who was vainly begging for his life, was slain. Men and women panted for breath, leaning on their swords, staring out over our lawn. Bodies lay everywhere, many had missing limbs as well. A few Santi were going from body to body, with their usual thoroughness.

Bard Tal and Renzo stood over the remains of the tall man, surrounded by a field of dead men and Santi fighters. "Grey Creature verified," Bard Tal commented, as he looked at the giant, which was now in two parts. His energizing belt had been cut in half, ending his illusion of a tall man.

"We should search him for other devices and for clues where Bethany may be located," Renzo ordered. "Oh yes, General Lem, body count, casualty count?"

Across the battlefield, the plate mail clad general saluted Renzo. He yelled, "Going to be a while coming."

The Guardians fired up some fifty blue lights, illuminating the field somewhat. Quickly, a search was made for injured Santi. Only four had taken sword cuts to their hands. These were rushed to the infirmary, where the Healers were waiting patiently for the aftereffects of a battle, expecting the worst.

Mary Dietz, Elona Po's Healer, said, "Where's all the rest of the wounded?" The four had just walked in, their hands bleeding profusely. "We're it," one woman bravely said. Quickly, the Healers began their work, trying to save hands and fingers, yet fully expecting to be bombarded with many more wounded. No more came, however.

Around two in the morning, General Lem walked into the manor house, where Tal and Renzo were examining the confiscated devices from the Grey Creature. "One thousand one hundred and five dead assassins, including the Grey Creature, unless it should count for more than one," he teased. He added, "Four light casualties; worst case, Sally lost a finger. We did well. Brilliant plan, Renzo, brilliant indeed. Any clues where Bethany and the kids might be being held?"

"One finger?" Bard Tal repeated in disbelief. Lem held up one finger.

"No, lots of strange devices, but no clues. At first light, send out riders and scouts. See where all these man came from, and see if you can find this alien's flying ship. He didn't walk here, that's for sure."

"Aye, sir. I'll see to it." He saluted and left the two, who were still studying the objects.

Paulette came into the room, "Elona Po's church was attacked. She has four wounded and asks if her Healer can return at once."

"Send her all our Healers as well," Renzo replied.

A short while later, Paulette reported another communique. "Fortress Seven, along the Barcella border, way up north, was attacked. A hundred three came over the walls there. Two light casualties; all assassins dead."

"Excellent, then Bethany was right; they are making an all-out effort to get our leaders everywhere."

"I think I will sit here near you, Renzo. This is going to be a long night! Yes, here comes another report!" Beth Ann began making a listing of the combat attacks and the results, sipping a cup of tea, trying to stay awake. The cooks began bringing everyone hot tea and biscuits, for they too knew it would be a long night.

Around four in the morning, Renzo dozed off. Tal had already fallen asleep. Paulette had to stay awake; reports just continued to come in from all over Tarra. She took pity on old Beth Ann, who had also dozed off, writing down the latest figures herself. At dawn, many horses thundered out of the estate, waking everyone up.

"Here's the list, Renzo," Paulette handed him Beth Ann's ledger. He stared at the many entries.

"New Barq? They attacked there as well? Damn, just about every fortress was attacked in some way. Good, uniformly our casualties are low. Only five dead? Incredible. Forty-nine wounded. Excellent, none critically. Two thousand six hundred and ten dead assassins? Unbelievable!"

Bard Tal yawned. "I think that we put a serious dent in their numbers."

"If we were lucky, we got most of them," Renzo sounded an optimistic note. He sighed, "But we're no further along on finding out where it took Bethany and the kids!" Paulette didn't hear him; she was sound asleep, leaning on Beth Ann, who had gone back to sleep.

Renzo and Tal headed for the dining room and some food. Both were dead tired, but Renzo had to stay awake until he heard from General Lem. He had to find some clue to our whereabouts! Finally, around noon, Lem entered the dining room, nearly asleep on his feet.

"No trace of the flying ship, sir. We followed their trail to a point two miles north of here, where they formed up ranks. Backtracking from there, they all came out of Velona by various routes, though we cannot follow their path once we got to the city cobblestones, unfortunately. Looks like we got rid of much of Velona's riff-raff. I've got six patrols still out, widening the search for the ship."

"Thanks. How's the burial project going?" Renzo asked, he'd forgotten all about this detail. The General had not.

"Pit's dug, 'bout a mile north of here, near where they amassed. Probably be sundown before all the bodies are carted there. I am going to get some sleep before I fall down." Renzo thanked him once more.

Bard Tal yawned, "Let's take a hint from him. Let's get us some sleep, shall we?" Both men headed to their bedrooms. Renzo laid down on our bed, crying until he fell asleep.

He awoke in the middle of the night, but there was little more news. The battlefield had been cleaned up, but a good rain would be needed to wash away the scars and remains, either that or a wet and melting snow. Already, several construction workers had begun repairs on the hole in the wall. Renzo ate a little and went back to bed.

The next morning, all of the regular inhabitants of the estate began returning, and the fighters had already returned to their normal stations. Renzo found Enyo studying the newly acquired devices. "Hi, thanks for getting me some new things to study," she said cheerfully. "I think we have here another type of mental scrambler, you know the kind that the mantis had which entrapped Bethany in the dome. We should experiment with it. Perhaps Paulette can find a way through the energy field."

"Okay, you turn it on, but be ready to turn it off if anything bad happens," Renzo said, ready to try any foolhardy idea to get clues to our whereabouts. "Iee, yes, that is doing pretty much the same thing. Ouch my head." Take it to Paulette and see if you can work out a way around this device so we can contact Bethany. If you can, Enyo, I owe you big time! You name it and it is yours!" She giggled, then picked up the device in her teeth and scampered off to find Paulette.

He went over the scouting reports; still no trace of the flying ship could be found. "This makes no sense! Its ship has to be here somewhere!" He left in search of the scout squads stationed here.

"Hi, Elinor, I heard that your Scout Squad followed the Grey Creatures trail."

"Yes, sir," the blonde scout squad leader jumped up from mending a bridle. "We lost the trail, though. I was so hoping to find some clue where our Supreme Commander is being held." A note of loss was in her voice, he noticed.

"Can you take me to where you lost it?"

"Sure, let's get saddled up. It's about three miles north of here." Ten minutes later, the two rode north from the main gates, while the rest of her squad was only a minute behind the two. No way were they letting Renzo go off on his own!

Soon, he had no trouble picking up the trail, even though hundreds of horses had passed along here in the last two days. The creature's steps sunk deeply into the soil. Renzo wondered how much the thing had weighted, resolving to ask those on burial detail when he got back. A few minutes later, Elinor showed him where the tracks ended. They had come upon a small hill. Trees grew around nearby, their winter branches lifeless, Renzo's heart fell, and he hoped they were not a harbinger of loss.

He dismounted. "I'm going to back track his footsteps," he announced. He turned in the direction the steps headed. Looking over his shoulder, he moved back into the next step the creature had made. Three steps later, there were no more. He was right up against the little hill.

"See, they just mysteriously end or rather begin," Elinor pronounced, baffled by the trail which made no sense. "Can he just appear at some location?"

"I doubt that. Maybe he jumped down to this spot, though I would expect far deeper prints here, but these are the same as all the others." Renzo thought a moment. "I think I will climb up here and see if I can see anything else. This sure is strange, Elinor." He stepped up the side of the hill and lost his balance. The rocky ground of the hill was not there. He fell forward, his hand flailing in total surprise. Oof. His body hit something cold and hard.

Elinor screamed, "Half of your body has disappeared! Are you all right?"

Sure enough, the front half of his body was not visible; at least he had no lower arms any more. He pulled one back and it reappeared. He stuck it down to the solid thing on which his other hand was resting, and it disappeared once more. "Eureka, this must be it! Elinor, we have found something, though I can't tell what." He began to feel around the object, which for all appearances was merely another stark hill here in the middle of the wintertime barren lands.

A minute later, the twenty women of the scout squad had all dismounted and joined him feeling their way along the hill, which was not a hill. "It is some kind of illusion," Elinor declared.

"I've an idea," Renzo said. He stuck his head into the hill. He saw a long, sleek flying machine, black metal skin. "Wow! Stick your heads inside the hill!" Suddenly he saw twenty heads of women looking this way and that at him and the ship, disembodied heads. He began to laugh at how silly they looked. It was contagious, Elinor claimed he look like a floating head.

An hour's study later, they concluded that it measured a hundred twenty feet long and fifty around, rather like an enormous cigar. It had no visible wings, perhaps they were retracted somehow. They also saw no way inside the ship. However, Elinor found a strange set of symbols at one spot in its side. Apparently, they didn't do anything, though she pushed some with her fingers.

Renzo was frustrated. He'd found the ship, probably the one which had abducted us, yet he could not get inside. He used the pummel of his sword and began tapping on the metallic sides. The whole ship echoed. "They might be inside," he said and all twenty-one of them began tapping all around the ship, hoping to hear a reply from inside. Nothing.

Still not convinced that we were not inside, Renzo decided to see if he could move inside the ship. He had Elinor watch over his body, and he slipped up to the black skin. After a pause, he inched forward, half expecting to get a shock or some nasty surprise. Nothing happened, except he began to slide through the metal hull. He moved all the way inside.

This was a strange world to him. Nothing looked familiar, but there was a faint night light illuminating the inside. He moved systematically through the whole ship. In what must have been a cargo bay, he found Adrien's scarf! Once certain we were not in there, he returned to his body.

"Adrien's scarf is inside there! This was the ship used to abduct them! Unfortunately, they are not here."

"Well, sir, you now know at least that much," Elinor tried her best to put a positive slant on the disappointing news. She had crossed her fingers that Renzo would find us all safely inside, awaiting a rescue.

"True," Renzo commented, and they all returned to the manor.

Now he became more and more worried. "Look, Enyo, Paulette, what if they are utterly dependent on the creature returning back to them? What if they are out of food and were waiting for him to return with more? What if he left them in a precarious position, expecting to return?"

"Look, you can 'what if' all night long, Renzo. It won't make a drop of water in the ocean's difference. We need to concentrate on finding a way to reach Bethany without causing her the excruciating pain she had just sending you her warning."

"True, Paulette. Any progress?" he said, realizing she was right.

# Chapter 15 H'Kan Makes His Move

A deep bass voice appeared in my head. I was fighting the damnable pulsating machine, while trying to sleep. The bass voice said it again. *Paulette here. Bethany, am I getting through?*

*That can't be you; your voice is below any man's voice. I'm hallucinating again.*

*No, it's me. I've found a way to break through the energy barrier preventing you from using telepathy. Thanks to your warning, Renzo managed to save the day. We killed the Grey Creature and a couple thousand of the assassins. They attacked nearly every one of our fortresses all over Tarra, even New Barq. Their main thrust was here at the estate. We took four light wounds; one fighter, she lost a finger. We eliminated every one of them. Renzo and Bard Tal used the mantis Stone Cutters to cut the Grey Creature in half. He's also found the thing's flying ship. He says that Adrien's scarf is inside. We also got a hold of the creature's devices that he was wearing. One is similar to the mantis device, which prevented you from using telepathy or moving out of the dome. Enyo and I worked out a way around it, a change in frequency. I've gone much lower on this first attempt to get through to you. Are you in pain while I am talking?*

*No, no pain; you just sound weird.*

*So do you, like super low man's voice. Anyway, how are you holding up? Any idea where you are being held? Kids all right? Do you know how many Grey Creatures we are dealing with?*

*Kids are fine. No idea where I am. They've blinded me, among other things. I think there are only two. One is here looking after us, you killed the other one? Really?*

*Yes, here are the images. I was watching the battle.*

*Wow, cut in half! Tell Renzo that was a fabulous idea! I am at some kind of experimental station. They've captured a number of mantis experiments, but I think they did this more than a quarter century ago.* I told her of the people here, their names, and what little I could of them. *Tell Renzo I love him and will make sure the kids somehow survive all this. I have to go. I hear footsteps coming. Thank you!*

The door opened and the lights went on, though I saw nothing but utter blackness. The friendly voice of H'Kan spoke, "Good morning Bethany, children. Time to rise and shine. Breakfast is waiting. See you there." I heard his footsteps diminishing; he left us alone, as he had been doing the last few days.

With a great effort of swinging my legs, I managed to get into a sitting position. Chamber pot. Badly needed. Ten steps to my left. Okay, here goes. I stood up, wiggling my body to keep my balance. After ten small steps, I began to feel for it with my right foot. I heard it hit the metal pot. I tried to imagine its location relative to me and moved to straddle it. A short while later, Lena exclaimed, "Yes, look everyone, mom did it all by herself!" I heard her come over to me and felt her arm leading me to my bed. She helped me get dressed.

"Okay, you kids go along first. I will bring up the rear."

"Are you sure mom?" Lena asked.

Taking small steps and counting quietly to myself, I made it to the doorway, but almost fell down as I bumped into it. After readjusting my position, I began again and eventually arrived at the table. Everyone was so cheerful this morning, chatting away. As usual, Lena fed me my breakfast.

H'Kan surprised us all when we finished, "Bethany, may I have a private word with you?"

"Sure, I am basically your prisoner. I can't survive without you," I replied rather sarcastically.

While the others and my children ran off to do chores or play, I could not tell which, H'Kan put his arm around me and led me down the hall. "Where is this direction? I mean I haven't been this way," I said becoming disoriented; my black space did not have anything in the way we were going.

"My private office, Bethany. A few more feet. Here, I have a chair for you." He guided me to the chair and had me bump the back of my legs into it. Gosh, it takes a strong heart suddenly to sit down without seeing a chair under you, no sense of space at all. I hit the bottom rather hard, jarring the device, which gave me a jolt of physical pain.

"Bethany, I wish to speak to you about something that I have been considering since you were brought here. Our race has always been about controlling other's bodies. In contrast, we know the Kronids, the mantis, are far worse off; they are into punishing other's bodies, torturing them — most sadistic creatures. We have lost all sense of ourselves as spiritual beings. I've come to this as a logical conclusion, though I have no real tangible proof myself. I've been here on Tarra for centuries now. I've watched my own people slowly sink down to the level of our enemies. G'Kar has sunk to the depths of a mantis or lower. I think he actually enjoyed punishing your body, your cell."

"Bethany, I can take this no longer. I have been watching and caring for all these people here for a half century now. Always, I see true love and humanity; they care for each other, something we have long ago lost completely among our people. Perhaps it is because we have been at war for centuries, I don't know. Yet, despite all the torture and mutilations of your bodies, you still love each other, are still being happy, still look out for each other, and still make sure those who need help receive it. I am humbled to admit this, Bethany, but the people here at this station are more human than we, the Grey Creatures as you know us. Somewhere along the line, we have lost that which once made us a great race. We've lost track of our own selves, becoming that which we hated, the Kronids and their perversions."

"Then, here you come, brutalized by G'Kar beyond all need, and you give out kindness and concern, hope, and guidance, even in your horrible, tortured shape. Indeed, you are more worthy of life than I am. Bethany, I am old and tired; yet I am also somewhat selfish. I must admit that I have spent these past nights thinking about your therapy and what all it has done for others. Before I lose this aged body, I would give anything to regain my self-respect, to know something of my spiritual nature, and to be free or outside of this body, though I can't imagine what that may be like. I have always thought of myself as being this body here."

"I know that you have promised to give all the others here therapy sessions as soon as you are able to do so. Yet, I ask you, I beseech you, would you be willing to give me those sessions first and soon? If you need time to think about this, I can understand. If you hate us, and you certainly have every right to do so, and if you do not want to freely do this to me, I can understand that too. I am certainly most unworthy to receive such a gift."

I was taken by surprise, shocked really is more like it. I said nothing for a moment. "Well, H'Kan, you have shown me and my family nothing but the greatest of kindness. I can tell from hearing the others speak of you that you have treated them like they were your own family. That your body happens to be one of those we consider our enemies, I would be a total fool to say that alone made you my enemy. What a person does makes the person. Yes, H'Kan, I will do what I can for you. Only at the moment, I don't think I can do it without being able to see my patients and their reactions. If I ever can get home, I have friends who can also perform the therapy, and I can monitor them by listening in and offering suggestions, even though I can't see. They will have to become my eyes."

"You would do this to one who is your enemy?"

"Yes, but you are not my enemy. G'Kar was. My husband killed him two nights ago when he tried to storm our estate."

"Yes, I know already. G'Kar is dead. I sensed it. He was to report and did not. His ship is still in chameleon mode. I believe it was your husband who searched it, though I can't be sure, only that some presence entered the ship. The ship logged it. I feel that it is good that your people have killed him. He got only what he sewed in life. I have been wondering how your people knew of the attack of G'Kar's?"

"I told my husband that first night I was here. It hurt me terribly to use telepathy, and I passed out from the pain, but I got the message to him. Your kind may torture my body, but I refuse to let my people down. There is more to life than a fleshly body, H'Kan."

"Bethany, you have put our entire race to utter shame. You are more than worthy to control and run your own lives. We certainly are completely unworthy of ever doing it again. Since you have promised me that you will give me your therapy, then I can talk more to you."

Now I was intrigued. What else was there to say? Unless he could get us all back to our estate and I could convince Beth Ann to run the sessions with me listening in, what else could I say?

H'Kan said, "Bethany, there is a huge galaxy of stars out there in the sky, around which many Tarras revolve. Tarra is a very, very long way from the inhabited portion. Yes, it is a penal colony, a dumping ground, where unworthy spiritual beings have been dumped for generations. Yet, have you ever wondered how it is that our flying ships and those of the mantis can even find such a tiny dot as Tarra, so utterly far from our inhabited worlds?"

"Well, I wondered how you could find us."

"On the moon above are two homing beacons that continuously send out a signal, much like your telepathy. Our ships lock in on that beacon and therefore know how to find this place. One is our beacon and the other is the mantis beacon. I will give you and all of the wonderful people on Tarra the greatest gift that I can, as a way of thanking you for trying your therapy on me first. With G'Kar dead, I alone have the access codes with which I can turn the beacon off or even destroy it. Actually, I was thinking more along the lines of its destruction. I know that the mantis beacon is close to ours. We rigged an explosive device on ours that will also destroy the mantis beacon. I suspect theirs is also similarly rigged. All I have to do is enter the codes and the beacons will be destroyed. Once gone, it will be next to impossible for other ships to find Tarra, out here in the depths of uncharted space. Will you accept my gift in return for my therapy?"

"Absolutely! H'Kan, this is the best, most incredible news that I have ever heard! Yes, yes, a thousand times yes!"

"Then, I will do so soon. Yet, there are some other small things that I can do for you. You and the men are not permanently blinded. Rather, grey caps have been placed over your eyes. I will remove them for you. At least, you can then see. I will also remove that deplorable device he put inside you as well."

"Not blind?" I could have screamed for joy!

"Here, spread your legs." I obeyed. Soon I felt something slide out of me. God did that ever feel great; gone was my entrapment! "I did that first because I know the other women are a bit sensitive to having men down there. Now I will fix your sight. Please hold quite still. Water will be flowing into your eyes. I need it to help break the tension on the grey globes." I felt water going into each eye, felt it drip down my cheeks. I felt a pressure on my eyes, as if they were being pulled out of their sockets.

Suddenly, light entered them. I blinked. I could see the room. "See, these were covering your eyes." I blinked and tried to focus, there were two small half spheres of grey.

"Thank you, thank you! H'Kan, I could hug you, but I've no arms. I guess thank you will have to do!" He smiled. I had another thought, "Can you do anything about these neck things, the corset, or the boots?"

"I can unseal the boots, but on this cold floor, you must wear them or your feet will eventually freeze to the floor. One minute." He walked over to a desk filled with equipment and gadgets. He picked up a device similar to the one G'Kar had used to seal them onto my feet. Soon, he was moving it up and down my legs. I felt the tight tension subside. "There, see if you can slip them off and on." It was difficult, constrained as I was, but I successfully got them off and on again.

He then said with a great sadness, "I'm afraid that I dare not undo the corset or neck collar. Both are made of metal and sealed onto your body for a reason, in your case. You see, G'Kar has disintegrated some of your neck bones and some in your lower back. That is why you were having such pains there. If I remove your neck support, your head will flop down to your chest, for there is no more bone structure to hold it up. You would either suffocate to death or choke to death, depending on which way your head fell down. If I take off your corset, the two halves of your body would do pretty much the same thing. I'm terribly saddened to have to tell you this horrible truth, but you must wear these two for as long as you live."

"What about the others?" I asked, fighting back the tears.

"I'm afraid that, while their bones have not been destroyed as yours have, they have worn them for so long that their muscles have atrophied so much so that the same things would result if I removed them. They can no longer support their own heads without the neck braces. Similarly for their waists. I am so truly sorry that I was a part of that experiment, the neck braces thing. I did not know the ultimate result. I discovered it some twenty-five years ago when I removed one from another woman here. Her head plopped to one side, and she died almost at once. I was so sickened by it that I refused to do it anymore."

"If you will go out and tell the others what I am doing, I would appreciate it. Start with the men, bring me them one at a time. Would you do me the favor of being with them when they finally can see the women whom they've married? I will feel horrible if they now reject what they are actually seeing in their mates."

"Sure, but I think you are not giving the men enough credit. Thank you, H'Kan. Thank you." I walked out of his room, light as a feather; a hideous black weight had been lifted from me. I could at least see now and could communicate freely with Renzo, who must be frantic with worry by now.

I was amazed to see how our habitat actually looked. Neat rows of growing plants filled one huge room, which had growing lights overhead. I found Pedro and Delia working in a plant bed. "Pedro, we can see again. H'Kan is giving us the greatest of presents, our sight back. Put your arms around me, and I will lead you to him. Delia, you can follow us. I'm sure that Pedro will want to see you immediately when his sight returns."

"You are joking with me," Pedro asked.

"No! Her eyes, they are not grey like they were. She has walked her herself with no one leading her. Go with her Pedro! Go! I'll be right behind you two." I positioned my body so Pedro could feel it, and he soon had his arm around me. Slowly with small steps still, we walked down the long hall. He was also disoriented as I had been, since this area was not known to him in his blind space. A little while later, Pedro could finally see for the first time in twenty years.

"Oh Delia! You are even more beautiful than I ever fantasized!" He grabbed her, and they embraced very passionately. I felt like saying to H'Kan, "See, I told you so," but didn't. I let him loosen their boots, while I went to find another pair.

I had Aduviri in tow, with Yida following behind, when Delia and Pedro came past us. Pedro said, "Aduviri, it is true, you will be able to see again. Oh, Yida, you too are gorgeous!" She smiled and looked at the floor. I was a little worried for these two, since she was very black. I suspected she had similar thoughts.

A short while later, Aduviri was just as wildly excited about seeing Yida as Pedro had been seeing Delia. "I swear you are so beautiful, Yida, I had no idea you were this pretty. Oh do I ever love you!" Once more, smiling to myself, I walked slowly back to find the next couple. Soon I was leading Lexos and Citalmina to H'Kan room.

"You are kidding me," Lexos kept saying. "I cannot see. How is it that I will be able to see again?" I didn't try to explain. He would soon be able to see for himself. Now I had to bring the two older women, who were encased similar to me. We three were now going to have the roughest time, unable to move waists and necks. However, being able to free our feet opened up many new possibilities for more independence, that much I knew.

After getting them to H'Kan, I went in search of my children. I found them playing games in a large open room. The girls were playing squares, where they tried to jump to certain squares, while the boys were playing hide and seek among the supplies in the supply room.

"Mom! You can see again!" exclaimed Lena. They all rushed up and hugged me tightly. I had tears of joy wetting my cheeks; I had thought I would never see their faces again. She added, "I can still feed you, mom."

"Maybe not, we'll see. He had fixed my boots so I can remove them myself. I may be able to feed myself once more. Don't know, what with this neck thing and corset. We'll see at lunch."

I added, "Now you kids play and have fun. I am going to give our host, H'Kan, some therapy sessions. Once I finish him, I will work on all of the others here."

Slowly I walked back to find H'Kan. He was still in his private room. As I entered, he said, "I am so sorry about the neck and waist, really I am, Bethany."

"Well, what's done is done. Come on, I promised you sessions, we should get started now."

"First, I must destroy the signal beacons as promised. Here, you can watch me. See this green light; it is indicating the beacon is operational. That smaller one there is monitoring the mantis beacon so that we know when they are coming as well." He entered some digits into a console device. "Here, you may have the honor, push this button and ours will explode, and that will trigger a similar explosion in the mantis beacon."

I walked to the console and using my nose, pushed the button. I had an awful time getting to it, however, unable to bend enough. I felt the button depress and backed up to watch. The green light suddenly turned red, within seconds, the smaller mantis light shone red as well. "Well, that seals my fate as well as yours," H'Kan said with a sigh. "I'm now stuck on Tarra along with all of you."

"Thank you, H'Kan. Now let's get started. Can you help me into a chair?" I sat across the table from him in his room. I explained the basic procedure to him. "Usually, we handle trauma the person has just undergone, such as my losing my arms. Here, we don't have such, but you've mentioned your obsession with controlling other people's bodies. Let's try this area. I want you to find the most recent time that you can where you actively were controlling other people's bodies." I surely hoped this approach would work. How else could I get started with this kindly alien? Would our techniques even work on an alien?

"Oh I well remember the day when the raider crews brought in Chimalma."

"Okay, I want you to go through it and tell me what is happening as you go along."

"Well, T'Ank said, 'Here you go, H'Kan, got another one for you to play with.' He was laughing. The poor woman is terrified, shaking badly. I pick her up and carry her down here. Of course, she had no arms; we got her from the mantis creatures. I thought I could really control her best if I encased her neck as I had done to Sophia some years before. I am fixing her neck brace so she can't move her head. I thought I am controlling that body rather well. Just as I am about to put the corset on her to further control her movements, I notice that she is pregnant, so I decide it is best to wait until the baby is born. Two weeks later, she has twins, which is why she is so large. Then, I am putting the tight fitting waist brace on her, effectively ending all of her struggling. Now I have her completely under my control. I feel satisfied, but then I discover that I have to help her with nearly every aspect of raising her newborn twins. I begin to regret what I have done, but there is no going back."

We went through it a couple times with nothing significantly new appearing and I asked for an earlier time. He then went through his initial episodes with Sophia, when she was brought here. From there, I began to get an education in his more distant past. He was three hundred sixty-four years old. We went through four more similar incidents from when he first came to Tarra, incidents where he had actively attempted to control other people's bodies, making them do what he desired.

What shocked me was that in one of these, he had convinced King Randolf of the Greenway to align with some thousand Galts, the horsemen of the Northern Steppes. He had been the one responsible for setting up the events in which my first body here on Tarra, Elizabeth Stanton, had been killed by these very men. We, in turn, had unleashed an incredible lightning bolt display, which wiped them all out. Now I understood why King Randolf had seemed insane, Grey Creature meddling.

We had to stop so that he could prepare supper for everyone. Naturally, the other adults wanted to know how it was going for him; they were most curious about this therapy of mine. "Wait until we get done, please," I interrupted his response.

"That's true. I can say this is *so* real. I hate to admit this to all of you, but I am seeing just how badly I have behaved in the past." He fortunately left it at that.

The next day we continued. I helped him face another dozen incidents during his long life where he had been reactively enjoying controlling people's bodies. Just before I was about to ask for yet another earlier one, he volunteered an observation. "Bethany, you know I just realized that when one sinks lower, they tend to become obsessed with punishing bodies. I believe that I stopped that vicious descent just barely in time. I hope that I can be saved. I don't want to end up being another G'Kar! Okay, what were you about to say?"

"Thanks for the observation. Now then, is there another one similar to this that is earlier?"

"Well, that last one was pretty much it. I mean I was just a wee giant when I did that. Earlier you say?" He began looking and looking. At this point, I simply faced him and waited patiently, casting the many doubts out of my mind that I had at night thinking about the effectiveness of therapy on aliens.

Suddenly, he doped off, sort of fell asleep. "Yes, have you found something there?" Normally, I would have touched him gently with my hand or more recently with my foot. Constrained as I was, I thought it better just to continue to see if I could coax him. Finally, he muttered something unintelligible.

"Okay, then I want you to begin at the beginning and go through that and tell me what is happening."

For the longest time, all I got were grunts and highly visible body jerks. Then, he began some incredibly huge yawns! I knew I had him now! I kept him at it. Slowly the details began appearing. "I am floating around this world. God, I am me. I am a being! Here I am floating along. I see these large, rather pretty, grey bodies down there, and I am sitting way up here watching them move around. Then, one sees me up here. He points something in his hand toward me. At once, I feel waves of energy swamping me. I am helpless, unconscious. I feel I am being sucked downward. I fight against it. No use, going down. Oh, I end up in one of these bodies. The body who did this to me says, 'There, now you can be a body too. See how great it feels to be a body? Make it run, come on.' He takes off on a jog. I follow him; it feels good. I get all these wonderful sensations from the body. He says that my name is Y'Far, and I don't have to remember anything else but that."

H'Kan began laughing heartily. "Don't remember anything else! Ha, ha, ha! That was a silly decision! Bethany, the Grey Creatures actually captured me when I was a free being and forced me into one of these giant bodies. I went around for years being this body, Y'Far! Damn, I slowly slipped on down into the controlling of bodies as the years went by! Bethany, I am not this body! I am me!"

Oh!" He looked at me strangely and added, "I am no longer in it! I'm me! Right here! I can see you too. You are there behind your head. I feel fabulous! Words cannot describe how I feel. Bethany, you have given me back my freedom!"

I saw him also above and behind his head and quietly ended the session. We wandered out to where the others were, and H'Kan began telling everyone all about it, laughing more than getting actual words out. His laughter was contagious, and soon everyone's spirits were soaring.

That night after diner, he came to me again. "Bethany, I have another confession to make to you. Only now do I fully understand what we did to you. You are like me, outside. When we constrained you, that is bad enough, but when he blinded you and put the device inside you to force you to be permanently inside your head — that is unforgivable of us! Come, I must show you some things."

"Here, this is how you operate the food dispenser. Oh," he realized that it took hands to do this.

I helped him out, "Why don't we show this to Citalmina?"

"Yes, yes, that would be better." I went to fetch her. He spent a half hour showing her how it all worked, where we should put the food inside, how to cause it to create the meals, and how to retrieve them.

"Now Bethany, will you please come with me to my room. I have something else that I must show you." I followed along behind him into his room, where all the various machine panels, full of knobs, dials, and switches was located.

His first question I found intensely interesting. "Do you know where you are being held? Where we are at?"

"No, only that we are underground."

"Let me show you. I have a map around here somewhere." He rummaged through several drawers until he found one, though not the one he desired. "This will do. Here is Tarra. You recognize where Velona is located?" When I was a little girl, I would have pointed to it with a finger. A month ago, I would have pointed to it with a toe. Just now, I could bend enough to get a heel up, so I described it to him.

"Yes, that's good. We are up here at the very top of your world, well mine too now. We are deep underground, however. I have entered the access codes that have unlocked all the gates. Now anyone can enter or leave at will. If anything should happen to me. . . Well, I thought you ought to know. I don't know how we can ever get back down there, though. I always took one of our ships, but there is none here now."

"Okay, so how do we get. . ." I didn't get to finish my sentence. H'Kan began holding his chest, as if in great pain.

Slowly he collapsed onto the floor, while I stood there helpless. I squatted down to be beside him. His voice was weak. "We have just been in time, dearest Bethany. My body is very old, even for one of us. I knew that my body was dying months ago. I was going to speak of it to G'Kar, when he returned. Our therapy has been just in time. Now I can let this body go, knowing now who and what I really am. Thank you for giving me the greatest gift anyone can bestow. I promise you this, Bethany, I will get a baby body in Velona, and when it grows up, I will do everything I can to help you Santi in your mission here on our home world. I swear this to you. I only wish the body could have lived a little longer so that we could get you all out of here and safely back to Velona. In this I have failed. . . His body slumped; he released one last breath of air. Slowly his eyes closed, and H'Kan, the gentle Grey Creature, floated up and out, heading south in the direction of Velona. Stunned, I sat there beside him for some time.

At last, with an effort, I got to my feet more slowly than ever, tears coming naturally. I went in search of the others. "Mom! What's wrong?" Lena asked. She, I found first.

"Our host has died. Please get everyone together in the dining room, will you?" Lena didn't need to be asked twice. Her heels clicking rapidly, she headed off to find all of the others here in this underground home. Fifteen minutes later, all of us were crying together. I told them of the passing of our host. Yes, H'Kan was more of a father or a host than a jailor. I never got the chance to tell him so.

I let everyone grieve for him for a while. Now we had to take stock of our situation. "Okay, he told me where we are located and has opened all the gate barriers so that we may leave. However, that is not going to be easy. Let me explain." I described where we were at, beneath the northern pole of Tarra. No Santi had ever been to the land of the Axemen, Volksholm, in the far northern area of our part of the dog bone continent. Yes, some sea captains of the Sea Princes had been there, trading with these hardy, burly men from the north, these powerful fighters whose weapon of choice was a mighty battleaxe. We had not. Yet from our mantis maps of Tarra, Volksholm was nowhere near the northern pole of Tarra.

"How will we get home, mom?" asked Ben.

"That is a very good question, son. I have no answer yet. Tomorrow, we must take stock of our supplies here; figure out how long we can live here before trouble comes. We need to see what cold weather gear, if any, we can find. We need to explore this entire complex to see what we might be able to use. We will need to see what it is like outside, above ground. Also, I will let your father know our location and have him put all of the Santi resources on the task of getting us home. Son — actually all you children — we are now going to be very dependent upon your help, if we are to get home. All the rest you are more than welcome to come to Velona and live at our mansion. If we can get us all safely there, then if some of you wish to return to your homelands, I will see that you get safely there as well. Once we know our situation, if we have time on our hands, I will continue with your therapy sessions. It was just in time for H'Kan. He made it and now is on his way to a new, far happier lifetime."

"Can't we do some of the searching tonight?" asked Lena. "I cannot sleep just now, not with the old man having just died. I like to think of him as an old man; he seemed that way to me."

"Yes, he did to us all, Lena. He was a good person in the end." Since everyone felt similarly, I decided to break up into groups and explore every inch of our site, particularly where we had never been. I took Lena and Ben with me, while the two older women looked after my younger two and Yida's and Deilia's youngest. We broke up into five search teams. I had the men find a place to lay H'Kan and cover his body.

"Where are we headed mom?" asked Ben.

"Up and out. I want to see what the conditions are topside."

"Makes sense, that's the first thing I would want to know," Lena said. I detected she was beginning to make use of all her knowledge and training from last lifetime, when she was Lenkova, one of the most powerful freedom fighters in Zargarb. "We must find the stairs that we originally came down. I will need you two to open the doors. Can either of you remember the way he brought us down here?"

"I do mom," Lena replied. "I remember being carried down this hallway here. Let's backtrack. Come on." Three sets of heels echoed loudly down the narrow hallway, carved from solid stone. I wondered how far underground we actually were.

"Say, slow down a bit, kids!" I panted for breath. "I can't breathe well at all in this. We have to go much slower or I'm going to faint. Hold up a minute please." I stopped and tried to control my desperate gasps for breath. At last, I recovered, and we continued at a much slower pace, one that I could handle, breath-wise.

Damn, Lena was good, very good. Unerringly, she retraced the path that G'Kar had carried us down here. We passed many side doors, but did not stop to search just yet. At last, she opened a door, and a dimly lighted set of stairs led steeply upwards. I looked up; gosh, it was a very long way up! "Kids, easy does it. I'm not able to breathe at all well. Neither will the other women who are wearing these restraining corsets. If I begin to faint, please catch me. I don't want to fall all the way back down here!"

Unable to bend my neck to look down, unable to bend at the waist, going up these steps was challenging, made all the more so by the heels. Even the kids remarked that their knees were aching before long. Worst still, I had to stop to gasp for breath every few steps. Gasping, I said, "This will never do!" I moved on up towards the top, a very long way up. Once at a landing there, I latched on to my body and those of my two oldest and lifted our three bodies up to this landing and sat them down.

"Wow mom! That was terrific! Can you teach me how to do that trick!" exclaimed Lena.

"Me too, incredible mom! These boots make my legs and knees ache so, but I bet going all the way down is going to be a knee killer!"

"Come on; open this door, and let's see what's beyond it. I hope not more stairs," I replied, smiling a satisfied smile. Ben did the honors, but none of us was prepared for what we found.

Yes, we were definitely outside, back on the surface of Tarra. A bitter cold blast of air hit our faces and bodies. Only our feet inside the boots were unaffected by the cold. In a very dim light, we saw nothing but snow, grey white in this light, a snow-scape stretching as far as our eyes could see. "Sh-sh-sh-shut t-t-t-the d-d-d-door!" I tried to say, my body shaking from the sudden cold. Ben did at once.

"T-that w-was c-cold!" he exclaimed.

Quickly, the temperature began to warm up. "We are trapped here, aren't we mom?" Lena said, heartbroken that we could not just walk out of here somehow. "Not even dad could travel through that!"

"We'd best continue our search, we need to find some heavy clothing to protect us from that cold," I suggested, unwilling to give up without a fight. I stared at the steep steps going down. "I don't think I can go down constrained like this and in these boots." Lena tried a few steps, Ben, likewise.

"God mom, my knees are aching already. We are never going to make it back down without your help," Lena said, looking back up at me. I smiled, and moved out and down and then picked up our three bodies and sat them back down on the lower landing safely.

"First, kids, we must find warm clothing, if we are to go back out there and head for home," I tried sounding optimistic for all our sakes. "We have to use our minds to get out of this one. Come on; we passed many side doors. Time to search."

Hours later and incredibly tired, we had found one room, which held a large collection of heavy parkas and gloves. The other rooms appeared to be barracks of some kind; the beds were exceedingly long and wider than normal. Some contained many other types of supplies, including ropes, strange axes, and other things too numerous to mention.

We were very tired and our legs ached from having done so much walking. The others were equally tired, and by agreement, we decided to compare notes in the morning. Back in our room, Lena undressed me and helped put me to bed, kindly pulling up the covers for me. She leaned over and gave me a kiss. "Thanks mom." Ben turned out the lights, and it was time to relax and ponder the situation.

I reached out and made my nightly contact with Renzo. My body drifted off to sleep while I was telling him about all that I had learned, all that had happened, and where we were located.

*You mean that with these signal beacons destroyed, neither the mantis nor Grey Creatures will ever be able to return here? Bethany, that is incredible news. Yes, I'll have Paulette let Julie and the Guardian know tomorrow! You and the kids have saved all Tarra. I'm so proud of you! But I want you all safely back here. How are we going to do that?* His excitement gave way to near grief as I showed him my images of the surface.

*We have found what may be warm clothing. Our boots protect our feet, only we might not be able to walk in the snow and ice without falling down. Dear, give us some time on this end to see what we can figure out, while you work on it from your end. I'm sure that there has to be a way, only we just don't see it at this time. I love you.* We said many personal things, and then I broke the connection, floated above my sleeping body, and began to think.

My body woke up, refreshed, but in a desperate need to use the chamber pot! I realized that we had been utterly dependent on H'Kan giving us our wake up call. Now he was not here to do so. It must be morning, because my body told me so. With a major effort from my legs, throwing them about, I was finally able to get to a sitting position. I walked over to the light and pushed it with my nose. On came the lights, waking up Lena and Ben, while I headed for the pot. It was nearly full; no H'Kan had come to empty it as before. Ah well, we now had new chores for the children to perform.

Indeed, everyone else suddenly discovered how much we now missed good old H'Kan. From the morning wake up call to waiting breakfasts, we suddenly had to deal with these ourselves. I took charge, as is my nature, getting all these little details worked out. I had Paulette once more give me a wake up communication so that I could then wake the others in the morning. Citalmina, who still had her arms, was in charge of handling the machine that made our meals. The men were put in charge of taking our garden produce and getting it put into the various machine hoppers. I concluded that this was a self-sustaining environment, where everything was reused repeatedly, a model of efficiency that I didn't fully understand, especially what was done with the chamber pot's contents. This remained a mystery to us all.

Over breakfast, we compared observations on what all we had found during the searches last night. They had found many unexplained rooms, some filled with equipment, some with supplies such as hundreds of pairs of boots, corsets, and neck bands, some with clothing, and some with unknown items. The women had been most concerned over the food supply and had found a large supply of stored food in labeled boxes with strange symbols on them. The men had broken one open to see what was inside and discovered what was probably our meat supply. It was dehydrated and would have to be put through the machinery to make it edible.

I couldn't help thinking how excited Enyo would be if she were here. There was so much that would hold her interest that she could spend months here investigating and experimenting. "We found lots of warm parkas. I would like to don them, go out into the world above us today, and see if we might be able to survive in the coats, and if we could walk anywhere, though I'm not sure where we would walk just yet. Pedro, Lexos, Aduviri, would you guys come with me? I need help getting into the warm coat, and let's check the outside world together."

A while later, we four entered the coatroom. Admittedly, I looked very strange wearing this big, puffy parka, with only the tiny portion of my face visible. The arms dangling at my sides looked rather funny to me. We four looked at our appearance and laughed. However, when we reached the stairs, the guys tried to climb them, but they too experienced great difficulties in these boots. Our knees would take a beating if we did it. Again, I lifted us all to the top landing. Yes, they were incredibly shocked, surprised, and now in awe of just what I could do. Later I overheard them telling their wives that I must be a goddess.

Pedro opened the door, and we four stepped outside onto the surface of Tarra. Moonlight provided the only illumination, a dim pale light. Snow and ice stretched as far as we could see, totally bleak and dismal. When we spoke, giant puffs of frozen vapors formed small clouds around our mouths. Yet, we were staying quite warm inside these parkas. One problem solved, we could now be out here. "Let's see if we can walk over to that gate and flat area," I suggested.

I took three steps on the icy ground before I my heels slipped out from under me, and I went crashing to the ground. I managed to latch onto my body just before it hit, softening the hard, unexpected landing. I watched as the guys managed five crazy steps, their arms waving like mad to keep their balance before they too hit the ground. No doubt about it, while these boots kept our feet remarkably warm, we could not walk on this ice in the boots. I could not even get up, constrained as I was. I laughed my head off watching the three men try repeatedly to get up and walk back to assist me. They'd get a step or two and their feet would go sliding out from under them again. At last, they were laughing as well, crawling back to me on their hands and knees. With a great effort, we made it back to the landing, got inside, and shut the door, still laughing.

"That was actually hilarious," Pedro said, still chuckling. "Can't even stand on our own two feet out there!"

"They keep my feet warm, though," I added. I lifted us back down the steps, and the guys took our parkas off, hanging them back up in the store room. "So much for walking home," I teased them. We roared again.

Back in the dining room, Delia asked, "If we cannot walk out there, are we trapped in here until we too die, like H'Kan?"

"No, we must find another way. Perhaps my husband will devise a way. We'll figure out some way to get out of here," I tried to sound optimistic again, though I had no idea how we could.

After they gave me a tour of what all they had found, I then contacted Renzo and brought him up to date on our situation. Then, I spent the afternoon giving the first of many therapy sessions to the adults, beginning with Sophia. The other adults often listened in, fascinated by what they heard, eager to have their own sessions with me.

At supper, Ben showed me his find. He had found a ball! "Okay, Ben, you are on. It's kick ball after supper!" He grinned; he loved our playtime as much as I did. Before our abduction, we usually played every night after supper. I had him explain the game to the others. While the dishes were being done, thus began the first of many kick ball sessions.

In fact, it was rather hilarious: all of us trying to run around dodging the ball while wearing these boots. It was more like slow motion kick ball, except the ball wasn't going slow. We laughed and had such a good time that soon the adults joined in with us. After this first night, evenings became a group activity, which we all enjoyed, a time to forget our plight and circumstances and just have fun.

# Chapter 16 Unexpected Help

"Well, Bethany is certainly in a fine pickle barrel this time," Alexa commented at the morning meeting. Renzo had just briefed them on her location and the frustrating attempt to walk outside this morning. "We know where they are at as before, when you knew where we were at, only there is no way to reach her this time. I don't suppose that there is an underground river that runs under the North Pole of Tarra is there?"

"Not likely," Renzo replied, imagining a frozen river of ice.

"I'm more worried about her physical shape," Beth Ann, the aging Healer of my mother's Circle. "I've been discussing what she said the creature said that the other creature did to her back and neck — the disintegration of her bones there. I've brought along a couple example bones from a skeleton here to show you." She held up the two vertebrae to show them the skeletal backbone that supported the muscles, which in turn supported the head and body. Now she pointed out what she presumed that the creature had done to Bethany.

"The key is her choice of words, disintegration," Beth Ann continued. "Are hers merely broken into a couple of pieces or at the other extreme completely smashed into thousands of little pieces? If merely broken, the intense pain she would be under is debilitating, though with the good support that she is wearing, perhaps she can get by. However, if they are both truly broken into tiny bits, that could be life-threatening, again in this case, the braces are the only thing keeping her alive!"

"Can anything be done for her?" asked Renzo, fighting back his grief.

Beth Ann longed to offer him hope, but knew she must speak honestly. "If they were merely broken in one or two places, like any bone, they may heal in time, perhaps leaving her in constant pain or a somewhat overall deformed body shape. If in lots of pieces, which seems more likely, there is nothing that can be done for her. I'm sorry Renzo."

Alexa came to his rescue, "Well, none of that matters one iota, unless we can get her safely back here. How can we do this?"

"We know next to nothing about lands north of the Greenway," Renzo replied, grateful for a change in topic. He smiled at Alexa, who returned it. "Hence, I spent yesterday afternoon wandering about Velona, making inquiries of those who have immigrated here from Volksholm. I've asked Olaf Grenwaldt to come and give us a geography lesson. He has sailed the northern waters off Volksholm and has actually set foot on that frozen polar land. He should be here soon." Everyone thought this was an excellent move on his part, and they chatted while awaiting his arrival.

"Everyone, this is Olaf Grenwaldt," Renzo introduced the tall, gangly man, whose weight was much more than Renzo's and he stood six inches taller. His hair was red as was his full bushy beard. Olaf was a jovial man and fun loving, but a good navigator and now a good worker. He'd brought his whole family with him to Velona a dozen years ago, citing much better opportunities for a good life.

"Olaf, we need to find a way to rescue some people who are trapped up here at the top of the world, the North Pole. They have warm parkas and the cold does not seem to pose a problem for them. At this time, they also have sufficient food supplies. I've asked you here to get your ideas and opinions and suggestions on how we much rescue them." He did not want to divulge just who were there, me and our children. Nor did he want to go into a lengthy discussion of the Grey Creatures, which would likely be wildly beyond his comprehension.

"In Volksholm, we have long, cold winters. Down here, this hardly counts as winter!" They chuckled. "I've been on this polar land mass once. I had to set foot on it just so that I could say that I have, you know? In the summertime, that's the best time to get there. From October through April, it is very tough or next to impossible, because even the northern sea freezes up. Once a boat delayed too long from leaving a northern island and it remained frozen in the ice all winter. Its crew had to walk out of there or starve."

"As far as going overland to the top of the world goes, I sure wouldn't want to try that! Its surface is always covered in snow and ice, treacherous to walk. Worse, I've heard that there are bottomless fissures scattered about the land. One misstep and down you go, lost forever. Getting there on foot would be about the most risky adventure I can imagine!"

"Now if that doesn't scare you, then imagine going for a long walk around here. You've got hills, trees, and streams, all sorts of landmarks to guide your progress. Up there, from what I have seen myself, you've got snow and ice and ridges of snow and ice, all greyish white, no landmarks that we know as guides anyway — and you propose to hike in any kind of straight line? Unlikely."

"Then, there is the problem of carrying along food and housing. You cannot sleep out in the open; you'll freeze to death. Moreover, there is a light problem. In Volksholm, the winter days are very short, while the winter nights are very long. I've heard stories from those unfortunate souls whose boats were trapped in the ice. They say that when the night comes, day does not. I believe they mean that the night lasts all the time until spring comes. Of course, they also say that in summer, the days are very long indeed, while the nights are only a few hours long. I do not understand why this may be. However, if you are going overland, I urge you to do it in the summer time, when you have long periods of light."

"I've seen a few hardy souls use what they call dog sleds. Large, powerful dogs, sometimes a dozen of them, are used to pull sleds carrying their supplies and canvas huts for the nights. Of course, one sled is only able to carry one adult. If you have many people to bring back, when you add in sleds for food and huts, that is an awful lot of dog sleds; maybe more than exist. Then, of course, you have to guide them and not fall into the bottomless crevasses."

"Where would we stand the best chance of finding a number of these dog sleds?" Renzo asked.

Olaf thought for a moment, running his hands through his beard, bringing it to a point. "Probably on the island of Gossenhammar. It's one of the most northern inhabited islands. They do use dog teams quite a lot during the long winter months. In the summer, the sleds are not used. In my opinion, that's your best chance. Try Gossenhammar."

The others questioned him for a while longer, but nothing more of significance came from that. They all thanked him for coming and for his frankness. After he left, Renzo seemed more distraught than before. "How do we navigate there? How do we find and avoid these hidden crevasses? It seems an overland mission is more of a suicide mission than a rescue mission. I'll let Bethany know the grim news when she contacts me tonight. We must find another way to reach them."

The bedraggled faces, one by one, left the meeting room. None had any bright ideas for an alternate method to rescue us. After hearing about the bottomless crevasses, I was glad that we had not gone exploring beyond the few feet that we had attempted.

During the following week, Enyo visited the concealed flying ship many times, inserting her head under the "hill" and observing the ship. She found what must be the entrance to the ship and a small mechanical pad, which held nine ciphers. At the next meeting, she volunteered, "You know, if we could get inside that flying ship, perhaps we could learn how to fly it and use it to rescue everyone."

"Enyo, how the devil do we get inside, let alone fly that alien thing?" asked Renzo.

"Well, I have found a set of nine ciphers on what must be the entrance door. Remember, Bethany said that there were several other similar pads, which they used to enter codes to operate the machinery. I suspect this one is similar. Of course, we don't know the codes to open it. I can speculate that if the sequence is nine digits long, comprised of any of the nine symbols, there are over three hundred eighty-seven million possibilities to try. Of course, it might not be nine ciphers long, which would greatly lessen the number of things to try."

"I'd be an old man before you got inside it," Renzo moaned. "Even if you got inside, how would we ever learn how to fly the thing? We know nothing about it."

Her face fell, "Well, yes, that is true. I don't know. It's a shame that H'Kan died before he could educate us in its operation."

The next day, Rosina, his sister, contacted him. She and the others of the Explorers Circle were on the Sleepy Hollow, heading back toward Velona. Currently, they were just leaving from the far south land of the peanut continent, having re-supplied there.

*Renzo, Benet, Michelle, and I have an idea. Why don't we four actually go and*
*look at this pole land, see it up close, skim over it. Perhaps these hidden crevasses are not as bad as Olaf made them seem. We owe it to Bethany at least to observe for ourselves.*

Renzo's spirits rose. *Great idea. When should we do it?*

*How about now? One minute while we come to you. Get prepared yourself.*

Five minutes later, the foursome was flying over the northern lands of the Greenway, heading due north. Renzo kept an image of the Tarra map in mind and shared it with the others. Sometime later, they were out over open waters again. Slowly, ice shelves began appearing, and then the sea turned into a sea of ice and snow. They slowed down to get a close look and were appalled at the actual surface. Great sheets of ice pushed up and onto other sheets, forming ragged ridges, which would be nearly impassable on foot. Further inland, they spied a deep, gaping fissure. Renzo headed down it for a look, but soon gave up and rejoined the others, saying it was exceedingly deep. Olaf had not exaggerated; one fall into one of these crevasses would spell death. This one was large enough to swallow an entire dog sled.

After traveling several hundred miles with little change in the surface terrain, Renzo called a halt. It was very real to all four that a surface rescue was out of the question, for it would be nothing more than a suicide trip. None would likely ever reach us alive. Sadly, the four returned to their bodies. Renzo laid his head on the table and cried quietly to himself for a very long time.

During these past few days, Enyo spent every waking hour at the flying ship, trying combination after combination, to no avail. Sadly, she decided to give this line up, because without more information on what the code might be, she had no real chance of entering the correct sequence. Enyo didn't bother to tell Renzo that she had tried, although he already knew of her efforts.

By March 1, 659, Renzo had sunk into the deepest of depressions. Not only had he been utterly unable to dream up any way to rescue me and the children, neither had anyone else. He stopped attending the morning meetings; what was the use anyway? With their new organizational setup, the Santi del Dio was at long last operating smoothly without heavy, daily control from the headquarters group. Alexa took over most of the duties for him anyway. During the daytime, he mostly laid in our bed alternating between a hopeless crying and violent anger.

Yet, at night, he would relish my mental contacts. This night, when I made contact, I really sensed his utter depression. *I know, my love, there just doesn't seem to be any overland way to get to us. We just have to find another way.*

He sent, *I've given this a lot of thought, Bethany. If you are doomed to spend the rest of your life imprisoned up there and our children too, I am ready to come and join you. I can drop this body off the roof and come and be around you at least. I cannot live without you and the kids.*

*Renzo, that's not a good idea. What if one day we do find a way to get back? Then what? The children and I would be without you. Our long sacrifice would have been for nothing. You just have to bear your part of our burden. Keep the Santi healthy. Don't let our sacrifice go for nothing.*

*I just cannot take it anymore, Bethany. The first time, I spent hours working out ways to cross the desert to get to you, and then later how to get through the underground river. I had something I could do to rescue you. This time, it is utterly hopeless. There is no way to cross that land of ice and crevasses. I know I have lost you forever. I just cannot take it anymore. I just cannot take it anymore.*

Hey, the red flags went off in my mind. No, not that he might just kill off his body to come join with us, rather he was saying something rather irrational, rather reactive, like some wording right out of a traumatic incident of the past!

*Okay, I want you to go to the beginning where you first realized that we had been abducted this time.*

*I'm still in it. Okay, I can see myself waking up.*

*Good. Now go through all that happened and tell me what you are seeing and feeling as you go along.* I had no choice but to run a therapy session on my husband from long distance. I could not risk him jumping off a roof top or similar silly action. We ran through it a few times, his depression only grew worse. I asked for an earlier traumatic loss and, of course, we began running through the earlier Desert of Desolation incident. After a few times through that one, I asked for another earlier one.

*It's all hopeless. I've lost her. I just cannot take it anymore. I just cannot take it anymore.*

*Okay, let's go through that one; tell me what you are seeing.*

*I've lost her. I'm jumping off a rooftop. I cannot take it anymore.* I had him go back to the beginning and we ran through it once more. *I have a wonderful wife. I'm an engineer or something. I build new things. They took her away and killed her. I cannot find her. She is utterly gone without a trace. I bury her body. I cannot go on without her. I jump off a building top.*

At least we were finding out more about it. I had him go back through it once more.

*Oh, she and I, we are sort of fighting the local government, trying to make life easier for our people. They are forcing our people into a sort of slave working life. They get up, go to work, work at the most mundane task. Our close friend, all he does all day is polish the brass doorknobs at the Legislature Building. All day, nothing else. No one is allowed to buy anything anymore. Everyone just eats the same things, dresses the same way. She and I, we are inventing new things, trying to give our people some hope for a future, something to look forward to when they came home from their incredibly boring workday. I mean he has to polish the same damn doorknobs every day. They didn't even need it but perhaps once a year, yet he has to do it every day! We invent a card game where he, his wife, and us could have some excitement each night.*

*The Thought Police find out about it and take her away. I find her body lying outside our front door in the morning. I search everywhere for her, but she is just not on our world anywhere. I realize that they had taken her off to the penal colony. They make me go to work that day. I have five minutes to bury her body! Like every day of my entire adult life, I have to sweep the Legislature Building's steps. Perhaps once a week, there might be some small amount of dust or debris in my pick up shovel at the end of the day. It certainly does not need sweeping every day! Now when I come home, I have nothing to look forward to. She is gone. I cry and cry and cry. I just can't take it any longer. I jump off the Legislature Building's roof in the morning.*

*Oh, then the Thought Police come and, using this hand-held device, suck me into a black box. A long time later, I remember falling out of the box. A voice says go get a new baby body. It's Tarra! I'm floating down toward the Sea Princes. That's Zargarb. I recognize its shape and location. So this is how I got here. I was a rebel; so was my wife. Oh gods! I know who that was! Bethany, my wife, she is Lena, Lenkova! No wonder I have always tried to be around her somehow, someway! Now I have two reasons to find a way to get you all back here!*

Renzo was now quite enthusiastic. His depression had vanished in a flash. *Thank you! God, you are the absolute greatest person on Tarra, Bethany. There you are entrapped, in a horrible physical condition, and you still take the time to help me! God, I love you and our children too. I will find a way to get you back here. I promise you, Bethany.*

Honestly, I didn't have a whole lot of choice. I knew that I was going to be unable to get us home from here on my own. I depended upon Renzo to find a way, and he'd never do it if he was depressed or took other drastic measures. Still, I felt great that we had blown his traumatic loss. I hoped he would now be able to find a way to get to us.

The next morning, Renzo found Paulette. "I need you to make a Mind Link for me. I must talk to either Julie or the Guardian of the Anuir at once."

"I don't know how to contact Jes, so let me see if I can get a hold of Julie."

A short while later, Renzo felt the presence of Julie. *Hi, I'm Renzo,*

*Bethany's husband.*

*Hi, Renzo. How is Bethany doing? Have you found a way to get her and the others back to Velona yet?*

*She is holding up as well as can be expected. The Grey Creature crushed her vertebrae in her lower back and in her neck, forcing her to wear some very constraining braces. She cannot even bend enough to feed herself. Yet, she is still doing all she can. She's done therapy on the last remaining Grey Creature, who opened all the security locks before his old body died. She's doing therapy now on all the others who have been held captive there for so many years.*

*Yet, I'm afraid that we're not going to be able to rescue her. There is no possible overland route from here to where she is at the North Pole of Tarra. We've taken a very close look at it. I can show you what I found.* He showed her some of the memories he had of their trip, including his dive into the deep crevasse.

*At this point, we have exhausted all the means that we have to get to her. The only wildly possible thing is for us to somehow break into the flying machine of the Grey Creature that I killed and then somehow learn how to fly it. That's farfetched and not doable by us. I'm afraid that we simply don't have the means to rescue her and the others.*

*Now I'm sort of thinking outside of the box, so to speak. Julie, can you tell the Guardian all this please? I hate to have to ask you for help, because I know that you are all so very busy down there freeing beings. Yet, I have no other choice. Can you all see if you can think of some way that Bethany and the others can be rescued and brought home? If you cannot, then let the Guardian know that Bethany will no longer be able to hold up her end of the bargain, that is, to help keep Tarra quiet and at peace so that you all can do your job. He'll need to make such a bargain with another of us Santi. I will volunteer, if he doesn't know any of the rest of us well enough to make a replacement choice for Bethany.*

*It's that bad?*

*Yes, Julie. She's in a whole lot of suppressed pain. I can tell when she links to me each night. Yet, she can endure the pain if only she can get back home here.*

*Okay, Renzo. We will discuss it and see what can be done. You realized just how vital her recent actions have been? She's ensured that no more aliens will come to Tarra to wreak havoc on us all. That is an incredible gift to us all. I'll get back to you later. Thanks for letting me know just how bad it is. Bye.*

"Thanks, Paulette. Mission accomplished."

"Do you think that they will have any bright ideas for us? Will he really replace Bethany?" she asked, terribly worried about the consequences of that.

"I am hoping that they can see a way where I cannot. If not, then honestly, Bethany will be unable to continue working toward making Tarra safe for the Guardian. He'll have no choice but to appoint someone else to that task. Since he probably doesn't know anyone else here, I volunteered. It will be the least that I can do for her, if I'm utterly unable to find any way of getting to her and getting her back, along with our children."

Renzo continued, "Look, even if we do get her back by some miracle as yet unseen, she'll spend the rest of her life in pain from the crushed vertebrae and horribly constrained by the waist and neck devices. As it is, she has to be fed by Lena. She can hardly do anything for herself anymore. I will be honest with you; I don't hold out much hope for her or my children. Yet, I simply will never give up."

"She married the right man, that's all I have to say," she smiled and left.

Renzo went to find Alexa. "Hi, Alexa. I've made a decision, if I don't hear any good ideas from Julie down in the Red Desert on how to go about rescuing Bethany, then I am going to make a dog sled attempt to reach her. I want you to take over the reins of the Santi until she and/or I get back. The Explorers Circle will be returning in a few months, they will be able to help tremendously. I am going alone, because it is a very risky move. If I can pilot a way there, then perhaps others can follow."

"You should have someone go with you, you know. I will volunteer. I know that Enyo would also volunteer, just as soon as she hears about it. We all want to help get them back, you know. You are not the only one who loves her." She saw him staring at her missing arms.

"So I don't have arms, nor does Enyo or Bethany. That has never stopped us. Don't be so biased. Buster, if you say we can't go with you because we're armless, then Enyo and I are going to have to teach you a big lesson!" She threw her body up against his and grinned. "I'll go find Enyo and warn her to keep a sharp eye on you. You're not leaving without us, period."

"But who will run the Santi? I need you here, Alexa," Renzo complained.

"Let Kallisto do it, unless she insists on coming along as well!"

"Maybe then I won't go," he teased.

"Hum, maybe then we three women will go by dog sled and show you men up!" feisty Alexa playfully retorted. "Maybe you, being a man, are way overdue for some pleasure and that's why you are so, so, well so whatever. If you want, I'll bring Enyo and Kallisto around your bungalow tonight, and we can relieve you. I'm sure Bethany will give us her permission." Poor Renzo, he could not tell if she were joking or if she meant it. Red faced, he left to go make some more plans for a dog sled trip.

He commented to our room's walls, "I think that Alexa and Enyo are just over sexed. God, they are beautiful women though! They pale compared to you, my dear." He'd just seen our Torque Ball sitting beside the bed.

An hour later, Enyo and Kallisto came storming into our house. "Renzo! What's this I hear about you going off on a dog sled mission to reach Bethany and you're not taking me along?" Enyo said angrily.

"And me too," Kallisto added just as mad as her friend.

"But. . ."

"Alexa said that you are prejudiced against us because of our lack of arms! How dare you think that!" Enyo declared. "Get him, Kallisto!"

Both women swarmed up to him and banged hard into his body, knocking him down on to our bed. Both immediately plopped down on top of him, pinning him down. Enyo wiggled around and began to kiss him, while Kallisto wiggled the other way, rubbing his pants. "Okay, okay, okay. I give up! Please. You are married. Think of your poor husbands. Think of your children. Think of poor Bethany." He was rapidly running out of ideas.

At last, they could not keep from breaking into a hearty laugh. "We did get you good, now didn't we?" Enyo said. "Now we three are coming along and that is that. No more talk about it, you hear?"

"But. . ."

"No buts, buster. Okay, Enyo, let's continue raping this man," Kallisto replied.

"Okay, okay, okay, you made your point! Now come here and snuggle, one on each side of me," he said. The women wiggled around, tossed their long hair back, and cradled up against him, one of his arms around each women. "You make the best of friends. It will be a very dangerous trip. I didn't want to risk your lives, but it would be nice to have some company."

"I told you he would see reason," Enyo commented to Kallisto, who smiled.

"Thanks, we want to help, Renzo. If you are risking your neck, we want to risk our necks as well. We love her as much as you do," Kallisto added.

Renzo couldn't help teasing, "No, Enyo, you just want to get a good look at all the alien devices Bethany has there." Both women rolled over, began rubbing their legs on his private parts, while kissing him. Only when he began to tickle their sides did they relinquish their attacks. All three began laughing.

"Okay, ladies, we will go just as soon as possible, if I don't hear back any bright ideas from Julie. Now will you please stop trying to rape me?" Both chuckled and gave him a kiss before getting up and leaving him still lying on our bed.

After they had gone, he asked our walls, "I wonder if they would have gone that far? We sure have dedicated friends."

That night, just after we all finished our kick ball game and I was putting the kids to bed, I had a very unexpected visitor. *Hi Bethany. It is good to see you once again.* It was Jes Amir, the Guardian of the Anuir and my husband two lifetimes ago.

*Hi. I've gotten myself into a real pickle this time, haven't I? How did you find me way up here?*

*Renzo told us. I came personally to thank you for getting the signal beacons destroyed. We've verified that they are gone. Well done.*

*Just making sure they can't come back. They are particularly brutal on our bodies. I'm rapidly running out of body parts to donate.* I jested bravely. *How is Linda doing?*

*Very well indeed. Now let me see what injuries they have caused. Renzo says your back and neck were damaged.* I felt him sliding into my body, then he backed out.

*You're suppressing a great deal of pain, are you not?*

*Yes, I have to, no choice. I have my children to care for and all these others here. I can't afford to wallow in my own pain.*

*I understand. Have you tried to look and see what has been done to those two locations?*

*No, the pain gets too intense when I even try to get close to inspect them. Why? Are they as bad as I was told?*

*I want you to relax and duplicate your back. Move into the center of the pain and duplicate what is there. I am here and will help you with it.*

*Okay, I'll give it a shot.* I moved into the dully aching lower back and began to observe it. Wham! The amount of pain that I was blocking hit me hard. I screamed as loudly as I could, though Jes muffled it so that not even my sleeping children could hear me. Later, I was thankful for that. It took ages for me finally to confront that level of pain and observe my lower spine. *Good god! One section is mostly tiny particles!*

*Thank you. Now where were you when he did this to you?* I tried to answer as best I could remember. *Where are you now?* Right here, I answered. He played these two back and forth for quite some time.

*Hey, the pain is subsiding.*

*Good. Now let's make a new vertebra where this bad one is at, shall we. Go ahead and see if you can envision a new one there. Okay. Do it again. Good. Now do it again.* He kept this up for a long time. *Are you satisfied that you have a good replacement one there now?* I wasn't, so he continued some more. At last, I thought that I was.

*Excellent, well done, Bethany. I'm now going to remove this waist constrictor, corset thing.* I heard a popping sound, and it had severed in half; he lowered it to the floor and moved it away from me. *Now how does your back feel? Move around a little, bend, and stretch.*

*It's a miracle, Jes! The pain is gone. I can move again! Truly a miracle!*

*Very well done. Now I want you to move into the center of pain in your neck.* Once more, I felt a huge surge of suppressed pain. I screamed violently, more so than before, because now I could get a deep breath. Again, he repeated what we had done on my lower back. After a long time, he removed the neck collar bands. I could move my neck normally. All pain was gone, and I had healed the shattered vertebra there.

*Jes, two miracles! How can I ever thank you enough?*

*You already have by ensuring that these beings that would enslave us will no longer be able to find us. This is the least I can do to thank you. While we were working on your body, I was also working on the other four women here. Their constraints have been removed and their muscles strengthened. I'm about finished with them, though they know me not. You'll have to explain what I have done for them. In no small measure, they did set the stage for H'Kan to realize his own spirituality. It is my way of thanking them. Now I must get back to the others. Keep up the excellent work. Tarra is now more stabilized than it has ever been in many centuries. Thank you.*

*Thank you for these miracles.* Then, he was gone. I realized how much I had missed him all these years. Perhaps when this body dies I will be able to join him again, I thought. Just then, I heard a light pounding on our bedroom door. I knew it must be the others. I walked to the door and opened it. Sophia, Delia, Chimalma, and Citalmina were standing there, free of their corset braces and golden neck rings. Awe shown from their eyes.

I stepped outside so we didn't wake the children. I spent an hour explaining what had happened to us. In the end, they still believed that a god had just touched them! I could do little to dissuade them from that opinion. It didn't matter though; we all were free. Now I could concentrate on showing them how to become independent once more. First action, to feed themselves! We five walked to the food dispenser, and Citalmina activated it, producing five drinks. I wish it were tea, however. She was about to carry them over to the table for us, but I intervened. "Do it like this," I picked mine up with my teeth and carried it to the table. The other three followed my lead, smiling all the way.

"Now slide off the boots and get your toes around the handle loop like this," I demonstrated how to use a foot to raise the cup and bending over enough to sip from it. Amazed, the three struggled to duplicate me. By the time we finished our drinks, they were starting to get the hang of doing it themselves. For the first time in way more than a quarter century, Sophia was able to drink by herself! The incredible surge in self-respect these women had was unbelievable. I promised to show them how to eat their own breakfasts in the morning.

Finally turning in myself, I was fully able to get into bed and get my covers up for the first time in months. Life had suddenly drastically improved. I know my children would be very excited about it in the morning.

"Jes did this?" asked Lena, in shock and disbelief. "Mom, you are completely cured! It's truly a miracle!" My four children just hugged me tightly for some time before we went off for breakfast the next morning.

Naturally, all conversation centered on our miracles. I spent some time discussing religion, putting Jes Amir in context, and just how we are all spiritual beings. Those who had my therapy sessions readily accepted this concept. From there, they accepted that perhaps beings could become more powerful, more able. Still, they considered Jes to have been a god. I just could not get them to see it otherwise.

After breakfast, I made contact with Renzo, much earlier than usual. I just had to tell him about our miracles, especially mine! *Hi, Guess what? I'm healed! I'm free at last. Jes came to us last night, and he worked his magic on me. I really had an enormous amount of pain suppressed in my back and neck. He had me confront just what was there. Renzo, the entire vertebrae were completely smashed into little tiny pieces! If it wasn't for the neck and waist braces, I would be dead for sure. I could never take them off, because I'd die at once. Now I am all healed. Somehow, he helped me make two new vertebrae. Pain's all gone, and he removed both braces. I've free at last! He also did it for the women here as well.*

Renzo was crying, I could tell. *This is unbelievable. I have no words to tell you how grateful I am for that! I was prepared to have you be crippled the rest of your life. I could live with that if only I could get you back! Are the kids still holding up okay? I asked Julie for help the other day. I guess she got Jes to help you. How will we ever be able to repay his miracles?*

*I have already done so by getting those signal beacons destroyed, Renzo. No more aliens will ever be coming here to mess us up! Had any more ideas on how to get to us?*

*If Julie doesn't have any bright ideas, then I'm going to make the attempt by dog sled. However, I just can't keep Alexa, Enyo, and Kallisto from coming. When I said they couldn't come with me, they attacked me, knocked me on our bed, and began to molest me. I had to renege and promise to bring them, before they would stop! They really are insisting on helping get to you, dear. I think they love you as much as I do.*

*Renzo, they wouldn't actually mate with you, but they sure might pleasure you into letting them come. I bet that was funny. I wish I could have seen them in action.*

*It wasn't funny, well not until I tickled them.*

*If we can get rescued, I probably should have Enyo come here to check out the various devices and see what, if anything, should be brought back with us. If you do come, make sure that you wear very warm clothing. It is very cold here. I've never experienced such a bitter cold.*

*It sure is interesting. The mantis creatures picked the hottest place on Tarra for their prison, while the Grey Creatures picked the coldest spot. Guess they didn't want the other side to get to them.*

*Yes, sure is remote up here. Well, I had better see to the training of the women here. More tonight. I love you.*

Renzo began searching Velona for four sets of very warm clothing. This turned out to be a bit of a challenge. It is never very cold in Velona, so heavy parkas were very hard for him to find. After visiting nearly every clothing store in the huge city, he finally found parts to make four sets, including warm boots. It took him all day to accomplish this task. I know that he doesn't particularly enjoy shopping; that indicated to me the level of his commitment to see this through.

He entered the manor house near suppertime. Enyo saw the large bundles and came to see what he had acquired. "Looks big and bulky. Winter clothes for us?" she asked in a probing way, though grinning.

Before he could answer, Alexa walked up to them, "What have you there, buster? Something for us all to try on?"

"What's this?" asked Kallisto, trotting up to the threesome. "What have you been up to all day? You've been gone nearly eight hours! Can we see?"

"I got myself some warm, heavy duty winter clothing," he replied, but with all three of them blocking his path, he knew that they must have been keeping watch for him. The three were conspiring with each other.

"What about us, buster?" Enyo declared, a mischievous look in her eyes.

Feigning surprise, Renzo asked, "Oh, was I supposed to get you a set too, Enyo? Maybe I don't know your sizes. I might get one that is much too small, then what, eh? Or maybe one so large that two of you could fit into it."

"Renzo!" Enyo stomped her feet on the floor. If she had arms, she would have snatched the packages from him.

His arms were bulging; he could barely see over the top of the packages. "Ladies, we must force him into his cottage, and we must attack him. I see no other option," Kallisto ordered. The three women bumped into him and began moving him toward the back door, which led to our bungalow. They kept on mercilessly pushing him all the way inside, finally pushing him into our bedroom, and he fell backwards onto the bed, spilling the many bulky packages all over the bed and floor.

By now, all four were laughing hysterically. "Okay, okay, I'll open them, but you got to let me up! If you don't, I will tickle all three of you until you laugh to death!"

"You wouldn't dare," declared Enyo, challenging him, "pick on three helpless, armless women, now would you?"

"Now you've gone and done it!" he declared, and began to tickle her sides. With his other hand, he tickled Alexa, who was also close to him. They giggled and wiggled to get free of his relentless hands.

Between laughs, Enyo said, "Get him Kallisto; he's only got two hands!"

She lunged at him, landing squarely on him; they both went down on the bed with Kallisto on top of him. She spread her legs wide pinning him down, and at once, the other two climbed onto the bed and threw their bodies across him as well. All three began to kiss him, and all he could do was wiggle under their combined weight. I would have given anything to see that!

Buried in piles of long hair, kissed relentlessly, unable to move, poor Renzo finally yielded. "I give up!"

Enyo stopped kissing him long enough to ask, "Are you going to show us what you got now?"

"Yes, yes. I got us all warm clothing and boots. Please, I cannot take this loving any longer!" The three wiggled loose and finally got to their feet. Their long hair was a mess, but they were more interested in the packages.

Renzo began opening them. One by one, he laid each set out on the bed. "Now you got me all flustered, and I don't remember which went with which!"

"Silly, these have to be your boots," Alexa replied. "And this one is probably yours; both are way too big for us."

"I'm the next largest," Kallisto added. "This one must be for me."

"We are the same size," Alexa said, "guess it doesn't matter which, Enyo. Come on; let's try them on. Golly, Renzo, why all the arms in these parkas? Haven't you noticed us yet? We don't need arms." He began laughing, so she quickly added, "In our parkas, I mean."

Renzo expected to have to assist each one into their parkas. However, the three, long used to helping each other, began donning them without his assistance. If nothing else, I believe they wanted to see if they could do it, and if so, prove to him that they would not be dependent upon him completely. Surprisingly, all three managed to get theirs on and buttoned up. Only their heavy boots they could not manage, because they had heavy laces. They needed their feet, as I did, to get the parkas buttoned up and their hair moved into its proper place.

"Well, they will fit you all right. I'll get the arms fixed up tomorrow. Maybe Beth Ann will lend her skills."

Enyo said in a serious tone, "Thank you Renzo. This means everything to us three."

"I know it does. Come on, let's get out of these, and get something to eat. Your kids will be wondering where you are. You three are the greatest."

After supper, Renzo sat for a time in our Torque Ball room, staring at the walls. "Walls, your Bethany will be able to play again. I know I told you before that she was so badly injured that she could barely move. Well, she has been healed. So one day, she will return and pound the ball against you once more." He felt more confident after explaining this aloud to the wall. One way or another, he was going to fetch me back, along with the kids and everyone else.

As he prepared for bed, Julie contacted him directly. *Hi Renzo. Julie* here. I have some good news for you. We've figured out how we can rescue all of them. What we need is for you to build us a large box, big enough to carry back all you who are going there to help them, all of them, and all the stuff you want to bring back with you. Make sure that those who are going there are dressed to withstand the incredible coldness.

I don't quite understand. Does it need wheels? Or skids like a dog sled?

No, just a box large enough for you to fit in. We will be carrying it there and back again. The trip time will be short, however, from what Jes and you have shown us, you will be exposed to bitter cold for a brief time getting from the box inside the complex and then when you return to the box.

Carry it? What shape? Handles or what?

Whatever shape you think best. It does not have to be overly large, nor does it have to be terribly sturdy. As I said, travel time will be short. It is not like a ship, so it does not need to be water tight, though if it has many holes, you might get too cold during the trip.

Something like six feet by six feet by maybe thirty feet?

That would be fine. Have Paulette let us know when you are ready. We will need you to guide us there, Renzo or perhaps the Guardian will guide us. We are glad to be able to assist Bethany. Bye.

Thank you Julie! Thank Karmanski for me too. You have saved us!

Renzo jumped around the room wildly. After he calmed down a little, he ran to find the others, but they were already in bed. Instead, he took a chilly run around the manor a couple times, before he felt like he could sleep.

The next morning, he got Enyo to get all her engineers to begin building the box. When I contacted him, I knew something was up. He was incredibly cheerful. A minute later, I shared his joy! We were about to be rescued! I told the others, and we began to try to decide what to being back with us. For the others, it was mostly a few personal items. I decided to wait for Enyo and get her opinions.

Two days later, one ugly rectangular solid box sat on the front lawn, resting on a fresh light snowfall. Each end had a large door that could be latched so that no one could accidentally fall out during the trip. Paulette contacted Julie to let her know that we were ready. She gave us a half hour to get ready, and they would then arrive.

Hastily, Renzo donned his winter parka and helped Enyo, Kallisto, and Alexa into their boots, allowing them to get their own parkas on by helping each other with them. Beth Ann had removed the arms, so those did not hinder them slipping on the bulky, warm coats. Satisfied they were warm enough and ready, Renzo carried his large gloves and escorted them to the box. Everyone around the estate stood around to watch this incredible event. The four walked into the box, and Renzo latched it, and then put on his gloves. "You three ready?"

All nodded, and they sat down to wait. *Hi Renzo, Alexa, Enyo, Kallisto.* It was Julie. *Are you ready to go?*

*Yes. Let's do it. Thank you both very, very much!*

*Okay, hang on. There, how was that?*

*We are fine. How long will it be?*

*We're there. The Guardian gave us good directions. Please check it out and make sure we are in the right location.*

*But we didn't move did we?* Renzo opened the door and felt a blast of the coldest air he'd ever felt!

Those at the estate saw the box suddenly levitate into the air and then it was completely gone! Vanished, right before their eyes! This became the talk of the day everywhere around the entire complex.

"Wow, this is cold. Come on, ladies. Let's see if we can get inside." Renzo walked out onto the snow and ice, a bitter wind was blowing. It was slippery, so he carefully kept an arm around each woman, making sure each made it to the door, before going back to fetch another. At last, with all four inside, he yelled, "Bethany! We are here."

They stood on a large landing. A room was to their right. Before them, an enormously steep and long stairs descended a very long way down. Suddenly, they saw Bethany's body floating up to meet them. "Hi everyone. Renzo!" I gave him a long passionate kiss, though his lips and face were quite chilled.

"Open that door, and leave your parkas in there, but wear your boots. The floor is icy cold below. If you don't, then you'll have to don a pair of these high heel boots, which is the only thing that keeps your feet from freezing down there. I hope your boots will do so anyway. If not, we've a crate of boots."

Renzo opened the door and the four stared at dozens of heavy parkas. While Renzo took off his, I helped unbutton Enyo's, while Kallisto aided Alexa. Shortly, the heavy clothes off, I said, "Okay, the steps go way down. I'll carry you all down and up. It is just too steep for a human to manage without killing their legs." One by one, I took them all down, Renzo first, because our children were waiting at the bottom for their dad. They swarmed all over him and he latched on to all of them.

I caught snatches of their conversations. 'Dad! Mom was hurt bad. We took care of mom, really we did," Lena explained. A few minutes later, I had the other three safely down as well.

"Okay, follow me. Let us know if your boots are not keeping your feet warm enough. Also, we all walk awfully slowly in these, as you probably can guess."

"Hi Alexa," Lena said. "Like our boots? I love them actually. Warm, but they are useless out on the snow and ice, though. Great in here."

"Yes, but you can hardly walk in them, not very practical," Ben countered.

"They are supposed to look good, not be practical," Alexa replied. "Sense of fashion, well they also attract attention. You look good in them Ben." Ben, now approaching nine, made an icky face. He wasn't interested in girls yet.

"Here are all the others," I pointed out the obvious. We had just entered the large open area that expanded into the huge underground garden plot. The others were lined up in family order, ready to meet their rescuers. I decided to introduce them in age order, giving Sophia, who had been here the longest, the honor of the first introductions.

"Everyone, I'd like you all to meet these four rescuers. Renzo is my husband." He bowed. "These two are also from the House of Right, Enyo, our resident engineer and Planner, and Alexa, a top leader in our Santi organization. This is Kallisto, also a top leader, from the southern country of Demokritos."

"Gang, this is Sophia, from the House of Right and her daughter, Delia, and son, Lexos." What happened next, I would not have guessed in a million years, though I ought to have had a clue, an idea.

"Mom? Delia?" Enyo said, her eyes popping out of her head, her mouth gaping.

"Enyo? My little Enyo?" Sophia exclaimed, her eyes lighting up and opening wide.

"My baby sister? Enyo?" exclaimed Delia, shocked.

Suddenly, I saw the family resemblance. How had I missed this? Okay, Enyo had not been here so I couldn't compare the three women's faces.

"I thought you both had died! That's what I have always been told. Is it really you, mom, Sophia, Delia?" Enyo exclaimed, barely able to contain her shock and joy, uncertain whether or not this could be true.

"We were taken away in the night by a Grey Creature. I was changing Delia's diapers, and Leona was watching over you, sleeping in the cradle bed," Sophia explained. We had already erased this entire trauma during her therapy. "I thought that I would never again see you! My baby is all grown up! Look at you, so pretty, so healthy!"

"I have my little sister back! Enyo! Oh Enyo!" Delia exclaimed. All three rushed to hug each other, well our trademark bump and head touch anyway. Three pairs of eyes were streaming tears of incredible joy and happiness.

The long arms of Lexos wrapped around all three women, holding them tightly. "Now I've got two big sisters! Mom told us about you, Enyo, but you were just a year old. I was born here after mom and Delia were abducted. That's why I still have arms left."

"I never knew I had a brother! Oh, hold us all tightly, Lexos! I've never been so happy!"

The rest of us also had very watery eyes. Finally, I said, "Enyo, your siblings are married and have families here. You are an aunt with nieces and nephews. Well actually, Enyo is married too, and you all are grandmother, aunt, and uncle too. Let's introduce the others. Golly, this is just too incredible! Now, this is the other older woman, Chimalma, from Wanakan, and her daughter, Citalmina, and son, Aduviri. They are twins and were born here as well. This is Yida from the Southlands, and this is Pedro Amirez from Bonilla."

"Now then, Deila has married Pedro here; these are their children, Alex, Iola, and Domali. Lexos has married Citalmina, and these are their children, Aria and Atl. Finally, Aduviri and Yida are married, and these are their children, Itali and Mili."

"Enyo married Frank Westhall, one of our Santi Planners as well, and they have two children so far, Erika and Ben. As soon as we return, you will get to meet those three. This is unbelievable! Wow!"

Aria, now ten years old, proudly said, "Aunt Enyo, you are like mom and grandmother. I have been looking after them, and now I will also help you too, when you need it."

"Hey, me too," said Alex and Iola in unison.

"Thanks, all of you. I am so happy; I am crying like a baby!" Enyo replied.

"I hate to break up this happy time, but Enyo is our senior engineer, and we need to have her quickly determine what we need to take back with us. Let's break up into teams and show them what is here. I don't want to make the two people, who are carrying us home, wait any longer than necessary. Let's get moving. Enyo, Lexos, you are with me. Let's show her the devices. Alexa, Lena, Ben, Pedro, check out the clothing supplies. Renzo, Kallisto, Aduviri, you check the rest of the stuff."

For once, Enyo was not suggesting we take back everything; she was rather distracted to say the very least. An hour later, we had six boxes of thing to take back with us. The men moved them all to the stairs. Now came the hard part, getting everyone and everything up these stairs made for eight-foot tall giants, not we humans. Fortunately, Julie and Karmanski lent me some assistance. One by one, we lifted everyone up to the top landing.

When everyone was there, we went into the coatroom. Those with arms helped the rest of us get into a parka that fit, well somewhat anyway. Renzo kept saying that the actual trip would be short; we just needed to stay warm for a short while. Another half hour later, everyone looked like poufy balls, with barely our eyes showing. Now came the transporting of everyone into the box.

While it was only a hundred feet from the exit, slippery ice and snow covered the ground, which was many feet below our feet. In the end, Julie and Karmanski ended up just carrying most of us over to the box. Once everyone was inside, the boxes came next. We left the remainder of the parkas here, just in case someone ever came back here and needed a warm coat. At last, Renzo latched the door shut and sat down beside me and the kids.

"How long does it take?" I asked, as I felt the box being picked up by the two powerful beings, Julie and Karmanski.

"Hum, I think that we are there now," Renzo said.

*One rescue complete.* It was Julie. *Thanks Bethany for all that you did for everyone. We need to go now.*

*Thanks for rescuing us, Julie, Karmanski. Bye. Tell Jes hi for me.*

Renzo opened the door. I could see the estate once more! Only I was staring at the partially rebuilt hole in the wall where the Grey Creature had smashed through, leading the waves of assassins into our home. The light snow had melted already. The sun was shining brightly. Already, we were melting in our parkas, so the first action was parka removal. We let the many arms extract us from these bulky coats. Then, we all walked out onto the lawn in front of the manor house.

Hundreds of our families, friends, and Santi were there waiting for us. Bard Tal had his band ready. As soon as we stepped out, the fanfare began, welcoming us home. After many hugs and greetings, I led our guests down to the dorms where many lived. Here was where I intended to house our new guests.

Enyo had already introduced a very surprised Frank and her children to her mother, sister, brother, and their families. As we walked down the quarter mile cobblestone path to the dorms, Enyo began to explain to her mother and sister about her inventions that made their lives so much better. These people, who had lived in the underground chambers for a quarter of a century in some cases, were simply in complete awe of everything. Sophia and Chimalma kept pointing their faces to the sun; it had been so long since they felt its heat, light, and warmth. I knew that they all would need a good period of adjustment.

When I finally got back to the manor house, Renzo and the others already had the boxes carried inside. Indeed, nearly all the children were now gathered around Alexa and our kids. It seems that Alexa had brought back all the boots. Many were sized for children, and our four were still wearing their boots. All the many other children were begging Alexa to let them try on some boots; she was busily handing them out, while younger girls were trying them on, Lena doling out walking instructions. What surprised me were the large number of boys who were also experimenting, congregating around Ben and Adrien. Ah well, our kids had been through a lot; time to let them tell their friends all about it. Honestly, I would not have survived without the help of Lena and Ben.

Renzo spied me watching the kids. He came over and put his strong arms around my waist. We kissed passionately for a long time. "Thanks for getting us," I whispered between kisses. It was so good to be home!

# Chapter 17 Changes

The summer of 665 brought Linda and Chaucer back to us. For the last number of years they and their children were in the Red Desert studying or learning from the Guardian of the Anuir, Jes Amir. Their goal: total spiritual freedom. Finally, they were returning to Velona and our estate. I wondered how my best friend would look now? I had not seen her in a half dozen years. What changes would I see in her? Would we still be close friends? I mean she probably now had so many more abilities than I had, so would we or could we still be close?

I mean, I've seen it happen so many times with others towards me. Most recently, after I lifted the people up the steep prison steps to the landing there at the North Pole, their viewpoint of me changed. I was now a goddess in their eyes, not a normal person. Well, okay, I admit that normal people don't go around lifting other people's bodies up several hundred foot tall stairs, not even by using their bodies. I remember my mother telling me about this so long ago. When you do something that exceeds the reality of another person, such as levitating their bodies, transporting their bodies from the North Pole to Velona in a matter of seconds, that tends to shatter their expected reality. They will either hold you in awe as a goddess or seek your death as a demon. You have created an effect that the person just cannot tolerate easily. You have become a threat to their existence or a savior, godlike. Either way, their viewpoint towards you is altered.

For days, I continued to worry about my dear friend Linda, even Chaucer for that matter. The day they were to dock, I had Renzo dress me up in my fancy gown and had him brush out my hair. I even decided to wear the fancy heeled boots that Alexa had turned into the latest fashion craze in Velona. Looking in my mirror and satisfied that I looked as good as I could, we loaded up the kids and headed to the docks to welcome them home. I was nervous, excited, and a bit fearful, all at the same time.

We were both thirty years old now. Golly how the time has flown this lifetime! Our twins are of age, fourteen, likewise, their oldest son, Zachary. Danielle is twelve and Adrien is ten. Linda's daughter, Marion is twelve, and her son, Samuel is ten. I know that they opted not to have more children while they were in the Red Desert. Interestingly, Lena had just become a full-fledged Protector, while Ben had opted to be a Planner. Danielle wanted to be an artist and was studying painting at the Laird Foundation. Adrien didn't know what he really wanted to be, except that the trauma of having been captured by the Grey Creature had made him keenly interested in also becoming a Protector. Other times, he just didn't know. I wondered what Linda's children were like now. Had Zachary been trained or had he also been assisted by the Guardian of the Anuir? Ditto with Marion and Samuel.

I had more unanswered questions than I had answers.

We spied their caravel slowly tacking into the harbor. "How do I look?" I asked anyone and no one in particular. I was nervous.

"You look perfect, mom," Lena replied. She, too, wore a fancy party dress and a pair of the heeled boots, compliments of Alexa. Lena was at that age when a young girl wants to be noticed, and she was definitely accomplishing that. "I haven't seen Zach for years, mom. Do you think he will remember me?"

I looked at my eldest daughter, full of the enthusiasm of youth, blossoming into womanhood. Lena was very pretty and had allowed her hair to grow long, taking after me. "You will definitely get his attention, dear. Half of the dock hands are staring at us already." She blushed, but stole several sideways glances to verify my observation.

The caravel hands tossed out the mooring lines, and the gangplank was lowered. I watched as they walked down onto the wooden deck, some three hundred feet from us. No mistaking her form or her lovely, long blonde hair, curlier now. However, I suddenly had my first taste of being around a spiritual being that is completely free and able. Instantly, as if Linda was right in front of me talking intensely with me, I heard her say enthusiastically, "Hi Bethany! It's great to see you again!" Yet, from this distance, she would have had to yell it at me if I were to have heard her. Further, I felt a great love flow between us; my attention was riveted on her completely. Linda, I discovered, could now put a communication onto a communication line with full and complete intention. It startled me to receive such a powerful communication, wow.

Rapidly, both groups closed the distance. "Linda, you look super!" I exclaimed. "Your children, they've grown so! Chaucer, wow, you look great yourself." He now had total poise, total self-confidence; gone was the indecision that I had often seen in him before.

"Bethany, you look even better than I remembered! Give me a hug," he said. "Renzo, you sure do have a hot one here!" I blushed. The two men began exchanging greetings, while Linda and I grinned at each other. Without any further hesitation, we traded our own special kind of hugs.

"I've missed you, Bethany. I'm afraid that we are all in dire need of a long, hot soaking bath. The desert sand, I swear I will never be able to get it all out of my hair. I love your dress, and those must be the boots that I've heard so much about. Golly, Lena, she's grown so." We looked at her, but we were both surprised to see Zachary and Lena passionately kissing each other.

"Well, I didn't know she missed him that much," I jested, but that was the truth. "I've missed you too, Linda. You've missed out on being abducted by the Grey Creatures." I joked.

She laughed, "I know, I go away for a little while, and you seem to find more troubles to get into! Sure glad you and the kids are all right. I know Zach was in fits for weeks when he heard Lena had been taken with you. That's when I found out that those two have had a crush on each other. Of course, we never had crushes on guys, now did we, Bethany?" We both laughed.

"I see you still have to take small steps in those boots. Is it true what I've heard, that Alexa has started a high heeled boot craze in Velona?" she asked as we slowly walked to the waiting carriages.

"Yes, it is the 'in' thing to wear to the dances and parties around here now. Alexa is running her own side business, supplying boots modeled on those we got from the mantis. The ones from the Grey Creatures are even higher and much more difficult to walk in, so thankfully she is not using them as her model. Linda, I am so glad to have you back with me."

"Glad to be back as well. We have so much to catch up on, we shall be talking for days, I expect, but I need a bath first," she teased. Everyone chatted as we rode back to the estate, but we had only begun to talk when we stopped at the mansion entrance. How time was flying! As we stepped out, everyone was gathered together outside on the lawn, hundreds of people waiting to greet Linda and Chaucer. Bard Tal and his group announced their arrival with a musical fanfare, and the crowd cheered, clapped, and stomped.

Again, I was amazed with both Chaucer and Linda. As they stepped out to receive the warm welcome, each said a few words, speaking in a normal tone of voice. Yet, so strong was their intention that each of the hundreds of people heard them clearly, as if they were being personally spoken to — amazing, I thought. As they then made the rounds of meeting with all of our friends, I saw all our children gathering around Zach, Marion, and Sam. I realized now how hard it had been for our Explorers Circle children to have been separated from these three for so many years. After all, this group of kids had grown up together, spending vast amounts of time on our caravel while we were exploring Tarra.

An hour later, Tonia, Rosina, Michelle, Natale, Mireio, Linda, and I headed to the bathhouse. Our combined objective: give Linda a bath she would not soon forget. Sitting in the warm water, Linda commented, "Ladies, this is what I missed most! A bath! I have not had a bath in six years or more! This is heaven." We chatted for some time. Finally, the others left to handle other duties, leaving us two alone, soaking still in the lilac scented waters. Her hair had already been thoroughly washed and rinsed. No more sand grains in it, we hoped.

Linda said, "Bethany, we need to talk in private. There is much that I must tell you. Can we meet after supper?"

"Sure thing, but if you stay in here much longer, supper will have to be delivered to us in here!" We laughed and she finally decided that she was clean enough. I had to dry her off myself, though I could have called for someone with arms to speed it up. She and I preferred to do it ourselves.

When it was her turn to dry me off, she said, "Hope you don't get too surprised by this." The towels moved as if controlled by some unseen servant, drying me off gently and quickly. "I'm doing it myself, Bethany. I've long ago stopped making the body here do things that I can do more easily and rapidly. I know others are going to be somewhat surprised or even shocked, but I'm going to just be myself anyway." Then, we each helped the other get into our fancy dresses and we slipped on our fancy boots.

"It sure is nice to be able to get them off when you want," Linda commented, remembering how hard our lives had been years ago when we had been abducted. "Yet, if this is a fashion statement, I'll go along with Alexa's plans," she said with a chuckle. "Besides, they drive Chaucer wild." Just then, Renzo and Chaucer came in to find us, and we put them to work brushing out our hair. At last, we four headed for the supper table.

Over supper, everyone got to see just what Linda meant. Again, instead of using her feet like so many of us did to feed ourselves, she did it herself, giving the illusion of another unseen servant lifting the fork and spoon up to her mouth, lifting her tea cup up, and so on. Yes, her performance rated the sole topic of table conversation this evening. She was besieged with hundreds of requests from others like us who wanted to learn how she was doing what she was doing.

After supper, she and I went to our bungalow. I informed my family that we were not to be disturbed unless an emergency arose. Inside, we again hugged each other. Yes, we both had missed each other very much. We took opposite seats so that we could face each other. Linda began, "Bethany, I am now a totally free being. I have regained all of my spiritual abilities that I once had millions of years ago. I cannot ever thank you enough for all that you have done over all these lifetimes for me, Bethany, to say nothing of having given me this chance to become free. I now know fully what you have done, not only for me, but also for all spiritual beings on Tarra. I thank you for that."

"I am now so powerful, Bethany, that if I desired, I could have new arms suddenly materialize on my body and even on yours. However, there is a limit to how much I dare shatter other people's reality. While I insist on feeding my body, I will not suddenly materialize arms for thee and me. That would be far too great a reality smasher around here. I know that you understand what I am saying."

"Wow. That's incredible, Linda. Yes, I know it would. They would elevate you to goddess status overnight, if you or I suddenly had new arms. Honestly, I've learned to adapt pretty well, especially when there are four of us in close proximity to help each other out."

"I understand. Another ability that I have regained is my ability to sense the near future. You see, if you group all the people of Tarra together, you will find some threads of group agreement that run through nearly everyone, or at least through a large percentage of them. Based on those agreements, then certain events are bound to happen, though just when remains uncertain, only that, unless the overall agreements can be changed, it will occur."

"This has now become very critical since we opened up the world's population to each other. It is as if the Explorers Circle sent a wakeup call to every country and people on Tarra. As you know, Tarra is a penal colony composed of criminals and the intellectual elite, both of which are now firmly convinced that they are physical bodies and only live one lifetime. Of course, there are a few exceptions," she grinned; I did too.

"The point I'm trying to make is that given the things that they are convinced is the truth, certain events are likely to happen in the future. The Galts of the Northern Steppes have been suppressed for many generations. Those millions in Tashien are blinded by honor. Even in Demokritos, things have been set into motion that will affect us up here. While I cannot yet predict with any certainty when these events will happen, unless group agreements can be altered, they will happen."

"I follow you, but like what kind of events?" I asked.

For an hour, she described the various causes and effects that would come about as a result. "So you see, Zargarb is once more the key to it all," Linda explained. "How many true Guardians do we have left? So many are very old, you know."

"I know, so many need to retire or have asked for replacements. I believe that we are down to less than two hundred of us, Linda. Yet, if we remove from that tally those who are old, it is more like a hundred of us yet fully active. In Zargarb, I have been using normal Santi officers to take over many of the daily operational details at the fortress there. However, Linda, I do believe that as their bodies die, we will have them back in the next generation or at least a good percentage of them may return to us."

Linda stated firmly, "Nevertheless, Bethany, the Santi, as an organization, will not last. Its days are numbered. We must find another way to maintain stability, while Jes continues to free us beings."

"Sure is kind of similar to what the mantis and Grey Creatures were doing here on Tarra. They were working behind the scenes to control groups of people, even whole countries, to get them to do what they desired. Now here we come and are doing similar things," I chuckled at the irony of it all.

"Their motives were to deny our own spiritual identities, to force us into being bodies and into harming others. We want to promote spirituality and harmony with others so that the world can be stable enough for beings slowly to go free. As long as we remain true to that lofty goal, I can support working behind the scenes to control people," Linda declared.

"This whole Jehosanity thing is going to reappear again. Just between us, Bethany, Jes now realizes just how big of a miscalculation he made when he was the Great Messiah. He now knows that he should have listened more to your advice. I believe he thinks that was his greatest mistake ever.

Jehosanity has just enough truth in it to entrap other beings, to make more worshipers and followers in the days to come," she explained.

I replied, "Well, if Zargarb is once more the key, perhaps I ought to be there and not here."

"Chaucer and I now are more than able enough to make our decisions hold true. We can take over the leadership of the Santi for you. If a man is now seen as leading the Santi, that will delay the events considerably. The uprising in Tewdwr was due in a large measure to having one of us as the visible Supreme Commander to the world at large, an armless woman. If the world sees Chaucer in that role, events can be slowed significantly, but not stopped, I'm afraid."

"Then, that gives us even more time to re-organize," I replied. "Would Chaucer and you be willing to take over here for me? I know Renzo and Rosina would dearly love to move back to their homeland, Zargarb."

"We have talked about this, and we both agree that we must do our part to help Jes and you. We do not need any Communicators here; he and I can communicate at will to anyone now. However, if we do this, can we please plan to visit each other at least once a year? I really do love you, Bethany. I still think of you as my mother, though that was lifetimes ago. You are still my best friend on Tarra." We hugged each other for a time.

I asked, "Is it really going to be as bad as you are predicting?"

"Bethany, I won't lie to you. It may be worse. Still with Chaucer and me here, we will preserve all that is valuable. You have our pledge on that. We both hope that between you and us, we can find a way to circumvent much of what is likely to happen during the next century. Bethany, it takes Jes around six years to free one of us completely; he has been working on three people at one time while we were there. Given his ceaseless dedication, a century from now, there will be three hundred of us not just a handful, compared to the millions upon millions who must be freed. Like you have always said, we must all work together to free man and woman."

"Okay, I'll let Renzo know that we will be moving to Zargarb say in three months, how does that sound? It'll give us enough time to get you up to speed on all that has been and is going on around here," I replied.

Just then, Renzo knocked on our door. I knew that he would only interrupt us if this were an emergency. We both looked slightly worried, as I opened the door. Renzo looked very concerned, "Excuse me, dear, but an emergency has arisen. I need you both to come. It's our children; they've grown up altogether way too fast!"

Our heels clicking on the cobblestones and then the hardwood floors, we followed him into the large dining room. The Explorers Circle's children were gathered along with our Circle adults. Many had grins on their faces, but no one clued me in on the emergency. "Dear, Zach wants to ask you and me something."

Zach, when I last saw him was only up to my chest, now he was a young man. He walked up to me, with Lena's arm in his. "Bethany, I'm now a full Protector." He got down on one knee before Renzo and me. "I wish to humbly ask you both for Lena's hand in marriage."

Instantly, memories of my own youth came back to me, Renzo asking for my hand, just as we turned fourteen ourselves. "Lena? I had no idea. . ." I began, looking at her flushed face, seeing a good deal of my own youth in her.

"I know mom, you never see others falling in love. We've been in love for ages now, and I am a full Protector as well. We are both of age and want to get married before you all decide to go off somewhere else, parting us again!"

While I was absorbing this, Ben came up with Aimee, Benet and Michelle's oldest daughter, in his arms. "Mom, dad, I have just asked Benet and Michelle for Aimee's hand, and they have consented. We ask your's and dad's blessings."

"Is this a conspiracy?" I grinned.

"Well, yes," Ben replied. "We figured to hit you with all of us at one time; that way none of you parents would be likely to say no to us."

I looked around. Felix, Rosina and Cedric's eldest son, was holding onto Ellaina, Tonia and Emil's eldest daughter. Charles, Natale and Henry's son, was holding onto Alwanianon, Mireio and Roberto's adopted daughter and musician. "All of you?" I asked dumbfounded.

"Yes," the four couples chorused in unison.

"Well, then, you have been reading my mind!" I decided to tease them back. "I'm just about to announce another big move that affects all of you. I'm giving control of the Santi del Dio over to Chaucer and Linda. Renzo and I and Rosina and Cedric will be moving back to Zargarb later this year. Lena, I thought this might make you much happier than living around here. Sorry for breaking this without warning, Cedric."

"You're joking?" Renzo said, a very surprised expression filled is face and eyes.

"Nope. Anyone who wants to come with us is most welcome, but we can talk more about this later."

"Whoopee!" exclaimed Renzo and Rosina together.

"Seriously, Lena, Ben, Zach — all of you. She's right. I didn't see any of this coming. I'm blind when it comes to others in love. Zach you certainly may have Lena's hand if she wants to marry you. When is the wedding date? When we all were your age, we had it all worked out, well mostly, well sort of, anyway."

Outdoing me, Lena replied, "Well, how about tomorrow morning, if that gives you enough time." All of us roared with laughter, remembering our conspiracy so many years ago, when we all got married together.

Ellaina spoke up, "I've already asked grandmother if she would marry us all, just as she did when you all got married together. She said that she'd be delighted to do it." Elona Po would live to marry off her granddaughter as well. Remarkable indeed.

Alwanianon added, "Bard Tal said that he will have Amiria and her subgroup sing holy motets during the service. Then, Chara and her subgroup will play vocal and instrumental polyphonic songs for the reception. Also, Cymone and her subgroup will play some of their larger instrumental works for the dance afterwards. It's all arranged, Bethany."

I began laughing, "And I knew nothing about any of this!" We older folks all laughed heartily, remembering our own younger years. "Okay, kids, you set your date, and we'll clear the calendar. Only if it's tomorrow morning, wedding presents will be very late." Now it was their turn to laugh.

"Now then, can I please meet with all the parents, along with Chaucer and Linda? You lovebirds go take a romantic walk or something. You younger kids — go find some mischief to get into for a while," I teased the younger ones, who were just as excited as their older siblings were. All scampered off, leaving we older folks to talk.

"Cedric, I'm sorry for springing this sudden move to Zargarb on you without warning."

"Hey, Rosina has wanted to go back for a visit for ages now. No problem with me. Why so sudden?"

"Let me explain a little. As you know, the Zargarb Fortress and Circle are very old; many have already dropped their bodies. Even Ariana and Ben are getting up there in years. More conflicts are in the offing, and Zargarb is at the crossroads here in the northern continent. We must do everything possible to ensure that Zargarb does not fall yet again. Velona is secure; Zargarb is not. I need to beef it up, Linda and Chaucer have graciously agreed to take over for us here."

"Anyone who wants to move along with us are welcome to come with us."

Natale said, "We should stay here; all of my work is at the museum here."

Emil said, "If Zargarb needs strengthening, perhaps Tonia and I should come with you."

Tonia added, "If we don't, you will not have a Healer with you."

Mireio and Roberto opted to remain here at the Laird Foundation. Benet and Michelle opted to come with us.

That night in bed, I've never seen Renzo so pleased. He was finally going home to his beloved Zargarb. I was the fond recipient of his enthusiasm. The next day, I made the formal announcement of our move and reorganization to everyone at breakfast.

After breakfast and lengthy conversations with many others, Enyo, Alexa, and Kallisto came up to me. Alexa spoke first, "So you are going to Zargarb. We cannot help but notice that you are violating one of your very own rules and orders!"

"Huh? What are you talking about, Alexa?" I asked, completely baffled. I could not put her words into any context.

"You've made it strictly a foursome: four of us living close so we can help each other out with daily chores. How is a one-some a foursome?" she replied.

Enyo added, "So we are moving along with you, Alexa, Kallisto, and me. You will be in a foursome once more."

"What? I cannot ask you to uproot your husbands and families and move to Zargarb," I replied, now grasping what Alexa meant.

"We know that," Kallisto replied. "So we are telling you that we will be moving with you. That's settled. We will, of course, discuss this with our families. Enyo's mother and extended family might like to come with her as well, but she's going to try to convince them to stay here for a year or two and learn as much as they can, before moving to Zargarb to join her."

"But. . ."

"No but's accepted. That's final. We are coming with you. Now when do we leave?" Alexa replied.

"Come here you three!" We four hugged each other for a time. "Thank you," was all I could say; I had tears streaming down my cheeks again.

Later, I held a short meeting with those who were going to move with us. I explained that anytime they wished to move back to Velona, not only could they do so, but that I would pay their moving expenses.

During the next three months, I began to realize what leaving this estate would mean to me. I grew up here. Mom built us our bungalow as our wedding present. I had the greatest inventors, artists, and musicians on Tarra on the estate with me. Here I was surrounded my hundreds of friends and supporters. We were only days from Mont Blanc and our museum. I was giving up all of this. Yet, the more that Linda and I talked, the more I realized she was right in her predictions.

"Remember, the beginnings will be when Elona Po dies," Linda cautioned me. "Her body is old and growing weaker, so it is extremely important that Tonia goes with you and does not stay behind to look after her mother."

"Why or how come?" I asked, not quite seeing her point fully.

"She has created Velona, brought it from a backwater country into the largest, most prosperous country here in the northern part of Tarra. A benevolent monarchy has been her rule."

"Of course, everyone loves her and would do anything to protect her. I once saw normal dockhands attack an assassin who made an attempt on her life," I explained.

"And what is the real problem with this type of rulership?" Linda asked. I looked rather blank. This was Judger territory, not that of a Wid. She answered for me, "Succession. Who will succeed her when her body passes away?"

"Well, if Tonia took over the throne, she would follow in her mother's footsteps," I said confidently. "She idolizes her mother and would continue doing what her mother would have done."

"Quite true, and if Tonia acceded to the throne, much strife would be completely bypassed. Yet, she will not be the one. It falls to the oldest of her brothers. Be forewarned, when the time comes, both brothers will likely vie for the throne. Keep Tonia safe in Zargarb until it's over." I promised that I would.

A month later, the four couples were married in a rather lavish ceremony. Elona Po Woodgrove presided over the actual ceremony. She really looked her age, sixty-nine; her hair had thinned and had turned nearly white. She'd put on a good deal of weight these last few years, and she was out of breath after only a little walking. Now I understood what Linda had been saying about her. Fortunately, Tonia was highly distracted with all the wedding plans for her daughter and had not paid her mom too much attention. For all of us, the large wedding brought back fond memories of our own weddings. Yes, Tal's music was fabulous. Renzo and I danced until our feet were sore. Funny, they had not gotten sore when we were first married and danced so much. Ah, we were their age then, but now I was thirty and he, two years older.

The move went without a hitch, smooth and efficient. Horses, people, possessions, all arrived safe in Zargarb on September 1, 665. The two caravels, which came from Zargarb to take us there, also brought back to Velona the remaining retiring Santi and Guardians, who had served the country well for nearly a half century.

Initially, Lady Ariana Zar Wilkins put us all up in her palace complex, which had originally been a Sisterhood inn. Ariana was thrilled to have us staying with her.

For you to understand the situation we found in Zargarb, you must understand how things have changed. Of the Zargarb Circle, only the twin's father remained: Andre Pazzio le'Goeur, who was now sixty-five. He wanted to retire and look after his grandchildren, but I could tell he was hoping to be a great-grandfather soon. The entire Circle, which had devoted itself to protecting Zargarb all these years, was gone.

At the Zargarb Santi Fortress just east of the city, the three Guardians were in their sixties. They greatly desired to be allowed to retire to Mont Blanc, which I allowed as soon as we got a better understanding of the personnel and situation here. Thus, the official Santi representation here in Zargarb was down to mostly aging fighters and support personnel!

Lady Ariana and her direct support staff were in better shape. She was now fifty while Ben was fifty-eight. Their daughter, Nicolina Sue, was now seventeen and a Loremaster herself. Tom was fifteen but could not make up his mind about specialization, a perpetual ninth year student. Jen was fourteen. Ariana had lost her hands to the Holy Paladins when she was in her teens.

Her two assistants, both armless themselves, were her constant companions and very much her assistants in all ways. Loremaster Julianna was forty-six now and her husband, Benigo Furri, was a painter of some renown. Franco was seventeen; Lisa, fifteen; Elisabeth, fourteen. Loremaster Rachele was forty-five and her husband, Rodrigo Decasas was a year older. Julia was sixteen; Raffaello, fifteen; Raquel, fourteen.

Mom had sent along some Guardians to assist Lady Ariana in running the country. One of these was my older sister, Donata, now thirty-eight. She was a Communicator and had married Cory Amir, a Protector. They used Rima as their last name to thwart assassination attempts from the Mano del Dio of the Church of Jehosanity, who were out to kill the entire Amir line of descendants. Their children were Rose, eighteen, Sam, seventeen, and Aleta, fifteen.

Besides these two, mom sent along Sarah Amber Amir, now thirty-six, their Healer. She had married a local man, Antonio Benito, a musician. Their children are August, sixteen, Enrique, fifteen, and Lilly Sue, fourteen. The final person mom sent was Sedwick Alyster, now sixty-five, who asked to be allowed to retire and return to Mont Blanc.

Finally, mom had sent along two married Santi fighter couples. Alessa and Adriano Zia and Celeste and Mahdi Almardi. These aging fighters were in their middle forties.

To prevent Zargarb from being overrun again, mom had ordered seven more Santi stone fortresses to be built along the border with Juda Arad. We found that these were fully built, but barely manned! Each held only twenty-five fighters plus some support personnel. Grim should we be attacked.

However, the economy was thriving. They had built up huge herd of the pacas from Wanakan and were now exporting the marvelously soft wool and even some pre-made clothing. With so many Loremasters at hand, Lady Ariana had turned the country around and it was now producing an excess of food! Their fleet of caravels now numbered thirty, most of which dealt with the exporting of paca wool and food items.

The population of the city proper was still only around thirty-five thousand, considerably down from its hey-day era when nearly two hundred thousand dwelt here. However, because of their turn to an agrarian society, another thirty-five thousand lived on small farmsteads and in outlying towns and villages. Florintine Junction, which had been the scene of the massacre of the Holy Paladins and their traitor supporters, and then burned down by the women who fled Zargarb Sector, had not been rebuilt. However, a Santi Fortress stood near the ruins of this once huge city.

Incredibly, we soon found that no one in the sector was living at the poverty level! Everyone had work and the pay was good, Lady Ariana saw to that change herself. Crime had dropped to all-time lows. It was safe for a woman to walk the streets of Zargarb at night, alone and carrying a money pouch. Indeed, Lady Ariana and her staff had worked miracles in this once crime ridden and forsaken country, decimated by the Holy Paladins, before they left.

After we were settled in, Enyo, who had brought a dozen toilets and six Bottom Washers with her, engineered their installation. As soon as others learned of this addition, orders for more began coming in to Rodrigo. Within a few years, every major building in Zargarb had these new facilities, as well as a number of outlying towns.

Lady Ariana took us all on a month long tour of the country. Of course, Rachele and Julianna had to ride their horses, along with Renzo and me. However, most of the others traveled by coach. Enyo and Frank took careful notes, paying close attention to what was needed most in this land. Water was scarce and necessary for their many crops. Hence, Enyo cleverly devised three reservoirs, damming up three small springs. From there, an aqueduct system fed the towns and eventually on into Zargarb.

For our part, we saw the dismal shape that the defense force was actually in and began to take steps to correct it. Lady Ariana paid almost no attention to such matters, leaving that to the Santi. I began a recruitment program, asking for young men and women who wanted a career in the Santi to join. I made sure that soldiering was a well-paid occupation. Additionally, with Linda's help, we began a strong recruitment program abroad. Within five years' time, we had two thousand Santi fighters manning the eight fortresses. Most were dual trained. Armed with longbows, they could man the defenses of the fortresses. They also could don their plate mail armor and withstand heavy hand-to-hand combat. For lighter missions, they could don their chain mail armor. Routinely, chain mail clad Santi now patrolled the border with the Arad.

Additionally, the Planners constructed ten heavy ballistae within each of the eight fortresses and added five heavy throwers, which could toss boulders or balls of flaming material a good distance from the walls. The Planners also built up the food and water storage systems in each tower, so that each could withstand a six-month siege.

Lena and Ben, along with their Guardian spouses and friends, took over the name Zargarb Circle. They took charge of the training and control of the entire Santi forces here in this sector. Lena was in seventh heaven, riding about the country nearly daily. She was back doing what she loved, defending freedom in Zargarb, just as she had done in her previous lifetime as Lenkova.

Alexa and Kallisto first educated Lady Ariana, Rachele, and Julianna on her new methods for designing and running of an organization. Next, the five of them began reorganizing the running of the country using Alexa's principles, which were working splendidly with the Santi back in Velona.

Once the three had Lady Ariana re-organized, they then helped Lena and Ben get the Santi here following the same principles.

Yes, we were all busy, and five years passed us by very quickly. In hindsight, these were extremely happy years for me. That ended with the message from headquarters on July 3, 670.

# Chapter 18 The Problem with a Benevolent Monarchy

Linda sent me, *Elona Po has left her body this morning. She is doing well and has a new baby body already lined up. You had best set sail yet today. Tonia must be here for the funeral. Tell her that her mother's heart gave out suddenly.*

I found Tonia feeding one of her grandchildren breakfast. "Tonia, I've some bad news for you. It's your mother."

"She's gone, isn't she?" she looked up at me; her eyes were slightly red. How could she know?

"Yes, this morning, her heart gave out; no one expected it," I replied. "Linda has asked that we set sail yet today. I'll see to the arrangements for us."

"Thanks, Bethany. I sensed it when I got up. Somehow, I just knew it had happened. Has she been located? Is she doing all right?" Tears trickled down her cheeks once more.

"Yes, Linda said that she already has a new baby body picked out and is doing fine."

"That is a tremendous relief. I was fearful that she would become confused and lost or mixed up or whatever. I don't know what all I was afraid would happen to her. I often thought that I ought to have been with her, but knowing mom, she would have ordered me back here. I'm the best Healer in this whole sector."

"I know. I'll go let the others know. As soon as I know when we can sail, I'll get back to you." I headed off to inform all the others. Many wanted to go to her funeral and Ariana graciously allowed us to use her personal caravel, saying this was an emergency, if ever there was.

At three in the afternoon, the Lucky Paca set sail for Velona. Besides my group of eight, Tonia's daughter, Ellaina and her husband Felix went on board for the trip. Hence, the caravel was very lightly loaded and the captain attempted to set a new speed record for the trip to Velona. We arrived on July 8.

With little to do, we spent most of the voyage chatting about the future of Velona. Tonia said, "Well, the rulership ought to go to Adrien, he's the oldest. He's forty-one now."

"Yes, but will Gascon allow that?" asked Emil. Gascon was thirty-nine, while Tonia was thirty-six. "You know how often we've heard them arguing about it. That's why we kept the two posted to opposite fortresses." Gascon was in charge of the northern one, close to the Appian Way, while Adrien was in charge of the one closest to the Med Sea. None was close to

Velona proper.

"Well, they are both Santi and ought to be reasonable about the transition of power," I speculated hopefully.

"They argued and fought when we were kids," Tonia added. "Why should they stop now?"

"Maybe you ought to take over," Rosina suggested. "That way there would be no bickering." We all laughed at that.

"Why didn't grandma just make it official whom she desired to take over for her?" asked Ellaina. "That would have made it simple."

"It would not have held up," Renzo commented. "They would still fight over it."

"Mom couldn't decide," Tonia explained. "She wanted to have me take over, but we both knew that neither Adrien nor Gascon would have accepted that. Tradition passes it on to the eldest son. Mom always thought that Adrien was too hot headed to rule in a manner similar to hers. Gascon always wanted to do things differently than mom. In short, she didn't want either of her sons to take over for her. I guess that's partly why she kept on running things long after she ought to have retired and just enjoyed all her grandchildren and life."

We talked about the situation for some time. Also, we knew that she wanted to be buried in her church. Because she was the most beloved of any ruler in the history of Velona, there was no other option. Linda relayed the news that the city had ordered a lavish crypt be built beneath the Rose Church for her body to lie for all time. It was the highest tribute to her that the city and sector could give.

When we arrived, the entire city flew black flags in her honor. The normally noisy docks were quiet and somber. Her death affected millions, for so many owed her so much. Elona Po had taken over control of the sector when its population had fallen to a mere twenty-five thousand and most of those were starving. Thievery was a way of life. During the many years of her reign, she had turned Velona into the most densely populated Sea Prince country and the most prosperous, bar none. Millions now lived here, not only natives from the Sea Princes, but also thousands of Axemen from the north had immigrated here, along with thousands from the Arad. Even some settled here from the West Reach Layamon region. The fleet of caravels and carracks of Velona numbered one hundred seventy-three, quadruple the combined totals of all the other Sea Prince sectors!

Further, as High Priestess, she had successfully joined many religions into one, combining ancient and modern Jehosanity, Tur, Blessed Holy Mother, and our own druwid concepts. Truly, Velona was the Gnostic capital of the world. Always, her high masses were packed; even the balconies were full. Ever since the introduction of music during services, people thronged into the church, if only to hear the holy motet music.

As we walked across the wooden docks to the waiting carriages, I wondered how her funeral could handle this many people who wanted to pay their last respects to this beloved woman, their monarch. How could millions attend a funeral? I hoped that Linda had already made plans for this.

Linda and Chaucer were waiting for us, two carriages at hand. "Please accept my personal condolences, Tonia, Ellaina, and those of all the Santi. If you will come with me, I will take you to see her body. We have it lying in state at the Rose Cathedral." We climbed into the waiting carriages for the short ride to the church. We were a very somber party; no one spoke during the trip. The two women cried considerably.

As we approached the church, we saw long lines of people lining the street, waiting their turn to pay their last respects. Somber music from Bard Tal's group could be heard even outside the massive chapel. Linda was met by several Santi guards, and we were quickly escorted through a side door. We walked down the long corridors that paralleled the huge chapel with its enormous high altar. Thankfully, we were allowed to cut into the front of those waiting to walk by her body. Her fellow priests had laid her out for viewing just in front of the high altar, where she had delivered so many sermons.

Solemnly, we all filed past her body, tears of grief flowing. The music was totally appropriate, spiritually uplifting, and helped hide the noise of so much crying. I nodded to Tal, who was playing along with ten of his fellow musicians. A few minutes later, we were escorted out another side door.

However, here her brothers were waiting for us. As soon as Tonia appeared, Adrien called out, "Tonia, good to see you again. You will support me in taking over the reins of power?"

Before she could answer, Gascon called out, "You know mom did not want Adrien to wield the power of Velona. You will support me in my challenge to Adrien?"

Tonia just bawled when she heard them. Ellaina yelled at them, "You should be ashamed of yourselves! We've only just got here. Grandmother is not even buried yet, and you two are arguing over who will rule. I say neither of you are fit to rule Velona. Now go away and leave us alone! We're grief stricken, tired, hungry, and just got here after a long boat ride!" With that, the Santi guards moved us on out of the side door, back into our waiting carriages for the short trip back to the estate.

Renzo made the only comment while we rode, "Of all the nerve. They ought to know better!" Ellaina just hugged her mother the whole way back.

"I think you will find a few things changed here," Linda said with a note of cheerfulness in her voice. I could tell she was making an attempt to change the mood in the carriage.

"Whoa! You can say that again!" I exclaimed as we approached the gates. The walls had been thickened. More guards were on patrol along the walls. Another walled complex lay to the north of our original compound.

Linda had greatly expanded the estate.

"Go around to the North Complex," Linda said to our driver, who veered from the entrance. "Stop here. Everyone out. This you need to see."

We all climbed out, those in the second carriage were wondering what was going on, why we had not gone in the usual gate. Exclamations of surprise came from all of us. Aella and Herbert were standing nearby, evidently expecting us.

Aella said, "Well, Enyo, what do you think of my latest project? The canal goes from the Med Sea to right here. Yes, that is a caravel you see docked between the two fortresses." Indeed, the tall masts of a caravel loomed tall above the two fortified stone walls.

Linda explained, "We needed direct access to the Med from the estate. I've doubled the size of the complex. We have another thousand Santi fighters housed in this North Complex. The canal is five miles long, deep enough for a loaded caravel to travel to our private docks. Draft horses pull the ship up and down its length. I got the idea from Sho Lin and her royal barges." We all could plainly see that Linda was making our Santi headquarters and the Laird Foundation insulated from the rest of Velona. We could be a separate entity, if the need arose. With the bickering of Tonia's two brothers, I now saw how wise Linda had been, how far reaching her planning had gone.

"Incredible, Linda. Well done indeed. I would never have thought of this, nor that it could even be done," I praised her.

"Couldn't have done it without Aella and Herbert. They were the engineers behind it," Linda shunted the praise onto the duo, who stood proudly before us.

"Sure, Aella," Enyo commented her friend from the House of Right. "Positively brilliant. You will have to share with Frank and me just how this was done. Incredible indeed." Aella beamed.

Linda then took us all for a long walk, touring the new fortress and the small docks. Eventually, we ended up at our old manor house. "I've got rooms all ready for everyone, just follow the guides. Your sacks are being brought as we speak. Everyone wants to chat with all of you, so take the rest of the day to renew all of your acquaintances." This was an excellent idea, because we were being besieged with friends and parents.

Dad, Hank Weston, looked so much older than I remembered him. We spent a lot of time just chatting. His legs were bothering him a good deal now, and we both knew that his days were numbered as well. This might be the last time that we would spend time together. Worse, I could not help noticing that dad was forgetting things. Five times he asked me the same thing, forgetting that he had already asked me about it. Beth Ann, who was nearby chatting with her children, winked at me. I knew that she knew what was happening with dad. Later she filled me in on his health, which was not good. He was sinking rather quickly.

I found it unnerving when he asked how Elona Po was doing. He'd forgotten that she had just died. I had to tell him about her death four times. It was painful to watch him react with surprise and grief anew each time. "Lizzy Ann, the old body is giving out," he said, "I think that my mental facilities are not quite right, though I cannot seem to pin it down. I see the reactions of others around me to me, and I can tell something isn't right with me. Beth Ann won't tell me, will you my Lizzy Ann?"

"You are forgetting things dad. You've asked me about Elona four times now. It's as if you aren't able to remember very recent things. You remember mom just fine and even the two apprentices you had, Rachele and Julianna, who send you their love and eternal thanks for what you did for them."

"Yes, I remember them well, like it was only yesterday, helping me in the large garden. Ariana did too." I could see his memories of them in full replay in his mind. He was smiling all the while.

"Dad, you have done so much for so many people to improve their quality of life that I just don't know how to thank you." He smiled.

"Yes, I do believe that I have, Lizzy Ann. I've always wanted somehow to make a difference in our world. I know it's not the same as Aella and her canal. Amazing canal, is it not?"

"On behalf of mom, me, and all the hundreds of others that you have helped, please accept our undying thanks. You have made our lives so much better." He looked at me and gave me a long hug. I just sensed that he was looking for some kind of closure on his life, an acknowledgment that he had succeeded in his goals. He held me tightly for a long time.

"I think I need to take a nap, body's getting old, Lizzy Ann." I helped him walk to his room and tucked him in for an afternoon nap. That was the last conversation I had with my dad while his body was living. He died that night in his sleep, but I didn't find out until the next morning.

Over supper, Linda explained how the funeral tomorrow would be conducted. "We are following her wishes to the letter. Tradition holds that everyone wears black to a funeral, but Elona stood for life. She wanted everyone to wear deep forest green, her favorite color, rebirth of life, she always said. Hence, we've got dresses made up for all of you women. You guys just wear your suits; we've made up green arm bands and neck bands for you to wear. Oh, yes, be sure to wear your fancy boots. It seems that we have Alexa to thank for this one."

"What? Me?" she said in an innocent, angelic tone.

"Yes, my dear. You have set a new fashion trend in Velona. Your boot company is making a fortune. Remind me to give you an accounting, and you can take your profits for the last ten years back with you, assuming you can find enough men to carry the heavy weight of all those coins!" She was teasing a little.

"Oh dear me," Alexa feigned surprise.

"Now where was I? Oh, yes. Tal will be providing the music. It will be standing room only for the funeral services. We're allowing the fifteen hundred most important people in Velona to attend the actual service. The visitation lines you saw last night have been like that ever since she was put by the altar, so folks could pass by and pay their respects. Six days of non-stop lines, even throughout the nighttime as well. It's incredible the outpouring of love and respect Elona has earned here."

"After the service, only the close friends and family will be at the interment ceremony. They are placing her body in a crypt beneath the church. Already, the stone masons are at work on the crypt's fancy lid. I believe it will be a life-sized representation of Elona on the stone top. Anyway, once that is done, per Elona's wishes, everyone in Velona will then attend one of the many feasts being held in her honor, all paid for by Elona. Her dying wish was to feed everyone in Velona one last remembrance meal. We will conduct ours here at the manor house. Questions?" No one had any.

The next morning, Renzo helped me get dressed in my new dark green dress. He brushed my hair out, flaring it out over my shoulders, Kallisto style. I have been taking a lot after her hairstyle of late, allowing my long hair to hide my missing arms. Frank and Renzo both say we look much sexier this way, and I am always willing to tease Renzo; he, me.

Just as we finished up, Beth Ann, crying, found us. "Bethany, it's your dad. He isn't waking up. Please come now." We followed her to dad's room. His pale corpse was lying in bed, right where I had left him yesterday afternoon for his nap. I went up to his body, kneeled down, put my head on his chest, and bawled. I felt Renzo's arms around my waist, lending me support.

"He went peacefully in his sleep," Beth Ann added, sobbing profusely.

"I know," I cried. Finally, sniffing, I relaxed and went in search of dad. I found him nearby, watching over a very pregnant Santi in the morning sunlight. She was preparing to go to the funeral ceremony.

*My mind is clear at last, Bethany. I cannot make up my mind whether to go searching for your mom or take this new body right here. What do you think?*

*I love you dad. You should do what you want to do.*

*I want to help. I think bad things are in the wind, and I should get back into the game as soon as I can. If Jenna needed me, I'm sure she would have gotten a hold of me before now. Look me up in a few years and make sure I am right on track. I hope I don't forget everything I know this time.*

*I promise I will, dad. Hey, just decide that you will remember everything and then do so. Oh, it's time to leave. I'd better get going. Talk with you when we get back.*

Hundreds of us filed out of the estate into the waiting carriages. I noticed that nearly every woman was wearing a pair of the high-heeled imitation black boots that Alexa's company was mass producing. Jeesh, she had started a trend in fashion. I was just glad that she had not opted to start a corset craze!

The funeral ceremony was impressive, from the stately music to the sermon to the vast number of people in attendance. At least Tonia's bothers didn't make a scene. They were present with their families and supporters, however. Later, in the basement below the High Altar, we gathered to watch as her remains were placed into the stone sarcophagus. After many holy words were spoken, the heavy stone lid was set in place. The ornate top cover would be added later when it was finished.

As we slowly filed out, Adrien said to Tonia, "We must talk later on!"

"No, *we* must talk later on!" Gascon insisted, glaring at his older brother. The two looked at each other, hatred flowing from their eyes. We ushered Tonia and Ellaina out as quickly as we could. No one said a word until we were back at the estate.

Next, we held our own funeral ceremony for my dad, burying Hank Weston in a grave beside my mother, Jenna Rose Weston. All those at the estate gathered around for the ceremony. Many said a few farewell words in his honor. Over and over and over, I heard someone say, "Thank you Hank for making my life so much easier to live." Yes, that was my dad's legacy. Always do what you can to help your fellow women and men who are in dire need — that was the motto my dad lived by, and those were the words I had carved into his grave stone marker, there beside mom's.

Fortunately, everyone just allowed me to grieve for my father the rest of the day. Still dressed in the same outfit I began the day wearing, Renzo came to me and said, "Dear, care to go for a long walk with us? We are going to take a quiet remembrance walk through Velona." How did he know that a walk was just what I needed right now?

A while later, Enyo and Frank, Alexa and Rene, Kallisto and Frank, and Renzo, and I climbed out of our carriage near the northern edge of the sprawling city. The guys put their arms around our waists, while we leaned our heads on their shoulders. Heels clicking on the cobblestones were the only sounds our passage made. As we passed by inns, the noise of those inside celebrating in Elona's honor reached our ears, though we paid that little attention.

I began looking at the trees, the buildings in the distance. Slowly my grief began to subside and move into the past, while I came up to the present. I needed this slow walk time. At last, I commented, breaking our silence. "You know, we are now at a critical junction in time and history here on Tarra. We are witnessing the end of an age with the passing of Elona and what she has accomplished in this country. I wish I could say that the future is bright, but we know that is not likely going to be true. I believe that Elona always knew that, while a benevolent monarchy offered her people the best possible salvation, in the end, the problem of succession would be a horrible affair. Yet, if she had not done what she has done, even we Santi would have been hard pressed to carry out our works all these many years. We owe her as big a debt as she owes us."

"Very Judger of you," Kallisto replied.

"Sure you are not one of us?" Alexa added.

"She might make a Judger yet," Frank, Kallisto's husband teased me.

"Kallisto, Alexa, Frank, what do you think will happen next here in Velona? I mean with Adrien and Gascon," Enyo asked. "They are brothers and even Santi as well."

"Power clouds men's minds," Kallisto replied.

"Always has, with men, that is," Alexa added.

"But I am a man," protested Frank. "Men are not the only ones who fall victim to a thirst for power."

"Okay, present company excepted," Kallisto teased her husband.

"There is a tremendous amount of power at stake here in Velona. Whoever takes over as ruler will be controlling well over a million people's lives, to say nothing of the incredible economy. Immense sums of money and power will be the prize at stake here, Enyo," Alexa explained.

"So that's why Linda had Aella make the canal, so that the Santi and the Laird Foundation can survive no matter what happens in Velona," Enyo concluded.

"But will the two brothers actually come to swords?" asked Enyo's husband, Frank. "They are both Santi and should know better."

"Linda would not have built the canal unless she had a strong suspicion that there may well be a civil war here over the throne of Velona," Renzo stated.

"We should probably get Tonia and Ellaina out of Velona as soon as possible," I added. "Thank you all for this walk. I really needed it. I think that we should be heading back now." An hour later, we arrived back at the estate; it was now full dark.

We found Tonia and Ellaina in tears. While we were gone, her brothers both came to see her. Emil explained, "They are both power hungry beasts! Each one wanted Tonia to support publically his bid for the rulership of Velona. First, they wanted to know where she stood. Was she going to make a play for the throne? She said she was not, of course. Then, each ordered her to come out and publically throw her support behind each of them."

"Mom said she would not support either of them," Ellaina said, tears still streaming down her face. "My uncles screamed at her for her stupidity. 'Who are you going to support then?' Adrien yelled at mom. I told him to get the hell out of here; she's still in grief over grandmother's death. My uncles are both heartless beasts! I told them so. They stormed out of here."

Emil added, "Honestly, I think that they both now believe Tonia is going to make a move to take the throne from them. Gang, I am getting very worried about the safety of my wife!"

The soft, yet commanding, voice of Linda took control. "Adrien and Gascon are fracturing the loyalties of many Santi fighters here. Adrien has the tacit support of hundreds here in the south, while Gascon has many supporters in the north. Both have been raising an army of loyalists for the last five years. If they come to blows over the throne, it will hurt the Santi as well. We'll have no choice but to fire all those Santi who join the brother's conflict. We cannot have divided loyalties among our fighters."

She continued, "As much as I hate to say this, Tonia's steadfast refusal to support either of her brothers has now got both convinced that she is going to somehow make a move for the throne as well. Her life is in jeopardy as long as she is in Velona. With so many Santi supporting one or the other of the brothers, anyone of them could make an attempt on Tonia's life here at the estate. Or perhaps just kidnap her to keep her out of their power plays. Either way, Tonia is at risk as long as she stays here in Velona."

I replied, "I've already concluded that. How soon can we leave?"

"The caravel is already loaded with your sacks. I took the liberty of getting your things packed for you. I think that it would be prudent to get them out of here immediately. We don't need another abduction on our hands nor an assassination attempt. It would be our own Santi members doing it! While I've tried, I cannot ascertain the loyalties of every Santi on this estate. Anyone of them could be looking to Tonia as a means of gaining immense favor for the new ruler of Velona. Can you go now?"

That was not so much a question as an order. "Let us make a quick pass to make sure we are not forgetting anything, then we can leave," I offered. Linda nodded, glad that I responded so well. "You'll keep us informed?"

"Absolutely. Get moving. None of us will be able to relax until your ship is on its way," Linda stated honestly. Of course, Tonia and Ellaina cried even more, but we all began checking our rooms. Linda and her staff had been very thorough. None of us found anything that had been left behind. All of us were still dressed in our funeral clothing and boots, and thus we walked slowly to the docks, assisted onboard by our husbands.

At once, the ten draft horses, five to a side, began to pull the huge ship down the canal. The moonlight gave us a dim view of this novel action. All of us stood on deck to watch as the horses moved the great ship the five miles to the Med Sea. The trickiest part happened once the horses reached the end of the land. The drag lines were undone; the ship, using only jibs, ever so slowly moved out from the mouth of the canal into the sea proper. It was a very challenging maneuver, especially at night. After two hours, the ship was finally on its way, mainsails lowered and pulling in the warm, summer breeze. Only then did we all go below to change clothing and shoes.

Once changed, we women took turns brushing out our hair once more, while Renzo went to the galley. We women later joined the men there.

"Tea, my dear?" Renzo joked with me. He knew that a cup of tea was just what I needed right now.

"Do you really think my brothers will abandon the Santi and fight each other over mom's throne?" asked Tonia, sipping her tea. She had at least stopped crying.

"The way my uncles treated you today," Ellaina answered defiantly, "I'm sure of it!"

"With you safely out of Velona, at least we do not have to worry about your safety, Tonia," I replied honestly. "She's probably right. Linda is very worried about it and the impact on the Santi. Something like this could cut our numbers by two thirds here in Velona."

"Why didn't mom just leave written orders on who should succeed her?" Tonia complained bitterly.

Kallisto answered her truthfully, "It would not have made the slightest difference in the outcome. If she had given the throne to Adrien, Gascon would have contested it. If she had given it to Gascon, Adrien would have fought against it. If she had given the throne to you, both of your brothers would have fought you for it. Either way, her orders would have availed nothing. I think that she also knew this, which is why she did no such thing."

"You know, Barcella and Zargarb are going to undergo similar problems in the future. When Jovanna and Ariana, both benevolent monarchs of their countries, pass away, the very same problem of succession will be facing those countries," I observed.

Emil added, "Throughout their long history, succession has always been a bloody mess here in the Sea Prince city-states. I think Ket Bethany's idea in the Southway was the best ever: hold elections, let the people themselves elect whom they wish to be their ruler. That has been working there well for quite some time now."

Six days later, a somber group arrived home in Zargarb.

# Chapter 19 Succession

July 11, 670, Adrien Woodgrove Po called all of his closest advisors, commanders, and local followers together for the most important meeting yet. For months now, Adrien had been working with the more influential members of Velona and those on his Santi staff whom he trusted. Finally, the time for action arrived.

"Gentlemen," he began, for the first time aware that there were no women present — he trusted none, not even his wife and daughters, "our time has come. It is my birthright as firstborn to take over the rulership of fair, prosperous Velona. Before you now, I claim that holy right. I proclaim myself your sovereign ruler." The group of some seventy men cheered and raised their fists in a "yes" signal.

"Tomorrow after breakfast, we will march to the Public Office and take over the governing of the sector. Are you with me?" Again, his supporters cheered their support.

"We can expect trouble from Gascon; he still refuses to give up. Commander Fillies, any word on his whereabouts now?"

The Santi commander of Fortress Number 2, just north of Number 1 at the Med Sea, which Adrien had long commanded, spoke, "Commander, our spies say that he is still within the city proper. However, as expected, the men we had tailing him lost him. Others at the gates have not seen him leave the city, so he is around somewhere."

"Let's make sure we have sufficient forces at the Public Office in the morning. I wouldn't put it past him to try to take the office by force of arms," Adrien ordered.

Someone called out, "What of your sister? Will she support us?" This was a particularly sore point for Adrien. He had long counted on Tonia lending her support for his bid for power, after all, she knew as well as he, the first-born had the right to the throne. Yet, she had rebuffed his every attempt to gain her public support.

"No, she continues to refuse to back me." If she had backed him, so much public opinion would be swayed onto his claim as to make Gascon's challenge become insignificant. Yet, she had not.

The same man asked, "Does this mean that she, too, is making a bid for the throne?" Adrien knew as well as every man here just what that would mean. If Tonia claimed the throne, she would at once have the full support of the female population of Velona, making it exceedingly difficult, if not impossible, for Adrien to secure the throne, unless Tonia met with an accident. Adrien liked his sister, as much as he liked any woman, which was not particularly much. He just didn't trust women, who preferred to talk their way out of situations, which clearly demanded a stronger hand, a sword hand.

"She has said that she does not. Although she is stationed in Zargarb, she is now here in Velona. Worse, if she does make such an attempt, she, unlike us, will have the complete backing of the Santi del Dio. You know what that will mean to you, my friends. Linda d'Grange will be ordering you to support her, not our bid. We will again have a woman pulling the strings. I say it is time for a change. Mom has had her way here for far too long. Yes, yes, she has done a terrific job of recovery. Yet, times change. We are now the most powerful country on Tarra, richest too. Now we need the strong arm of a swordsman to lead us forth against the many challenges we will be facing, what with all these new lands to control."

"My sister, however honorable her intentions, must not be allowed to interfere with our succession to the throne. Is that clear?"

"Yes Commander. Should we send out the word to have our supporters arrange for an accident tonight?" asked another of his Santi supporters.

Adrien sighed, wishing that it had not come down to this. She was his own flesh and blood. Nevertheless, she represented the greatest threat to Velona and his claim to the throne. He could not let that happen, "Yes, make it a quick and painless accident, such as falling off the third floor balcony of the Laird Foundation." The man nodded and left the meeting to carry out the order.

Adrien issued more orders. "Tomorrow, I want all of the main streets leading to the Public Office building totally secured with our forces, not the ordinary city guards. I anticipate Gascon to make his move then too, so let's send word to our fighters back at the fortresses. Have all those who support me arm themselves for battle and ride here. They should arrive within four to five days. I want as much force as we can possibly bring to bear right here, just in case Gascon tries something. Any protest on his part must be terminatedly handled immediately. Give those who might be swayed into his camp no chance to be so moved." They talked for another half hour, making detailed plans for the morning.

Across town in an inn frequented by the dockworkers, Gascon and his men held a similar rally. He said to the crowd of supporters, "We all know why mom did not leave written orders for succession. She would have had to violate tradition, naming me as her successor, not Adrien. She couldn't bring herself to break with the historical president, and so left it up to us to do it for her. Tomorrow, we can all expect Adrien to lay his claim to the throne of Velona. We all know what that would mean for Velona, a return to the dark ages where might made right!" The crowd cheered this point, for Adrien's temper was well known in the city, as was his propensity for outright anger and violence.

Many wondered how he ever had been allowed into the Santi del Dio.

Gascon continued, "We cannot allow him the throne of Velona, never in a thousand years, not unless we desire a return to barbarism!" Again, cheers interrupted his speech.

"Even as we speak, thousands of fighters who support us in our drive for the throne are on the move from the northern fortresses. Within a week, we will have more fighters in Velona than Adrien can muster. Time, gentlemen, is on our side." Many again yelled their support.

"Now some of you know of my attempts to gain my sister's backing. Yes, I admit freely that if Tonia lent us her full and public support, our task of unseating Adrien would be much easier. However, she remains adamant, she will not lend us her support, nor to Adrien either. Which brings up the question: is she too planning a move to gain the throne?" Many "yeh, right's" echoed in the room.

"I can say the answer is likely no; she has no such plans. I know my sister; she is a Healer and is stationed in Zargarb, where she is vitally needed. I believe her allegiance lies with Bethany le'Goeur and will not interfere with anything that we do. Consider Tonia to be out of the running, so we get no support or hindrance from her. She has become a non-entity in this power play. We can safely dismiss her entirely from our thinking. I know my brother well enough to know that he will not do so; he may even make an attempt on Tonia's life. So I would like a volunteer to go to the Santi headquarters and tell Commander Linda d'Grange that we suspect Adrien's men to make an attempt on Tonia's life." One man nodded and left to deliver the message to Linda.

"Now in the morning, I expect Adrien to make his move, probably after he eats breakfast. Adrien has always been fanatical about doing nothing before breakfast. We must make our move before then. He will undoubtedly station his many fighters along the main streets leading to the Public Office. You know what their orders with respect to us will be." Many boos resounded in the room, along with stamping feet.

"Here's what we do, we get our supporters to the Public Office at dawn. It is important that we let him make the first move. We will just stand there acting innocent. Above all, do nothing to provoke either him or his men. Our retaliation will come once our fighters arrive a week from now. Instead, once he has staked his official claim to the throne, then it is my turn to lay claim to the same throne. We follow tradition strictly, gentlemen. Only when the first-born is dead or is proven unworthy or incapable of leading does the second-born rise to the throne. He must make his claim first, and then I will challenge it by naming him unfit for office. That is all that we must do tomorrow, challenge his claim by saying he is unfit."

Gascon knew what that would mean. Once the unfit challenge was raised, the city officials would have no choice but to form a fitness committee and then set about gathering the necessary data to either prove or disprove that assertion. Such would occupy everyone involved at least a month, maybe longer, far more time than Gascon would need to muster all his fighters here into Velona proper from the northern towns and fortresses. Then, he could make his move by force, if need be.

Linda thanked the messenger from Gascon, who delivered his dire warning. She neglected to tell him that Tonia had already left Velona, only hours before. "Just as you predicted my dear," Chaucer said, after the man left.

"Yes, now how about you handling the trap that you've devised? Let's get all the facts that we can gather. In the end, I still don't think it will matter, but we owe it to Tonia to try."

"I know, we've seen this coming. I will see to it now. Back in a while." Chaucer left and went to the main gates and left a very specific message. Then, he met with the night watchman, who patrolled the outside of the manor house. Linda and Chaucer had stepped up their nighttime security, not wanting a repeat of the assassination attempts that Renzo had had to handle. Next, he stationed another woman Santi guard near the door of the bedroom, which had been Tonia and Emil's room earlier this day. He went over what she was to say and do. Satisfied that she knew her part perfectly, he went to his private room, grabbed the dummy he'd been fabricating, and returned to Tonia's room. He carefully placed the dummy in the bed.

He drew his sword and took up his position, hiding behind a cabinet. Now he merely waited. Both he and Linda had glimpsed the likely near future, and he was thankful that Linda had been able to get Bethany to leave at once on the caravel. Time passed.

Hours later after the noise had died down completely and everyone had gone to bed, he heard footsteps coming down the hall, booted steps. He heard the whispered voices outside Tonia's room. "I have got an urgent message for Tonia," a male voice said. "I was told she was in here somewhere."

"Oh yes, sergeant. This is her room here. I believe that she is sleeping. She's taken the loss of her mother rather hard. She is probably sound asleep, but you can check if it's urgent. If you will excuse me, I have my rounds to make." She walked on down the hall and headed up the steps to the second floor. The hallway was now totally deserted. Chaucer heard the door opening quietly, heard the tiptoe of the man's boots as he entered. He heard the telltale sound of a sword being drawn. He heard the sword being thrust into the chest of the dummy body he'd made.

"That will do." Chaucer said commandingly, as he stepped out from behind the cabinet. "I've been expecting you. Drop the sword. You are under arrest." He uttered his commands with his full intention, a total expectation that they would be followed to the letter, without any doubts on his part that they would not be. He heard the sword clank onto the stone floor as he commanded the oil lantern to light itself. Yes, Chaucer had become far more able as a spiritual being. "Sergeant Fellweather. What a shame. Come with me now." The man stared at the dummy, stared at Chaucer. He had an impulse to flee, but could not make his feet work. Chaucer had complete control over his body, walking him out of the room.

The Santi guard had arrived, along with a dozen others, who surrounded Fellweather, searching him for additional weapons, removing a dagger and a knife. "You work for Adrien, correct?" Chaucer asked. While Fellweather tried to hold his tongue, his voice replied that he did. "Take him away. Put him on the next boat to Isla Roca," Chaucer ordered. At once, the Santi obeyed, marching the sergeant out of the manor. Chaucer walked out back to his bungalow, where Linda was patiently waiting him.

"It is done," he said to her.

"I know. Well done. Now how about helping me undress?" Linda replied.

At dawn, Gascon and three hundred men, mostly dockworkers, stood just outside the Public Office building, munching on the breakfast, which they had brought with them. Soon, they saw numerous fighters, whom they knew to be loyal to Adrien, come marching down the street, intent upon taking up their assigned positions. They were startled and surprised to see all these men and Gascon standing where they should not have been allowed to be located, not this close to the building. "Good day," Gascon said to the men as they sized up his numbers, too many to confront openly. Dockworkers were strong, burly men. Even though they were not fighters, Adrien's men would be out-numbered thirty to one. Instead, the fighters formed a barricade line between the building's entrance and these men. Gascon knew that they would merely wait for revised orders later on.

Around nine, Adrien, accompanied by several hundred fighters and local influential men came marching up the street to the Public Office. The two brothers glared at each other, but Gascon said and did nothing, but watched his brother climb the steps of the building. There, Adrien had to make his official speech.

"I stand before you today to announce that I am the rightful heir to the throne of Velona, the eldest son of Elona Woodgrove Po. I accept my birthright to be the sole ruler of our fair country." On cue, his supporters yelled and cheered, showing him their support. By now, a very large crowd of curious people had gathered to watch the simple proceedings. Some of them also joined in with their support for Adrien, who seemed to cherish and welcome this outflowing of public support.

Once the noise died down, Gascon spoke loudly. "As the second-born, I lay challenge to Adrien's claim to the throne of Velona on the grounds that Adrien is unfit for office. I so declare." Now his supporters yelled and cheered even louder than Adrien's had. Gascon also noticed that some of the hundreds of public who had gathered also cheered for him. Indeed, he had some other supporters as well. "Let the city official decide upon Adrien's fitness, following the long tradition of Velona," Gascon ended his speech.

The public, as expected, took up the cry, calling for public hearings of Adrien's fitness. Adrien fumed, his face was red, he was livid. Yet, now, he could do nothing, though he wanted desperately to attack his brother right where he stood. The nerve Gascon had to openly block his rightful place as ruler of Velona. Adrien resolved to have Gascon beheaded as a traitor as his first official action once he took the throne. Fuming, he and his men retraced their steps back to the meeting hall. Once out of sight, Gascon and his party did likewise, only, during the walk, Gascon slipped aside, going to another secret location. He was not about to be attacked by his brother's forces, whom he knew would be following his dockworkers. Gascon needed to stall, time for his mighty army to reach him here.

A while later, Adrien screamed, "What do you mean you lost him? Damn you all. Send out men everywhere. Find that treacherous brother of mine and kill him any way you can!"

By noon lunchtime, everyone in Velona was talking about the historic events of the morning. At the manor, Lilly Ann asked, "Linda, that was a shrewd move by Gascon, claiming Adrien is unfit for office. They must conduct an investigation into those charges, right? Won't that side in Gascon's favor, especially when we present the botched assassination attempt on Tonia last night?"

Linda replied calmly, "Don't put much faith in the investigation. It is merely a ploy on Gascon's part to make his ascension to the throne acceptable. It buys him time to get his soldiers down here from the north."

Beth Ann gasped, "That can only mean a civil war in Velona!"

"Yes, as Chaucer and I have foreseen, civil war has indeed come to Velona. Now we must see what we can do to minimize that war and its effect on the millions who live here. Otherwise the trauma will be unmanageable here," Linda said softly.

"We must first get the Santi members, who would betray us and join with one of the brothers, identified," Chaucer added. "We cannot survive with traitors in our midst. So we give them time to make their choices: Adrien, Gascon, or us."

"I am too old for wars," declared Beth Ann. "If they fight among themselves, I totally refuse to do any healing on any participant in the civil war. It's their stupidity. Let them heal themselves."

Linda added, "I support you, Beth Ann. No Santi Healer will be allowed to heal any casualty of this civil war. They have deserted us, so let them suffer the consequences of their actions." There was a certain coldness in her voice that made even Beth Ann shutter a little.

"What do we do now?" asked Lilly Ann.

"Nothing. We wait and let the traitors make their move," Linda said. "Now how about some tea everyone?"

July 20, 670, civil war broke out in Velona. Gascon entered the northern part of the city with over a thousand determined fighters; many were Santi. Adrien had not been idle. Unable to locate his brother, he sent word for every available fighter loyal to him to ride to Velona immediately. He too had nearly a thousand heavily armed fighters behind him. Fully half of the men on each side wore plate mail, while the remainder wore chain mail. The battle would take place primarily in the City Park and the surrounding streets. During the morning, both sides moved their men into position.

Both brothers were Guardian trained Protectors but neither had been able to convince other Guardians to support them. Hence, walls of flames would be minimal; this would be a bloody hand-to-hand combat, for there was no room for archers in this confrontation, rather a match of brute force against brute force.

Of course, both brothers would be leading their sides into battle. Aides assisted Gascon into his plate mail, while Adrien was assisted by his aides. Their hatred for each other mushroomed, both swearing to slay the other. Meanwhile, vast crowds of ordinary citizens took up every available position from which to view the spectacle, which was about to unfold. Rooftops were mobbed by people trying to catch a glimpse of the action. All windows of all buildings anywhere in the vicinity were packed with onlookers. In fact, the owners of these buildings had already made a tremendous fortune by noon, having sold viewing locations to the highest bidders!

Yes, if a million people could have watched, they would have. However, only several thousand could afford the price of admission into one of the choice viewing positions. Interestingly enough, none of the ordinary citizens of Velona joined either side. Had the Axemen thrown their support behind either one of the two brothers, then that would have totally tipped the scales. Instead, both brothers had carefully promised the world in favors to these burly Axemen of the north, who now chose to wait and see which way the wind actually blew this day. They would support the victor, who had promised them much.

The bell on the giant Rose Cathedral struck noon, the signal for the battle to commence. Mail clad men on both sides, charged towards the other, both brothers leading forth their forces. Sword fell upon sword and mail, a giant cacophony of sounds echoing loudly through the streets of Velona. Battle was joined.

At the estate, Chaucer, sitting in his saddle, turned to face his loyal Santi fighters. "Okay, they have all committed themselves. Now let us go and end this fiasco!" A great cheer arouse behind him, nearly two thousand strong. "Remember your orders. Contain them; let none escape our net. Allow Linda and me to end this first, then you are to arrest all the participants." He looked down on Linda, who stood on the ground next to him. "Are you sure that you don't want to ride up here with me?"

"Oh well. Okay," Linda agreed; it would look too silly for her to walk along side of him, she realized. She lifted her body up and sat it behind her husband's body. "Let's get this over with." Chaucer gave his arm signal, and the troops moved out, heading down the five mile road into Velona.

Actually, the city had grown and the manor was now actually at the northern edge of the city. The City Park lay in the center of Velona, some two miles south, so it would be a short ride. The many Santi fighters behind Chaucer stared in awe at Linda's unusual way of mounting a horse. Many said that she just floated up and onto the horse. It gave them something to think about and discuss as they rode into the city. Following orders, group by group, they peeled off to take up positions blocking all possible streets, all possible exits from the combat zone. Chaucer and Linda made straight for the heart of the battle, the grassy park.

Chaucer arrived at the rear of the battle. Both could see that already many men had fallen. The combat noise was incredibly loud. Still, neither took any action, awaiting certainty that their forces were in their assigned positions on all the other streets. Chaucer had been utterly insistent that every traitor be apprehended. He need not have worried, for these loyal Santi agreed; none wanted a traitor in their midst!

When Linda felt certain that their forces were in place, she floated down to the ground and Chaucer joined her. "Are you ready my dear?" he asked.

She grinned. "Time for some fun. Show time. This day will not be forgotten for a long time. Let's do it."

Suddenly above the hideous and loud noise of the battlefield, the voices of Chaucer and Linda bellowed, like the scream of God above. Twice as loud as the battle noise were their voices, seemingly coming from straight above the battlefield. They spoke only one word in unison, "Stop!"

The thousands of onlookers watched in complete shock and awe as every fighter instantly ceased fighting, ceased all movement. It seemed like the hand of God, or Lord Jehosa, had just spoken! Then, came more words, "This battle is over. Every participant in this battle is now under arrest for high treason against the people of Velona. Drop your weapons and surrender now."

Again, the onlookers gaped as the fighters began dropping weapons right and left. They then saw Santi, dressed in the familiar black tunics with red crosses appear behind the fighters from all sides of the huge group, From every side street, the Santi swarmed in. They watched as the fighters offered no resistance, and had their arms tied tightly behind them. With normal Santi efficiency, they were placed into long lines.

At the very center, the two brothers fought against the commands of Chaucer and Linda. After summing all of their will power, they broke free and turned to attack Linda and Chaucer, determined to kill them both for interfering in their power grab. Linda, armless and armorless, stood beside

Chaucer, who wore only light clothing; it was the heart of summer after all. The onlookers watched as the two brothers charged the two, swords raised high in a deathblow stroke. Chaucer had yet even to draw his sword.

As the two brothers came close to the two, Linda simply said, "You will stop now. Drop your weapons. Chaucer will accept your surrender." Again, she spoke with such intention, such presence, and such certainty, that both men stopped in their tracks, their swords clanking onto the ground. Chaucer quickly tied their arms behind their backs.

Quickly, several other Santi ushered the two brothers away, moving them into the long lines. "What a mess," declared Linda as she looked at the fallen men that littered the middle of the park. There were hundreds of casualties already. While some Santi began marching the prisoners down to the docks, others brought up wagons and loaded the casualties, whether alive or dead, onto the wagons in piles. None offered the slightest aid to these wounded men; instead, many spat on the traitors that they personally recognized. An hour later, the last of the fallen were rolling out of the park, heading towards the docks.

Again, Linda and Chaucer spoke in their "godlike" voice, this time so that the thousands of onlookers could hear. "Neither of these two brothers is fit to rule your fair country. We will soon help you choose a far better ruler. We will be in touch with the city officials shortly. That is all."

With that, Chaucer floated up and onto his horse, followed by Linda. Yes, they were making a dramatic statement here today. They wanted the power of the Santi to be highly visible, so much depended upon this show of near godlike power. "Do you think that we overdid it?" Linda asked as they rode slowly back to their estate.

"Hard to say. We had a very large audience, and all the proper people witnessed us. That is what we desired, so I think that we did fine. How about a cup of tea, my dear?"

Around suppertime, as we finished eating at the palace in Zargarb, Linda and Chaucer made contact with us. *Hi Bethany, Tonia, Ellaina. Linda and Chaucer here. Got some news for you.* Tonia still had not gotten over the fact that Adrien had tried to have her assassinated while she slept.

Slowly, Linda replayed the events of the day for us. *They have all been taken by caravel to Isla Roca. The civil war has been ended as it barely began. So much for that one. Tonia, Ellaina, the ball, to use one of Renzo's expressions, is now in your court. Tonia, you are the next in line for your mother's throne. What do you want to do?*

Tonia sent, *I've never wanted mom's throne. I don't like being a leader. I don't want to be forced into doing it. I love Velona and our people, but I am a Healer, not a politician. I don't have the patience mom had. Why don't you all listen to me? I really do not want to be the ruler of Velona!* She began crying. Everyone kept assuming that Tonia would, if given the chance, assume her mother's role. Yet, no one accepted her true feelings about it.

*How about me?* Ellaina timidly sent. *I'm willing to try to fill grandmother's shoes. Would I do in her place?*

*Honey, surely you don't want to get involved in all that, do you?* Tonia protested.

*Sure, mom. While I love Healing, I also love how grandmother worked her magic. I think that I've studied her long enough to do what she would have done. I am willing to try it, if they will let me.*

*Will they accept Ellaina?* Tonia asked.

*We are very certain that they will welcome her with open arms, Tonia. Will you allow your daughter to become the ruler in your place?* Linda replied.

*If she wants to do this, I will be eternally grateful to her. Are you sure, Ellaina?*

*Sure mom. Felix will just have to go along with it. Besides, he's known all along that one day I might have to rule, though we thought it wouldn't happen until your body died, many years from now.*

*Thank you Ellaina. We will make the preparations. How soon can you and your family move back to Velona?* Chaucer asked.

*Give them a week to set sail,* I replied. Now we began filling in everyone else about what had just happened in Velona. Felix was as excited as she was about the prospect of Ellaina becoming the new monarch of Velona. He was a Planner, and this position offered him tremendous opportunities for very far reaching constructions!

Our son Ben and Aimee decided to return with Felix and Ellaina, to be their Protector and Loremaster. I encouraged Ben to do this, knowing how much support Ellaina would need. A week later, we all said our farewells and watched their caravel set sail.

That night, Chaucer whispered to Linda, "That went perfectly according to our plans. Ellaina jumped at the opportunity, just like we thought she would."

"Yes, but more importantly, Chaucer, she is only nineteen. We can look forward to a coherent, continuous rule of Velona for at least another fifty to sixty years, if all goes well. If Tonia had taken it, we'd be right back where we started in less than twenty years. We should take a well done on this one, dear. How about a kiss?"

On August 15, 670, Ellaina Dietz Po ascended to the throne of Velona, its sole ruler. Though Felix was always at her side, she made the decisions. True to Linda's words, the citizens of Velona gladly accepted Ellaina Po as their new monarch, especially when they soon saw that she would rule just as her grandmother had before her. A total disaster for Velona had narrowly been averted, solely because of the intervention of Chaucer and Linda d'Grange.

     I now began to see that those two were somehow working behind the scenes of society, controlling and directing it along a certain path, one that led to greater freedom, stability, and prosperity. Perhaps one could control we humans and not in a suppressive manner.

# Chapter 20 Prophesies of Demos

When the caravel, which took Ellaina to Velona, returned to Zargarb, the captain brought a top priority package to me. Linda had sent it, though Chaucer had wrapped the package, had written the to-from note, and had sealed it in with our seldom-used official seal. The address label asked me to notify Linda when I received it and if the seal was still intact.

*Hi, Bethany here. Package arrived. Seal is unbroken. What is this all about?*

Linda sent, *Have Renzo open it for you. Then, if you can read it, do so, but bring Kallisto in to read it to you if needed. She may have lots more knowledge of this book than we do. Once you have read it and gotten Kallisto's opinions on its contents, contact us again.*

Why all this secrecy, I wondered. I had Renzo open the package for me. While I could have probably managed it with my feet, the time required would be prohibitively long. I was entirely too curious to wait that long. Inside we found a book, leather bound, with a highly ornamental covering, strange symbols embossed in the old leather. This was a very old book for sure. The writing I could not read. As instructed, I went to find Kallisto and brought her into my room to see if she could read it.

"What's this? A rare old book? Wow! This is a find indeed," she said as her foot opened the book to the cover page. "This is one of the dozen original, hand-copied printings; it is worth a fortune!"

"Yes, but what is it?" I asked.

"The Prophesies of Demos," she replied. "Demos was one of the legendary founders of my homeland, Demokritos. This book dates from that period, shortly after writing was developed. It is likely six hundred years old and in incredibly good shape. Nowadays, copies of this work are a dime a dozen; it is common reading for our children. This one would sell for at least a hundred thousand gold coins," Kallisto explained.

"Yes, but Linda didn't send it to me as top secret unless there was something vitally important in it. Can you read it to me or teach me how to read your language? I wish Natale were here. Oh," I remembered that Natale was at Mont Blanc now and had probably already read it to Linda.

"The founder of our country wrote of things to come in the centuries that lay ahead of us. So many of them have indeed come true that many believe utterly in its accuracy of future forecasting. Me, I think it is rubbish. How can someone know what will be happening five hundred years in the future?" Kallisto said with an antagonistic air.

"Look Linda has left us a bookmark. Why don't we start there?" Kallisto suggested. "Renzo, will you hold it and turn the pages for me? With a book this rare and valuable, I do not want to risk damaging it with my clumsy feet." He gladly obliged.

She read the first passage aloud.

In the middle of the Sixth Century, travelers from the north will discover Demokritos, bringing news of the rest of the world and of our lost colonies.

A few years later, the Emperor, having learned of our lost colonies, will return to the nearest one and reclaim it for us, through the use of force. Yet, in doing so, he will contract a disease, which will ultimately cost him his life. His son shall become Emperor and his Old Way wife shall be the Empress.

Three-quarters through the Sixth Century, the Emperor will return to the remaining lost colony and reclaim it for us. Learn from the past. Wisdom dictates a new approach. The Empress adopts the new religion, so paving the way for the reclamation.

In the year 686, his son will claim the throne upon his death. However, the Empress will be of the New Way, and she shall bear him this year the son who will become the Ruler of All Tarra. During the formative years of her son, the New Way Empress shall demonstrate to him the importance of maintaining the Old Way. The Sixth Century thus ends upon the sad note of change, demonstrating for the last time the necessity of the Old Way.

The beginning of the Seventh Century marks the beginning of a new era for Tarra, one that will see a grand, great unification, one never before seen on our world. This century opens with the uniting of Demokritos and Annelise into the whole it was this day meant to be. The Boy-To-Be-Emperor, who will be of Gavril lineage, must seek a woman of the Old Way and thus must turn to our neighbors in Annelise. There the Boy-To-Be-Emperor will find a Woman of the Old Way. She shall be of the Ryker lineage. By making her the Empress, the Boy-To-Be-Emperor shall become the Emperor and the two halves of countries shall forever more be united into a single whole.

Now the Emperor, with his Empress of the Old Way at his side, will move north, reclaiming the northern lands, forming a Unified Empire of wealth and beauty that has never been seen before on Tarra. Wisdom dictates leaving the Yellow for last.

"There is more, but maybe this is enough," Kallisto suggested. "As I said, you can interpret these pronouncements in many different ways. Most of us don't really put much stock in it."

"True, fortune telling often is nothing more than the seer sensing what the requester desires. I suppose we should contact Linda and see what this is about," I replied. A few minutes later, I had Linda Mind Linked to us three.

*We read the marked pages. Kallisto says this edition is extremely valuable. Is this the point?*

Linda sent, *No. We've found it uncanny and correct, as far as we can tell up to now. You did open up all Tarra in the middle of the Sixth Century. We did some research via our Fortress down in Demokritos. It seems the reference to the 'Lost Colonies' may refer to that island you were not permitted to explore, Acropolis, at least that may be one of them. We have just learned via returning caravels from the south that Emperor Andreas Gavril has indeed landed on the island with a large force of Centurions. He's defeated the islanders there and added the island to Demokritos. He did this about five years ago now. I've sent a trade ship to the island with a secret purpose to determine if there are any armless women there or similarly mutilated women. We don't expect to find any, based on our own brief survey that we did when we discovered the island. They will also recheck that mantis base to double-check it is not operational any longer.*

*What has really gotten my attention in all this is that this week Emperor Andreas has come to our Fortress with a very high fever, seeking help from our Healer there. He has Jungle Fever as far as she can tell, incurable, but controllable perhaps. No, wait a minute. I am being contacted by the Healer there. Hang on a second.*

I said, "Kallisto, this is getting a bit weird."

"Yes, maybe there is more to this fortune telling that we think. Nah, look, you remember how interested Emperor Andreas was when you were telling him about discovering that island and about Megalos? Well, since everyone reads the Prophesies, Emperor Andreas probably just decided to follow that, using it as a justification for attacking those people."

"You are probably right. If everyone reads this, then it is easy to make it come true simply by doing what the prophesies say. You make them come true," I suggested.

*I'm back. Sad news, Emperor Andreas has just passed away from the fever. His son, Axos Gavril, has accepted the throne and is the new Emperor. Incidentally, his wife of some twenty years Adelpha, is also of the Eighth Degree. Curious isn't it? That makes the first two accurately predicted.*

I sent, *Probably just Andreas making it come true, nothing more.*

*The next one involves Megalos. I am sending several spies down there to keep an eye on things. If Demokritos joins forces with Megalos, though I can hardly see that happening, given the fiercely independent nature of Megalos, they will become a powerhouse, a force to be taken seriously. We have been barely able to keep Megalos at bay all these years. With the overwhelming power of Demokritos behind them, we will not be able to stop them. The alluding to taking over the control of all the northern lands has me very concerned, Bethany. If the next prophesy comes true, the beginning of the Seventh Century has Chaucer and me extremely worried. We may have a mission for you to attempt at that time.*

*Meantime, Kallisto, please educate Bethany on all of the history and culture of Demokritos that you know. It may amount to nothing, but then again, it may be vital for her to know. I can't tell you how worried we both are over these prophesies, Bethany. Oh yes, one other thing you should know. Demokritos has successfully copied our caravel design. They have made a successful test run. We anticipate that they will now begin building their own fleet of caravels. This will give them much more mobility than they previously had. It only raises our concerns.*

We agreed to do as she asked, and Kallisto began educating me in the history of her country. I don't believe in prophesies, but these were a bit uncanny.

# Chapter 21 The Conversion and the Pact

In the hot summer of 675, the Royal Arc, the Emperor's official caravel, docked in the port of Athos, near Constanza City. Emperor Axos Gavril and his wife, Adelpha, had come to visit the last of their Lost Colonies. He had one hundred legions of Centurions accompanying him in a flotilla of caravels, which were lying at anchor just off the port. One legion landed with him to protect their sovereign. Axos would conquer this island and bring it back under Demokritos control, one way, or another. Yet, the prophesies were ever in his mind, which was why he had brought his magnificent wife, Adelpha of the Eight Degree with him. The prophesies could not be ignored, though he did not personally believe in them.

The Eight Degree referred to the old practices founded hundreds of years ago in Demokritos. At that time, marital infidelity was at record levels. The Oracle at Aylon Orthos had for centuries spoken prophesies of the future. A mantis creature, unknown to all, had taken up residency there and had gained control over the Orthee, the seers. Through them, the mantis created the Holy Eight Degrees of Matrimonial Binding. This scheme had been in operation some three hundred years, and the broken marriages were at an all-time low. Generally, the only broken marriages to be found are among those of No Degree.

When a couple decided to get married, assuming that they were not extremely poor, they would journey to the Temple of Orthos to sanctify their union. The woman would sacrifice an appendage and the man would thus be bound to her for their lives. Only if they possessed wealth and power, would the Orthees allow the woman to become of the Eight Degree, losing both arms at the shoulder. This then ensured her new husband of total fidelity for the duration of their lives, as he would have to assist her with everything in life, providing many servants as well. These were the women who were held in the highest regard by everyone, their sacrifice visible to all. They also wielded great power, but of that in a moment.

The Seventh Degree women sacrificed their arms at the elbows. The Sixth Degree, at their wrists. The Fifth Degree women gave up one entire arm. The Fourth Degree lost one hand. The Third Degree, three fingers of each hand, leaving only the index finger and thumb. The Second and First Degrees, two and one finger on each hand, respectively. Thus, as the degree of sacrifice rose, so did the power, respect, and honor of the union of the women, and the men who were so pledged. While the scheme sounded utterly barbaric, here it had achieved its goal, for couples remained faithful to each other for life. Never in the history of Demokritos had an Eighth Degree couple been unfaithful to each other! (Well, that is not true; the Kali assassinated those who were unfaithful.) The penalties were too great to consider even having an affair outside the marriage. If the man did it, the woman was given everything that the cheating husband had, land, property, money, even his job. Similarly, if the woman was unfaithful, she would be sent out into the world to survive on her own, and none dared do this.

Now only the very poor had unions of No Degree, those who could not afford to make the trip to Aylon Orthos. Here were found the few unfaithful marriages. All this has changed when the Explorers Circle first came to Demokritos. We effectively stopped this awful practice. Since that time in 652, no further women were thusly mutilated. Adelpha had become of the Eighth Degree several years before we came and was one of the last of her kind.

While we were there, Kallisto was the leader of the Kali Assassins, whose goal was the elimination of these Holy Degrees and those husbands who proved unfaithful to their wives. With our help and Kallisto's, the barbaric practice had been ended in Demokritos.

Emperor Axos was forty-three and getting a rather late start on being the Emperor. His father, Andreus, had simply lived too long, and Axos was glad that the Jungle Fever finally brought his father down. Now it was his turn to put Demokritos back on the map, according to the ancient prophesies. To that end, he'd brought an initial invasion force. However, Adelpha had consoled him that the prophesies dictated another way should be found. He helped his wife off the caravel and onto the docks.

"My, it's hot here, Axos. I am melting in this heavy dress," she commented.

"Perhaps it will be cooler once we get to the meeting place. Look at the architecture! It is so much like ours; white marble is everywhere. This must be our lost colony!"

Just then, a man dressed in a black robe with a white cross walked up to them. His Centurions had disembarked and had formed a line around the two. "Emperor Axos I presume. I am Supreme Prelate Anatol; I am in charge of security for the church. I have coaches waiting to take you and the Empress to Constanza City and the Holy Church, where His Holiness Pope Aison is anxiously awaiting your arrival. If you and your men will follow me, it is but a short ride; Constanza City abuts the western edge of this port city of Althos."

His arm around Adelpha to steady her, the Emperor followed Anatol to the carriages. He lifted his wife up and into the carriage and climbed in beside her. Anatol joined them. "Forgive me, Empress, but I cannot help but be so amazed at your beauty. I had no idea you were, well so impressively beautify. You must be terribly proud of your wife, Emperor Axos. She is a fine woman indeed."

"Thank you, Supreme Prelate. I do hope the meeting room is cooler. I am so hot in this dress. If not, I may need someone to fan my face," she replied.

"Aye, there is only one Adelpha. I am so very lucky to have her as my wife," the Emperor made small talk. His attention was on the passing buildings and people outside the carriage. He could not get over how similar this all looked to his homeland. Even the color of their skin was the same, bronzed.

"Ah, here we are, the Holy Gates of Constanza City, an entire city dedicated to the Church of Jehosanity on Tarra," Anatol explained. Both passengers stared out the window at the huge, white marble walls surrounding the huge city. Before them, massive oaken gates, heavily carved with frescoes were open. Inside, they got their first view of the enormous mother Church of Jehosanity. Both found it breathtaking indeed, from the white marble pillars and columns to the gold foiled dome that shown like the rays of God in the afternoon sun. Spectacular indeed was the mother church.

Soon the two entered the main entrance, which opened into the massive foyer, whose domed ceiling stood fifty feet over their heads. Great marble columns supported the dome, and it was cool here inside, much to the relief of the Empress, who was helpless, dependent upon others caring for all her needs.

As they entered, they were greeted with Holy Hymns, sung a capella. The echoes in this massive chamber magnified the sound, as if the very heavens above had opened up into song, praising the Lord Jehosa. Resplendent in his purple robes with white crosses on its front and back, Pope Aison walked forward to meet his very special guests. Aison was thirty years old and only recently voted in as the new Pope. This time, the Cardinals wanted to elect someone who stood a good chance of reigning for a long period. They had become tired of constant change from popes who only lasted a few years before they died.

Over the singing voices, Aison said, "Welcome Emperor Axos, Empress Adelpha. I am Pope Aison, your host. If you will follow me, I have prepared a room, which is cool and quiet, where we may discuss matters of the highest importance. Your Centurions may follow or Supreme Prelate Anatol can take them to a room where they can take some refreshments, your choice." Axos had two men follow him, while the rest went with the Prelate. After a short walk, they entered a plush meeting room. It was indeed cool inside here; great tapestries adorned the walls, and golden candelabra provided the illumination. Six oil paintings depicting the life of Lord Jehosa's Son, Jes Amir, hung on the walls. Pope Aison, who had never seen an armless woman before, much less one this pretty, could not help but watch her closely, as Axos pulled out her chair and helped her be seated comfortably.

"Wine, ale, water, juice?" asked Pope Aison. Both took a cup of juice. Again, Pope Aison watched carefully to see how she would be able to drink. Axos held the cup for her to drink.

"Shall we get down to business?" Axos said, noticing the Pope staring at his wife.

"Ah, yes. Perhaps I should tell you a bit of our long history," Pope Aison began his well-rehearsed speech. He outlined their illustrious history. "You see, we used to have an Emperor and Empress much as Demokritos has. However, over the years, they became very ineffective in leading. Before our Church of Jehosanity was founded, they all believed as your people, in the Sun God. However, decadence set in, promiscuity ran rampant, vile, unholy acts were condoned and done in the very throne room! Our Church has put a total stop on such unholy, promiscuous acts! The Senate was given the added responsibility of leading our vast country. Yet, they could never seem to reach any decision on important matters. In the end, our church with our Holy Paladins had to step in to defeat the enemy, which had invaded our island and bring order back to our land. Now the Church of Jehosanity effectively runs the entire country. Yet, we still allow the Senate to make the laws of the people. As long as those do not violate our religious beliefs, we see that they are followed."

"Nearly a quarter of a century ago now, we set sail to the south to try to find our lost relatives. We found them at Acropolis, though they refused us to land and meet with them. At that time, we did not know that more of our relatives lay even further to the south; hence, we turned back in great sadness. I cannot begin to tell you the joy that we all felt here when your ambassadors first contacted us last year. This is so incredible, so hard to believe. We welcome you here, brother and sister."

"Thank you for the warm welcome," Adelpha replied, before her husband could respond. "Tell me, do you also have women of the Holy Eight Degrees here in Megalos?"

"Not as such, though we have tried twice. Each time, our enemy, the Santi del Dio, keeps interfering and stealing them away from us. Once they even came here and ordered us to stop creating women of the Holy Degrees. We had little choice but to obey their wishes," Pope Aison replied half truthfully. He hastily added, "Now that I have met one of the Eighth Degree and seen just how beautiful you are, I only wish that we could somehow get the Holy Eight Degrees going here in Megalos. It would solve so many problems."

"Yes, it has kept our marital unions totally faithful. I enjoy being doted upon by my husband too. It is the highest honor that I can provide for him, you know. Yes, these Santi have been instrumental in ending the Holy Eight Degrees in Demokritos as well. You are not alone, Pope Aison. We have this in common."

Emperor Axos had heard enough now. He knew that the source of real power in Megalos now lay with this church and their leader, this Pope Aison. "Demokritos is at least ten times the size of Megalos; each of our kingdoms is larger than your island. My father retook Acropolis by force of arms, since they refused to allow him to land. Now it is my duty, following the prophesies of old, to get our other lost colony, Megalos, back into our folds. As you know, I have many caravels lying at anchor; ten thousand Centurions await my signal to invade and use force if necessary to get Megalos back into our loving fold." He studied the Pope's reaction to his veiled threat. Surprisingly, the Pope did not bat an eye!

"Ah, that you have, we know. Yet, Emperor Axos, you are demonstrating a profoundly great wisdom in not using them. Megalos has never been taken yet by force of arms in all its long history. Megalos is guarded and protected by Lord Jehosa himself! Let me tell you of the two attempts. Many years ago, the barbarians rode out of the Northern Steppes, intent on conquering the entire known world. They swept through the land of the Seven Sea Princes, conquering them with great ease. They swept through Juda Arad and entered the Southlands, taking control over all that they conquered. In fact, they had gotten as far south as Sud, just across the Narrow Firth from Megalos. Sud is one of our largest cities, off island, of course. There, when it looked like we were doomed, the hand of Lord Jehosa intervened on behalf of our first Pope, Yazi I, who founded this very church. Lord Jehosa struck down the enemy leader, and our Centurions then drove them back into the steppes, never to be seen again."

"Then, just a few years ago, the Yellow Men came to invade Megalos, from somewhere far to the east. Again, we are sure that they are in league with the Santi del Dio. These savage barbarians sacked nearly half of our island. Yet once more Lord Jehosa directly intervened on our behalf. He brought down a typhoon, which swept the entire enemy army off our lands, never to be seen again. In short, Emperor Axos, Megalos is indeed protected by our Holy Savior, Lord Jehosa. God will not allow anything to harm his most holy church here in Constanza City. Of that, you can be utterly certain. Lord Jehosa has intervened twice now on our behalf, and I only need to pray to him and he will yet again defend our island. Thus it is that I say, Emperor Axos, you have shown great wisdom in not trying to take Megalos by force of arms."

"It seems your God is more powerful than our Sun God," Axos replied with a sigh. "Yet, you do see my dilemma. I must find a way to unify our two countries into the whole that it once was in ancient times."

"And I too must find a way to unify Megalos with our lost relatives," Pope Aison answered. Both men stared at each other, neither willing to alter their viewpoint.

Adelpha stepped in to break the deadlock. "This Lord Jehosa of yours — he must be awfully powerful and caring to have watched over your church and country."

Pope Aison welcomed the change of topic, "Yes, he is the God of every one of us. Routinely here in our churches on Megalos he works miracle cures. Once each month, we conduct the Holy High Salvation Mass, in which we try to get at least ten of our people who are in need of healing, you know, the lame, the blind, those who have lost the power of speech, and during the High Mass, Lord Jehosa heals one or two who have totally opened their hearts for forgiveness of their sins and have embraced Jehosa as the One God. Our founder, Pope Yazi I began these special masses and began the Official Miracle Ledger, which we have faithfully maintained all these years. In it, we document each of the wondrous miracles Lord Jehosa has given unto us. While I don't recall off hand the actual number recorded there, it is over one hundred people he has cured or healed so far. The number grows each month."

Adelpha looked at Axos and grimly asked, "And how many miracle cures has our Sun God given us, Axos?" He squirmed, not wanting to admit it, so she answered for him. "None, zero, that's how many."

"The sun is just another part of the physical world that we live in," Pope Aison offered. "Many of the uncivilized mariners of the Sea Princes believe in their Sea God, Tur, assigning unto him all their troubles at sea. Yet, is not the sea also only a part of the physical world that we live in? I've heard that the farmers of the Greenway up north above the Sea Princes believe in some kind of pagan fertility god, which helps them have children and good crops. We educated men and women — we know this is just superstition at work, just as the barbarian horsemen of the Northern Steppes believe in some pagan horse god. Superstition. Yet, there is a real God of Mankind, Lord Jehosa."

"What does he stand for? I mean what kind of beliefs do you have, the faithful of your religion," Adelpha asked, a little unsure just how to phrase her question, perhaps because she had never really thought much about religious matters before.

Pope Aison rattled off, "The Holy Decalogue of Lord Jehosa states for us all:

There is no god but Jehosa.

Do not worship any other god but the One God, Jehosa.

Do not build statues of Jehosa, for Jehosa has no form. One may build forms of the Holy

Son and the Holy Mother of the Son.

Set aside the Holy Day, Sunday, from your labors and worship Lord Jehosa upon that

day.

Respect and serve thy mother and thy father, for they have labored long in your raising.

Do not kill another who worships Jehosa.

Do not steal from another who worships Jehosa.

Do not commit adultery or lay with a woman before you are married.

Do not lie to another who worships Jehosa.

Do not desire another's house, possessions, or wife, if he worships Jehosa."

"We do fully appreciate the adultery or bedding before marriage or desiring another's wife," Adelpha replied. "It was because those were running rampant centuries ago that the Holy Eight Degrees came about.

"Here, we know that everyone of us possesses a most precious soul, which is not of this fleshly body or world. When the fleshly body dies, the soul goes to meet with the Keeper of the Holy Ledger. The soul's name is then checked against this ledger, which has two columns. One is labeled Good Marks, the other, Bad Marks. Lord Jehosa watches over every action a person makes in their lifetime. Every time the person does a good action, such as helping another who is in distress, he places a checkmark in the Good Marks column. Every time the person does a bad action, such as you mentioned, sleeping with another's wife, a checkmark goes into the Bad Marks column. Thus, when the soul arrives at the Keeper, if the ledger contains more Good Marks than Bad, the soul is allowed to enter Heaven, the realm in which Lord Jehosa lives. However, if the ledger contains more Bad Marks, the soul is denied entrance into this Holiest of Realms, instead it is sent into Hell, where Lucifer dwells, there to be eternally tormented in the fiery pits of burning sulfur."

"Adelpha, here we have seen so many women who rebel against society, who continually commit numerous offenses, whose Bad Marks ledger continually grows beyond count, that we had to do something about them. You see, our entire purpose, the totality of our church's teachings, is to help all people earn nothing but Good Marks so that their soul can enter Lord Jehosa's Heavenly Realm, when their mortal body dies. Oh, have we tried to reach these women, so desperately we have tried. Yet, they do not see reason or listen to us. That's when we began to implement something akin to your Holy Eight Degrees. Yet, no sooner had we begun this, than the Santi del Dio intervened and stole all these women from us, taking them to Velona. By force of arms, these Santi forced us to stop. Yet, we refused to yield to these unholy Santi. Instead, we tried an alternate solution, encasing their arms in a metal device so that they no longer had the use of their arms. I know, this is so unlike your wonderful Holy Degrees, yet it was the next best idea we could try, given that the Santi refused to allow us to continue the correct and proper way. Yet, even this they denied us, again stealing away those whom we were trying to bring to their senses and begin to earn Good Marks."

All this, Adelpha greatly desired to hear. These religious people were not so different from her. In fact, she deeply regretted the abolishment of the Eight Degrees, for she knew that if she had not been of the Eighth Degree, Axos would have left her for a younger woman years ago. She had seen the lust in his eyes, but only the binding contract of the Holy Eight Degrees had kept her marriage intact.

Emperor Axos commented, "You say that these Santi stole your

Eighth Degree women and refused to allow you to continue your Holy Ways. How is this possible?" He was beginning to believe these people here were terribly weak — their fighters hardly worthy of the name Centurion.

"Emperor Axos, two factors have led us down this path. First, this all occurred just after our last Emperor Justinian personally led his ill-fated assault on the Santi in Velona and was killed on the battlefield. Our entire army of brave Centurions had nearly been completely wiped out during those battles. We were at their mercy. Second, some of these Santi, the Guardians, they call themselves, are evil witches, possessed of evil magical spells, given unto them by Lucifer's spawn! Poor Justinian was unable to save himself from their magical fires. The few Centurions who managed to survive reported that these witches entirely encased his body in burning flames! Others report that they can command the very sea to capsize a huge ship. One of our own Popes witnessed these evil witches lifting giant marble columns and swinging it as a giant club, crushing the bodies of our brave fighters. I say unto you, what chance has the bravest, strongest Centurion against such evil spells from Hell? None."

"I see, yes, none at all. Yet, may I ask how many legions of Centurions did this Justinian have at his command and how many of the Santi did he face? This is a very significant question that I am asking," Emperor Axos stated very seriously.

"Alas, I am not a fighter. I believe that he had around seventy legions at that time and was facing perhaps fifty legions of defenders. If you truly desire a more accurate accounting, I will send for the Holy Historian, who can find those numbers for you. We keep accurate historical records of all events here at the Mother Church."

"No, that estimate is entirely sufficient, Pope Aison." Axos saw his opening and took it. "Pope Aison, what would you say the outcome of that battle might have been had the Emperor had not seventy legions but two or three or four hundred legions?"

"Oh my, the world would be so very different now! Evil witches or not, the Santi would have been destroyed once and for all time! Never in our long history have we ever had such numbers of Centurions. Four hundred legions? Incredible."

Axos knew that he had him now. "Well, Pope Aison, I can field four hundred legions in one month's time. If I need more than that, give me a year, and I can triple those numbers. That is how strong Demokritos actually is. Unlike your small island, Demokritos is a very large country indeed. To prevent such ills happening to our lost colonies is just why I and my lovely wife have made this incredibly long journey so far north. We are here to help."

Pope Aison knew that this Emperor could easily conquer the entirety of Megalos with half of those numbers. Still, his focus was not on politics or armies. He was the Pope, after all; men's souls were his prime motivation.

"Our people here on Megalos simply would not accept Sun God worshipers. Your people would always be seen as pagans, barbarians, not as the true elite that you actually are. Might I make a suggestion?"

Axos nodded, Aison continued, "Now if it were widely seen that our cousins from Demokritos also believed in Lord Jehosa, then your presence here would be seen as fellow believers, lending us a helping hand. You and your people would be totally accepted far and wide throughout all our many conquered lands."

"Dear, that seems most reasonable, given that Lord Jehosa is protecting Megalos. We should denounce the Sun God as a false god and accept Lord Jehosa as the One True God. Dear, we could use some miracle cures back home. Think what that would do for our positions?"

She looked at the Pope, "You would send some priests to help get the Holy Church established in Demokritos?"

"Why nothing would give us more pleasure, more satisfaction than helping so many more souls be able to enter Heaven upon their fleshly body's death. We would be highly honored by such an invitation!"

"What would you demand in return?" Axos asked, not believing that anyone was this altruistic. There had to be a hidden motive.

Pope Aison looked at the beautiful Adelpha and replied, "Would it be possible for some of your Orthee, who used to perform the Holy Operations to create the various Holy Degrees, to come here and teach us how it is done? Teach us the ways and means to properly perform such a ceremony, to broadly educate our people in the workings of the Holy Eight Degrees of Matrimony? We know nothing about it, yet, I can see with my own eyes how wonderful it actually is — for you two are shining examples of its complete success!" He laid it on a bit thick, but this new Holy Degrees offered him a solution that he greatly desired, though he did not mention that they had been doing similar mutilations to only the recalcitrant women of Megalos and elsewhere. Here, it was done to nearly all women whose men had means. Surely, with this widely implemented in Megalos and their controlled lands, all women would end up earning nothing but Good Marks, and their souls would have a free pass into Heaven!

Axos replied, "Ah Pope Aison, if we did indeed do as you ask, what would keep these Santi from once more stealing away these women and forcing you to cease and desist?"

Pope Aison squirmed, did he dare ask? He decided to try anyway, for he had nothing to lose and everything to gain. Eventually, this Emperor would learn that the Church of Jehosanity and the Pope were the actual rulers of Tarra. "Could you possibly spare enough legions to come here to ensure that the Santi cannot do so? Of course, they would have to convert from pagan Sun God worshiping to Lord Jehosa or our people would ostracize them."

Axos thought, "This is like taking candy from a child! He's given me precisely what I came here to obtain! And for what? A silly religious belief change and the re-implementation of the Holy Eight Degrees!" He tried to act as if this might be troublesome for him to do. "Well, yes, I do believe that I could spare you some legions. I do not know the size of your forces at present. Would say seventy more Centurion legions stationed here be sufficient to dissuade these Santi from intervening?"

"I do believe that number would give them something serious to think about before they acted. If they did attack, surely our southern cousins would send us more aid?"

"Oh absolutely! No hesitation. You are our northern lost colony. We want you back in our fold. You have my word. Should the Santi threaten, let me know at once!"

"Then, I see nothing standing in our way!" Pope Aison declared. The two men shook hands. He attempted to shake the Empress's hand, but had awkwardly forgotten she had none to shake.

"Oh, silly. You give me a hug. I've no arms to shake. That is how it is done, by hugs," Empress Adelpha graciously explained, as she often had to do so in the past when around those who were unfamiliar with women of the Eighth Degree, the women who wielded great power in Demokritos.

Stiffly, Pope Aison gave her a hug. Inwardly, he enjoyed it immensely. He thought, "If only our women were as wonderful as this woman!"

That afternoon, at a special High Mass, Pope Aison baptized the couple into the Church of Jehosanity. For the next two weeks, the Emperor and Empress visited many of the cities and nobles, sharing their great success with the Holy Eight Degrees of Matrimony, among many other political details. Everywhere they went, as soon as it was known that they were officially baptized into the Church of Jehosanity, the two were accepted as long lost nobility and accorded great status. Many men listened carefully to their every word. More than a few women talked openly and frankly with the Empress about her situation, and she had nothing but praises for her Eighth Degree.

When the two finally set sail for home, on deck, his arm around his wife to help her keep her balance, he said, "We did it, dear. This has worked out just like the prophesies foretold. You were wonderful, as always."

"Yes, we got everything we could possibly have hoped for and then a whole lot more! I am so excited! The Holy Eight Degrees of Matrimony shall not die with me! Kiss me. I feel very passionate at this moment!" The two lovingly embraced long, before they went below deck to enjoy each other more fully.

# Chapter 22 Shock and Response

Late August 675, Linda once again linked Renzo, Kallisto, and me together for a very serious discussion. *It's worse than we predicted, you guys! Damn these prophesies anyway.* Linda was angry; she seldom got angry since she had returned from the Red Desert.

*Our spies in Megalos verified that Emperor Axos and Empress Adelpha have indeed taken over control of Megalos. They have publically adopted Jehosanity as their religion and will be converting all Demokritos over to it. Priests of the Pope's are already heading there to begin teaching the citizens and converting them. We've heard various numbers bandied about, but somewhere around seventy thousand Centurions from Demokritos have landed on Megalos and are taking up full time residence there. I cannot believe that Megalos welcomed them warmly!*

*I guess that is not so bad. We are on excellent terms with Demokritos, unlike Megalos. Yet, if their perverted religion gains a foothold, I can see trouble brewing,* I replied.

*Bethany, it is far worse! Something completely unexpected. Megalos has asked that they be allowed to implement the Holy Eight Degrees of Matrimony! Axos agreed and he and his wife have been actively promoting it on Megalos! Rumors have it that Axos will be sending Orthee to teach and advise those on Megalos who will do such a horrible thing to others. With seventy more legions of Centurions there, the Santi will be powerless to stop such butchery of women, let alone come to their aid.*

Kallisto put in, *Calm down, Linda. Only the very wealthy can afford to do this. Always it has been a mutual decision between marital partners. As long as we can somehow insist that it be an unforced, knowing total commitment, the Degrees will not become the horrid mess that you had to handle with the so called recalcitrant women of the Sea Princes and Megalos. If a woman is willing to do this to herself of her own volition, then I say let her. It is her life. We draw the line when the victim is unwilling and it has been forced upon her. People choose their own punishments. After all, how many men drink themselves into a stupor or worse? As long as they are doing it willingly of their own choice and not being pressured to do this thing, let them.* Kallisto had a hard heart when it came to people knowingly harming themselves.

*You are right. I was thinking how damnably hard we have all suffered and are suffering every day. Yes, you are right; it is their choice to make, as long as they are doing it knowingly and freely. I won't tolerate even the slightest coercion though.* Linda calmed down.

*The main reason for this chat is what Chaucer and I have been seeing more and more clearly as the years go by us. Recall the next prophesy. I'll quote it from Natale's translation.*

> *In the year 686, his son will claim the throne upon his death. However, the Empress will be of the New Way and she shall bear him this year the son who will become the Ruler of All Tarra. During the formative years of her son, the New Way Empress shall demonstrate to him the importance of maintaining the Old Way. The Sixth Century thus ends upon the sad note of change, demonstrating for the last time the necessity of the Old Way.*

> *The beginning of the Seventh Century marks the beginning of a new era for Tarra, one that will see a grand, great unification, one never before seen on our world. This century opens with the uniting of Demokritos and Annelise into the whole it was this day meant to be. The Boy-To-Be-Emperor, who will be of Gavril lineage, must seek a woman of the Old Way and thus must turn to our neighbors in Annelise. There the Boy-To-Be-Emperor will find a Woman of the Old Way. She shall be of the Ryker lineage. By making her the Empress, the Boy-To-Be-Emperor shall become the Emperor and the two halves of countries shall forever more be united into a single whole.*

> *Now the Emperor, with his Empress of the Old Way at his side, will move north, reclaiming the northern lands, forming a Unified Empire of wealth and beauty that has never been seen before on Tarra. Wisdom dictates leaving the Yellow for last.*

Linda said, *These children, who are to be born around sixteen years from now are pivotal — their actions will decide whether the Sea Princes remain free and independent countries or not, whether the Santi del Dio continue to exist or are destroyed, whether the northern lands all become one vast Demokritos subject to the rule of one Emperor or not. Bethany, we can see some of the future track of civilization here on Tarra, but not quite that far ahead, there are too many variables at play in the world.*

After a pause, she added, *Bethany, I don't know how to put this to you or even if I have the right to ask this of you.*

*What?* I had no idea what she had in mind.

*Remember long ago, Alabaster Benjamin Crowley, having heard of the birth of the Great Messiah, asked you to go there and, well, you know the rest. Some of us truly know the magnitude of what all you did for us all by accepting that mission. I sincerely believe that we are once more at a similar crossroad in history.*

*You want me to go down to Annelise, take this female baby body, and become the Empress so that we might sway the Emperor, change his plans somehow, or even kill him if he is about to destroy the Santi?*

*Well, yes, but I doubt that you would need to kill him, persuade him would be far better.*

*I married Jes because I fell in love with him. We had or have the highest admiration and respect for each other. I don't know if I could marry a man under such false pretenses. Yet, too much is at stake for me to refuse, Linda. Everything we have worked for all these years could be destroyed. Heaven help us if all Tarra is subject to one man's whims!*

*Thank you for considering this. We have at least another eighteen years to watch and observe. Perhaps it will not be needed, other things may change,* Linda sounded a hopeful note. As far as I was concerned, if these people put such faith in blind prophesies, they would surely attempt to make them come true.

Linda added, *I will have our Santi down in the two countries monitor the situation there. We must identify the people who will be involved in the prophesies, especially in Annelise. We must find the mother who will be giving birth to this woman who will become Empress. The boy will be obvious, Alkaios is the son of Axos; it must be his son that will be the boy Emperor.*

Renzo, who had been quiet up to this point, asked, *Why could I not go and take this boy Emperor's body? Then, I could completely violate the prophesy, doing everything possible to support the Santi.*

*We thought about doing just that Renzo,* Linda answered honestly. *There are two huge problems with this approach to the problem. One: when you pick up your next baby body, you must be able to remember everything from this lifetime. Renzo, as you grew up as a young boy, did you recall everything from your previous lifetime, what you had seen and done, what you had been in your prior lifetime? I'm not picking on you. Most people completely forget their last lifetime when they are established in their new baby body and identity. We know that Bethany has always been able to do this. Yet, we cannot ask her to take the Emperor's baby body for the second reason. The whole country appears to be slavishly following the prophesies; hence, the Emperor will be under extreme pressure to follow the prophesy. If Bethany or you were to become this Emperor and attempt to do something completely different, the political forces would counteract any such openly direct move. No, I am afraid our best chance is to influence this Emperor by using his wife. I know it feels like we are now becoming the mantis or Grey Creatures, controlling society from the sidelines, but our goals and intentions are to help humanity not pervert it.*

Renzo sighed, *I understand, but I want to help my Bethany somehow, someway.*

*I know you do. This is a hard decision for us all. We will find a way for you to help, Renzo, I promise.*

*Hey, I am going to help her too,* Kallisto added. *Look, she is going to need real help down there. My current body is aging fast. It's already fifty-*

*two. By the time this new baby body is born, it'll be in its sixties. Perhaps, Linda, I could go ahead of her, maybe be her older sister. That way, Bethany will not be on her own.*

*Thanks all of you, but we are forgetting one big factor. Just how do we know that this supposed Annelise woman will actually have a baby at the right time? Further, it is fifty-fifty that it will be a male baby. Aren't we jumping the gun here?* I threw in my thoughts.

Linda's answer surprised me. *Bethany, both Chaucer and I are able to predetermine the sex of a newly conceived baby, even cause one to miscarry. I promise you, Bethany, if you find the marriage so awful that you do not wish to have his children, we will see that you do not. That is the least that we can do for you. It is likely to be an awful situation we are asking you to put yourself into down there.*

*Wow!* I was amazed at just what all these two could now do.

*Yes, either of us could have that boy Emperor's body die instantly and at any point in its life. Yet, doing so would make no difference, if the others are slaves to the prophesy. They would just elect another Emperor who would insist on following it. Our best chance is to influence events from behind the scenes. Yet, we all have at least another dozen years to find better ways of handling it.* We all agreed to put our minds to the task.

Later Renzo called a special meeting of all the Santi leaders in Zargarb. He outlined the high probability of yet another war coming our way. "Look, for the first time in history, we know the war is coming nearly thirty years ahead of time. We should use this opportunity to prepare well in advance of its arrival. I swear this time Zargarb will not be sacked!"

"Amen to that!" declared Lena, who, in her last lifetime, had seen Zargarb conquered and the horrible consequences thereof.

Lady Ariana, who was now sixty, exclaimed, "Oh no, what am I leaving to you, Nicolina Sue, another devastating war? What can we do? Surely, there is something that we can do about it? I am so sorry, daughter, that I am leaving you to face yet another war."

"Don't worry so mom. We will find a way to deal with it," Nicolina Sue consoled her mother. She was slowly assuming more and more of the daily duties for her mother. She was now twenty-seven and married to a fine painter. Already she had three children running all over the palace, much to the pleasure of their grandmother. Unlike Velona, there was no question of the power transfer. Her younger brother of two years, Tom, didn't want anything to do with ruling the sector. He was primarily a Loremaster, caring little for politics. While Nicolina Sue was also a Loremaster, she also had been helping her mother, along with Rachele and Julianna, all these years. She knew just how to run the sector, following her mother's lead.

"Lots of Santi fighters, all wearing plate mail, lots of ballistae and throwers in each fortress — that will help," Renzo stated.

"No dad, we need something more," Lena replied. "We need

something that can hit them long before they can get to us, something absolutely devastating."

"Dad, I have an idea," Adrien, our youngest suggested. "Enyo and Frank gave me the idea. It's a modification of the Tashien fireworks. Can I work on it?"

A month later and several rather severe burns later, Adrien called us all over to the Zargarb Fortress, where he had his grand experiment now operational. Adrien was very excited and very proud. For the first time in his life, he was not taking the back seat of the carriage and was about to contribute to our defense. "Imagine out there on the empty grasslands to the east lies the enemy army marching towards us here. If you will look closely out there, I have put a dozen dummy mock ups of soldiers, some wearing armor. Imagine they are coming towards us. This is what I call a cannone assassino. Watch what happens when I light this fuse. Hold your ears! Oops, mom, here I'll cover yours."

We watched as the flickering flames rapidly entered the long metal tube, which he had setup at a forty-five degree angle from the floor here on the wall. Boom! A tremendous explosion occurred. Smoke covered us all. However, I saw a projectile, much like a fireworks fly out, arcing high into the sky. As it came down over the dummy men, the firecracker exploded with a loud bang. "There, now come on, everyone. You must walk out there to see what has happened. You will not believe it unless you see it!" Black soot covered his hands and face, but Adrien was extremely pleased.

A few minutes later, we all arrived some thousand yards out from the fortress on the grasslands. The dummies had been literally blown apart, dismembered. "I put metal nails in the explosive charge; see they have penetrated even the plate mail. Given the blast radius clearly visible here, ignore all those older ones, you can see I've wiped out everything in about a seventy-five foot circle. If we had a dozen of these all working together, that would cover a line almost a thousand feet long. One shot and at least a legion of the enemy would have been wounded or killed." Impressive, yes. I'd never seen such a lethal weapon before.

"Son, this could well even the playing field for us. This is absolutely brilliant! How far can it shoot, this cannone assassino of yours?"

"Right now, this is as far as I've been able to get it to go. I've blown up a number of barrels trying to make it go farther. I think I need to find stronger or thicker metal for the cannone assassino, if they must shoot farther. Also, dad, if they come at us with siege towers, I can switch projectiles and shoot a heavy lead ball, which will splinter the towers long before they can reach the walls."

Lady Ariana gave Adrien her complete support and finances. The initial order was for a dozen of these cannone assassino for each of the eight fortresses. Later on, that number doubled and three dozen more were also stationed along the outer walls of the city.

News of Adrien's cannone assassino soon spread to Barcella and Velona, who ordered several to use in their tests. Captain Henry, visibly impressed with the test firings, ordered two for every caravel in the Santi fleet. Ellaina followed suit and had two cannone assassino mounted on each of her many caravels. Soon, Barcella and Zargarb did so as well. Not far behind these sectors, Solamina and Pieta followed suit, though not in the numbers that Velona and Zargarb had.

Later I commented to Renzo, "Well, the cannone assassino will give us an advantage in one war, one battle. After that, the enemy, whomever that may be, will copy them and use them on us. With a number of these cannone assassino, they could well breach our stone fortress walls or the city walls. Inventing better ways to kill the enemy will not guarantee security nor peace, only larger numbers of casualties on both sides."

"I know, but maybe it will not come to war this time. Yet if it does, I want our children and grandchildren to survive and not become Megalos or Demokritos slaves. Let these Centurions come and die here. I'll worry about what comes later at that time."

Typical justification, I thought. Live for today; let tomorrow take care of itself. That is precisely what we were attempting to undo. Create a sane, safe future.

# Chapter 23 So It Begins

Ambassador Nikos Drakon, now twenty-two, bronzed skin, handsome, with a wiry frame, black hair, and eyes, loved his new appointment as Ambassador to Megalos. He'd been here in Galantas, their capital city, for nearly five years. Following his Emperor's orders, he had been searching for a suitable, locally born wife, a woman to marry. Already, the Orthee women had come and had been training the local physicians in the methods of Holy Eight Degrees of Matrimony creation. For months now, the priests of Jehosanity had been preaching the complete and utter virtues of the Holy Eight Degrees of Matrimony. However, no couple had yet stepped forward to undergo this ceremony. Nikos was under orders to change that, but he had to find a suitable wife.

Worse, he knew that this union would be permanent. His finances had been guaranteed for life by the Empress herself, as long as both he and his wife stood by their matrimonial vows, of course. He also knew that if he broke them, was unfaithful to his wife, he would lose that extensive access to funds as well as his soft job here, besides which he'd probably be sent to the marble mines, there to pound stone until he died. While he had met many fair maidens, none had yet to make an enduring impression upon him.

Melissa Patra was about to change all this. She was twenty-one, tall and thin. Her well-formed bosom always caught men's attention, which she desired. Her perfectly formed bronzed skin bore no blemish to mar her beauty. She kept her curly black hair shoulder length and always used a bit of black on her eyelids to accentuate her keen black eyes.

She was neither an artist nor a politician, like her Senator father, who had recently passed away. Melissa hated doing housework like her mother, who had always forced her to do while she was a child. Somehow, she had to find a way out of being yet another housewife. She hated cooking, though she enjoyed eating, particularly at the fancier inns about the city. "Why should I cook when there are so many excellent chefs in Galantas?" was her motto that she often told her friends, most of whom had already married and settled into a housewife career. Melissa wanted something different, something more fun, something — well she didn't quite know what.

As was her wont, around six, she was dining alone at Kleo's Inn, one of the fancier inns in Galantas. It was the summer of 675, a hot one at that. She wore only the lightest of grey togas, one that allowed even the dark of her nipples to show through. She enjoyed the stares of men. Nikos, for reasons unknown to him, likely chance, had decided to dine at Kleo's Inn this same night, but was running late, having to handle a last minute meeting with one of the Jehosanity Priests. He looked around and found the establishment packed. Only one seat remained available, a lone young woman was quietly eating at that table. His stomach growling, he decided to see if the seat was available.

"Excuse me, miss, is this seat taken? I am running late tonight and there seems to be no other chairs available. If you are expecting someone, I will understand." He found himself staring at the hint of her nipples protruding from her gauze of a toga. Grey, so she had to be nobility.

Melissa had never met Nikos, but had both heard of him and had seen the ambassador around the city. "No, please, ambassador, dine with me. It is such a lovely night, and the food is superb here. I know the chef. The eel is fabulous. Oh, I am Melissa, Melissa Patra, the late Senator's daughter."

"Thank you, Melissa. I am so sorry about your father," he replied using all his charm. Since she was eating the eel, he decided to try that dish as well. All during the dinner, the two chatted. He found this woman very easy to talk to, and she seemed interested in him, which he enjoyed as well.

An hour later, Melissa, who was fascinated with the ambassador, asked, "Would you care to go for a stroll around the city with me? The night is becoming cooler now, quite pleasant for a stroll."

Before the night was done, Nikos swore he was in love with Melissa! She, in turn, became infatuated with him and his role. That he had both power and seemingly unlimited funds also appealed to her. Soon, the two were inseparable, dining daily with each other, going to the various parties and socials to which the ambassador was always invited, even to the plays held in the giant coliseum.

A month later, Nikos gave Melissa a diamond necklace with matching earrings, which pleased her immensely. Over the next two months, their love blossomed, and finally, Nikos was convinced that she was the one for him. At dinner at Kleo's Inn, their favorite dining establishment, he finally proposed, "Melissa, will you marry me? I am madly in love with you."

Already, Melissa had set her sights on Nikos. As an ambassador's wife, she knew that she would never be expected to cook, sew, or even do normal house chores. To her, this seemed to be a perfect, golden match! "Oh yes, Nikos, I will. I love you too."

They embraced long, before Nikos realized that he had to tell her what he was obligated to do. Inwardly he hoped and prayed this beautiful woman would agree to it all. "Melissa, there is just one hitch to our getting married." Her face fell; she could not even guess what the problem might be. She was of noble birth and even had funds of her own; a dowry would also come to her when she at last married.

"You see, my Emperor has ordered me to partake of the Holy Eight Degrees of Matrimony. You know, to set an example here on Megalos for everyone to follow. After all, if the official Ambassador of Demokritos does it, then surely others will see that this is a terrific and important thing to do to seal our marriage vows. In my homeland, no couple who have been joined in the Holy Eight Degrees of Matrimony has ever betrayed their spouse, ever, quite a remarkable record, don't you think?"

"Well, yes, I've heard the priests talking about it during their masses. I thought it was a horrible thing to do to a woman," Melissa replied.

"Oh it is mostly painless, as I understand the procedure. Yet, think of the impression that you would make at all of the parties, socials, and plays that we attend! Everyone would be looking at you and your beauty. Other women would die to emulate you. Besides, I would then have no choice but to dote on you, to care for your every need. Never would you have to wash our clothes or change our bed sheets." Nikos wondered what he could say that would convince her to do this for him.

However, Melissa heard the start of the magical words. "You mean that I would never, ever have to do housewifely things?"

"No, never, never. Our union would have to be of the Eighth Degree of course, which means that I would also be responsible for making sure that you always have enough servants around to help you with everything, though I would also be doing the same for you as well. They would help you, for instance, when I am off in a meeting with the priests. Melissa, I do not ever want my wife to have to do normal housewifely things. I hate home cooking. We both love to dine out, only I would be obligated to assist you in all things. We would show the world how great and strong our love for each other actually is!"

"Well, as I understand this, I would then be completely helpless," Melissa thought aloud.

Nikos misinterpreted her statement and countered, "Melissa, if I ever was unfaithful to you in any way, if I ever mistreated you, then two things would happen at once. My entire fortune would instantly become yours alone, and I would be fired and sent off to hew marble from the mountains until I died! That is the hard, invariable rule of the Holy Eight Degrees of Matrimony. Whoever breaks their vows loses everything instantly, with no recourse possible."

"Nikos, let's do it! When can we get married? Do we do it before or after we do the Holy Eight Degrees of Matrimony ceremony?"

"Er, I don't know. I suppose that we can do it either way, but let's get married soonest. I cannot live without you, if you haven't noticed."

The Pope personally married the two one week later. The largest cathedral in Galantas was standing room only, so many wished to see the two united, primarily because everyone knew that they would be the first to undergo the Holy Eight Degrees of Matrimony ceremony. Curiosity had packed this church, coupled with seeing the Demokritos ambassador marrying a local woman.

Two days later, the new couple entered the infirmary of the Church of Jehosanity in Galantas, prepared for the official ceremony. Again, because of the enormous importance of this first couple, not only being the first but also because he was the official ambassador, the Pope performed the Opening Ceremony personally, reading from cue cards prepared for him by the Orthee, who watched from his side.

"Do you Melissa Drakon desire to undergo the Eighth Degree of the Holy Eight Degrees of Matrimony of your own choice and volition, that someone has not put you under any pressure to do this, that this is your own free will and choice?"

"Yes, I do. No one is forcing me to do this. I do it out of love for Nikos." She replied as she had been coached. However, the words were her own.

"And you, Nikos Drakon, do you desire your wife Melissa, to undergo the Eighth Degree of the Holy Eight Degrees of Matrimony of your own choice and volition, knowing that once done, there can never be any going back, that this is a permanent seal, a bond between you two that can only be broken upon death?"

"Yes, I do."

Nikos Drakon, do you swear that from this point onward you will provide for Melissa's every need, whether in public or in your own home? That you will care for her and provide others to assist her when you are not present, so help you God?"

"Yes, I do."

"Nikos and Melissa Drakon, do you both realize that should one of you ever be unfaithful or mistreat the other, then their entire fortune is irrevocably the property of the one maligned and the perpetrator shall be cast out of society forever?"

"We do," the two said in unison.

"Then by the powers invested to me as the Pope of the Church of Jehosanity, I accept this desire to show forth to all the world the eternal symbol of your undying love for each other, your undying wish to obtain only Good Marks, that your precious souls will forever after be joined in the Blessed Holy Realm of Heaven, where the Lord Jehosa dwells. You may now kiss each other, and Melissa will be taken from you for a short while, during which time, Nikos, we shall pray together for her safe recovery."

The two embraced lovingly, though Melissa felt a nervous knot in her stomach. What was she doing? She began to panic slightly, but followed the Orthee out of the room and down the hallway. In the operating room, the women undressed her and had her lie down on a table. "This will only take a short while. Breathe deeply while I hold this over your nose." She did as instructed and soon fell unconscious. Now several male physicians entered.

This first one, the Orthee performed, while the others watched. "First, we liberally inject the aesthetic in a pattern all around her shoulder," one explained. Soon the messy part began. True to their word, the operation did not take very long, primarily because the arms were merely being removed from their sockets. They carefully left sufficient tissue below to seal the holes cleanly and neatly. Once done, they bandaged her shoulders and then washed Melissa off.

Then, the women redressed her, and one man carried her into the recovery bedroom, where she would be staying until the wounds had fully healed. There were two beds here; Nikos would also be staying here alongside of his wife, getting familiar with her special needs. Per their instructions, the physicians were never to allow a patient to leave before her husband had learned how to care for her and before her wounds needed no bandages. Usually, the Orthee explained, this would be a couple of weeks.

Some hours later Melissa woke; her shoulders ached, and she needed to go to the bathroom badly. She tried to sit up, but she no longer had any arms. Panic struck her and she screamed. Nikos bounded to her side. "It's me honey. I'm here. What do you need?" Thus, the stark reality of just what this meant finally struck home to both of them.

Two weeks later, the bandages gone, they were allowed to leave for their home in Galantas. The Orthee woman who discharged them said, "Remember, Nikos, give Melissa at least a month to get used to her new condition before you two start going out into the world. I know that you two love to dine out and go to many parties and such. Please, give her time to adjust. She will have a lot of adjusting to do, and so will you Nikos. I wish you both the very best of love and happiness." He promised he would and the two left the infirmary. He helped her into the waiting coach.

"I feel so helpless, Nikos."

"I know. I am here for you. I hope you can adjust rapidly, Melissa. Because we went through with this, my salary has just been quadrupled, for life! We shall never want for a thing. I do love you so; I cannot wait for us to go out again and do all the things that we love to do. I will hate dining in our home, and I know you will too." She grinned; yes, that she would.

"When we go out, everyone will be looking at me, at us, won't they?"

"Sure will, you look just fabulous, dear."

"Well, I am going to need some appropriate new clothes, don't you think?" Already, Melissa was thinking ahead.

Thus began the usage of the Holy Eight Degrees of Matrimony in Megalos. There was nothing that the Santi del Dio could do to stop this barbaric practice at this time. Our only consolation was that the women undertook it freely.

# Chapter 24 Bitching, Bickering, Bashing

The spring of 685, Emperor Axos met a premature death, a hunting accident. While some doubted that, no one could prove otherwise, and his son Alkaios became the new Emperor. His wife, Ligeia, became the Empress, the first in many centuries who had arms. Both were in their twenties, childless thus far, by choice. Theirs was not a happy marriage.

"Well maybe now you will stop drinking," Ligeia called out loudly. They were in their Royal Bedroom of the palace. They had just been officially sworn in as the new leaders of Demokritos.

"Why? The Emperor can do any damn thing he pleases! You should be happy I kept you with me all these years. Now you can be Empress and stop bothering me," he retorted. Alkaios smelled of stale wine.

"Yeh, right, you hear me, Alkaios, you stop messing around with all those whores of yours. I'll not be the laughing stock of Demokritos, you hear me?" she screamed at him. Since he didn't respond, she slapped him hard on the side of his face.

"Damn you bitch! I should have dumped you years ago. I'm going out for a drink!" He stormed out of their new bedroom on this, their first night in the Royal Bedroom.

Later that spring, drunk again, Alkaios stormed into their bedroom, "Damn it woman, you will give me my heir. You know the prophesies as well as I do. If you won't do it now, I will find many others more than willing!"

Ligeia knew the prophesies as well as the next person. She knew that she had to bear him a son and soon. Reluctantly, she allowed the Emperor on top of her, while she held her nose from the stench of alcohol on his breath and sweat from his armpits. He finished rapidly, much to her satisfaction. "Now get out of here until you take a bath, you stink." He left for more wine.

Finally, Ligeia knew that she was pregnant with his child. She was sure that it was his, well nearly so. Unlike her husband, who slept with any willing whore, she prided herself on sleeping only with the finest looking young dandies, and that done on the sly. At least for the next nine months, she did not have to suffer this beast having his way with her. Ligeia wondered why she had not thought of this before, but quickly realized that she would not be having much pleasure at all for nearly a year. Ah well, perhaps the prophesy will be fulfilled, and she wouldn't have to go through with this any longer.

In the early part of 686, Ligeia gave birth to a son, whom they named Deimos. At first, her feelings of motherhood kicked in, but soon she was more than ready to give up feeding Deimos, allowing midwives to care for her son.

While Deimos was growing up, the two parents fought nearly every day. Often Ligeia would throw things at her husband. Later on, she began to wise up and scratch him with her nails. Thus scarred, he was less likely to visit his whores, for he looked a mess. Poor Deimos saw nothing but utter domestic strife for the first fourteen years of his life.

Yes, he was duly educated by the court sages, especially in the prophesies, which he might follow. The best swordsmen of the court trained him in the fighting arts. Retired generals drilled him on battlefield tactics. Court advisors trained him in the fine arts of ruling a country, specifically Demokritos. Thus, by the turn of the century, Deimos was properly trained to become their next Emperor.

During the extravagant new century celebration at the Imperial Palace, Emperor Alkaios got drunker than normal. Some say that he was so drunk that, while he was watching the fireworks imported from Tashien, he fell off the palace roof to his death. Secretly, some said that Deimos might have pushed him, while others suggested that Ligeia gave him a push. In any event, Alkaios died, and Empress Ligeia left the palace, taking with her a sizeable pile of gems and jewels; she was now free at last to seek out a far better husband or perhaps party, for she was not yet too old.

The next day, Deimos was sworn in as the next Emperor. Immediately after the ceremony, his advisors, who used to be his teachers, came to him. "Deimos, it is time that we see to the fulfilling of the age old prophesies. We know that there was no love lost between your father and you, so we are of the opinion that you should take a vacation trip to Annelise soon."

"Damn it, I loved my father! It was all that bitch who birthed me — her doing. She abused my father, drove him to drink, and drove him to the whorehouse. The prophesies are right! No Empress ever should be allowed to have arms! Not ever! Damned Santi have convinced our people to abandon the Holy Eight Degrees, so I have two choices open to me. Either I go to Megalos and try to find someone there or believe in these silly prophesies written seven centuries ago by who knows who. I say there is more chance of finding an appropriate woman to become Empress in Megalos than in Annelise. They are totally hung up on proper dress! God, even their farmers dress in business suits! Stupid, stupid, stupid!"

"You Highness, stupid or not, the prophesies say that now is the time for unification with the Annelise. A Royal Marriage between the two ruling houses would unite our two countries. Surely, you do not doubt the great wisdom and foretelling of the holy prophesies?"

Deimos knew they were right, "All right. All right. I will go to Annelise and see what is there. But believe me when I say we are not going to find an armless woman in that country. Besides, what am I to do, marry the first armless person I come across? The hell with all of you. I am going to choose whom I marry, and I'll be damned if I am going to marry a bitch like my mother, whether or not she has arms!"

"Think unification, Deimos. Our goal is to unify and bring the Annelise under our dominion and control. Regardless how they dress, they are a wealthy nation and have much to offer us. If we are to conquer the world, we will need their resources to back us up. So think unification, Deimos, unification." He glared, but thought unification.

# Chapter 25 Endings

By 684, things were looking more and more like war may well be coming to Tarra once more. Centurion legions from Demokritos had been steadily, although slowly, arriving on Megalos. The Santi could do little about this, except continue to spy on their slow yearly buildup of forces and how they were armored. Indeed, reports of plate mail clad Centurions began filtering into headquarters in Velona. While Linda and Chaucer had long ago predicted this would happen, still everyone found it alarming indeed. Gone would be our distinct advantage on the battlefield. Only Adrien's newly invented cannone assassino offered us any real hope of defeating such a huge army.

Worse, from my point of view, Kallisto's body died here in the springtime. She had become like a sister to me, just as Donata was my actual sister also stationed here in Zargarb. Hank took her loss very hard indeed; he loved her as much as I loved Renzo. Interestingly Hank also lost his body but a year later, some said that his heart could not go on living without her around.

When Kallisto's body died, Linda joined us together once again. I knew that it was decision-making time at last. We had not come up with any other viable plan. I would have to go down to Annelise soon , take this prophesy body, and try to become the Empress, hoping somehow to influence events so that we Santi were not destroyed. Somehow, I needed to maintain the peace and tranquility on Tarra that Jes, the Guardian of the Anuir, needed to work his miracles of spiritual freedom. If Chaucer and Linda were indicative of his final products, it was totally worth the effort!

Linda said, *I'm sorry about your body, Kallisto. You have done so much for the Santi, I want to thank you personally for everything, including looking after my best friend all these years when I could not. Thank you from the bottom of my heart, Kallisto.* I think that Kallisto spiritually blushed, if that is even possible.

*I hate to bring this up, but it is time for us to make major, far-reaching decisions. Steadily, day by day, those ancient prophesies are coming true, probably because those in Demokritos are working overtime to make them happen. However, what shall we do?*

I answered, *Okay, I'm ready. I'll go down there, take this baby body, and try to make it become the Empress. Once I succeed in that, Linda, I'll need your guidance on just what I'm to do with my influence, mind you.*

*Thank you, Bethany. I will never let you down. We have determined who the woman in question is who is going to have said baby girl, probably in the year 682. Kallisto, do you still wish to go there and help Bethany with this project?*

*Absolutely!*

*Then, we must act now. If we delay even a year, the woman may get too excited, jump the gun, and decide that Kallisto is to be the one, not Bethany. If you are willing then we will arrange it now. Do you prefer to have another female body or perhaps a male, Kallisto?*

*Hell, for god's sake, don't have it be male!* she replied with a passion. I chuckled, so did Renzo.

*Okay, one minute. There, she is pregnant with a female child. Damn, this is so easy to do, make a woman pregnant or not. Ah well. When you are ready, Kallisto, I will take you directly down there to her. We cannot have any possible mixups.* We all chuckled over this thought! I also began to wonder just how on Tarra Linda managed to get a distant woman pregnant in a flash and with a female baby at that!

*Hey, can you also get this mother to name me Kallisto? Also, can you make sure that she does not jump the gun and try to make me the woman to be Empress?*

Linda's body back in Velona chuckled. *Yes, Kallisto it shall be. I will make very sure that she doesn't jump the gun on this, Kallisto. I suppose that you want her to name you Bethany as well, right Bethany?* Now I laughed.

*I don't suppose that is a proper Annelise name now is it? Kallisto, I will stay in touch with you too,* I added. *I know Linda will be keeping an eye on you, but I will too.*

*Thanks. Once your new body is born, I will look after you as well, Bethany. Take care of Hank; he is going to take my body's death very hard. I know that I would if he had lost his before I lost mine. I never thought that I could ever love a man again, but Hank changed that in me forever!*

Linda added, *Bethany, we think that you have at most another two years before you must take this new baby body. Now, Kallisto, let's get you into position. The Santi strike once more!*

It is weird knowing that your body has but two years left to live! Strange indeed. Yet, I knew that I would relish having a body with arms once more. Being armless isn't all that it's cracked up to be — that's a joke, by the way. Anyway, I spent my time with my family, with Renzo, our kids, and my grandchildren. My sister also took over helping me with things, now that Kallisto was gone.

As the time approached, I had a long talk with Renzo. "Look my body is going on fifty-one now. I am depending on you to help our children and grandchildren prepare for the worst. I know that when the war comes here, your body will likely be at least sixty-seven years old, if not more. Just do everything in your powers to keep our children and grandchildren safe. They must somehow survive the coming war. Promise me that you will do this for us."

"My most treasured love, this I will do for us. I promise you. I will not promise that I won't cry for you every day that you are gone from me." I knew that he would miss me very badly, but the survival of us all depended upon our being able somehow to circumvent the coming war of conquest.

"Renzo, I will make you this solemn vow. When this is all over, somehow, someway, no matter what does happen, I will come and find you once more. We shall be together again in the future. I promise you this. I will have Linda make it so, if I am unable to do it myself. I won't let you down!" We embraced long that night.

At last that day for change came. I gathered all of those whom I loved together and we all said our last farewells. Yes, everyone was bawling like babies, but it had to be done. Linda made the Mind Link with all of us, and we all shared a last conversation with Linda, who did much to quell everyone's grief.

At last, she said, *Are you ready, Bethany?*

*Yes, how do I die? Does Renzo have to stab me?*

*Oh don't be so melodramatic, Bethany. All you need to do is back out of the body and severe the connection. The body will die without a spiritual being activating it. However, to make your death plausible to the others, I will make it appear that you have suffered a viper bite to your neck, instant death. Are you ready?*

*Yes, let's do it.*

*I'm ready here.* It was Kallisto! Her body was now two years old, but she was fully aware and waiting for me. Her mother, or rather ours, was pregnant once more.

*See that thin line there, break it. Yes, like that. See the body is dying rapidly now. Okay, one, two, three, and here we are. Can you see her standing there?*

I saw a woman dressed in a large hoop skirt, nearly twelve feet across. She was ironing baby clothes. Crawling around a penned in area was another baby girl, also wearing rather fancy clothing for a baby anyway. *Hi Bethany.* Kallisto looked up at me.

I had almost forgotten just how overly well-dressed these people insisted on being, to the point of ludicrousness. Ah well, I now had time to reflect, think, and chat with Kallisto. We still had fourteen more years for Linda and Chaucer to come up with a better plan than the one on which we were now embarked. It was comforting to both Kallisto and me to know that if we were needed elsewhere for a better plan, Linda could come to us instantly and rescue us from these new bodies.

She and I knew that so much depended upon our success down here in this southern continent. All our loved ones, our dearest friends, and families — all were in dire peril from this new Emperor to be, who would be born at nearly the same time as my new body would be. I had no idea just how I would manage to alter this Emperor's plans for the conquest of Tarra.

I only knew that I must do it or we would lose everything.
The End.

# A Favor to Other Readers

How about helping other readers? Many readers rely on reviews to make the decision whether to buy a book. You can help them make their decision by leaving your opinions and viewpoint in a short review of the positive things of this book. Writing the review and expressing your opinion only takes a few minutes, and other readers will appreciate your efforts.

Click this link: Volume 7 Abducted
scroll down to Customer Reviews; click on Write a Review, and enter your review. Thank you.

# Author Information

## Visit My Amazon.com Author Page
Vic Broquard Author Page

## Follow My Blog
Vic Broquard's Blog

## Follow Me on Social Media
Facebook
Google+
LinkedIn
YouTube

# Other Books by Vic Broquard

The Return of the Wizards: Twelve Companions – The Making of Wizards (fantasy)

www.ingramcontent.com/pod-product-compliance
Lightning Source LLC
Chambersburg PA
CBHW080819250626
47159CB00011B/3436